THE WILL

Jane Mann

Matador
9 Priory Business Park,
Wistow Road, Kibworth Beauchamp,
Leicestershire. LE8 0RX
Tel: 0116 279 2299
Email: books@troubador.co.uk
Web: www.troubador.co.uk/matador
Twitter: @matadorbooks

ISBN 978 1785893 865

British Library Cataloguing in Publication Data.
A catalogue record for this book is available from the British Library.

Printed and bound in the UK by TJ International, Padstow, Cornwall
Typeset in 11pt Aldine401 BT by Troubador Publishing Ltd, Leicester, UK

Matador is an imprint of Troubador Publishing Ltd

THE WILL

For my family

Chapter 1

"I don't understand."

Hannah frowned, bewildered, as she skimmed the single page of her father's letter a second time.

It was a neatly typed letter which struck her as unusual since her father enjoyed displaying his italic hand and rarely used either his typewriter or computer for personal correspondence. But it was more the style and the content of the letter that struck her as strange. There was none of his usual enthusiasm for the books he'd read, the friends he'd seen, the changes he'd made to the garden. The letter was a list essentially of visits he'd made to museums and art galleries, the details dry and laboured, more as objects of proof than enjoyment. Then at the end, coolly matter-of-fact, the statement that Emma Mason, his housekeeper, had given in her notice and left.

"She'd never leave like that. She was devoted to Dad, had promised to stay."

"She could be ill," Richard offered. He tried to sound interested but his thoughts were preoccupied with his coming meeting that morning with Stanley Chan. Chan was pleased, Richard was sure, with the computer system he'd already installed at his main factory in Kowloon. There'd been some teething troubles though with the present

1

installation in Chan's office on the island and the long term contract he wanted for updating the systems in the rest of Chan's offices and factories still hung in the balance. He had somehow to persuade Chan that the present problems were now virtually sorted and would not recur.

As his eyes swept over Hong Kong's harbour below, over the skyscrapers bordering the water and reaching up into a brightening sky, Richard was drawn into a mood of optimism. The rumble of the Peak tram, the roar of traffic, the steady plying of the Star Ferry between mainland and island, all reached him as the heartbeat of a city – a city where, if he played his cards aright, he could have a stake, a future long enough to make some money. It was even possible, he reflected, he could one day be like Chan and have his own growing enterprise.

"No." Hannah was adamant. "She would have told me if she was."

"Not if she hadn't got your address." Richard savoured the remains of his coffee, resolved to dissipate any drama. There was often some practical oversight he'd found behind Hannah's worries and he didn't want a promising day shadowed. It was essential he remained coolly focused and aware if he was to secure the contract with any certainty and on favourable terms.

"But I showed her where my address was in Dad's desk. She could have got it anyway from Dad or Hugo. No, I feel there's something more, something wrong."

"What do you mean exactly?" Richard glanced at his watch, immediately regretting his question. He should be leaving very soon now for his meeting. He couldn't afford to be late, to be diverted. Yet equally he felt he couldn't

abruptly dismiss Hannah's concern. There was an edge of fear now in her voice demanding more attention – a fear he had somehow to allay or resolve to a decision before he left. He didn't want her to feel, as she'd once accused, that he didn't take her seriously.

"I don't know. That's the problem." The word 'exactly' irritated, making her feel she was in court. "But this letter's not Dad. It's not Dad at all."

"You felt the same with the last letter – if I remember rightly,"Richard pointed out he thought reasonably.

"That was at least his own writing."

Or was it, Hannah now wondered. The shaky lower case letters, the abrupt endings to his words, the downward drift of the lines – had they really been, as the letter had claimed, only the effects of a new pen? And why had he taken so long to reply – a full twelve weeks when she'd written five times? It was so unlike him. They'd always been close, had communicated either by letter or phone every week till now for the past five years and he'd promised always to let her know if anything was wrong, if he was ill or needed her in any way. It had been one of her main conditions of agreeing to come with Richard to Hong Kong. Was he in fact ill?

Hannah sat up, feeling the need suddenly to act.

"I think I ought to go back, Richard, and see what's happening."

"What now?" Richard's dark blue eyes sharpened in alarm. He didn't like surprises especially those based on what he considered irrational grounds. "On the strength of an uncertain letter and before we've finished?"

"Finished?"

3

"The present contract. It'll take me at least another month to make sure the computer's working and then there's the next contract to consider. I couldn't possibly go back to England now."

"I wasn't implying you should, Richard. I only meant I should go."

"What on your own?"

"Why not?"

"You've still got your teaching commitment. You can't just go without good reason."

"The term's nearly over. There's only a couple more weeks. Besides, I'm not indispensable. I'm only part time. It's not a job of any great significance."

"Even so," and he knew looking at her, at the beauty of her finely shaped features sharpened by concern, her dark brown eyes intent yet faraway, her dark brown hair lingering over her shoulders, the soft pallor of her skin strangely untouched as yet by the sun, that it was for himself that he wanted her to stay, that he feared losing her, that she might cease to need him, to depend on him. "You know you hate travelling on your own. And how are you going to get out to Yadrahna without a car?"

"There are buses from Oxford."

"Not right to the house though." The thought of her walking the long mile from the bus stop up Winter Hill alone appalled him. "It's absurd and what's going to happen if you get there and find everything's normal – as no doubt it will be."

"Then I'll come back."

"Isn't that rather an expensive exercise when the object of being here I thought was to save money?"

He noticed her flinch as if he'd struck her, felt her withdraw from him, disapproving. Why, he wondered, were her feelings for her father so intense. Surely she should have grown away from him by now. It wasn't as if she was on her own. You have me, he felt he wanted to assert.

"He may need me, Richard."

He was conscious of an appeal and sadness in her voice now and knew he should respond, agree with more willingness to let her go but to agree, his business sense told him, would be to weaken his own commitment, his own position and the future he was trying to nurture with Chan, if she decided not to return.

"I need you too." He didn't wait for her denial or confirmation. Conscious of the time passing, he stood up, reaching for his jacket. Tall and tanned, with his neatly cut fair hair, his even features and determined eyes, he dominated, as he stood over her with his air of confidence and well being. "I understand how you feel. You need to know and you can know. Your father's usually in his study, you say, every morning till 10 which means if we ring when we get back around 6 this evening, we can catch him then and you can speak to him direct."

"And if for some reason we can't speak to him?" Hannah tried without success to hide her scepticism, hesitant to confront him, in all his certainty, with the fact that she had already tried ringing her father, that each time the phone had gone on ringing or been answered by a strange woman who'd curtly told her that her father was unavailable, then rung off.

"Then we'll try Hugo or your Aunt Eileen or Sally. Sally seems a sensible and reliable person and she lives near your father, doesn't she? She could go over and investigate. I'm sure anyway we'll get to the bottom of all this without your having to travel half way round the world." He bent over and kissed her. "You mustn't worry. It'll turn out all right. We'll get in touch with them all this evening and sort it all then."

Would they, Hannah wondered, watching Richard go, or was he trying as he always did to comfort and reassure?

She felt suddenly tired and drained, the clammy June heat, an unseen furry presence, enclosing her again. She poured herself another coffee, then taking the rest of the post drifted out onto the veranda.

It was no cooler here but she had the illusion from the height of greater space. The flat was on the top floor of one of Chan's ten storey blocks just above mid level. The view Richard prized as being one of the best on the island with its broad sweeping overview of Kowloon, the harbour and the commercial centre of skyscraper banks and offices, the symbols Richard claimed of "enterprise and progress".

But the skyscrapers, detached as they were from any visible anchorage of earth or green, seemed to Hannah strangely unreal buildings, aggressive and hostile, like well–filed teeth biting into the sky. How much further, higher would they bite she wondered. Would the sky eventually become one vast dome of concrete?

She could feel the sun already burning her arm, the gleaming white of the concrete tower block just below hurting her eyes; from the flat below the persistent clatter of mahjong.

With longing she thought of the quiet and cool of Yadrahna, the green of its trees and shrubs and the surrounding fields and as she wandered in her mind then down Yadrahna's driveway, seeing before her its mellowed ochre facade, its classic proportions, the wisteria in bloom over the wall of her father's study, she felt an intense need again to see her father, to know that he was well.

It was over six months now since she'd last seen him on the afternoon before her evening flight from Heathrow to join Richard in Hong Kong. It had been New Year's Day, a crisp clear day with the sparkle of frost on the lawn, the kind of day her father would have rejoiced to be out in walking or gardening. But a bout of flu had kept him indoors and as they'd sat by the fire in his study, it had struck her that he'd aged suddenly, that his tanned craggy face was more lined, more drawn, his discerning brown eyes more reflective, more subdued.

Uneasily she'd wondered whether she should leave him then and had offered to postpone her flight and see him through the effects of the flu. But he'd insisted on her keeping to her plans, assuring her that Emma would look after him. She had, after all, been a nurse, he'd argued, and been with him five years. As if to underline his health, her father had poked the logs of the fire into action, wanting her to see his resilience rather than the vulnerability of his lines.

It had been a strange parting. Despite the effects of flu, her father had expounded with enthusiasm on his plans for the kitchen garden and his fantastic crop of leeks but he'd carefully, Hannah had noticed, avoided talking about Richard and her planned life with him for the year of his contract in Hong Kong.

She'd sensed from the first moment she'd introduced Richard that he'd never really approved. But since she and Richard had not made any specific plans to marry but rather to see how their relationship worked out, her father had not been involved in any official sense. It was not in his nature, anyway, she knew, to interfere. But his self–imposed restraint about Richard had made their parting seem oddly artificial as if she was going into a void.

Then abruptly, while they were still sitting by the fire, only an hour before her friend Sally was due to collect her to drive her to Heathrow, her father had told her that he was leaving Yadrahna to her in his will.

Yadrahna had been the Delaney family home since her grandfather Herbert Delaney had bought it in the 1930's on retiring early from various successful business ventures in the east. It was from a period of trading in India that he had given it its name – Yadrahna, meaning a place to be remembered. It was a name which had caused some irritation locally, Hannah had learned, but which was an improvement, she'd thought on its more prosaic previous name, Stoneleigh.

Built in the 1840's, it had been designed much as any other Cotswold country house at the time, along simple but spacious classical lines in mellowed ochre Cotswold stone that harmonised both with itself and its surroundings. It was in fact Yadrahna's surroundings that made it special in Hannah's view and she often thought of what the Delaneys owed to the far sighted Victorians who'd not only planned and assembled an unique library of first editions but who'd planted the great oaks and limes and copper beech that sheltered Yadrahna now from the

road. Those who'd come after had sustained rather than created but each had left footprints, Hannah sensed, on the flagstones of the house's history, linking them. Even her namesake, Hannah, the elusive maid, who'd mysteriously disappeared in the summer of 1912, had left her mark, cryptic though it was, in the message of love she'd carved on a beam in the north–facing attic.

Often Hannah had wondered what had happened to the other Hannah. She felt in a strange way linked to her through her name as if the other Hannah was whispering to her down the century, trying to hold on; not as a spirit – she no more believed in spirits and ghosts than her father did – but as a person who should have been recognised, her unhappiness known. She'd resolved that one day, when she had more time, she would investigate Hannah's disappearance, check the records. She might even, she thought, write a book on the history of Yadrahna.

When her father had told her that he was leaving her Yadrahna, it was not, therefore, entirely a surprise. She knew that he'd recognised that Yadrahna was far more to her than just the place where she'd been born, that it was the place where she felt she belonged, where she was most at ease, in tune and which she wanted, as he did, to protect for the years to come.

But she had mixed reactions to the news of his bequest. She felt deeply honoured and moved that he had trusted her with what he valued most beyond his family but at the same time a chill inside her at the thought of his ceasing to be at Yadrahna. He had always been at Yadrahna, always been a part of it in her memory, as she had, and she couldn't imagine either the house or grounds without

him, nor did she want to. She felt also uneasy about what he'd said because of Hugo.

Though technically a brother by her father's first marriage, which had been dissolved after her father had met her own mother, she'd seen very little of Hugo since they'd lived as children at Yadrahna. Now 38 and 11 years older than herself, he'd been married for three years to Laura, an artist like himself, but for some reason that Hannah had never fully fathomed it hadn't worked and they now shared between them their son Marcus who was 12, Hugo having him at weekends and Laura in the week. Hannah hadn't seen Laura since their divorce but she'd heard that Laura had remarried and had a little girl. Hugo meanwhile had returned to living in Windsor with his mother, an embittered woman, Hannah had discovered, a woman with hawk eyes and a permanent grudge against her father for leaving her.

How much Hugo was affected by his mother Hannah wasn't sure. It was difficult with Hugo, she'd always found, to know what he was thinking or feeling, to reconcile the affability in his voice with the detachment and remoteness in his eyes. But she sensed that his mother with her hawk eyes would not herself be too detached when it came to her father's will and could become an unpleasant directing factor.

Playing devil's advocate, she'd asked her father whether he'd yet discussed the matter with Hugo.

"Not yet but I will," he'd replied with some surprise.

"Don't you think," she'd hesitated, "that he might be resentful, try to challenge?"

"Hugo will have no cause to complain." Her father's voice had been tired she'd thought but unequivocal and

clear. "Apart from some capital I've set apart for the upkeep of Yadrahna, I will be leaving him all my investments – which will be more than enough for his needs. No, I want you to have Yadrahna. There are too many speculators about now wanting the land for development."

"You've been approached then?"

"There's a whole raft of them out there – writing, telephoning. Most of them thankfully have at last realised I'm not interested. But there's one, a Hugh Jamieson, one of these new–fangled estate agents cum legal boffins – he won't give up. He's even called."

"But obviously not convinced you," she'd smiled.

"Certainly not. You can see it in his eyes. He has no feeling for the past, no interest. Yadrahna's just so many bags of money to him in the bank. It would be a tragedy if it ever fell into his hands."

"You're afraid then that Hugo might succumb?"

"Let's say rather that I think you have more of the family stubbornness in you to resist the blandishments."

It was a compliment that Hannah found difficult to reply to and they had both sat in silence for a few minutes, each absorbed in their own thoughts about the significance of what he'd said against the pressure of coming departure and separation.

Then Emma had come in to collect the tea things and the conversation had turned to practicalities. Hannah had written down Richard's address in Hong Kong and put it in the top drawer of her father's rosewood desk where both he and Emma could find it, hurriedly whispered to Emma to let her know if there was any problem while she was away. Then Sally had arrived and they were all immersed

11

in goodbyes. Nothing more was said of Yadrahna and her father's will. Sixteen hours later she was with Richard in Hong Kong.

It was wonderful, Hannah had found, to be with Richard again. They hadn't seen each other for three months and couldn't have enough of each other. Richard had specially taken a week's leave with the intention of showing her the sights and Macau. But sightseeing had become a low priority once they were together. All day and nearly all night that first week they made love, leaving the flat only for meals and an occasional walk round the peak.

Then Richard had had to go back to work on his contract for installing the computer for Stanley Chan in his main office – work that demanded long hours. But it was work that Hannah could see Richard enjoyed and found a challenge. He enjoyed in fact, she noticed, the whole fast lifestyle of Hong Kong, the edge it gave to competition, the atmosphere it had of further possibilities to make money. And the flat with its ease of living suited him. He liked its modernity, the freedom it gave him to concentrate on his work and building up contacts.

Hannah could see his point but once the idyllic first week was over and she'd explored the island and most of Kowloon and Lantao, she found the flat dull and confining. It seemed an unreal life without a garden – even her London flat had had a garden – and there was mostly literally nothing to do. Chan had even arranged for contract cleaning of the flat as part of Richard's perks in the contract and as she and Richard were increasingly being invited out for meals by both Chan and other contacts, only rarely did she have any cooking to do. Eventually,

feeling rather useless during the day, she got herself a part time post in a technical school teaching English.

Richard had ambivalent feelings, she knew, about her working. He had the traditional view of the male as the main breadwinner and was reluctant, she sensed, for her to have an independent life of her own in Hong Kong. At the same time he was money conscious and wanted them to save all they could so they could afford a pleasant place in which to live when they returned to England. There was a growing assumption in the way he talked that they would soon get married.

Hannah had no doubt that Richard loved her. He showed her every night that he loved her and when she was close to him, she felt that she too loved him. Physically they satisfied each other's needs.

Hannah wasn't sure though that she wanted to get married in any official sense. She had the feeling that at 27 she perhaps ought to get married. Her Aunt Eileen had indeed urged her age as a main reason, emphasising that Richard with his good looks, his drive for success and competence, was a good match, which might not come her way again and at 30 she could well be on the shelf.

But what was the point, Hannah wondered, if one didn't immediately want children. Most of her friends, even at 30, were in long standing relationships which seemed to work as well as marriage but without the official sanctions, the involvements and ties. It was the sense of being tied Hannah knew she feared, the limitations on her freedom to change and make new relationships if she chose.

And yet she was in a sense she knew already married to Richard, had shared his bed, his everyday life at least

in the evenings and at weekends for over 6 months now. And mostly they got on well together, harmonised over practicalities, gave each other space. In bed Richard was an attentive and considerate lover. He didn't excite her but he made her feel she mattered and in every other way she knew she could depend on him to do what he'd said he'd do if at all within his power. He never let her down if he could help it, was always there to take charge of the practicalities she dreaded.

But increasingly she found herself unable to express herself with him, to question and explore new ideas, new concerns and the six months, despite their harmony in everyday living, had not brought the certainty she'd hoped would come from the experience.

As the months wore on she found herself, too, feeling more and more alien in Hong Kong itself. The competitive, money orientated city centred life style which appealed to Richard did not appeal to her and seemed damaging to the natural world and she was aware of their mentally drifting apart, separating, as she realised with greater certainty that she didn't want to be a part of it.

Her part time job helped the time to pass more quickly but she was not deeply involved and as Richard worked, it seemed, increasingly longer and longer hours, her thoughts returned ever more frequently to her father and Yadrahna.

As she sat on the veranda, reflecting, her remaining post unopened, Hannah was wondering whether she might ring her father before she left for her teaching, when she was conscious of the phone itself ringing. So strongly focused were her thoughts on her father that she was sure it must be him.

To her surprise, for it seemed he'd only just left, it was Richard, his voice buoyant with undisguised relief and satisfaction.

"Guess what?"

Instantly she knew but with a sense of dread rather than elation. "You've got the contract."

"Signed, sealed and 25% up on the last one."

"Congratulations." And he deserved it, Hannah knew. He knew his job, was skilled, competent, had put in the work, often more than was needed, but she couldn't summon up the enthusiasm she felt she should express and he'd expect.

"Chan, moreover, has agreed to my having a month off in September between contracts which will give us time to get married back in England. He really seems to want me."

"I'm not surprised."

"Oh yes, and he's invited us both out for drinks this evening to celebrate."

"This evening?"

"Yes. Why? We've nothing else on, have we?"

"No, but we agreed to make the phone calls home, Richard."

"We still can. If we get on the case as soon as we get in, they'll be completed by 7 – no problem. But the drinks I think are a priority. We can't let Chan down – not now."

"No," Hannah forced herself to agree. "Of course not."

"I'll try and get back early."

"Thanks." Hannah put down the phone, then, making herself some more coffee, went back to the veranda and opened the remaining post.

15

It was bills mostly and advertising leaflets but at the bottom was a letter from the Blackstone Management College at Oxford, accepting her for a Personnel Management course. Thinking she was unlikely to be accepted, she had largely dismissed the course from her mind. It was a course she'd applied for in a mood of desperation after teaching in an inner city school and being unable to cope with the ill discipline. She'd felt at the time, just before leaving for Hong Kong, that she couldn't bear to go through such an experience again on return and, if working in England, would have to change her career. Personnel Management had appealed – the chance to work with people, solving problems but on a more one to one basis. Reading through the letter again – a decision needed within a month, she felt again that she would like to do the course.

But how could she, if she was going to stay with Richard, now that the contract was confirmed and Richard would definitely be staying on in Hong Kong another year? It would be unlikely, she reflected, he would willingly agree to her doing the course so far away – a course he would probably consider even a waste of time. It would mean being separated virtually for nine months. No, she couldn't see Richard agreeing, especially if they got married.

As Richard's words on the phone penetrated, Hannah's doubts about getting married returned with a sense of panic and alarm. September was only three months away. She was in no way ready, prepared. She still wasn't sure. But would she ever know for sure? Could one, did one ever feel truly certain about anyone else?

Abruptly from the past there came back to her words she hadn't thought about for over five years now – words from her mother a few months before she'd plunged to her death in her car accident on Winter Hill. "You'll always know, Hannah, when it's the right person. It's like a flame inside which never dies. You may quarrel, disagree, be of a totally different age or opinion but you'll never be indifferent. The flame may flicker, even subside but it's always there."

Yes, Hannah reflected, her mother had been certain about her father but then her father was an exception, had always let both her mother and herself be themselves, had never closed doors or sought to mould either action or mind. Even in his more uneasy relationship with Hugo he'd shown respect. In the army, that was different. There he'd retained, as Lt Colonel, his control. But at home, there'd always been love and understanding, never an iron hand.

Had her father perceived, Hannah wondered, that ultimately her relationship with Richard was not right. Was that the reason for his reticence on the evening she'd said goodbye to him in his study and left to join Richard? If only, she longed, she could talk to him again, question him more closely about what he really thought.

Restless, Hannah got up and took her coffee cup and post through to the kitchen. If only, she thought, she could ring him now. But it would be past midnight in England and he could well be asleep. She didn't want to worry him. No, it would be better to wait, as Richard had suggested, till the early evening, she decided, and, taking a shower, she got ready for her two hour morning session of teaching at Ho Tung College.

The morning passed, as it always did at the college, smoothly, pleasantly. The students in all the three classes she took for oral English were all quietly well-behaved and attentive, anxious to make the most of their opportunities to develop and perfect their English. All, without exception, had learnt the phrases and vocabulary she'd given them the day before. No one spoke out of turn or tried to disrupt. Sometimes she could hardly believe it after her previous year's experience in London in trying to get some order, let alone teach. Here she could talk in a normal voice and didn't feel like a rag that had been wrung out and trampled on. Here, though she sometimes wished they asked more questions and were more challenging, she felt she could be herself and feel the achievement of getting the points across and being able to make a difference to their lives and help them on.

Many of them she knew lived in tenement blocks, a whole family sometimes crowded in one room and she couldn't help but admire the way that, supported by their families, they turned out always immaculately clean, organised, their homework done, despite the hardship, the poverty, the crowdedness and noise.

Their resilience amazed her and sometimes she wanted to tell them so but they kept their distance as far as life outside school was concerned, seeking approbation only in their work for her. She never felt she got to know them. They liked her, wanted her, she recognised, for what she could give them – a passport to a security beyond mere survival in one of the companies that kept Hong Kong going.

At the end of the morning, the headmistress, Jenny Wong, took her aside and asked if she would like the next

year to work full time and take charge of the fifth form English. It would have been ill mannered, Hannah knew, to reject the offer out of hand and there was a clear benefit in accepting if she stayed on with Richard in Hong Kong. But the uncertainty about her father made her nervous of any commitment and she said, trying to smile, that she was honoured by the offer but would like a few days to think about it.

She decided, before returning to the flat, to go down to Wanchai to buy her father a present. What she would buy she wasn't sure but it would pass at least some time till the evening when she would ring him.

It was a burnt languid day with the weight of other burnt languid days behind it and by the time she reached the main street, though only a short distance, the bodice of her dress was soaked and perspiration was streaming freely between her thighs.

Usually she enjoyed wandering through Wanchai and taking photos of the colourful stalls with their exotic fruits and foods, their strangely shaped remedies. She liked the bustling atmosphere of cheerfulness and resilience, the weather beaten hawkers defying with their toothless smiles and raucous voices the drag of poverty and age. She loved the small children with their black hair and neatly cut fringes and calm almond eye on the backs of their mothers or playing amazingly free of tears their palatial games on the pavements.

But today she found herself noticing more individuals who were not cheerful and resilient; a boy scratching his head which was covered with prickly heat sores and garish purple ointment, a listless girl in a doorway and a beggar

without shoes lying asleep on a narrow plank. Jostled within the shifting stream of sightseers and shoppers, she was conscious more of angry drivers hooting, of hammer and drill from a nearby site overriding the laughter of children and jangling on her nerves.

Suddenly, the desire to be back within the peace and surrounding green of Yadrahna swept over her again and from the past she heard her father's voice calling her from the garden in the gentle but urgent tones he used when he had something to show her or confide. She had an overwhelming sense of her father trying to reach her, needing her, yet at the same time an awareness that she was anchored in a gravity beyond his reach, that she was unable to respond.

Withdrawing from the crowd, she stood still for a moment in the doorway of a Chinese art store, her father's voice still echoing in her mind. Despite the heat, she felt cold, the muscles of her skin contract as from the effect of a chill breeze.

As she tried to calm herself, to readjust, she noticed then beside her in the window of the store, a scroll with a black and white water colour painting on it of a horse galloping forward. She'd seen the scroll before but not in such proximity and she was struck by the energy and life it conveyed, the nobility of the horse's head, the tail flicked up and the mane in the wind flying. It was the perfect present, she knew instantly for her father, which would reflect his sense of optimism and moving forward. Without hesitation, she went in and bought it together with a rice–patterned bowl for Hugo and a red lantern for Sally.

Returning to the flat an hour later, she found a message from Richard on the answer phone saying he'd be back later than planned but in time for Chan's party. There was no mention of the phone calls they had planned to make. Had he forgotten, Hannah wondered. She couldn't she knew logically blame him if he had. Once he was in a business setting he became totally involved and wasn't he after all trying to do his best for them both? She felt disappointed all the same that he'd discounted what was important to her. She wanted to talk to him about the odd sensation she'd had in Wanchai, to get his reaction, another perspective. If only, she wished, Sally was in Hong Kong or someone she could really talk to so she wasn't so dependent on Richard.

The time until she felt she could reasonably ring her father, knowing he'd be settled for the morning in his study, seemed to drag on forever. She made herself a snack, endless cups of tea and prepared her oral lessons for the next three days in advance. At 6.p.m. when she felt she could wait no longer, she dialled her father's number.

She waited on edge as it went on ringing, ringing for at least three minutes, then she heard, to her dismay, not her father's voice as she'd wanted but again the strange woman's voice that she'd heard the week before – sharp and in control.

"Olga Slade speaking."

Hannah braced herself. "I'd like to speak to Mr Delaney, please."

"Do you mean," and there was a plum in her voice now, "Thomas Delaney or Hugo Delaney?"

"Thomas Delaney, of course. It's his residence." Why on earth, Hannah wondered, should she mention Hugo.

"And who may I ask is calling?"

"It's his daughter, Hannah. And I'm speaking from Hong Kong," she added beginning to feel exasperated. "It's a long distance call. Can you get him quickly, please?"

There was a long silence in which Hannah began to feel she'd been cut off. "Hello, are you there?" twice she called down the phone. She was aware then of other voices in the background but couldn't distinguish them or make out what they were saying. "Hello, could you please answer? I want to speak to my father."

Another silence, then the same clipped voice returned. "I'm afraid your father's away at present."

"Away? Where?"

"He's staying with some friends in Scotland."

"What's his address and telephone number?"

"He's travelling around. I haven't got a precise address for today."

"But you must know basically where he is. Who are you anyway and what are you doing at Yadrahna and where's Mrs Mason?"

But the questions went unanswered and what Hannah had feared now happened and the phone went dead. "Hello. Hello." But it was no use. Whoever Olga Slade was, she had put down the phone.

Hannah stared down at the receiver for a moment in helpless anger and disbelief. She felt she wanted to stamp on the phone, crush the voice of the woman who'd put the receiver at Yadrahna down. What was happening and what was she doing at Yadrahna anyway? Where above all was her father and how was she going to find out?

Chapter 2

"I think you should ring Hugo, then your aunt, then Sally – in that order."

Richard poured himself a whisky and soda. The flat was hot and clammy. Hannah had forgotten again to switch on the air conditioning but he felt too elated by the way the day had gone to make a point. He could still hardly believe it. Not only had he secured the contract but a fee well beyond what he'd expected.

It had been touch and go at first and he thought he hadn't convinced Chan, then at what seemed the last moment Chan had come round. Or had it been always from the start his intention and he just enjoyed the game? Well, Richard reflected, he'd never know now for sure but perhaps he could congratulate himself to a degree. His pinpointing of pressure between socialising – hadn't it after all paid off?

He'd be able to afford now the wedding and a holiday – if only he could get Hannah to stop worrying.

Richard looked down at her pale strained face, her long brown hair clinging damply now to her neck, her eyes focused on the phone and he wanted to force her to acknowledge him and what he'd achieved. But it wouldn't work, he knew. Nothing mattered to her now but the facts

relating to her father. All he could do was to get her to act, to get the facts, expose them and with luck bury them.

Decisively he took his whisky through to the bathroom. "You ring while I have a shower. Then we'll discuss the outcome."

Hannah hesitated, staring down at the phone. Richard was right, she knew. Hugo was the obvious person to ring first but for some reason she could never define she was always reluctant to ring Hugo. As brother and sister, they'd never been close. His mother with her bitterness over the divorce had seen to that. Yet despite his remoteness, she and Hugo had nevertheless over the years evolved a working relationship without quarrelling as far as family matters were concerned and she felt she could trust him basically to tell her if her father was ill or if anything was wrong. Why should she not trust him now?

Overcoming at last her hesitation, she dialled his number but as she'd expected she heard the click again of the answer phone and instead of Hugo the impersonality of his rehearsed plummy voice recorded on tape. "This is Hugo Delaney. I'm beavering away in the studio at present. If you would like to leave a message, I may ring back when I have my coffee break."

May, she thought, or won't? Rarely had Hugo been known to ring back for short distances, let alone long. It was extremely unlikely she knew that he'd ring Hong Kong. She left a message all the same asking him to find out the whereabouts of her father and to let her know.

She tried then, as Richard had suggested, her father's sister, her Aunt Eileen at Hampstead, but there was no

answer. There was only one thing for it. She would have to ring Sally and enlist her aid.

Sally, an old friend from university days, had always got on well with her father. Would she though, with the demanding marketing job she had, have time to go over to Yadrahna, even though it was only 20 miles away? Was it fair to ask her? Well, she could always say no.

But as she knew at heart Sally wouldn't and didn't say no. Getting through to her eventually in her office, Hannah expressed her concern as briefly as she could about the strange woman at Yadrahna.

"You'd like me to go over and check then?" Sally's voice came back to her immediately involved.

"Could you, Sally? I mean if you've got the time."

"Of course I've got the time. I'm very fond of your father, as you know. I wouldn't like to think he had a problem we didn't know about. I expect he's all right but it's as well to check. I tell you what. I'll go over in the lunch hour. It'll only take an hour or so and I can eat my sandwiches en route. I've already got your number, haven't I? I'll ring you back in 2 – 3 hours. How would that be? Will you be there?"

"Yes, of course. And thanks, Sally, thanks."

"Try not to worry."

"I'll try."

"So you got through then successfully." Richard smiled as he emerged swathed in a polar designed towel from the bathroom. It was a smile she recognised that didn't want to know of doubts, drawback or disaster – a smile that wanted to know that everything was all right and she told him that, yes, Sally was going to investigate for her.

"Good. So for the time being we can relax."

Water from his hair flecked onto her breasts as he leaned over and kissed her.

"Well, are you pleased?"

His face was shiny, boyish as when she'd first known him, free for the moment from the strain of striving and she felt herself wanting him back again in the past.

"About the contract you mean?" she asked stalling.

"And the fact that we can have a break long enough."

"Of course – it's great."

"But not of great consequence compared to your father I think – "

"I'm sorry. I just need to know, Richard, to be able to get in touch."

Again the strange experience she'd had in Wanchai came back to her, her father's voice insistent, calling. What did it mean? Did it have a meaning or was it just imagination, wishful thinking? She felt she wanted to discuss it with Richard but the time seemed wrong and she feared his dismissal of the subject, even mockery. She felt she ought to tell him too about the course she wanted to do and her doubts but hadn't the heart to puncture his obvious success. Tomorrow, she decided, when she'd heard from Sally.

"You'll be in touch, you'll see." Pushing aside the phone Richard knelt down beside her. "In another month, even week, you'll be laughing at your fears." Gently, firmly he stroked her legs, her thighs, then discarding his towel, taking her hand, he led her through to the bedroom.

She felt more relaxed after they'd made love, more assured and able to tell him that she needed to stay in for

Sally's call, that she couldn't go to Chan's party. He wasn't pleased and made her promise to ring him at Chan's villa as soon as Sally had rung so he could come and collect her but, at least, she thought with relief, when he'd gone, he hadn't been insistent as she'd feared.

An hour before Sally was due to ring, she sat by the phone, ready waiting, her thoughts focused on her father.

Then her eyes closed and, momentarily dreaming, she was back again as a child in the garden at Yadrahna. There was no one else in the garden but herself and she was searching for signs of tadpoles stirring in the spawn of the long established pond enclosed by willow and alder at the back of the house. It was spring and she had a sense of life magically unfolding in the tadpole spawn and the willow buds opening – a sense of the infinite yet enclosed in a safe secret world where she could explore at will on her own. Then she heard in her dream her father again, calling in a voice compelling in its urgency and concern. Running through the trees, she found him in the drive, his eyes wide staring at her with sadness. Looking up then she saw flames and smoke billowing from Yadrahna's windows, heard the penetrating siren of a fire engine advancing up the drive and she awoke with a start to hear the phone beside her ringing.

Shaking, she reached out for the receiver.

"Hello."

"Han, it's Sally. I've rung a bit early I'm afraid but I thought I ought to let you know that I went over to Yadrahna as planned and I couldn't see any sign of your father. I tried the front door but there wasn't any answer and his car wasn't in the drive. Hello are you there?"

"Yes."

"You sound a bit odd. Are you all right?"

"I just had a dream about Yadrahna, that it was burning."

"Goodness. You are in a state. Well, I can assure you that it was solidly there two hours ago so there's no need to worry on that score." Sally continued briskly, "To cut a long story short. There was no sign of the strange woman you mentioned either but I had a look round the garden while I was there and I came across a young chap in the vegetable garden sorting plants. So I asked him if he knew where your father was. He was a bit reluctant to talk at first, even hostile I'd say. But eventually I got it out of him that your father had been confined for some weeks to his room and had recently gone into hospital."

"Hospital? But why? What's wrong with him? Did he say?"

"He said he didn't know, that he was just a part time gardener and not welcomed in the house."

"Did he tell you the name of the hospital?"

"He said he'd no idea, adding rather sarcastically that he wasn't informed about family matters and if I wanted details I'd have to ask Madame Slade who was out for the day or Lord Hugo Delaney who would be there at the weekend."

"Hugo? But he hardly ever goes to Yadrahna."

"Well, apparently he is this weekend."

"There was no sign then of Williams?"

"None. Apparently he left when Emma Mason went some three months ago."

"How odd." Williams, her father's old gardener, she'd known had intended to stay till he retired. Why should he

28

feel the need to go early? Another thread it seemed was cut. Williams had been someone she could talk to and trust, someone she could have talked to and trusted now.

"And who's this young chap who's taken over?" Even without knowing him she felt a latent hostility that he'd taken over from Williams, that he'd indulged in sarcasm for something important to her. Surely he must know the name of the hospital. How could he not know, from simple curiosity working there?

"He's a student he told me, trying to keep himself on some environment course."

"Well, he hasn't exactly been helpful, has he?"

"No, but it could be genuine he doesn't know. It sounds as if there's no love lost between him and the new housekeeper and she's the one in control. Anyway, I felt I ought to check first that the story's true. I tried ringing Hugo but couldn't get hold of him so I decided to tell your aunt. I felt she'd have more right than I have to get information and see your father. She's got some kind of virus at the moment and feels she can't go visiting but said she'd ring round the likely hospitals and get through to Hugo on another number. Either way she'll ring you shortly. I'm sorry I've got nothing more definite to report."

"I'm sure you've done everything you could, Sally."

"Wait and see what your aunt says, Han. You can ring me back then if you need further help."

"Yes, yes, I'll do that and thanks, Sally, thanks."

Dear Sally – all the trouble she'd taken, Hannah reflected, but what was really going on and why had the situation, as it appeared, been kept from her hidden? Why hadn't Hugo at least told her? Surely her father couldn't

have persuaded him not to? It was all so uncharacteristic of her father, of his trust in her, of his openness and the promise he'd made to let her know if anything was wrong. Could it be that he was in fact seriously ill, in come way incapacitated?

Hannah felt she couldn't bear to sit any longer by the phone waiting and decided to ring her aunt instead of waiting for her to ring. To her surprise, her aunt responded on the second ring but not with her usual cheerful, confident voice.

"Hannah, dear, I was just about to ring you. Your friend Sally told me the situation so I rang immediately through to Hugo's business number. I'm afraid the news is not good. Your father is very ill. Hugo's just told me in fact he's in intensive care."

"Intensive care?" It was what deep down she knew now she'd feared. "But why?"

"Hugo didn't seem to be able to explain but I got the impression it's touch and go. So I think you should come, dear, if you want to see him just in case."

"What hospital is he in?" Again she wanted to ask why, why no one had told her, a helpless sense of anger rising through her fear.

"It's St James's Hospital, dear, Windsor."

"Right." Hannah forced her voice to a decision. "I'll get the next flight I can."

Chapter 3

"Please, let me be in time and find him still alive."

Hannah leaned forward in her seat, repeating the words silently to herself, willing, desperately wishing they were already at Heathrow. It was seven hours now since she had boarded the Boeing and left Hong Kong – seven hours of inactivity, not knowing and there were still six to go.

Her eyes dulled with tiredness, she stared out at the now familiar grey section of the Boeing's wing. Fleeced by cloud, it gave the impression of static rather than forward motion.

She should sleep she knew while there was still a chance so she could cope when the plane arrived. But every time she closed her eyes, the telephone call with her aunt came back to her, renewing her unease and apprehension.

"It's touch and go so I think you should come, dear, if you want to see him – just in case."

Despite another phone call, her aunt had been unable to indicate the nature and cause of the illness which Hannah had found strange. Surely Hugo must have been informed by the hospital.

But she hadn't pressed the matter. The overriding need in her mind was to get home as soon as possible to be with her father and to help him.

By good fortune, ringing immediately round the airlines, she'd found a cancellation on a Boeing leaving at 6 the next morning and she was already booked and packing when Richard returned from Chan's party.

He hadn't been pleased, she could tell by his questions, and hadn't wanted her to go. She'd taken him by surprise and acted without consulting him and on the way to the airport pointedly he'd observed that he could have negotiated a better deal for her, a cheaper rate through his contacts, if she'd left the arrangements to him.

But by the time they'd reached the departure lounge, his eyes were strained with more than the tiredness of their early rising. "You'll come back, won't you?" he'd pleaded as they'd said goodbye. Concerned how she'd manage on her own and where she'd stay, he had insisted she'd taken the key to his flat in Hampstead in case of problems and as a base where he could contact her. She'd taken the key but more to please him from a sense of guilt she'd doubted, undervalued him than because she'd felt the need for the key. Yadrahna, despite the strange woman there, was after all her home. Why should she not stay there? It was inconvenient now that she'd sold her car but she'd manage somehow by public transport.

When Richard had gone on to express his concern that no one had been asked to meet her, she'd told him not to worry, that she'd be all right, better on her own. Now, uncertain again about what she'd find at the end of the flight, she began to wish she had rung Sally and asked her to meet her at Heathrow.

"Coffee?"

Beaming with efficient ease, an air hostess handed her a tray and Hannah felt the aroma of the coffee tempting, reviving her.

As she drank it, refocusing, she noticed that the Indian man sitting beside her was smiling with his eyes closed. Was he awake, she wondered, or asleep or in the world of dreams between?

She had no idea of his name, his work or why he was travelling but he had spoken to her earlier of the beauty and timelessness of the Indian countryside and its remote villages and the need to conserve them close to the soil from which they'd grown, had spoken with a Welsh like lilt in his accent with a quiet conviction that had impressed. She'd told him then about her father. He'd listened without comment but with an empathy that reassured.

He wasn't a young man. His hair, though still dark, was turning to grey and there were lines of ageing sketched across his forehead and down his cheeks but they were lines following the contours of his smile and reflections, rather than disappointment or striving which she usually associated with middle age and there was a calm peacefulness about his face generally that made her feel a surge for a moment of hope.

Her father was after all, she reasoned with more optimism, a basically healthy man, had never had a day off in his working life and though he was 76 now, this was not old considering present day life spans. He was still young moreover in spirit. True, he'd looked drained from the effects of flu before she'd left but there'd been no obvious signs of deterioration in his faculties.

Or had she missed something in all the rush of leaving, some sign he'd kept hidden? There was something strange certainly about his letters. The first one which she'd received some three weeks after she'd arrived in Hong Kong in response to her own, had been quite normal, reflecting her father's usual resilient self, describing visits to friends and further plans for the garden. There'd been a long gap then – eight weeks before the letter with the shaky handwriting she'd doubted. Then a gap of twelve weeks, despite her writing five times, before the strange stilted typewritten letter dated the 16th June which she'd just received.

Why hadn't he written for such long periods of time? It must be, she reflected, that he'd been ill. But why hadn't he told her? He'd made the point himself that she'd hear if there was bad news, if he was ill. Why then hadn't she heard before and what was it that was wrong? Had he been trying through the strangeness and irregularity of the letters themselves to tell her something was wrong that she'd failed to notice, failed to comprehend?

She felt suddenly a constriction in her throat, a fear she wouldn't make it, wouldn't reach him in time, that she could hardly breathe; then a hand gently laid on her arm and the dark brown eyes of the Indian beside her, awakened now, regarding her with kindly concern.

"I think you should sleep now. You have a problem that will not go away when you arrive and you will need the strength to deal with it."

There were no questions, to Hannah's relief, no demands or need to explain and Hannah felt her throat relax again in tune with the calmness of his voice.

Beyond the window, the clouds enveloping the Boeing were darkening into night and, at the Indian's bidding, she closed her eyes and for the first time since the news had come to her of her father, she slept.

Six hours later, she awoke to the glint of sunlight on the Boeing's wing and an announcement that the plane was about to land at Heathrow.

As she sorted her hand luggage, the Indian handed her a card with his name and address. "Come and see me if you come to India and I'll show you the villages and the countryside where I work."

"Thank you." Taking the card, she read: Dr Madan M. Ganga, Mobile Leprosy Unit, Kalavati Colony, Haldwani, Dist. Nainital,U.P.India.

She'd guessed, though not defined, that he was some kind of healer from the way he spoke and empathised but the leprosy took her by surprise. It belonged in her mind to an ancient prejudice and time, not a jet set age – a disease that should surely by now have been erased. But what did she really know of disease, indeed anything in India or other parts of the world? So much she didn't know, so much she had to learn. So much she felt she could learn if she stayed long enough to try.

"Thank you," she repeated, touched by his offer. "I'd like to. I'm not sure when though it would be." Her father, the need for resources, another job, Richard – the obstacles in her mind mounted.

"It doesn't matter when," he smiled, dismissing the exigencies of time. "India will still be there waiting for you. Close to the earth, in its heart it doesn't change and you will know when it is right for you and you can learn and understand."

"Yes." Carefully she put the card in the inner pocket of her bag. It wasn't impossible, she thought. Perhaps one day she would go – when her father was well again.

Briefly later as they passed through customs, he said goodbye, then merged as another Indian claimed him into the anonymity of the crowds at the exit.

Uncertain for a few moments she hovered, missing his presence, his reassurance, wishing she'd asked Sally to meet her; then trying to subdue her anxiety and fear, she manipulated her two suitcases through the crowds to the phone.

There was no reply from Hugo's number – only the same message on the answer phone that he was "beavering away" in his studio. Her aunt's number likewise gave no reply. She decided to waste no more time and go straight by taxi to the hospital.

"St James's Hospital, Windsor, please."

The taxi driver, to her relief, seemed to know where the hospital was and was not anxious to give his opinion or to ask hers on the state of the British economy or Europe.

Free with her own thoughts, Hannah tried to visualise the possibilities of what she'd find and what she could do. If her father was better, she would try, she decided, to get him moved back to Yadrahna. It would be what he'd want, she was sure – to be in his own home and surroundings. But supposing he wasn't better?

The thought threw her into a panic again of fear and she could no longer concentrate. Places where she could stay to be near him all jumbled in her mind without resolution.

The closer they got to Windsor, the more the uncertainty weighed and pressed against her temples,

giving her a headache rather than the calm she wanted. But at last the taxi entered the carefully designed grounds of St James's Hospital. Hannah took in a compact building of concrete and glass before the taxi stopped in a prescribed place before the main swing door.

"Would you like me to wait?" the driver offered.

"No thanks. I'll be staying some time." She paid what seemed an exorbitant fare then struggled to the reception desk with her cases.

"Good morning."

A receptionist, with sleek shoulder length black hair and the coolly efficient manner of someone used to conveying people to their destinations with minimum fuss and involvement, smiled brightly at her.

"Can I help?"

"I've come to see my father, Mr Delaney, Thomas Delaney."

"Do you know which ward he is in?"

"No, I'm afraid not."

"It's all right. I'll check."

"Thanks."

Nervously Hannah watched as she tapped with long thin fingers on the keys of her computer, then scrutinised several lists on the screen, tapped then scrutinised again, finally shaking her head.

"I'm afraid there's no Delaney recorded for any of the wards. Are you sure he's in this hospital?" Her voice assumed a note of tact and caution. "There's another St James's Hospital in Reading."

"No, I'm sure it's this one. My aunt rang me and told me only yesterday."

Or was it the day before? Hannah felt confused, disorientated by the time change.

"Do you know the date on which he was admitted and what for?"

"I'm afraid I don't." Hannah felt suddenly ignorant and exposed, a sense of being through the receptionist's eyes an object now of suspicion and she felt compelled to explain. "You see I've been abroad. I only came back to England this morning. I haven't been given any information."

"Just a minute. I'll check admissions." Her long thin fingers flickered again over the keys and she frowned again at the screen, then, to Hannah's relief, resumed her bright smile. "Right here we are. Thomas Delaney admitted to Ward B 6th June."

"He's still here then?"

"I'll have to check with the sister of Ward B. It may take me a while to get hold of her. I suggest you wait in the waiting room and I'll give you a call when I've got through."

Sitting in a comfortable armchair, Hannah felt she could easily drop off again, at the same time a realisation that she was on her own now and had to manage alone, be alert, that she had to look after the suitcases and couldn't go to sleep. Richard was no longer at hand to watch with her, for her and for the first time since she'd left Hong Kong she found herself missing him. He'd always known how to deal with situations of doubt, could take charge, get results. He'd have found out instantly where her father was and what had happened. Why couldn't she?

Despite her resolution, her eyes were closing when she was abruptly aware a half an hour later of the receptionist tapping her arm.

"Sister Jones from Ward B is coming down to have a word with you."

"You've found out then where my father is?"

To Hannah's surprise, ignoring her question, the receptionist picked up her suitcases and led her across to a small reception room behind the reception desk.

"It'll be more private for you here." Seeming anxious not to be further involved, the receptionist retreated to the door. "Sister Jones will be with you shortly."

It was an oppressively small room with minimum furniture and bare white walls and a stale smell of perfume – a room Hannah instinctively wanted to escape from.

Though only minutes, it seemed like hours before the door eventually opened again and the expected Sister Jones, dressed in a traditional royal blue uniform, came in, carrying an official file.

"I'm sorry to have kept you waiting, Miss Delaney."

Her voice was quiet, reassuring. She had greying hair and an experienced manner but there was a sympathetic concern in her blue eyes that immediately filled Hannah with apprehension.

"You've got bad news for me, haven't you?"

Sister Jones nodded sadly and sat down beside Hannah, taking her hand.

"I'm sorry to have to tell you, Miss Delaney, but your father died with us in Ward B three days ago."

Chapter 4

"Three days ago! But he can't have. It can't have been my father if it was three days ago. He was alive when I got the message about him and I came straight away. That's less than a day. There must be some mistake. You must have confused him with someone else. It's impossible. It can't be him – " Hannah felt her voice at last falter.

Sister Jones was continuing to regard her steadily with sympathy and concern.

"There's been no mistake, Miss Delaney. Your father was the only Delaney in the hospital." She hesitated a moment before continuing. "I think unfortunately the messages to you didn't get through as they were intended."

"Messages? What messages?"

"I asked your brother to contact you at the beginning of June when your father was first admitted when we realised his cancer was terminal."

"My father had cancer? Then why – "

"I tried to let you know, Miss Delaney, and your father – he was concerned in the last two weeks that he hadn't heard from you so I asked your brother to contact you again. Why the message got through so late I don't know but what I said about your father is true. There's been no confusion."

"I'd like to see him." There could still be a mistake, Hannah clutched in despair. People were always making mistakes. One could never be certain.

"I'm sure you will be able to see him if you wish." Sister Jones tried to sound encouraging. "But I'm afraid he's no longer in the hospital. The funeral director, I understand, has taken him to the mortuary."

"The mortuary?" Suddenly it was real and Hannah could feel in her heart the coldness of the slab on which he lay, could feel a numbness that froze her resistance, the firmness of her features, the hope she'd held since first her fear had risen.

Sister Jones glanced discreetly at her watch. She had to get back to some urgent cases on her ward yet felt she couldn't leave Hannah. Even the paleness had drained from her features and there was a stiffness in her stance as if she'd been immobilised by the shock or empathy was it? There was an unusual intensity, Sister Jones sensed, in her feeling for her father and something wrong about the way the messages had been withheld which could rebound later.

"I think," she said at length, trying to get through to Hannah, "that we should contact one of your friends to come over and be with you and take you home. Is there anyone specially you would like me to contact? Perhaps you could give me a number." There was bound to be someone, Sister Jones thought. She was very attractive with her fine features, her large brown eyes and her long dark hair. There must be someone who cared for her. But she had to press Hannah's hand before she responded.

"Perhaps Sally would come." Hannah fumbled in her bag for her address book.

"Right. I'll go and ring then."

Vaguely Hannah was aware of Sister Jones returning with some coffee and the news that Sally would be with her within the hour, then a huge vacuum of time alone with the frozen white walls of the reception room. Trying to drink the coffee, she felt alternately nauseous then hungry, tired then alert, then a gnawing pain accumulating in her belly and rising in her heart.

Her head throbbed with unanswered questions but she felt she couldn't focus, couldn't think. Nothing seemed to make sense though she knew she had somehow to resolve some sense, some action. But how and what and why – why had Hugo not told her?

"I don't understand." It was all she could think to say to Sally when she arrived.

"We'll find out. Don't worry." Fashionably dressed in a beige two–piece with a positive smile, wavy blond hair and cool grey eyes, Sally Thompson gave the impression at once of what she was – efficient, calm and able to take charge. "The main thing just now is for you to have some peace and quiet."

Never, Sally thought, had she seen Hannah looking so desolate and drained. "I suggest we go back to my place. We can discuss things later when you've had some sleep."

"I slept on the plane. There was an Indian. He..." Hannah could still recall his effect but the words to describe it eluded her.

"Cast a spell on you?" Sally ventured, trying to divert her.

"Something like that." She's like Richard, Hannah thought, even her eyes unswerving and in control and she

felt unsure again. "I don't want to disrupt you, Sally, if you've got calls to make."

"You're obviously forgetting I'm my own boss now. If I want to take a day off, I can. And I'm going to take a day off now. Besides, it's due to me anyway, so you don't have to worry on that score. Right now, before we go. Is there anything you need to find out or do either here or in Windsor? The funeral director, for example, have you got his name and address?"

"No, I haven't."

"Right then, I'll check that out with the sister you saw. And Hugo – he lives in Windsor, doesn't he? Shouldn't we perhaps check with him what arrangements have been made before we leave?"

"I suppose so."

"We needn't if you don't want to."

"No, you're probably right. It's just that," Hannah struggled to express the unease she felt through the pain, "I feel Hugo has let me down."

"In what way?"

"He didn't tell me that Dad had cancer."

"Why ever not?"

"I don't know. That's the problem."

"Wouldn't it be better to find out? He may have a good reason for not telling you and if you don't see him, you won't know."

"True."

"I tell you what," and feeling the need for action, Sally picked up the two suitcases. "Let's get these to the car. Then I'll go and see sister and ring Hugo and see if he's there."

As Hannah had expected, the only answer from Hugo was the answer phone. But Sally was undeterred. Consulting the map, she decided Hugo's house was on their way out of Windsor and no problem.

They stopped in a secluded road of terrace houses close to the river. Hugo's was the end house with a garden wall and a larger back garden than the others in the road and distinguished by its immaculately painted white window frames and door, by its carefully nurtured pots of geraniums and purple clematis trailing over the front windows, by its gleamingly polished brass door knocker and brass Victorian insurance sign. Parked outside and equally polished and gleaming, as if awaiting an important call, was Hugo's 1952 Daimler with its pre–reflective number plate with embossed silver letters.

There was no room to park nearby so Sally parked in the only free parking space at the other end of the street from which they could just see Hugo's door.

There was no sign of Hugo himself but then Hugo wasn't, Sally reflected, exactly a "street man", inclined to pass the time of day chatting to neighbours and passers by – more an individualist, she remembered, a collector of valued or artistic objects but not a collector, she guessed, of women. On the few occasions they'd met, she'd sensed instantly a withdrawing, as of someone fearful of being involved. He'd later made, she'd noticed, on one of her visits to Yadrahna, some snide remarks about dominating women. She took Hannah's arm and they walked to the white door.

As she rang the doorbell and then rapped the brass door knocker, Sally was sure she saw movement behind

the net curtain of the window beside the door, the twitch of a curtain at the window above but no one came to the door though they knocked and rang three times.

"We'd better go. There's obviously no one here," Sally enunciated as clearly as she could towards the net curtain. She sensed eyes following them then as they walked back down the road and she diverted Hannah for a few minutes away from the location of the car to another road.

"Let them think we've gone and we'll watch for a few minutes and see if anyone comes out."

Back in the car some twenty minutes later, Sally was confirmed in her expectation as they saw the door of Hugo's house open and Hugo himself emerge with a shopping bag and head towards them in the direction of the town.

He was dressed in exactly the same outfit he'd worn, Sally remembered, when she'd last seen him at Yadrahna – the same olive green corduroy jacket, green trousers and cap as if he was playing the country gentleman rather than accepting an urban role; only he was redder in the face and more overweight and he was walking with less steadiness and composure and glancing back every few moments over his shoulder as if uneasy about being followed or observed.

"Now," Sally nudged Hannah when she assessed Hugo would not be able to avoid them and opened the car door on Hannah's side, stepping out herself also so as to block his pathway. For a moment she thought he was going to flail her aside with his bag. His eyes shifted in alarm, then coolly taking control again, he focused on the space between them and smiled.

"So you're back then."

"Yes, I'm back." Confused by his stance, Hannah wasn't sure how to express her concern. She felt she wanted to trust him but he wasn't looking at her and she needed to know the truth not only about her father but about Hugo himself.

"Why didn't you tell me, Hugo?"

"Tell you?" His voice sharpened with a hint of irritation and unease. It was a dry voice, detached. "Tell you what?"

"That Dad was so ill."

"I did tell you. I told Eileen and she said she'd phone."

"When it was too late, Hugo. He died three days ago."

"Well, that's hardly my fault, is it? I can't be responsible for when he died."

"No, but you knew a month ago when he first went into hospital that he was very ill. The sister told me she asked you to let me know. Why didn't you?"

"Why?" Hugo paused. Hannah could feel him oiling his voice for reassurance as he went on. "Well, you wouldn't have thanked me, would you if you'd come all the way from Hong Kong to find a false alarm. It wasn't clear how long he'd live at all. He could have lived any time – 6 months or a year. Some people live months, even years beyond what they've been told." Hugo gave a gesture of expanse with his bag.

"That's not the point, though, is it? Don't you see? I needed to see him. And Dad in the last two weeks the sister told me – he asked you specially to let me know." Hannah felt she wanted to shout now at his obtuseness but the pain was too great inside her and she felt too weak, too drained. Why couldn't he see or was it that he didn't want to see? Exhausted, she leaned against the door of Sally's car.

"You obviously didn't get my letter then." Oiled, his voice had taken on a purr.

"Letter?"

"I sent a letter. Let's see – it must have been ten days ago, explaining how things were."

"Why didn't I get it then?" She felt she wanted to believe him, needed to believe, but his voice didn't convince.

Hugo shrugged. "I can't be held responsible for the inadequacies of the Hong Kong postal services."

"Surely though if you hadn't heard from me you must have wondered. You could have rung me. Dad had my number in his desk."

"Look, I did my best to contact you." Hugo's voice started to rise on the defensive. "I can't be blamed if you go off half way round the world to some place with a dubious postal service."

"I'm not blaming you, Hugo. I just want the truth."

But the truth Hannah could feel hanging in a balance of silence between them, unresolved, unresolving. She was silent as Sally suggested they went back to Hugo's house to discuss the funeral.

"I can't stop now." Hugo waved his shopping bag with dismissal. "Mother's not well. She needs medication. The funeral's all sorted anyway. 2.30 at St Mary's Church in the village on Thursday."

"Thursday!" Hannah echoed, amazed that he could have gone ahead without consulting her. "But it's already Tuesday. There's not time enough to let people know."

"You'd better tell that to the vicar then. He's the one who gave the date."

"But why the great hurry? There must have been another date."

"Well there wasn't. And as far as letting people know goes, I've put an advert in the local paper which comes out tomorrow."

"But most of his friends are not local. We need to put it in the national press."

"Do you know how much it costs in the national press?"

"What does it matter how much it costs? Don't we owe it to him to let his friends and colleagues know?"

"Go ahead then and put a notice in but you'll have to pay for it yourself."

"I'll contact the executor. Who is he, by the way?"

"Hugh Jamieson."

"Hugh Jamieson?" Hannah echoed, remembering then the name of the man her father had warned her about, the estate agent who'd pressed him to sell Yadrahna. Surely it couldn't be the same Hugh Jamieson. There must be some mistake or had she got the name wrong, remembered it falsely? "Well, how do I contact him then?"

"You can't. He's not around at the moment. He's on holiday."

"On holiday where?"

"God only knows. Some exotic resort, no doubt."

"You've not seen the will then?"

"No, nothing. Haven't a clue. We'll obviously have to wait till he returns."

"When will that be?"

"I've no idea."

"But surely," Sally felt compelled now to intervene, "someone will be taking over in his absence."

"Apparently not." Hugo gave a disclaiming shrug. "I know it's all very frustrating. It is to me too but what can we do? We'll have to wait till he decides to return."

"I'd better go down to Yadrahna then," Hannah said.

For the first time Hugo looked at her direct and she sensed a trace of menace in his voice. "I shouldn't do that if I were you."

"Why not? We're his children for heaven's sake. It's the family home."

"We're not supposed to touch things till the executor gives the go ahead. After all, we don't even know what's in the will yet, do we? The house might have been left to some company or other. We don't know."

Don't you, Sally felt like challenging. Her instinct was not to trust Hugo. What he'd said about the executor and the house didn't ring true but she didn't want to challenge to the extent of upsetting Hannah still further. Already she was distressed enough. The conversation with Hugo was clearly an ordeal. They could always go to Yadrahna anyway without Hugo knowing. They were obviously not going to get any further with him now. He had some agenda of his own which they'd have to prise open by other means than direct contact.

Trying to sound cheerful and convinced, hiding her doubts, Sally suggested that Hugo kept his phone off the answer machine so they could keep in contact. Meanwhile they'd go to her house and she wrote down for him her telephone number and address.

"That sounds a good idea. I'll see you then at the church on Thursday. And do, of course, ask more people to come if you like." With a benign smile of relief, Hugo

turned and waved back at them as he made his way on into the town.

They stared for a moment without speaking watching him go, Hannah puzzled and distressed, Sally angry and full of suspicion and doubt.

"Why do you suppose he doesn't want you to go to Yadrahna?" She helped Hannah back into the car and drove on out of Windsor.

"I don't know. Hugo's sometimes like that. He feels he has to stick to the letter of the law."

"There isn't really a law though about you going to Yadrahna."

"No, I suppose not. Yadrahna's meant to be mine anyway. Dad told me the day I left for Hong Kong that he was leaving Yadrahna to me in his will."

"Really? Do you think Hugo knew that? Did he tell Hugo?"

"He said he was going to but I don't really know for sure. From what Hugo has just said it sounds as if he didn't tell him. But there's no reason for Hugo to feel jealous. Dad told me he was leaving him all his investments."

"So he shouldn't have any reason to be on the defensive?"

"No, he's probably just upset. I know he seems a bit odd and his manner's off putting but I don't think he intends any real harm."

Doesn't he, Sally wondered. There was something about the cold grey eyes that made her doubt Hannah's assessment. Nothing obvious, certain. She could be wrong and certainly she didn't want to worry Hannah unnecessarily, cause her greater distress. There were things

though that obviously needed to be clarified and Hannah's interest protected.

"You've every right all the same to go to Yadrahna."

"Yes, but I don't want to cause any upset before the funeral. I'll go after the funeral."

"If you want some support, I'll be only too pleased to come with you." There was so much more Sally felt she wanted to ask Hannah, aspects that needed to be probed but in the seat beside her Hannah had turned away, with tears streaming down her face now, wanting only her father.

Chapter 5

"Colonel Delaney was a man of many talents, who gave himself in service both to his country and to the local community." Reverend James paused, letting his eyes pass gently, unobtrusively, over the congregation gathered in the parish church. He felt mildly surprised that more people hadn't come to the funeral, that he himself had been asked to summarise Thomas Delaney's achievements when there were obviously others who knew him better. He was conscious that he had only a few sketchy facts from Hugo Delaney, not a comprehensive base on which to elaborate. He had wondered about asking Hannah if she wanted to say a few words about her father but she'd been and still was too distressed when he'd spoken to her. And it moved him – her grief as she sat alone in the front pew, spurred him to try for her sake to remember more of the facts and lift them to a higher plane.

"At the outbreak of war," he continued," he volunteered at the age of 19 and became a private in the Royal Ordnance Corp. He served with the British Expeditionary Force in France in 1939 and after Dunkirk was among the last to be evacuated. In 1943 he was promoted to Major and became the assistant military attaché in Russia. The year after he was assigned to the important task of marshalling men

and supplies along the south coast ready for the D Day landing.

After the war he joined the Territorials in the 53rd Infantry division and was subsequently promoted to Lt Colonel to command an army reserve unit. In 1956 he led the unit in Egypt during the Suez crisis and was awarded the Emergency Award Decoration.

Since his retirement, Colonel Delaney has given himself tirelessly to the many conservation societies that he has supported – The National Trust, the CPRE, the Wynton Naturalists Society and more globally Friends of the Earth and The World Wide Fund for Nature. He was particularly dedicated to helping the conservation of the tiger in India.

After the death of his dear wife some five years ago, Colonel Delaney withdrew to some extent from public life to his own privacy but it was never a privacy that kept out those who wanted his advice and he will be long remembered as a very kind, well loved and good humoured man – a man who will be greatly missed."

Reverend James paused before reading the Lord's Prayer. He was conscious of Hannah looking at him as if reflecting on what he'd said, conscious that what he'd said seemed inadequate, that Thomas Delaney had been a good man and deserved more of a personal tribute. He would suggest, he decided, a memorial service. There was something wrong about the rush, the pressure from Hugo Delaney to have the service so soon and it seemed strange that he was hovering at the back of the church rather than being in the front pew with Hannah.

After the prayers he explained that they would go for the rest of the service outside. The pallbearers picked

up the coffin and to the singing of "The Lord is my shepherd" Hannah, at his signal, followed him to the grave outside.

It was a clear blue, cloudless sky, the graveyard lush with uncut grass and wild flowers. After the cold grey light of the church, the sunlight dazzled her, hostile, glaring, and she had a strange sense of unreality as they grouped round the grave as if she was acting in a play that had no relation to either herself or her father.

She was aware of words, phrases, coming in waves from the vicar, words familiar yet remote, belonging to the past, to people who'd lived and died before:

"The days of man are but as grass:

he flourishes like a flower of the field;

when the wind goes over it, it is gone:

and its place will know it no more."

Hannah could feel the vicar trying to reach through to her, to give her hope as he scattered earth over the lid of the coffin. "We have entrusted our brother Thomas to God's merciful keeping and we now commit his body to the ground in the sure and certain hope of the resurrection to eternal life through our Lord Jesus Christ who died, was buried and rose again for us."

Sure and certain hope – could anything, Hannah wondered, be certain. Resurrection and eternal life – they didn't fit the facts, the inevitable laws of nature. Her father had never believed in resurrection and eternal life, nor had she, nor could she now. The only certainty was that he was in the coffin in the earth and would not return.

Inconsolable, as she scattered earth over the coffin, Hannah started to cry.

Watching her, Sally wanted to put her arms round her and comfort her but her Aunt Eileen had taken on the role and Sally felt it would not be diplomatic to intrude. On the opposite side of the grave, she noticed Hugo turn briefly and say something under his breath to a black haired, well–built woman in her early fifties standing beside him, garishly dressed in a suit of purple and emerald green and with innumerable rings that sparkled in the sunlight on her plump fingers. She had thick sensual lips, beady eyes and coarse features, heavily caked with make up. Who was she, Sally wondered. She could see no signs of grief on Hugo's face. The sunlight seemed to accentuate even more its coldness, a quiet satisfaction rather than sorrow and despite the warmth of the afternoon Sally felt a chill go through her. On the other side of Hugo, looking rather bored, stood a boy she guessed in his early teens with the same profile as Hugo and the same cool grey eyes.

As the mourners drifted to the church hall for refreshments, seeing Hannah and Aunt Eileen wanting to stay by the grave, she offered to bring refreshments back to them.

In the queue in the hall, trying to be unobtrusive, Sally edged her way forward to be within earshot of Hugo. The woman in the purple and green suit was still with him and they were talking quietly but more with the intimacy of business contacts, Sally sensed, than that of lovers. They were talking, she soon realised, about Yadrahna and repairs to the house and work in the garden. She missed several words and phrases through the clatter of teacups, then heard the word 'locksmith' and Hugo saying quite distinctly, "I want him to come to Yadrahna next week. I

thought perhaps Wednesday. Could you guarantee being in on Wednesday afternoon?"

"I'm afraid not Wednesday, Hugo. I've an appointment in Oxford to have my hair done on Wednesday afternoon."

"What about Thursday then?" There was an edge of impatience now in Hugo's voice.

"I could be in on Thursday, yes."

"Right. I'll make an appointment then. I'll be down, of course, at the weekend with mother but remember what I said about letting certain people in."

"I've been very careful I can assure you."

"Good. Just try and keep it that way."

Sally strained to hear more of what they were saying but a couple had shifted in front of her and she felt she was stretching her luck keeping close to them for too long. Hugo had already turned round and noticed her with the same cold look in his eye. Collecting some tea and sandwiches, she went back to Hannah and her aunt.

They'd moved to a seat at the far end of the graveyard. Aunt Eileen had her arm round Hannah and was comforting her. Gratefully Hannah took the tea but said she didn't feel like eating.

"You must have something, dear, to keep your strength up, "Aunt Eileen urged.

Smartly dressed in a black Jaeger suit, with her fine features and silvery grey hair swept back in a French knot, Aunt Eileen cut a distinguished figure. At 72 she still ran her own decorating business, working a full day and Hannah admired her for it, for her persuasiveness, her curiosity and her forthright stance but the very qualities she admired in Aunt Eileen she found now tiring and felt she wanted to be alone.

"I'm sure Richard would agree with me. How is Richard by the way?"

"He's fine – fine."

"I know it's none of my business, dear, but why isn't he here with you?"

"He couldn't leave Hong Kong just now. He has to finish the contract."

"I see. So when are you going to get married then?" Aunt Eileen's eyes were the eyes of her father, brown and discerning, disconcerting.

"Married? I never said anything about getting married, Aunt Eileen."

"No, but it would be unwise at your age not to think about it. Richard has good qualities as well as good looks, you know. He'd look after you, Hannah, and you need looking after, especially now."

"Do I?" Hannah could feel a huge emptiness inside her as if her womb had been ripped out, leaving a void instead of hope, again the need to be alone. "I'm not sure I'm the marrying kind."

"Not the marrying kind! Whatever next? You surely want children, don't you?"

In a world already overpopulated, Hannah wondered, but she felt she hadn't the energy or inclination to launch on such a global perspective. Aunt Eileen was bound to challenge her. Without thinking she said, "You don't have to marry to have children."

"So you're going to be one of those lioness types – managing without the male, is that it? It's not a good strategy for children, Hannah."

"I'm not sure I want children."

"Of course you want children. You may not realise it now but you will do. It's in the genes. You can't just disregard evolution. Your purpose is ultimately to reproduce yourself. And you're already 27 remember. In my day..."

"It's different now, Aunt Eileen." I must hold on, Hannah told herself. I mustn't alienate her. She's the only relative left who was close to Dad, who knew him, knew what his wishes were. If only she would see. "You really mustn't worry about me. People, if they marry at all, marry much later now."

"Do they? Well take my advice," Aunt Eileen conceded at length, smiling, "and don't leave it too late. Don't let someone like Richard slip through your fingers." Affectionately, she squeezed Hannah's hand. "Have you seen the will yet?"

"No, the executor's away."

"There must be some deputy who could let you see it."

"Apparently not, according to Hugo."

"Well, you shouldn't take no for an answer," Aunt Eileen asserted. "You were promised Yadrahna – Tom told me – and you want to make sure you get it. Have you been down there yet?"

"No, Hugo seems to think it's not a good idea till the will's known."

"Well, I shouldn't take any notice of that. You've every right to go."

"That's what I said," Sally joined in supportively. She liked Aunt Eileen and her no nonsense approach. It disconcerted her that Hannah had been so noncommittal about Richard. What did Richard himself think, she wondered.

"And as far as that new housekeeper's concerned," Aunt Eileen continued. "I wouldn't trust her as far as I could throw her."

"You know her then?" Sally asked.

"I don't know her, no, and I don't want to know her. But it's my belief from a brief visit I made at Easter that she was trying to get Tom to drink and befuddle his senses."

"She made him actually drunk, you mean?"

"If not knowing what you're saying is drunk, then yes. Of course I didn't realise then he had cancer which might have had some bearing. But I had the distinct impression she was trying to get a hold over him and keep other people at bay. I wouldn't be surprised if getting his money wasn't the prime motive in getting there in the first place. Which is why you need to find out as soon as possible, dear, about the will and ensure you get what is due to you."

"You really think she may have influenced him?"

"I'm certain of it – if she had the chance. You can see it in her eyes – the grabber instinct. I can't think what Tom and Hugo were about employing her."

If only, Hannah thought, Emma had stayed. Why hadn't she? And why wasn't she here today, one of the people her father had most trusted?

"Why isn't Emma here?" she voiced aloud.

"I don't know, dear. Why not ask Hugo? He should know. Look he's just leaving. You could catch him now."

Aided by Sally, Hannah stumbled across the graveyard to the waiting cars by the Cotswold wall surrounding the churchyard. As Hugo approached his Daimler, she asked directly.

"Where's Emma, Hugo? Why isn't she here?"

Sally watched Hugo hesitate, affably shrug, then smile.

"I've no idea."

"Did you let her know?"

"She didn't leave her address."

"She must have. She wouldn't have gone without leaving Dad her address."

"Well, she did and there's nothing more I can tell you." Determined Hugo moved with his keys ready to the Daimler. "I'm afraid I have to go. I've got to get back and take mother to an appointment."

"What about a stone for the grave? What shall we arrange?"

"I'll leave that to you. You were always the one for words, weren't you?"

With a shifting smile, Hugo stepped into the Daimler and without looking back smoothly manoeuvred his way out from the remaining cars by the Cotswold stone wall and out onto the Oxford road.

Sally's eyes were drawn to the woman in purple and emerald green who'd accompanied him, now watching him go. Perspiration had stained the folds of her suit and blotched the make up on her face. She looked tired and strained from the heat and Sally thought she detected a sense of pique at being left abruptly on her own, then the dark beady eyes were turned on Hannah and herself with suspicion and she was pushing past them to a blue Renault which had been parked behind the Daimler. The rings on her plump fingers sparkled in the sun as she opened the Renault's door, then she heaved herself inside and drove off in the opposite direction to Hugo, up Winter Hill.

"You realise who that is, don't you?" Sally turned to Hannah, making a note of the Renault's number. "It's the housekeeper you rang – Olga Slade."

"Are you sure?" Like hard bright plastic on an ancient shore, the woman had jarred in her garish attire against the mellowed Cotswold stone and Hannah couldn't visualise her at Yadrahna at all.

"Yes. I heard her talking to Hugo about keeping people out of the house. There's a locksmith going apparently on Thursday because she said she'd be out on Wednesday. You've got your key for Yadrahna, haven't you?"

"I've got the front door key, yes."

"Good. Well, I suggest we go on Wednesday next when glamour guts purple is out. Are you ready to leave now?"

"I'll just go and say goodbye to Rev James. I won't be long."

"Ah, Miss Delaney." Rev James was standing, as if waiting for her, by the grave. "I was hoping to see you." He gave a tentative smile of concern. "I was wanting to tell you how sorry I am that it's all been such a rush for you. I would have liked to have consulted you about the service."

"I gather it was the only time that could be arranged."

"Well actually I suggested next week to Mr Delaney but he seemed anxious to have the service as soon as possible. I realise now that it may not have been suitable for all your father's friends and former colleagues from afar."

"So my brother specifically requested it early then?"

"He said he wanted it today, yes."

"I see." But Hannah felt she didn't see. She didn't see at all – only that Hugo had lied to her.

"It's not always easy," Rev James hesitated, conscious of Hannah's disquiet, "I mean to come to terms with the way things have happened. If you ever feel you want to come and talk about your father or anything related, please remember I'm always here and available, should you feel the need. Perhaps you might like to consider later a memorial service for him."

"Thank you. That's kind of you." And he had, Hannah thought, a kind and sensitive face, the same expression in his eyes as the Indian healer she'd met on the plane, the same empathy and calm. And like the Indian, she knew, though she didn't share his beliefs, that he was a good man, that he meant what he said and it came from the heart.

But she couldn't dispel the sense she had of a darker force, close, enclosing her – a force she didn't understand and couldn't prove but which instinctively she felt in the circumstances of her father's death, in the shadows and glaring light now over his grave.

Chapter 6

In the days following the funeral, Hannah stayed in her room at Sally's house mainly sleeping. Even when she'd slept twelve hours at a stretch, she still wanted more and often when Sally was at work in the afternoons she would go back to bed and sleep another three hours. She felt too exhausted even to walk, though Sally urged her for her own wellbeing to get some "fresh air and exercise."

Still she found it hard to take in her father's death. She knew it as a fact but not a fact she could accept; she knew she would have to investigate but couldn't bring herself to do it. She felt as if her energy and will power had been drained like blood out of her veins and found it difficult to talk, to communicate especially to people unknown to her. Though she appreciated Sally's support and efforts on her behalf, she was relieved in the day when she could be alone and not have to make an effort.

At Sally's insistence, she rang Richard to tell him about her father. Richard was duly sympathetic, as Sally guessed he would be, but his probing questions upset Hannah and she broke off the call. Richard rang back the next day full of apologies and concern saying he was making every effort to get the computer finally installed and running so that he could come back and be with her, he hoped, in September.

She wasn't sure that she wanted him with her. All she felt she wanted was her father back again, to be with him and be able to talk to him again. The pain, as she thought of him in her waking hours, increased instead of diminishing. She longed to go to Yadrahna yet feared what she would find.

"We must go," Sally urged, hoping that Hannah might be spurred to act and find out what lay behind Hugo's actions once she'd seen Yadrahna again and realised what she might lose. At last she managed to persuade Hannah and on the Wednesday after the funeral, the day Sally understood Olga Slade would be out, she drove Hannah over, parking her Golf in a lane nearby so they could approach unheard.

Hannah could see smoke rising from the kitchen garden to the west of the house, which made her suspect that Olga Slade might not be out after all but there were no cars in the drive, no blue Renault, no Daimler. As they quietly approached through the shrubbery, avoiding the gravel drive, and she saw Yadrahna before her again, its familiar mellowed ochre facade and classic proportions bathed in sunlight, house martins nesting already she could see in its eaves, her heart lifted with the hope that all might be well after all, that Yadrahna in its substance had not and would not be changed, that it would still be in essence her father's and as he'd wanted.

She couldn't resist then coming out of the shrubbery into the sunlight and going up to the front door, the key in her hand. She didn't care now who saw her. It was her right to be here, her right to remain.

More apprehensively, Sally followed, touching Hannah's arm as she turned the key and the door opened into the hallway.

"I think I'll stay and keep watch just in case." Sally transferred the key to the inside and locked the door, then positioned herself by the hall window, looking out at the drive. "I'll whistle if anyone comes."

"We're not burglars you know," Hannah responded, half indignant, half amused. "This is my home."

Or was it?

Nothing had changed in the hall. There were the same familiar Bokhara carpets and Chinese scrolls depicting the seasons on the wall, the same carved teak chest she'd known since childhood on its flagstone floor.

But in the study where her father had spent so much of his time, there was no sign of him at all. His extensive collection of antique books were still encased in their walnut shelves but all his personal belongings: his pen, his glasses, his binoculars, his pipe, the letters and cards that had strewn his desk, his slippers by the fire, all his photos on his desk and mantelpiece were all gone. The only photo remaining was one of Hugo and Marcus with his air gun. And in the lounge, there was the same sterile tidiness – the books he'd had ready to read, the photo of herself and her father which she'd particularly liked on the piano – gone as if a cold invisible had had sought to erase her father from any association with Yadrahna, from herself and the past, as if he had never been.

Only she knew he had been and she wasn't going to let him be erased. They had no right – Olga Slade and Hugo – for she was sure it was them now – no right to touch things as Hugo himself had claimed.

Shocked and shaking, she tried to calm herself by acting, looking in cupboards and drawers but none even of

the cards and letters she'd sent from Hong Kong could she find, let alone his belongings – only at the back of a coffee table drawer the photo she valued of herself and her father, scratched and without its silver frame. Carefully she put it in her bag and went upstairs.

Her father's bedroom she found as cleansed and organised as the lounge. Even his clothes had gone together with the collection of old watches he'd inherited from his grandfather in the top drawer of his mahogany chest.

Yet she felt reluctant to leave his room, felt there must be some place she hadn't searched, that there must be something else left of him but at the same time conscious that the time was passing. She would return later, she decided, and passed on to her own room. Trying, however, to open the door, she found to her dismay that it was locked and without its key. Why? Her room had never been locked. Why should it be locked now unless someone else was using it? Who? The obvious answer was Olga Slade but why should she need to with all the other rooms there were in the house? And what right had anyone else to take her room anyway?

Hannah felt she wanted to bang at the door with desperation, a growing sense of injustice at what was happening, the way her home and her father were being taken over.

She was conscious suddenly of Sally behind her.

"How's it going?"

"Not well. Not well at all." She tried to hold back her tears. "I've been locked out of my room."

And a lot more besides, I shouldn't wonder, Sally thought. It was even more ominous than she'd imagined

– the cleared tidied rooms, suggestive of more than usual determination. But she didn't want to linger with speculation. Their time was limited and she urged Hannah to check the remaining rooms, following her into the spare room that Hugo had customarily used.

It struck them both that it was no longer spare – more the settled province of someone in residence. Hugo's dressing gown was on the peg behind the door, the wardrobe full of his clothes and shoes. There were pens and stationery on his desk, a newly installed answer phone and a map spread out over the centre of the desk.

Hannah had never found map reading the easiest of pursuits and it took her a few minutes to realise that it was in fact a map of Yadrahna and its grounds but the grounds had been sectionalised as if detached as a separate entity from the house and there was a pencilled sketch of a minor road into the special site of scientific interest that was within Yadrahna's grounds and comprising its pond at the back of the house. Over the pond was a sketch of a building.

"It surely can't be a plan for development." Hannah looked at the map aghast, wanting to will it away.

"Not an official one – no." Carefully Sally checked under the map to see if there were any related documents, any letters but there was no correspondence, only some rough sketches of sectionalised buildings and a further draft of the road. "There's obviously though a wish on your brother's part, an intention. He hasn't done these sketches I imagine for fun." Sally looked at the map again. "It could be what he's intending to send as the base for a formal draft."

"But he can't," Hannah protested. "He doesn't even own Yadrahna. He's no right to."

"We don't know that though, do we?"

"You mean you think Dad may have changed his mind?"

Or had it changed for him, Sally thought cynically. It was all so obvious now what Hugo was aiming at. It all added up, made sense of his actions, his carefulness in trying to keep Hannah away. Yet Hannah in her grief couldn't and didn't want to take it in. Nor could she, nor could they know for sure till she'd seen the will. Trying to be positive, Sally urged,

"You need to see the will, Hannah, as your aunt said. It's imperative you see the will so you know how you stand."

"Yes, I see that. I.."

Hannah broke off suddenly as the phone beside her started to ring. The ringing seemed so loud, so compelling in the silent house she felt she had to pick the receiver up and stop it but Sally had laid a hand on her arm, restraining her. "Let's just listen to the message."

The ringing to Hannah's relief then stopped. There was a click followed by a preamble from Hugo, then to her surprise the name of the executor Hugo had given her.

"Hello, Hugo. Hugh Jamieson here. I got your message. Friday 15th will be fine for both myself and Gerald. Could we possibly make it 7 though instead of 6.30. And thanks, yes, we'd like to stay to dinner. There's obviously going to be lot to discuss. I anticipate some opposition from FOE regarding the special site. If there's anything you want to discuss first, then leave a message with Sheila, my secretary, on 447792 or you can phone me direct at home 891436. I'll look forward to seeing you."

As the message ended, Hannah stared down at the receiver in disbelief. "But he's supposed to be away on some exotic holiday."

"Well, obviously he's not and we'd better make sure while we're about it that we have the number." Sally replayed the tape, wrote down the two numbers Hugh Jamieson had given, then looked at her watch. "I think we'd better go. We don't want old beady eyes finding us here. It could negate the info we've got for Friday 15th."

"Yes." And Sally was right, Hannah reflected, and she felt grateful for her quick thinking, being with it and taking charge. She probably wouldn't even be here if it wasn't for Sally. She'd felt too drained over the past week to drag herself from the past to the present, let alone the future. But it depressed her, the feeling she had of helplessness, of not being able to cope, the sense she had from both Sally and Richard that she wasn't up to it, couldn't manage or decide for herself.

Following Sally down to the front door, it occurred to her that perhaps her father's belongings had been put in the attic. On impulse, she turned, telling Sally she wouldn't be long and ran up the main stairway along the landing and up the narrow stairway to the two rooms that had once been servants' quarters, which she'd used as a child for her hobbies and collections.

To her relief, they were still there, untouched, exactly as they'd been before she'd gone to Hong Kong – all her fossils and stones and dried fragments of insects she'd collected, laid out and labelled in the cabinets her father had made for her, all the boxes of bones she'd dug up from the garden: cows' thighs, jaw bones, skulls of mice and

badgers, boxes of books she'd had from childhood and hadn't wanted to part with.

But there was no sign, to her disappointment, of her father's belongings – only the sign still of Hannah, her namesake, carved jaggedly at the end of the main beam as it entered the stained white wall: "J in the waters of death with all my love Hannah."

As she stared at the cryptic message, trying as she'd tried many times before to elucidate its meaning, a large spider dropped from the beam beside her onto the floor and scuttled away behind a box of bones. In the beams of sunlight, penetrating the small eaves window, she noticed then other spiders and their webs, skilfully patterned, slanting the corners of the cabinets and beams.

The air smelt musty and stale and it struck Hannah afresh how confining it must have been for the other Hannah, how much she must have yearned to spread herself, own and determine more of her life instead of being so confined. She felt she had to open the window, let in freshness, movement.

Standing on a rickety chair, as she leaned forward to undo the catch, she noticed smoke again coming from the kitchen garden. Looking down, she could see where the fire was now at the bonfire site at the far end of the kitchen garden near the sheds, could see a man with thick, longish dark hair, tanned and stripped to the waist, forking into the fire the contents of a barrow. Hannah couldn't see exactly what was in the barrow but it seemed more like paper and clothing than plants.

Suddenly she recognised the distinctive red and blue striped dressing gown of her father as the man lifted it up

on a fork and deposited it in the fire which responded, as if in protest, with a billow of smoke. He grabbed then a handful of paper from the barrow, poking the fire at the same time with the fork till it burned more brightly.

Hannah slammed the window shut and, banging the attic door behind her, ran back downstairs past Sally and out into the kitchen garden.

"What the hell do you think you're doing?"

She was beside the man before he even noticed her approach, so intent he was on feeding the fire. He turned then with mild surprise as from a dream. He thought for moment he was imagining it – the beautiful face with dark brown eyes flaming at him with grief and rage. But the voice was real and accusing him and he didn't like being accused without justification.

"Why are you burning these things?"

It was too late she could see at once to rescue the dressing gown. Already the flames had taken hold in the centre of the bonfire, had consumed and were consuming the remnants of socks, shirts and trousers but it wasn't too late for the pile of ties waiting in the barrow. Hannah noticed then under the ties a bundle of letters and cards – on top a letter still unopened in her own writing which she'd sent in May to her father. She snatched up both the letters and ties, stuffing the letters in her bag, the ties down her blouse. Hastily she scavenged then at the edge of the fire's base, pulling out anything, everything that wasn't burnt or scorched, one a letter to her father in her mother's writing.

"How dare you touch these things! Who are you anyway?"

She turned her face to him, unable to rescue any more. She was too angry, she knew, to do him justice. The grime on his face, in her mind, was the grime of intent to destroy yet more of her father. The sweat on his chest glistened in a dubious cause. She hated the energy his muscles exuded on his bare tanned back as he forked the fire, encouraging the flames, the ironical gleam in his eyes, doubting her.

"I could ask you the same question."

"All right then I'll tell you. I'm Mr Delaney's daughter."

"Oh are you?" He gave a mock bow. "Good afternoon, Mr Delaney's daughter."

"It's not funny." She felt she wanted to hit him. "Do you realise these are my father's things?"

He didn't reply this time.

"Were you told to do this or did you decide yourself?" angrily she pursued.

"I make no decisions here. If I did, it wouldn't be for burning. I'd recycle or give them to Oxfam."

"Then why have you burnt them?"

"I was told there was an infection and it was necessary. I was told if I didn't that I'd lose my job. I need the money so I had no choice. Does that satisfy your ladyship?"

There was a resentment in his voice as if he'd been humiliated, a faint trace of Yorkshire made to toe a southern line. He seemed out of place to Hannah, alien to the role of gardener that Williams had assumed. His mockery told her she'd misjudged him but she felt too confused, too distraught to apologise.

"Have you been given other things to burn?"

"There's a couple of long things."

"What do you mean?"

The man turned back into the shed and a few moments later emerged with a long black dress and a grey cloak with a band of silver, white and grey edging. Hannah at once recognised the cape. It was the cape her father had wanted her to have, the cape he'd given to her mother when first they'd married and which held a special significance for him. How could Hugo, who knew this, want to burn it or was it the Slade woman behind all the destruction?

Hannah held the cape close to her a moment, unsure what to do with it. It had a glossy sheen that shimmered in the sunlight, a strange scent she didn't recognise. Carefully at length she folded it and put it down beside her bag.

"Is there anything else?"

"Not at the moment."

"If there is anything," she hesitated, wondering how much she could trust him, "will you please keep it for me? Documents, letters, books, clothes – anything – please don't burn them or throw them away."

"If there's no one around." Tentatively he smiled. "It's difficult to pretend that plants are paper and clothes from close quarters."

"You could use other paper. They won't be standing over you, will they?"

"They do sometimes on Saturdays."

"Is that when you're here? Saturdays and Wednesdays?"

"Sometimes Sundays if here's work to do."

"What's happened to Williams then?"

"Williams?"

"He was my father's gardener for 30 years. I need to know why he's gone."

73

"Where have you been that you don't know? I mean," he added with a hint of mockery again, "if you're the daughter of the house..."

"You don't believe me, do you?"

"I neither believe nor disbelieve." He shrugged, turning back to the fire.

"Well, anyway, I'll tell you. I've been abroad in Hong Kong. That's why I don't know and why..."

Hannah broke off, abruptly aware of Sally striding towards them from the entrance to the kitchen garden.

"There's a car in the drive, Han. We'd better go."

"What car?" Hannah felt she didn't want to go now. There were things still she wanted to do, to find out.

"The blue Renault. Olga Slade." Sally lowered her voice. "She's back unpacking some shopping by the garage."

"I don't see why we should go," Hannah asserted. "We've every right to be here."

To her surprise, the man turned from the fire at her protest.

"If it's the Slade, I'd go if I were you."

"But you're not me."

"No, but she's been told to report any intruder to the police."

"You think I'm an intruder?"

"It's not what I think that matters. It's what she can do."

"It's not her property. There's nothing she can do."

"Can't she? She'll be onto the police as soon as she sees you. She had a couple of them out the other day just because a friend of the family called."

74

"I think we'd better go, Han," Sally urged again, not wanting to see Hannah humiliated. "Until we've seen the will and a solicitor, we don't in fact know where you stand."

"That may be but I'm damned if I'm going to be booted out as an intruder in my own home when it's this so called Slade who's the intruder. I think in fact I'll go and see her."

"You've already seen her, Han, at the funeral."

"You won't achieve anything seeing her," the man said. "She doesn't listen. She's a guard obeying orders."

"He's right," Sally agreed. "If she knows we've been, she'll only talk to Hugo which will make it more difficult another time."

"Won't she be told anyway?"

It was a stupid remark, Hannah knew, as soon as she'd said it. The man wasn't the type to talk but he awoke, in a way she couldn't define, her defiance.

"If you're meaning me," he looked at her direct now, "we don't talk, the Slade and I, if I can help it."

"There you are, "Sally confirmed reassuringly.

But Hannah was in no mood for compromise or slipping away now unseen. All the frustration she'd felt, the grief and bewilderment, the pent up feelings of anger, despair boiled up inside her as she strode back to the front door. Finding it locked again, loudly she rang the bell.

She hadn't really taken in Olga Slade at the funeral, and seeing her now with her heavy features, her thick sensual lips and beady eyes, her hair so obviously dyed and contrived, standing guarding her childhood home, incongruous with everything her father had valued, with her glittering rings, her blatant perfume mixed with the stale smell of sweat,

she felt overwhelmed with anger that such a woman could presume to be there at all, let alone keep her out.

"I'm Hannah and I've come to stay for the next few days. I notice my room has been locked and I want it unlocked for me now."

It was as if an electric current had shot through the woman's eyes and zigzagged down through her overweight body. Her lower lip quivered. Then, to Hannah's amazement, as if a mask had been swiftly placed over her face, the doubt and fear had gone and the beady eyes were in charge.

"I've no proof you're Hannah." The voice had assumed a plum quality, not unlike Hugo's. "In any case, I have my orders from the executor that no one, no one is to stay till the estate has been sorted."

"But Mr Delaney, my brother, is staying, is he not?"

"That's different." She stopped as if afraid suddenly she'd said too much.

"I don't see why."

"You'd better ring the executor then."

"I thought he was supposed to be away."

"That's none of my concern."

"Isn't it? If you're supposed to be looking after the place? Now will you please let me in."

Hannah stepped forward ready to push past Olga Slade. But Olga Slade, despite her ungainly form, was too quick for her and slammed the door shut in her face. Quickly Hannah felt in her bag for her key but at the same time heard the two bolts in the door being drawn and knew it was too late for the key to be of use.

At her elbow Sally urged her again, "You're better away from here, Han."

"It's my own home, Sally."

"I know and we'll be back. You'll see. Now, have you got everything – the clothes you rescued?"

"I left them by the fire."

Dispirited, she followed Sally back to the kitchen garden and picked up her mother's cloak. The man was standing in the doorway of the shed now but said nothing.

"You will remember, won't you?" Hannah called over to him. "Please save any papers."

"If there are any more papers to save." The man folded his arms.

A gesture of rejection was it or compliance? Hannah suddenly realised she was dependent on him now, someone she didn't even know, for gleaning what remained of her father's possessions and possibly information even.

"I think there will be." She forced a smile. "What's your name, by the way?"

"Does it matter?" His voice came back to her hostile now, not wanting to divulge or be involved.

"It doesn't matter, no." She felt his hostility arousing her own. "But it's easier, don't you think, to associate someone with a name, rather than thinking of him as just man?"

"It depends, doesn't it, on whether the name fits?"

"You mean yours doesn't?"

"I didn't say that."

"Then why not tell me?"

"All right." He shrugged noncommittal now. "Call me Luke."

It probably wasn't his real name, Hannah thought, but what did it matter? She was unlikely to have much to do with him once he'd saved, if save he did, further papers

and clothes. Once she'd established Yadrahna as hers, according to her father's promise, she'd find Williams and restore him.

"Luke then, you won't forget, will you?"

"Will I be allowed to?"

He stared at her as she picked up her mother's cloak. He was still staring she noticed as she looked back following Sally out of the kitchen garden.

"What do you make of him?" she whispered to Sally as they made their way back through the shrubbery avoiding the drive and being seen from the house. So far with luck, she estimated, Olga Slade wouldn't know they'd been to the kitchen garden and seen Luke.

"I don't know. I can't say I'd trust him too much." Nor indeed anyone, Sally thought, relating to Yadrahna now. She'd always remembered Yadrahna as a place of laughter and light. Now, despite the abundance of foliage and flowers, the warmth of July, there were shadows where the light had been.

Shadows in Hannah's eyes.

Concerned she touched Hannah's arm as they got back into the car. "It's urgent you get a copy of the will, Han, now and see where you stand."

A few moments later, as they drove away, a police car passed them on the opposite side of the road, heading for Yadrahna.

Chapter 7

Over the next three days while Sally was at work, Hannah tried ringing the office number of Hugh Jamieson which she and Sally had gleaned from listening to the answer phone during the visit to Yadrahna. But every time she gave her name she was told that Mr Jamieson was unavailable. No one was able to tell her when he would be available. She was assured by a polite woman's voice that her message would be passed on to ring her at Sally's number but no return call came.

It was Sally, returning from lunch on the third day, who had the idea that they could try making an appointment in her name and try to get a copy of the will that way. To Hannah's amazement it worked. An appointment was made immediately for Sally to see Hugh Jamieson two days later. The reason Sally gave for seeking the interview was a planning matter, her intention being that once she was face to face with Jamieson she would ask for a copy of the will with the authority of a covering letter from Hannah. She would persist, she assured Hannah, until Jamieson gave it to her.

It was a way through, the only way it seemed through Jamieson's evasions. Hannah felt uncomfortable though that Sally, who was already stretched at work, was taking

on an extra burden which she should do herself. She felt also uneasy that Sally's boyfriend, Howard, a civil engineer, was due back any day from Jordan and that she would be in the way. Not that Sally had said anything. She'd been, Hannah thought, unusually reticent about Howard. There'd been no mention of their getting married, none of the exuberance of the year before. Had they finally slipped into a married state taking each other for granted or was Howard still using his good looks, his caressing blue velvety eyes to effect in other directions? Either way, Hannah decided, it would be best if she went, that she shouldn't be depending so much anyway on Sally and certainly she didn't want to depend on Howard and be left alone with him in the day.

"You must be looking forward to Howard coming back," she tried broaching the subject while they were eating.

"Must I?" Sally's voice, to her surprise, abruptly sharpened. "I'm not sure that I am." There was a tense silence for a few moments as Sally consumed the rest of her lasagne. Then she pushed her plate aside at length in a gesture of relegation. "You may as well know. I've decided not to marry Howard after all."

Hannah couldn't pretend that she was sorry because she wasn't. Howard had more than a reputation for philandering but she felt sorry that Sally's expectations of the year before had not been realised.

"No doubt you've guessed the reason." Sally's voice hardened. "I didn't realise it at the time but when he went to Jordan he took someone else with him – what he refers to as his 'ex'."

Sally lingered on the 'ex' with an attempt at scorn but it wasn't in her nature to linger or scorn. She knew of his betrayal and had revealed it and already her heart had moved on. She'd not forgiven him. He'd deceived her but she didn't want to waste her time regretting him. She'd find someone else, she told Hannah, someone more reliable and dependable. "Like Richard," she ventured. "You don't know how lucky you are having Richard. He's not the type to have affairs and he doesn't let you down." Less tense she added, "So there's no question of Howard coming here now."

"You don't think he'll try to see you?"

"He may try but I've decided this time – no. He's messed me about too much, Han, and I can't see any future with him. He's best forgotten now. So you can stay as long as you like, as long as you need."

"Thanks, Sally, thanks." And Hannah couldn't help admiring Sally for her resilience, her decisiveness, the way she resolved to get on with her life. She must feel bruised, Hannah thought, but she doesn't show it. Perhaps it would be better if she did show it but it seemed mean even to imply criticism. Sally had been so good to her, had shown unstinting support. She couldn't think what she'd have done without Sally at the funeral and their visit to Yadrahna and Sally had provided in her new red brick cul de sac house, a refuge that was quiet, convenient and undemanding. As in Richard's flat, with its tidiness, its modern gadgets, its fridge and freezer full of convenience foods, there was most of the time literally nothing to do. Even the garden seemed to run itself with its paved patio more extensive even than the lawn.

But it was a house, Hannah knew, like Richard's flat, she could never feel at home in and increasingly she longed to go back to Yadrahna. Yet the more she thought of Yadrahna, the more she felt disturbed.

Particularly upsetting she found the way her father's belongings had been so ruthlessly removed without any consultation with her at all and the way Hugo was obviously planning something behind her back which meant she couldn't trust him. Yet her father had assured her that he would leave Hugo comfortably off. Why then? What was driving Hugo and why had he employed someone as repulsive as Olga Slade? None of it made sense in relation to her father and his wishes. Yet how was she going to have a say without spending money on legal advice – money which she wouldn't have if she took the course at Oxford? Desperately she felt she wanted to go back to Yadrahna again but there was no point, she knew, until Sally had obtained, as they'd planned, a copy of the will.

She wondered again about doing the course at Oxford and mentioned it for the first time to Sally.

"It sounds a good idea," Sally responded with enthusiasm. "What does Richard think?"

"I don't know. I haven't mentioned it to him yet."

"But you are going to, aren't you?"

"When I see him – yes."

"It's none of my business, of course," Sally paused, regarding Hannah with concern. "But you are going to marry Richard, aren't you? I got the impression when you went out to Hong Kong that that was the idea."

"I suppose it was clearer then."

"It's not now, you mean?"

"I don't know why but I find it difficult to think of Richard – here I mean in England. I know it sounds odd but he seems to belong more to the east."

"An eastern tiger you mean?"

"In a way – yes."

"But you're not an eastern tigress?"

"We don't think alike on economic matters – no."

"Does it matter? One doesn't have to think alike to be in love or get on."

"No, but some things are fundamental, aren't they? Like Yadrahna. For me, it's my past, my future. I feel my spirit's there and the past matters to me. To Richard the past is irrelevant. He has no feeling for it. What matters to him is the now and the future – a future he can control."

"Well, there's nothing wrong with that surely." Frowning, Sally added, "You know you sound as if you didn't like Richard sometimes."

"Do I? I suppose I love rather than like." Hannah felt awkward now as if she'd betrayed Richard unnecessarily but having started felt impelled to go on. "He has an energy I admire. He doesn't sit back. He makes things happen but there's something destructive about the whole process. I mean one can't go on forever filling the world with skyscrapers and computers, can one?"

"I don't know. Maybe Richard can."

"That's what I mean, what I'm afraid of."

"I don't believe you're afraid," Sally said. "I think that you're just not sure because he's not here."

"Can one ever be sure?"

"Probably not, "Sally conceded, "not a 100%. I couldn't

certainly with Howard. I should have thought though you could with Richard."

"Perhaps." If I thought as he did, Hannah mused to herself, but I don't. Richard was reliable, yes, in the conventional way one measured reliability in time and commitment but what if one didn't take the same things for granted, if one's aims were different? And did she love him really enough to overcome such difference? There was no answer, she knew. She would have to wait till she saw him again to gauge her feelings and gauge his. Even then, would she, could she know with any certainty? Was certainty ever even possible?

"You'll feel different, you'll see," Sally reassured her, "once you're together again. It's natural you should feel uncertain with things as they are with your father and the estate." Trying to be positive she added, "But we're on the way to a resolution."

"Yes, I suppose so," Hannah felt obliged to agree.

Plans were then made for Sally's visit the next day to Hugh Jamieson and Hannah wrote the covering letter asking for a copy of the will. Sally's appointment was at 4 p.m. and she would stay with Jamieson, she assured Hannah, till he produced the will. She would be back by 6 p.m. hopefully with a copy in her hand.

That night Hannah slept badly. It was 4 a.m. before eventually she got to sleep. She overslept then long after Sally had gone, awakening from a dream of Yadrahna and her father in which her father was calling from the attic room where she kept her collections. She was climbing up the stairs to the attic and she could still hear his voice but when she threw open the door, the attic was empty with

no sign of her father and her collections gone. Over the area where the cabinet had been housing her collections, a huge black spider had woven a web from the floor to the beam overhead and crouched in the centre of the web was devouring the remnants of the insects she'd collected as a child. As she ran terrified back down the stairs she tripped and fell down into the morning to find herself awake and trembling in her bed in Sally's spare room.

It was light and she was safe. Below downstairs she could hear the rattle of Sally's post flap as the postman rammed in her letters. The spider wasn't real but she could feel the fear still as if it was real and a terrible sense of emptiness and unease that she'd heard her father's voice but never reached him or known why he'd called.

What did it mean – the emptiness of the attic, the spider? Did it in fact mean anything? Logically it made no sense and weren't dreams merely a sifting of the debris in her mind? Yet hadn't they sometimes pointed a way, suggested deeper unconscious reasons and explanations? Could this not perhaps be pointing to what was happening at Yadrahna, to what was going on behind her back, initiated, woven by Hugo? What exactly was going on though and why?

Lying still in her bed, reflecting, she knew she had to face the fact that she didn't really know much about Hugo at all, that there were layers below the surface of his character and mind instinctively she hadn't wanted to know. Always, even in her teens, Hugo had seemed remote to her and cold. She'd been aware of a cynicism and self interest but they hadn't impinged on her and she hadn't given them much thought. She had rarely in fact in recent years seen

much of Hugo at all. There'd never been a close bond. With Hugo eleven years older, their games and stages of interest had never coincided and Hugo had spent, in any case, most of his teenage years living with his mother away from Yadrahna. At family parties and birthdays he'd made jokes sometimes that had amused her by a flash of wit but the flash had usually also been one of cynicism and she'd never been drawn to confide in him on a personal subject or to explore a problem with any analysis or depth. Like ships passing in the night she'd long recognised they'd kept their distance, neither quarrelling nor drawing close. The centre for her of family life had always been her father and her mother when she'd been alive. Hugo had been a presence, a grey presence on the edge, not of any great significance to her.

Now with apprehension she sensed that she would have to communicate with him on a different level about the use of Yadrahna. Uneasily, she wondered if Yadrahna, as her father had promised, would be hers at all. If only, she thought, Sally would come back and she could be assured.

Looking at her watch, Hannah realised that it would be hours yet before Sally returned and she decided to pass the time by sorting through the correspondence she'd brought back from Hong Kong. On the top of the bundle was the acceptance letter from the Management College in Oxford asking for confirmation that she was intending to accept. To her alarm, reading through the letter, she noticed that the date she was supposed to reply by was that very day – July 7th. What should she do? She still hadn't discussed the matter yet with Richard and there was little chance of that now if she was to reply in time. Should she decline and

go back to Hong Kong or confirm and get herself set up for a change of profession in the U.K. and risk Richard's disapproval? Looking through the prospectus, she thought that the section on trade unions looked rather daunting but the course, as a whole, especially the communication and the management aspects looked useful and interesting. If she could get an equally interesting job as a result, it would mean she wouldn't have to go back to teaching. It was fine teaching in Hong Kong where the students for the most part were keen to learn and well behaved but she dreaded going back to the type of post and school she had in London with all the problems of ill discipline which she hadn't been able to cope with and which had worn her down.

The main problems of the course, she decided, were money and winning Richard over. Money – she'd probably have enough – just, she reckoned if she lived simply, perhaps on the outskirts of Oxford; she certainly wouldn't be able to afford to run a car. Richard was more complex. He might agree, yes, if he was back in England. It was all arranged though now that he would spend the next year in Hong Kong. But perhaps, if she tried some persuasion, he'd see the sense of the course. They weren't after all going to live in the east for ever and it would be far better, he must agree, if she could earn a living in a more congenial way. As far as the course was concerned, she could in any case, always go to Hong Kong for one of the holidays. Yes, she decided, she'd take up the offer. It was an opportunity which might not come again. Ringing up the college, she gave her verbal acceptance, promising a letter of confirmation for the next day.

She wrote the letter straight away, fearful she'd be diverted though she wasn't sure by what. A few minutes later, the postman called and she handed him the letter, receiving in return one for herself from Richard.

It was a letter of affection, which made her feel at once guilty for not consulting him about the course. "Dearest Hannah," she read, "I was so sorry to hear about your father and will very much miss him myself. He was a great character, whom I very much respected for both his wisdom and integrity. I do wish I could have been with you both for the funeral and afterwards and been able to share what you are going through. Hopefully, I shall soon be able to get away. I will let you know exactly when later. We can make our plans then. I thought perhaps Christmas would be an appropriate time now for the wedding. Hopefully you will feel able to return to Hong Kong in the autumn with me when your father's affairs have been sorted. I'll be in touch. I keep thinking of you. I miss you. All my love Richard."

Folding the letter, Hannah felt she wanted him then back in bed with her, close to her, sheltering her from the web of the spider and the sinister events at Yadrahna. With her head she knew that her decision on the course was right but her heart could not free itself from the guilt she felt regarding Richard. She decided, however, to say nothing to Richard as yet but to tell him when he returned so she could explain the situation more fully to him face to face.

With a jolt then she realised she would have to find somewhere cheap to live in the vicinity of Oxford and retrieve her bicycle from Yadrahna. Where was her bicycle though now at Yadrahna and how was she going to find

out and retrieve it with all the barriers to getting in?

Perhaps the gardener 'Luke' might be able to help her. He hadn't been too adverse about saving the papers and he was clearly anti Olga Slade. How much though could she trust him? The irony in his eyes and voice suggested an antagonism but there was something attractive about the way his muscles flexed themselves on his tanned back in tune with the movements he made with the fork and in the way the muscles of his face responded as if the irony was an overlay. He was an attractive man – the kind of man she liked physically – dark with a latent energy and strength. He might well help her. It was worth a try if she could get to Yadrahna. She would go, she decided, as soon as possible to Oxford then take a bus out to Wynton and walk on to Yadrahna.

After writing to Richard, Hannah wandered into Shawton and bought herself an Oxford paper to check the possibilities of accommodation for the course. She then prepared as much as she dared for Sally for the evening meal. After what seemed like days of hours, she saw Sally's car at last in the drive and Sally emerging with an envelope in her hand.

"You managed then?" Hannah ran to the door to greet her.

"Eventually." Sally handed her the envelope with a weary smile. "He's like an eel with barbed wire guts is Mr Jamieson."

"How did you persuade him then?"

"I said I was staying put until he handed the will over and if he tried throwing me out I'd report him through the complaints procedure and publicise his action. He's

obviously not wanting publicity for some reason so it worked. But with your letter he had no valid reason to refuse. Well, aren't you going to open it?"

"Yes, yes, of course." Yet now she'd got the will in her hand, Hannah was afraid to open it, afraid of what it would contain. She felt she wanted to be alone – alone with privacy and green around her, alone in the library or the shrubbery at Yadrahna – not exposed on the lawn here where everyone could see. "I think I'll read it upstairs though if you don't mind."

"Of course not. You go ahead. I'll make some tea."

Upstairs in her room Hannah sat still staring at the envelope unable to bring herself to open it. Then the whistle of the kettle boiling warned her that Sally would soon be up with the tea. Her fingers trembling, she forced herself at last to open the sealed envelope.

Slowly she read:

THIS IS THE LAST WILL AND TESTAMENT
of me
THOMAS JOHN CHARLES DELANEY
of Yadrahna, Wynton, Oxfordshire

1.   I REVOKE all Wills and testamentary dispositions I have previously made.
2.   (a) I APPOINT Hugh Jamieson of the firm H. Jamieson & Company of 31 High Street, Chadford to be the executor of my Will but I should like not more than two persons to prove it.

_____

2.   (b) I APPOINT the persons who take out the first Grant of Probate of my Will to be its Trustees and the expression

90

3.　I GIVE the following legacies free of Inheritance Tax

　　A (i) To my grandson Marcus the sum of £10,000

　　　(ii) To my daughter Hannah the sum of £1,000

　　　(iii) To the Stanton Hospital for Animals of Weybridge Surrey the sum of £1,000

　　B (i) To my sister Eileen my antique collection of watches.

　　　(ii) To my son Hugo all my household furniture and effects absolutely.

4.　I GIVE to my son Hugo my property Yadrahna and my investments.

5.　I GIVE the residue of my estate out of which shall be paid my funeral and testamentary expenses, my debts and any Inheritance Tax payable in respect of the property passing under my Will to my son Hugo absolutely.

There followed a long section on the powers of trustees which Hannah couldn't follow. The words she'd read blurred and shifted, then jagged out at her mocking, then blurred, shifting again – senseless without connection to anything her father had promised or told her, without connection to her father it seemed at all.

It occurred to her then that she had misread or there was some kind of mistake – a joke even. It couldn't be true. Her father had told her quite definitely he wanted her to have Yadrahna. There was no doubt. The words had stayed with her, were imprinted on her mind, part of her. She hadn't imagined them, she was sure. She couldn't have and he wouldn't have changed his mind.

Trying to steady her hand, she read the first section of the will again, clutching at the hope that there was some

mistake, that she'd misread a crucial word. But no – there was no mistake. The words were there in black and white clear – Hugo was to have Yadrahna. "I give to my son Hugo my property Yadrahna." Yadrahna would not be hers.

As the implication dawned, a deep down protest welled up inside her. "I don't believe it. It can't be true. It's not what he told me." She felt she could hardly breathe, a pain twisting in her heart as the words twisted in her mind – a strange sensation as of a hard gloved hand uprooting her as a weed and casting her aside.

Then she was aware of Sally, holding out a cup of tea for her, her large grey eyes looking down at her with concern. "What's the matter? What's happened?"

"He's taken everything."

"What do you mean?"

"Hugo – he's got Yadrahna – everything – the investments, the residue, the lot." She handed Sally the copy of the will.

Carefully Sally read the will through. She was angry rather than surprised. It was what at the back of her mind she'd guessed ever since she'd been to Yadrahna with Hannah to investigate but had not wanted to admit, least of all to Hannah herself. The signs had all been there even when they'd seen Hugo in Windsor. Why else had he wanted to stop Hannah from going to Yadrahna? But why did Hugo so want Yadrahna which he'd openly confessed he'd never even liked and how had he managed to overrule Hannah's father?

Sally sensed with growing unease the odds stacked against Hannah and, though she was not sure why, that the situation was more complex than it seemed, needing not

only challenging but investigating. She noticed then that Olga Slade was one of the witnesses, which seemed odd for someone of Thomas Delaney's standing. Surely he could have got someone more acceptable than a temporary housekeeper. The other witness was a woman Sally recognised as one of Thomas Delaney's old friends, Sadie Shaw, a widow of 80 or so who lived in a neighbouring village, Chadford, and occasionally played bridge with him. Neither Sally reflected with disquiet were promising witnesses from Hannah's view. But something clearly needed to be done as soon as possible.

"We need to find you a solicitor, Han." Sally hesitated, hoping Hannah had a name ready to hand, her father's solicitor perhaps. But Hannah was lost in thought processes of her own, her face distraught and Sally had a horrible feeling she was going to be too distraught to act. If only, she thought, Richard was here to take charge and look after Hannah. He'd know what to do to get things moving. Hannah had always been rather impractical when it came to a crisis. But she couldn't be allowed to be now. The sheer injustice of it all – the insult to Hannah with only a minimal legacy just to show she'd not been entirely forgotten – the blatant manipulation. Something had to be done or at least attempted to stop Hugo in his tracks.

"Did your father have a solicitor?" Gently Sally touched Hannah's arm. "Is there anyone we could contact who knows the situation?"

"I don't know. He had someone called Davies I think his name was but he retired. I don't understand, Sally. How could he? How could he change his mind?"

"He probably didn't," Sally tried to reassure. "He probably had it changed for him – which is why we must urgently find someone for you to consult."

"I don't know anyone."

"In that case, why don't we try James Ashford of Ashford and Swan? I've heard people talk of him. He's in Oxford and specialises apparently in Wills and Probate."

"You mean get a solicitor to challenge it in court?"

"What else?"

"It'll cost a bomb. I can't afford it, Sally. Not if I'm going to do the course."

"But I thought you'd still got to discuss it with Richard."

"I have but I'm still going to do it. I've decided now."

"I see." But Sally felt she didn't see, didn't see at all and someone would have to steer Hannah to take action – legal action. The whole situation was monstrous, totally unfair and probably criminal. It had to be put right. "Well, anyway, whether it's expensive or not, you've got to get some legal advice. Hugo's cheated you of your inheritance."

"I know but I don't want to be drained of the little I have by lawyers' fees."

"Look – I've got an extra £1,000 saved which I won't be needing now I've finished with Howard. You can borrow it and pay me back when you can."

"I can't take your money, Sally." Hannah felt for a moment close to tears from Sally's offer and the generosity of it. "You've got a mortgage and demands of your own and already you've done more than enough driving me around and supporting me. If I need money, I'll ask aunt Eileen." Or Richard, she added to herself as an afterthought. He

would help her, she was sure but for some reason she couldn't define, she didn't want to ask him now, didn't want to depend on him in the way she had.

"Well, the offer's always there." Sally wasn't sure whether she felt hurt or relieved. She wanted to help but wondered now if she really could. She'd never fully understood, she had to admit to herself, Hannah's deep attachment to both her father and Yadrahna. It went beyond the norm of anything she'd known with her other friends but all the more reason perhaps that she should help Hannah put things right. "There's a scheme I believe whereby you can have half an hour's free advice. Why not try it at Ashford and Swan? I know it's a bit of a trek to Oxford from here but I could take you over before going to work if that's what you decide to do. I could even come with you if you don't feel like going alone." Sally smiled, trying to sound casual as she collected up the cups and made for the door.

She was being kind, Hannah knew, putting herself out as she always did, doing her best, being supportive, making one feel valued. And Hannah did feel valued by her and she was grateful for all Sally had done. No one could have done more but she felt at times an unease, the same unease she felt with Richard, as if she wasn't quite up to it, not capable of managing and deciding for herself. Was she incapable, she wondered.

As Sally went back downstairs, Hannah looked over the will again. The words that had mockingly shifted and blurred had settled back on the page like hard cold stones.

Stones she wanted to throw back into the depths of the past. And she was back again in the shrubbery at Yadrahna

throwing stones as she'd always done into the centre of the pond, watching with fascination as the ripples grew and spread. And she felt her father beside her, the promise of his words renewed that Yadrahna would be hers.

Then why?

The hard cold words on the page glared back at her and with dread in her heart she knew she would have now to find out what had happened and try if she could to put it right.

Chapter 8

'ASHFORD & SWAN ESTABLISHED
SOLICITORS OF REPUTE SINCE 1890'

Hannah regarded the well–polished brass plaque with a mixture of scepticism and awe. The idea of generations of solicitors dispensing advice in the same high ceilinged, mahogany furnished rooms both appealed and impressed. She liked the late nineteenth century yellowing stone facade and portal; it gave an air of substance and restraint. How restrained though, she wondered nervously, would the fees be. The Personnel Management course was going to take virtually all her savings. The most she would be able to afford would be £1,000 but would that be enough for a serious challenge? Aunt Eileen on the phone the night before, though supporting her, had warned her that the cost of the case was often more than was won – if one was lucky enough to win. Of course, she'd agreed, it was all totally unjust and wrong and Hannah was right to get advice and she would help if she could but one had to be prepared for disappointment.

But what alternative was there, Hannah wondered. She had at some stage to seek advice, to know her chances, to assess from someone who knew from experience the

facts and grounds for those chances. She had to know or not know and not knowing meant leaving things, meant leaving Hugo to sweep the board and take away from her what she'd been promised, what by right was hers.

Hesitating outside, she wished for a moment she'd asked Sally to come with her instead of coming on the bus alone. She felt afraid of what she'd been told, afraid of the money involved. Then she thought of her father's study inside, of her father sitting at his desk in his Victorian chair. A sense of anger then impelled her and she walked up the stone flagged steps and through the door to reception.

"Can I help?" A woman with grey hair and glasses and wearing a smart navy blue suit with a blue flowery scarf, beamed on her a trained smile from the reception desk.

"Yes, I'd like to make an appointment with Mr Ashford, please."

"Mr Ashford senior or junior?"

"I'm not sure..."

"What is the matter on which you wish to consult?"

"It's about a will."

"I suggest then Mr Ashford senior. It's his particular speciality. When do you want to see him?"

"As soon as possible."

There was no computer. The receptionist studied a large brown leather bound appointments book with the days highlighted in italic brown. There was something strangely reassuring and solid about the book, Hannah found, as if it had always been there since the firm began in 1890, guaranteeing in the consciously written name a personal service. But would her name be written down?

"Unfortunately Mr Ashford senior is booked up for the next ten days but we've just had a cancellation for later this morning in an hour at 11.30. Would you like to take that?"

Hannah hesitated, feeling she hadn't properly prepared what she'd say or dressed appropriately for the occasion. Would she ever though be prepared? In any case she had the will with her, which was what mattered, and she could outline what she knew of the situation.

"It'll be quite a long time otherwise," the secretary persuaded, wanting to fill the gap.

"I'll take that one then."

"Please take a seat. I'll let Mr Ashford know you're waiting."

"Thank you."

Hannah hadn't brought anything to read except the will, which she didn't feel like reading yet again. She sat watching the receptionist for a while, amazed at her patience in answering endless calls with the same efficient polite voice.

After a while she couldn't bear to listen and as a client next to her was called she picked up the Oxford paper he'd left behind and started to look through the advertisements in the accommodation section. The rooms for rent in Oxford seemed rather expensive she thought – almost as expensive as cottages in the country and she decided to look at places in the outlying villages and countryside. She could always cycle into Oxford if it wasn't too far. Better to have space and a garden than to be cramped in one room however convenient.

Suddenly she noticed a house advertised in Wynton, a two bedroomed cottage at the end of the village. The

picture was not very clear but Hannah was sure it was old Mrs Blake's cottage which she remembered being modernised by the daughter after Mrs Blake had died. No rent was stated but Hannah knew immediately she wanted to see the cottage and check it out. She could cycle into Oxford from Wynton just and there were buses at crucial times in the day – not many but enough. She would also, she reflected, be near Yadrahna which would enable her to find out more about what was going on. She could slip up to Yadrahna from Mrs Blakes's cottage through Rassler's Wood without being seen in less than half an hour. She would also be near her father's grave and be able to look after it. Yes, she decided, she'd go and see Mrs Blake's cottage. Carefully she wrote down the contact telephone number and address, hoping it hadn't already been taken. A few minutes later, the secretary called in her polite voice, "Mr Ashford will see you now, Miss Delaney," and she led Hannah up to a quiet spacious office on the first floor.

Hannah noticed the desk before the man behind it. It was a large imposing mahogany desk, polished to perfection to a rich deep brown, with carefully crafted panelling and gold filigree patterning on its olive green leather working surface.

Mr Ashford by contrast gave an impression at once of greyness. He wore a grey suit and had greying hair neatly combed back from a wide forehead, a neatly clipped moustache and grey eyes that would not venture, Hannah sensed, beyond the confines of rational judgement. His voice had the calm and confidence of detachment rather than warmth as he greeted her.

"Good morning, Miss Delaney. Take a seat, please." He waited as Hannah seated herself and then sat down himself and continued," I understand you wish to consult me regarding a will."

"Yes." Hannah drew the will out of her bag, conscious that it looked now rather crumpled and there was a smudge on the first page.

"And this is the will?"

"Yes."

He took it from her then straightened it out in front of him, his fingers moving with the care and precision of surgical instruments about to perform an operation. His hands were very white she noticed and his desk very orderly and neat with an A4 notepad carefully placed at right angles in front of him – a pen ready beside it, a telephone to the right, an in tray to the left – no extra clutter, nothing extraneous or unwanted, no sign of a personal life. Behind him on the mantelpiece she noticed though a photo of a woman with delicate features and a tentative smile but she couldn't be seen by him while he was working.

She waited as he read the will through.

"Right." He put the will to one side and picked up his pen. "I'd like you to outline to me first, Miss Delaney, the nature of the problem as you see it."

She told him then all she knew – the promise her father had made, the nature of their relationship, the circumstances of her being abroad, the facts of her father's two marriages and Hugo's circumstances. She expressed her doubts about Jamieson being her father's true choice as an executor with his fear of the property being sold for development, her doubts about her father's state of mind during his illness,

her doubts about his illness itself and Hugo's failure to tell her about it. She conveyed to him her sense of the total injustice of the will and the whole situation, that it could never, she believed, have been his intention after his words to her before going to Hong Kong.

While she spoke, James Ashford wrote – neat notes in small very controlled legible handwriting. When she'd finished, carefully he checked over what he'd written.

"Right." He looked up then. "I'd just like to clarify a few points, Miss Delaney. Firstly, do you have any previous wills or letters of your father showing his intention to leave the property, Yadrahna, to you?"

"No, I'm afraid I haven't. My father only told me of his intention just before I left for Hong Kong. He may possibly have made a will previously to that effect but I haven't seen it."

"Do you know where such a will might be?"

"It would probably have been at Yadrahna but as I explained most of my father's things have been removed."

"But he had a solicitor presumably?"

"He had one who retired from ill health. I'm not sure if he found another one. My aunt might know though."

"I suggest you try and find out from your aunt and try and think too if there's anywhere in the house where he might have put a will for safe keeping." James Ashford permitted himself a brief smile. "Older people sometimes put wills in strange places so they can't be found except by a certain intended person. Your father if he was under pressure might possibly have done just that. You need to try and think carefully where such a place might be. Obviously you need to get to together evidence of your father's

intention towards you and a previous will would help."

"Yes, I can see that. I'll try and see what I can think of." But nowhere convincing could Hannah think of that Hugo himself would not have searched. Was there such a place and how could she know if her father had made a previous will or a later will in her favour?

"You told me," James Ashford continued," that your father had cancer in the last six months of his life. Have you managed to see his doctor yet to find out the nature and course of the illness?"

"No, I'm afraid I've been rather preoccupied." Hannah was conscious of making excuses, at the same time aware that she'd in fact wasted precious time at Sally's. Why hadn't she thought of going to Dr Griffin before? He was an old friend after all.

"I suggest you make an appointment to have a preliminary discussion with him. It's quite normal for close relatives to discuss with their doctor the circumstances of a patient's last illness and death so I don't think there should be an objection."

"What would I be trying to find out exactly?"

"Basically whether your father was of sound mind when the will was drawn up and signed, whether for example there were any drugs which could have affected him or the illness itself. We would write of course officially later asking for a report but it helps sometimes in a preliminary discussion to know it it's going to be worth it. You haven't seen the witnesses yet I presume?"

"No, I've only just in fact found out who they were. One of them, Mrs Slade, I don't think she'd be willing to talk at all."

"It's not always easy to judge, Miss Delaney. Some witnesses respond to an official letter, others to an informal discussion. One has to try both I think in some circumstances to get results so I think you should try at least to see both witnesses and ask them simply to tell you what happened during the signing, what the circumstances were regarding your father, what his health was and who was present. It can be difficult I agree." James Ashford's grey eyes for a moment lightened. "But if you give them a due sense of their importance, I think you'll find in most cases they'll respond."

"I'll have a try then." Hannah forced a smile. The visit to Olga Slade was not one she could anticipate with any optimism or calm. She'd try, she decided, Sadie Shaw first.

"Another point I need to ask you," steadily James Ashford pursued his questioning. "Was your father supporting your brother in any way or does your brother have relations to support as this could be a factor?"

"He has his son Marcus who is 12 but his mother who also lives with him has money I've always understood of her own. My father did continue to pay her alimony but it stopped once she'd qualified for a pension."

"And were you in any way dependent financially on your father?"

"No."

James Ashford checked the will again, made a few more notes, then turning to the bookcase behind him extracted a thick black leather bound volume entitled "Theobald on Wills" and placed it carefully on the desk in front of him opening it at a well thumbed page.

"We need obviously more help by way of information from the doctor, the witnesses and any other documentation

you can find but I need to emphasise to you at this stage certain aspects, Miss Delaney."

Hannah was conscious of his grey eyes penetrating with a more warning message.

"First is the basic principle that an individual can leave his or her property to whomsoever he or she likes, provided that the requirements of the 1975 Inheritance Act are satisfied. However, bearing in mind this basic principle, there are nevertheless certain reasons why a will can be questioned. The first question is: was the will formally valid, that is executed by your father and attested by the two witnesses in the manner the law required? I will quote "Theobald on Wills" to you a moment."

James Ashford leaned forward quoting from the thick black volume he'd extracted from the shelf but it was obvious to Hannah from the ease and emphasis of his words that he had no need of the book at all, that it was merely an expression of style, an externalisation of what was already familiar territory in his mind. 'The signature of the testator must be either written or acknowledged by the testator in the actual visual presence of both witnesses together before either of them attests or signs the will or acknowledges the will.' Ashford turned back again to the will itself. "On the face of it," he commented, "it looks as though it does appear to be duly executed, signed, dated 1st May and witnessed. However, as I've already mentioned, it's worth asking the witnesses personally what happened.

The next question is whether your father had what is called testamentary capacity. I'll quote to you again from Theobald." Ashford leaned forward turning to another well thumbed page and read: 'In order to have testamentary

capacity a testator must understand a) the effects of his wishes being carried out at his death b) the extent of the property of which he is disposing and c) the nature of the claims on him. The testator must have a memory to recall the several persons who may be fitting objects of the testator's bounty and an understanding to comprehend their relationship to himself and their claims upon him so that he can decide whether or not to give each of them any part of his property by "his will." We need to know in other words if your father was compos mentis at the time of making the will and signing it. This is the reason for needing to consult the doctor to see if he is willing to testify your father was not of sound mind."

"I'll go and see him as soon as I can. He was our family doctor for many years so it shouldn't be difficult to speak with him."

"Good. Right. We come now to the third possibility, which is undue pressure. The law states that 'persuasion is legitimate but coercion is not. A testator may be led but not driven.' Coercion, however, I have to say is difficult to prove. You want a reliable witness to this effect. The point is that you would have to satisfy the court that your brother had poisoned your father's mind so that your claims were not recognised. The fact that you are mentioned – albeit to a very minimal degree – suggests he did recognise a claim. I'm not saying this," Ashford paused looking at her intently, "because I disbelieve you, Miss Delaney, but to show what you are up against. If there is any doubt, the court will let the matter stand.

The next question is whether your father was under a delusion. Again the position may be simply stated and

I quote again from Theobald. 'A testator suffers from a delusion if he holds a belief on any subject which no rational person could hold and which cannot be permanently eradicated from his mind by reasoning with him.'

To Hannah's relief, James Ashford at last closed "Theobald on Wills." She felt she hated that black volume which made even basic justice seem such a problem. Wasn't coercion obvious in the outcome without one having to find a non–existent witness? No criminal with any intelligence would let his coercion be witnessed. Her hopes were not raised as Ashford sought to explain himself.

"I've quoted to you at length, I'm afraid, Miss Delaney from Theobald, not to overawe you but to show the difficulties you are up against and which I feel must be stated. I realise of course how you feel and the sense of injustice experienced but this does not mean you could satisfy a court that the rigorous requirements that the law imposes have been met.

As I said, I think that the best course now is to visit the doctor and witnesses and to think carefully if there is anyone else who could throw light on possible pressure."

"There was a housekeeper before the present one who was close to my father."

"Do you know why she left?"

"No, I don't. It's something I need to find out but she didn't leave apparently any address."

"A private investigator could help if you draw a blank but they can be quite expensive."

"Regarding the expense, Mr Ashford," Hannah felt impelled now to put her cards on the table, "I need if

possible to keep expenses to the minimum. I mean I don't want to go to court unless there's a real chance of success."

"I quite understand, Miss Delaney – which is why I've suggested that you do quite a lot of the preliminary investigation yourself. When you've found out all you can, I suggest you come back to me and we will reconsider the situation in the light of what you have found out.

But I have to warn you, from experience, I am somewhat pessimistic about the chances of success; I don't feel it's fair to mislead you with false optimism." Seeing her downcast face, he added, "However, that doesn't mean to say we can have no optimism. One cannot always tell what will happen as one pursues an investigation. In this respect, it will be worth it, if you can, unearthing any previous correspondence of your father as well as older wills and documents."

"Does that mean I'm allowed to go back and search Yadrahna?"

"Officially I'm afraid not."

"And unofficially?"

James Ashford smiled briefly for a second time.

"That's up to you, Miss Delaney." He straightened his pad. "I suggest you contact me in two weeks time when you've seen the doctor and witnesses." He looked at his watch, then extended his hand. The interview was over.

Ashford was only doing his job, Hannah tried to reason with herself as she walked back downstairs and out of the building. He'd explained clearly the situation and possibilities and given appropriate advice. And he was probably right not to be too encouraging, to be cautious about the outcome. She'd wanted a frank assessment of

her chances and he'd given it to her. He hadn't deluded her, given her false hope, led her on just to make money and she liked that – his professionalism, his honesty. She knew where she stood regarding the difficulties involved. But it didn't eliminate the despair she felt growing at there being apparently so little hope nor the overwhelming sense she had of the task before her.

How was she going to do it – to uncover, let alone prove in a matter of days and weeks what had taken years probably to plan? And where to start in the hope of finding information – information that could be of actual use? Where to find people who would know: Emma, Laura, Hugo's wife, her father's various associates and friends? For many she didn't even have a full name, let alone address. And how was she going to be able to find out about Jamieson's manoeuvres and how he came to be the executor at all? How was she going to be able to get back into Yadrahna to make the thorough search that seemed necessary?

Standing in the street again by the shiny brass plaque of Ashford and Swan, Hannah felt herself to be standing at the base of a mountain where the summit was in cloud and where even the foothills were beyond her reach.

Irresolute for an hour she wandered round Oxford, uncertain where to begin, whether to sort her accommodation first and provide a base, whether to ring Dr Griffin direct or whether to consult first with Sally or even Richard. Nothing seemed clear, promising or resolvable. Depressed, she found even walking after a while an effort.

Unexpectedly, it had grown hot – not the overpowering heat she'd experienced in Hong Kong but enough to make her feel dizzy and tired. If only, she thought, she could sit

down somewhere cool and remote away from the crowds and noise. She remembered then the museum and its inviting coolness, which she'd visited some years before with her father.

To her surprise and relief, nothing of significance in the museum had changed. There were extra security devices, more developed labels and directions, a shift here and there in the layout but the russet urns she remembered looking at with her father were still there in the same glass casements. Even the same small second century urn she remembered from a Naqada grave, perfect in shape and delicately decorated with a double horn ensign, a man carrying an oar, a man with flowing hair, two bovines with twisted horns, flamingos and a crested bird. All the urns amazingly preserved for nearly two thousand years.

And they would remain, she knew that now, long after her life span, timeless and cool as they were now in their harmony and design. They would remain because people cared that they remained, had set an aesthetic and historical value on them above gain.

Should she not all the more ensure that Yadrahna remained? Wasn't Yadrahna as important in its way as the vases were and who if not herself would ensure it remained? Wasn't that the reason why her father had specially spoken on the evening of her leaving for Hong Kong, entrusting her with its future?

Contemplating the urns, Hannah felt a cool wind down the centuries stirring her energy and resolve. She would act now. She had to act. She would go to Wynton and try to see Dr Griffin, her father's doctor straightaway. Then she would go and see the cottage.

Chapter 9

"I wonder if I could have a few words with Dr Griffin, please."

"Dr Griffin?" The receptionist arched her eyebrows, then smiled at Hannah apologetically. "Dr Griffin, I'm afraid, no longer practises here. He retired last year."

"Retired?" Hannah stared at the receptionist in disbelief. The idea of Dr Griffin retiring just didn't fit. Ever since she could remember Dr Griffin had always been at the surgery, always there to call on and consult and she'd consulted him over the years on matters well beyond health. Her father had always been sceptical, seen the medical profession generally as a last resort but she'd always thought of Dr Griffin with his broad shoulders, his untidy sweep of hair and expansive smile, as a friend, and though she hadn't seen him much in recent years – as a friend she could always turn to for advice.

"Dr Craig has taken over most of Dr Griffin's patients. Would you like to see him? I take it you were registered with Dr Griffin."

"It's not about me I've come. It's about my father. I wanted to discuss the circumstances of his death with Dr Griffin."

"What's your father's name?"

"Delaney. Thomas Delaney."

"Delaney." The receptionist quickly checked the computer then announced with satisfaction. "Yes, he was taken on as a patient by Dr Craig on January 1st. Dr Craig will have the information you want. I suggest you see him."

After some negotiation it was agreed that she could see Dr Craig for a few minutes after the last patient in the present evening surgery but it would be, the receptionist warned, a long wait.

It was a wait of two hours but better, Hannah reflected, than having to return the next day and repeat the same long wait for a bus and the same long meandering journey through the neighbouring villages. She'd never manage, she decided, relying on public transport for the course and it came back to her then, the need to go back to Yadrahna to retrieve her bike. Could she manage though without Luke's help?

Flipping through the magazines on the table as she waited, she saw again the ripple of his muscles in the sunlight as he'd forked the fire, the ironical look in his eyes, the way he'd stared as they'd left, as if challenging her and she knew she had to go back and find out if he'd saved her father's papers as she'd asked him, had to test him out.

She saw at length the last patient get up and go into Dr Craig's room and tried to sort out in her mind what she'd say to him, tried to imagine what he was like. She still felt disorientated and put out that it was someone unknown to her she was to see and not Dr Griffin and it all seemed much more complicated now than seeing the solicitor. There it had been straightforward – a matter of presenting

her view and gaining information into a possible course of action. Now she was on more delicate ground – probing a mind, a confidentiality, wanting an answer in a sense she didn't want to hear for how could her father have become mentally incapable in so short a time when she'd known him all her life as the most capable of men?

She felt tears coming into her eyes as she saw him again in his chair by the fire. What had really happened? Desperately she felt she wanted to talk to him, hear his explanation, hold onto his sturdy hand.

She was aware of a light suddenly flashing beside Dr Craig's name and the receptionist coming over to her. "It's your turn now, dear."

Dr Craig was clearly a younger man than Dr Griffin had been – in his early rather than late middle age. There was no grey in his carefully cut sweep of thick wavy brown hair, none of the tell tale facial lines that had betrayed Dr Griffin's close involvement with disillusion and pain. Dr Craig had handsome, clear cut, clean shaven features and a well cut suit but his eyes and his voice as he greeted her struck Hannah at once as being detached and tired.

"I gather you wanted to speak to me about your father's death." He motioned to Hannah to sit down.

"Yes, that's right. I should explain that I was in Hong Kong at the time of his illness and so there are aspects that aren't clear to me because I was away, you understand."

"Of course." Dr Craig regarded her with caution. "Perhaps you'd like to tell me what in particular you'd like to know."

"I understand he had cancer of the stomach."

"Yes, that's right."

"How long had this been known?"

"Your father first had symptoms, as I understand it, back in January – that is difficulty in swallowing, going off his food and vomiting. His housekeeper at the time was very concerned and tried to get him to come in January to see me but, as you no doubt already know, he didn't take kindly to coming to the surgery – I'm afraid to his cost. By the time he came in March, the cancer was well advanced."

"What happened then?"

"I understood from Mrs Mason that you were in Hong Kong so I got in touch with your brother. We discussed the possibility of an operation. The chances of success were frankly limited but still there but your father was not keen and your brother felt he was rather too old for the shock so it was left from lack of consent. It was then discussed whether he should go into hospital or stay at home. Your brother seemed to think he would prefer being at home and so arranged a full time housekeeper cum nurse – Mrs Slade. But I'm sure he has already told you this. Your brother I understand then moved in with him to keep an eye on him when Mrs Slade had her time off. I think he was reasonably taken care of though I should have liked the chance of an operation but as I said both your father and brother disagreed."

"I see." Had her father really been against an operation, Hannah wondered, or been persuaded. "When did he actually die?"

Dr Craig checked the notes on his desk. "June 21st in the morning at 10."

"And when did he go into hospital?"

"On the 6th of June. It had become quite difficult you will understand by that time managing him at home and there was little hope by that time of any real improvement or change."

"So he had two whole weeks in hospital when it was known he was dying."

"That is correct, yes,"

"Why then wasn't I sent for?"

For the first time Dr Craig looked mildly surprised. "But you were sent for, Miss Delaney."

"By whom?"

"By your brother. I asked your brother both before and after your father had gone into hospital, at your father's request, to send for you."

"But you didn't think to check that he had?"

Hannah could feel Dr Craig again weighing his words. "We don't usually feel it necessary to check what relatives tell us in these circumstances."

"But it was odd, was it not, that I hadn't turned up at the hospital?"

"I didn't know that you hadn't turned up, Miss Delaney. The hospital is considerable distance from here. I managed to visit your father on two occasions but I clearly could not go every day."

"No, but you could have checked that I had got the message. Do you know what really happened?" Hannah challenged, feeling the anger in her mount. "I didn't get the message at all. I was told nothing of my father's illness. I had an uneasy feeling that something might have happened, because he hadn't written in his normal way but by the time I got here it was too late."

"I'm sorry to hear that, Miss Delaney. But I don't think I can be held responsible for a failure of communication on your brother's part."

"Can't you – when my father specially asked you to contact me? He needed me here, don't you see, and I needed to be here."

Hannah felt she wanted to give in and cry. But Dr Craig was not a person she wanted to give in to and she jolted herself upright. Her father deserved more than tears. She'd come for a purpose and must stick with it.

"There's something else I'd like to ask you."

"Please go ahead." Dr Craig regarded Hannah, then his watch with apprehension. He was already an hour over his usual finishing time. He'd been up half the night and felt all he wanted to do now was to get home and have some sleep.

"My father made a will – a new one on May 1st in which he changed what he told me he was going to do. I wonder if you were present when the will was signed or asked to be."

"No." Dr Craig shook his head. "I had no association with your father regarding a will. I was neither present nor asked to be."

"Do you think that my father knew what he was doing at the time?"

"That he had testamentary capacity you mean?"

"Yes." She was conscious of Dr Craig withdrawing into more caution again.

"As I said, I wasn't directly involved on May 1st so I couldn't comment on his state of mind that day."

"Perhaps you saw him though roundabout that time?"

Craig thumbed through his notes. "I saw your father on 28th April and 4th May. I made no visit on 1st May."

"Do you think though that there were any signs on the days you did see him that he was not himself, not mentally alert?"

"I don't think there were any signs of senility – no. Of course, older people do vary and are not always consistently alert. His pain killers could have had an effect on some days and he did drink a lot in the last few weeks of his life."

"Drink?"

"Yes. I strongly advised him not to and I told the new housekeeper not to get any in for him but when I visited unexpectedly it was always there. I can only presume he used his persuasive charm."

"Or been persuaded. He wasn't a drinker, Dr Craig."

"Obviously you knew him better than I did, Miss Delaney. As you know I took him on as my patient only in January this year and rather late in the day for his cancer."

"The alcohol must have had some effect though surely?"

"It didn't improve his stomach certainly."

"And his mind? Would it have distorted his judgement?"

"It certainly could have. But if you are referring to his capacity on 1st May you would need a professional judgement other than my own. To make a firm and fair judgement about a mental state, one needs to be there at the time. I'm sure you will understand that."

"Would you be able to comment in a general sense though," Hannah tried to persuade. "I mean about the effect of his drinking at the time?"

"I could write a general letter – yes, but it would not be sufficient for your needs for evidence. One can't avoid the

facts that your father was not senile and I was not present on 1st May. I'm sorry. I have every sympathy with your predicament but you can see my position, I'm sure." Craig sighed inwardly to himself. He'd seen it all before – the careful manoeuvring around the dying, the careful timing and nudging aside in self–interest. Why hadn't he seen it here? He could have bypassed the brother. It was obvious now – the control over Thomas Delaney's movements and his drinking and Thomas Delaney had trusted him, pleaded with him to send for his daughter who obviously cared for him. "I'm sorry," he repeated.

"Supposing my solicitor writes to you?"

"He can write by all means and I shall respond but I wouldn't be able to say any more than I've said to you now. I can see what you're driving at." Briefly Craig wondered what was in the will. "But the situation is not definite enough to stand up in a court of law. As I said I sympathise but my hands are tied. I suggest you try the witnesses. They may be better able to help you."

"May be." Hannah didn't try to hide her doubt. Too disappointed for pleasantries, curtly she said goodbye and left the surgery.

Outside in the street, she felt again both depressed and alone. If Dr Craig couldn't or wouldn't help, who would? There was logic in his points, she recognised, but a caution and reluctance, she sensed as well, as if he didn't in any case want to be involved. If that was the case and almost certainly it would be with Olga Slade, what hope was there of any real challenge to the will?

Hannah felt disturbed also by Dr Craig's disclosure of her father's drinking. He'd never been a drinker, never

wanted to be. The only explanation was that he had been persuaded or coerced. What means though had Hugo used? For it could only have been Hugo – she was sure of that now – Hugo and Olga Slade. Was it the cancer, his pain, his sense of helplessness in a situation ever deteriorating? If only, she yearned, she could have been there to stop it, to comfort him. If only Dr Griffin had still been his doctor. He would certainly have phoned her and let her know. He'd have recognised how important it was, have recognised the scheming. One phone call and she could have been at her father's side.

Hannah walked for a while, trying to shed her anger and frustration at the way the interview had gone. Hot and tired, she hesitated at length at the corner of the main street in Wynton wondering whether to abandon the idea of visiting the advertised cottage. She didn't feel like talking to anyone, let alone strangers. On the other hand, she tried to reason with herself, she had to find somewhere to live near Oxford if she was going to go ahead with the course and soon. There was no harm, she decided at length in looking.

She found the cottage as she'd visualised on the main road leading from Wynton to Oxford, a picture book cottage of Cotswold stone with a thatched roof and a garden of lavender, lobelia and thyme. It was a cottage she saw at once well cared for – newly thatched, freshly painted with a polished brass door knocker and neatly trimmed hedge but these were assets and aspects that would have to be paid for and she sensed the cottage would be beyond her price range.

As she stood hesitating beside its wrought iron gate, a chirpy woman's voice from the upper window of the cottage on the opposite side of the road called out to her:

"You want to look round?"

Before she could reply, the window was shut with a bang. A few moments later, the front door of the cottage opened and a small sprightly woman, with sharp features and a fuzz of grey permed hair like thistle down, emerged, waited for a moment for the traffic, then sprinted across the road to join her.

"I'm Annie Hobbs." She extended a claw like hand. "I look after the cottage when Mrs Flinders's not here." Extracting a bunch of keys from a deep apron pocket, she led Hannah without more ado on a lightening tour of the interior.

Like the exterior, it was immaculate – rather too immaculate, Hannah thought, with too many china ornaments that could be knocked off their perch and when she enquired about the price, it was, as she'd anticipated, beyond what she felt she'd be able to afford.

"I'm sorry I was looking for something more," she tried to find the right word, "more wild."

It wasn't the word exactly she wanted but Annie Hobbs, to her surprise, immediately pounced on the word as on some vital ingredient for a brew.

"If it's wild you want, there's a cottage down our lane." She pointed back across the road to a narrow lane alongside her own cottage. "Bramble cottage – that's wild."

"Bramble Cottage," Hannah repeated, trying to recall the association. And suddenly it came back to her – old Mrs Webb, hunched with osteoporosis and arthritis, over her jars of blackberry jelly, jams and wines. Witch Webb they'd called her as children for her hunched back and hooked nose, not realising the effort and need that had gone into

the spurting red juices that had stained the kitchen walls. And Hannah saw again the brambles that had clambered over the porch and front windows and the wicker gate that had given the cottage its name.

"You mean old Mrs Webb's dead?"

"You knew her then?" Annie Hobbs focused her beady black eyes on Hannah's face. "You're from these parts?"

"No, no," quickly Hannah denied, realising her mistake. Hadn't her intention been to remain incognito? She'd never known Annie Hobbs nor, it appeared, had Annie Hobbs recognised her and she wanted to keep it that way. If she was to stay in Wynton it had to be without the association of the Delaney name, without Hugo's knowledge. "No, I just heard someone talking in the pub," she tried to sound casual, "about Bramble Cottage and a Mrs Webb. She was quite old, wasn't she?"

"Eighty four when she died," Annie Hobbs pronounced matter-of-factly.

"When was that?"

"Last winter in the freeze."

"You mean she died of cold?"

"More like blackberry wine." Annie Hobbs gave a knowing smile. "They found her stiff on New Year's Day in a pool of frozen wine."

What a way to die, Hannah reflected, degraded in such cold and alone. Would old Mrs Webb though have wanted it otherwise? Would she have wanted the comfort and warmth of a hospital bed with strange solicitous faces around her? Had she not kept to the end defiant her way of life, her independence, in a way heroic?

"Who owns the cottage now then?" Hannah asked tentatively. She could recall no family at Bramble cottage, no husband or children, though Mrs Webb must once have been married. Mrs Webb had always in her memory been alone – alone with her jellies, her jams and wines.

"No one who appreciates it – more's the pity – a niece who lives in London."

"She doesn't want to live here then or use it?"

"God bless me – no. She wants to sell and get a good price if she can."

"And meantime?"

"She's asked me to look after it and find a tenant if I can – someone without children. She doesn't want children." She gave Hannah a sidelong glance of persuasion. "I can show you if you're interested."

Hannah looked at her watch. The last bus was due to leave Wynton in only 30 minutes – a bus she couldn't afford to miss.

"It won't take long." And Annie Hobbs was taking her arm as if it was already arranged, leading her across the main road and down the narrow pathway that had served as the main thoroughfare before the advent of cars, past two other well kept cottages like the one advertised till they came at length to the wicker gate of Bramble Cottage, the last by the pathway before the river.

The gate sloped down off it hinges as Hannah nudged it. Before her she saw a garden transformed from her childhood memory. Where lawn had been, long grasses grew, golden in the evening light, like a cornfield, interspersed with poppies and thistles. Where well–kept herbs had flanked the narrow stone pathway, thyme had

gone to seed and oregano roamed ragged or struggled in the clutch of bindweed. And where Sarah Webb's pride of lupins had been, her sweet peas and roses, nettles now stood like sentinels six feet high as if guarding the cottage.

But the brambles still clambered over the porch and windows, resiliently extended on over a struggling hedge to make it their own, thriving in the air of neglect and withdrawal.

Hannah felt sadness that Mrs Webb had no more influence now yet, intermingled with it, a joy at the sight of the golden grass and the poppies and the brambles which brought back the past yet spoke of continuance long after people were gone.

The cottage itself, as she followed Annie Hobbs inside, she found more sombre. The wood of the porch and windowsills was rotting beneath the brambles; the paint work on the door flaked to mere patches like an ulcerous skin. The kitchen was dark from the overgrowth outside and the extended branch of a yew, its walls blackened from decades of blackberry stains. Upstairs the north facing bedroom had walls oozing with damp and mould where the thatch had leaked and continued to leak and everywhere there was a chill dank smell that warned of the deeper coming chill of winter.

Yet an attempt had been made to clear and clean the cottage and to make it habitable. There were no obvious signs of spider's webs – the one creature Hannah dreaded finding alone. Even the ancient tub that served as a bath was scoured and free of insects and on the bed of the south facing bedroom, bed linen and towels had been ironed and neatly piled on a bed that seemed both comfortable and dry.

"Everything's ready, you see." Annie Hobbs regarded Hannah with her head to one side as if she was listening to telltale sounds in the floorboards. She's like a bird, Hannah thought, and she wants me here. But why? She doesn't seem to like the niece so it couldn't be for the niece's sake to look after the house.

"There's no heating but you can make a fire. There's plenty of logs you'll find free in the woods nearby."

"What about electricity?"

"There's a power point in the kitchen and one up here." Annie Hobbs indicated with a nod a brown stained socket in the wall by the fireplace. It didn't look too safe to Hannah and she asked if it could be checked if she decided to come.

"I'll ask young Jack Ryder to have a look. He knows about these things."

Who Jack Ryder was and whether an electrician or mere handyman Annie Hobbs didn't elaborate. Seemingly confident the matter was settled, she told Hannah the rent – ten pounds a week.

"Ten pounds!" Hannah could hardly believe it. It was a fraction of the rent she'd have to pay in Oxford, a rent she knew she could afford without worry, a rent that would enable her to be sure of being able both to do the course and complete it. The cottage had drawbacks. It was isolated. It would undoubtedly be cold but as she looked out again at the golden grass and poppies she knew she wouldn't find anywhere so quiet and free nor anywhere so near to Yadrahna that she could predictably afford.

"You think it's too much?" Annie Hobbs looked at her anxiously as if she'd have to take up again a load she'd thought disposed of.

"No, it's fine. So I wouldn't have to deal direct then with Mrs Webb's niece?"

From the deep apron pocket from which she'd extracted the key, Annie Hobbs drew out a folded piece of paper and a biro pen. "Just write down your name and address and telephone number and where you'll be working while you're here and I'll tell Mrs Webb's niece when she rings this evening."

"And if she approves I can come straightaway?"

"You can come tomorrow, anytime."

"And I just deal direct with you, pay you the rent?" There must be some catch, Hannah thought. It all seemed too easy. Then she looked at the piece of paper and realised she'd have to give a name.

She decided to compromise, to keep Hannah but change her surname and wrote Robinson, the first surname that came into her head. Then she gave Sally's telephone number and address and explained that she intended to do the Personnel course in Oxford.

Carefully Annie Hobbs scrutinised each word, making sure she could understand each letter, then, to Hannah's relief, refolded the paper and put it back in her pocket. No more was said till Annie Hobbs had turned the rusty key in its lock behind them. Under the brambles of the porch she peered again into Hannah's face.

"You know you're just like another Hannah who used to live near here."

"Really?" Hannah smiled, trying to assume an air of innocence and surprise.

"Mr Delaney's daughter from the large estate up on the hill. She hasn't been seen for some time. She went

abroad they say to get married. She'll no doubt return now her father's dead to get her share in the estate."

"It's a large estate then?"

Hannah felt alarmed that Annie Hobbs who didn't even know her had made the connection. What about those who had known her? She was obviously too easily recognised as she was and would have to change her appearance but wasn't it already with Annie Hobbs too late?

The mention of the estate had the added effect of renewing her sense of urgency. She had somehow to get back into Yadrahna and search for more evidence, rescue what she could from any remaining belongings and documents of her father and find out more about what was going on there.

"Larger than is ever likely to come to ordinary folk, like you and me, my dear."

Annie Hobbs regarded Hannah more wistfully but had she really, Hannah wondered, been deceived.

Chapter 10

Two days later it was all arranged. Hannah was to collect the key from Annie Hobbs and pay her the rent for the rest of July. From then the terms were that she would pay on the first of the month in advance and would be given a month's notice to quit if the cottage was sold.

"It's a real bargain, Sally. I can't believe it."

But Sally was more apprehensive as they struggled with Hannah's suitcases down the narrow pathway now muddy from a downpour and spoiling her new court shoes. The sight of Bramble Cottage's rotting woodwork and overgrown garden set against a now grey sky did not reassure her nor the primitive limited facilities of the kitchen inside and its blackened walls.

"You're mad, Han, mad! No telephone, no heating, all this damp. Whatever's Richard going to say?"

"Richard?" Tentatively, Hannah started to wipe the shelves of the tiny larder to lay out the cereals and fruit she'd brought. To her surprise, they were already clean and everywhere the signs that Annie Hobbs had been back to the cottage again clearing, trying to prepare. "What's Richard got to do with it?"

"He's coming specially to see you, Han, and this will be your base." Sally regarded her with concern. "Maybe

you'd better come back to my place when he's home."

"Why? I don't see why he can't adapt for a few days. It's a bit primitive, yes, but it has other assets." Sally's idea of their going back to her place, though well intentioned, she didn't doubt, seemed a retreat – a retreat to which she didn't want now to succumb. She'd made a break and wanted to give it now a fair trial. If Richard didn't like the cottage, well they could cross that bridge when they came to it. "There's no need to worry. I'm sure we'll work something out."

"It's not just Richard coming I'm bothered about." Sally looked apprehensively out at the yew tree and nettles, the darkening sky above foretelling more rain. "It's the fact of your being isolated here and alone without even a phone. And is it wise, do you think, to be so close to Yadrahna, when you're doing all this investigating? Won't it make it more upsetting and frustrating for you? And what if Hugo and the Slade woman find out you're here? If things get tense, they could turn nasty. It's not a good place for you to be alone."

"It's cheap though which means I can manage the course."

"You're still seriously intending to go through with the course then?"

"Yes, I am. Why? Don't you think I should? I thought you were in favour of retraining."

"I am but there's Richard too surely to consider. I mean if he's staying on in Hong Kong, it means you're going to be separated for a year. Do you think that's wise?"

"Richard knows I don't want to teach back here. He'll see the sense of it when I've had the chance to explain. I

can't anyway go back to Hong Kong yet if I'm going to mount any kind of challenge to the will."

"Yes, I can see that. But have you told Richard yet about the course?"

"No."

"Don't you think you ought to?"

"I suppose so." It would be fairer, Hannah knew but she was afraid deep down that Richard would argue her out of the course and she wanted to reach a point first of no return. "I'd rather though explain it all when he's here. It's difficult on the phone."

"Yes, I can see that. You need to be careful though, Han, that you don't lose him. There aren't too many men around like Richard who'll look after you."

Hannah felt Sally's eyes regarding her as a child not knowing what was good for her.

"I'm not sure I want to be looked after," she defied.

"Oh well, you always were a law unto yourself." Sally wondered if she should warn Richard what to expect but deep down she was too fond of Hannah to go behind her back. No, she'd have to let them work it out, she decided, for themselves. "But please accept you're more than welcome to stay with me even when you do the course. There's really no need to come here for the winter. It's obviously going to be very cold."

"I can make a fire. I love wood fires. They're so much more natural than central heating." Hannah stopped, feeling she was now criticising Sally's hospitality and home. "Please don't think I'm not grateful, Sally, for all you've done. I just need to be able to work things out for a bit on my own, that's all."

"Well no one can say I didn't at least try to put the other view." Sally attempted a resigned smile, then looked at her watch, ready for the next task in hand. "Hadn't we better get going to see this witness of yours?"

Back in the car, Sally felt as if she'd shed a mouldy skin and was in control again. "So where exactly does she live then – Sadie Shaw?"

"She lives in an apartment block right in the centre of Chadford." Hannah pointed at the map to Duke Street, the address she gleaned from beneath Sadie Shaw's name on the will. Sadie Shaw herself had been rather vague on the phone, both as to time and place and Hannah wondered as they drove to Duke street whether she had in fact registered the planned visit and would be there and how useful, vague as she'd seemed, she would be.

Hannah had only met Sadie Shaw once at a drinks party her father had given for members of the National Trust. Pretty rather than striking with silvery curls, she wasn't a person who'd been, to her knowledge, of any great significance in her father's life – an acquaintance rather than a friend, which made it surprising she'd been chosen as a witness, Hannah thought.

Trying to find out more about her, Hannah's phone call to Aunt Eileen the night before had not increased her optimism as to Sadie Shaw's usefulness. "She's not the most observant and alert of people," Aunt Eileen had caustically remarked, "but she hasn't had to be. She's always had money on her plate, though I've heard since her husband's death, her means have been rather drastically reduced. You may find her somewhat less patronising now her circumstances have changed. But I doubt you'll get much out of her. She's now 80 plus – an obvious

choice for Hugo for a witness – not likely to be long around and not likely to be of much help when she is." But Aunt Eileen, whom Hannah knew to be sympathetic to her view, had nevertheless wished her luck. The only other information she'd gleaned was that Sadie Shaw had once been an actress.

"An actress!" Sally responded to the information with enthusiasm. "She should be easy to record then."

"Record?"

"Don't tell me you're not recording these visits, Han."

"I hadn't thought of it, no."

"Honestly, I can't believe it. How naive you are sometimes. How are you going to prove a point if you don't have some kind of record? It'll just be your word against hers. You know what people are like; they change their stance to suit the circumstance. Besides you need to be sure you've heard yourself correctly and don't miss anything."

"I suppose so."

"Look, you'd better take this," Sally urged, taking her own dictaphone from her bag.

"Am I allowed to though?"

"Whether allowed to or not, after what Hugo's done, I think recording a witness is the least of your rights."

Sally was probably right, Hannah reflected. She usually was when it came to practical matters. She felt uneasy all the same with the dictaphone in her pocket as they drew up outside the Georgian style three storey block of flats where Sadie Shaw lived.

"Would you like to come in with me?" Hannah hadn't mentioned Sally in her phone call to Sadie Shaw but it seemed mean now to leave her outside after she'd driven her all this way and to the cottage with her luggage.

131

To Hannah's relief, Sally declined. "No, it might intimidate her if there are two of us there. She'll probably speak more freely to you on your own. You can play the tape to me after. Don't forget to switch it on though."

Am I that hopeless, Hannah wondered, thinking she might well still forget the switch. She still felt discouraged by her visit to Dr Craig and wondered pessimistically, as she rang the doorbell of flat 4, whether she'd do any better with Sadie Shaw.

On the door outside two plaques were affixed, one saying 'Beware the dog' and the other 'No callers or salesmen'. There was no sound, however, of a dog as Hannah rang the bell. After three rings and a long wait between, she was about to give up when the door abruptly opened and she was confronted by a sturdy middle-aged woman with dark suspicious eyes who rapped her fists against the plaques on the door.

"It says no callers. You can read, can't you?"

Hesitantly Hannah tried to smile. "I rang Mrs Shaw yesterday to make an appointment. I've come to see her on a personal matter."

"Mrs Shaw's resting. She doesn't see visitors in the afternoon."

"I'm sure she'll see me." Determined not to let the opportunity slip, now she'd got so far, Hannah stepped forward putting her foot in the door as the woman was about to close it on her. "She's agreed to see me. It's about my father, Thomas Delaney."

To Hannah's surprise, the woman suddenly dropped her guard and called back into the flat. "It's a girl come to see you about Mr Delaney."

"Delaney?" Hannah heard a wavering voice from inside. "Oh, yes, oh very well – show her in, Mrs Brown."

Hannah had a strange sensation of stepping into a confusion of time as she entered the main living room of the flat. It was a room with all the comforts of the 1990's with gas fired central heating, double glazed windows, a wide screened television and video with remote control and plush mushroom wall–to–wall carpeting.

But the decor with its faded chintz curtains, its aspidistra and chaise longue, its bamboo table and fringed shawl draped over a wicker chair harked back, wistfully it seemed to Hannah, to the Edwardian age. And on every available surface, on the mantelpiece, bookcases, television, the walls and floor, were Victorian ornaments and memorabilia – a portrait even of Queen Victoria herself.

As if trying to hold the different periods of time together, Sadie Shaw sat in a Victorian upright chair by the window with a copy of the day's "Times" on the table beside her and an Edwardian walking stick in her hand.

She was, as Hannah had remembered, with the same silvery curls round a fine boned face, the same delicately lined skin and innocent looking, rather bewildered, china blue eyes – eyes that sought protection from the outside world. Could she really though have been so innocent about Hugo's intentions, Hannah wondered. Like the chintz curtains she seemed to be fading but her voice carried a trace still of command through its wavering as she asked Mrs Brown to make them some tea.

"So you're Thomas Delaney's daughter?" Sadie Shaw leaned forward, resting her frail bony hands on her stick as if she was about to use it for support to rise, peering at

Hannah as at an exhibit in a museum whose presence and meaning were not yet clear.

"Yes, that's right."

"Have I seen you before? I don't seem to remember.." her voice trailed.

"You've seen me once at a National Trust meeting." Hannah was conscious of Mrs Brown clattering and banging resentfully in the kitchen, conscious that she might not have much time with Sadie Shaw alone. "But it's about my father I've come to see you, Mrs Shaw." Trying to sound calm, as she felt for the switch of the dictaphone in her pocket, Hannah explained, "He made a will in May which changed completely what previously he said he would do. It's fallen to me, therefore, to find out more about the facts and circumstances in which he made the new will."

Hannah paused, aware of a sharper light in Sadie Shaw's eyes – a reluctance in her voice as she responded.

"I had nothing to do with the making of your father's will, Miss Delaney."

"You don't remember signing as a witness then?"

"A witness?"

"Is this your signature?" Taking a copy of the will from her bag, Hannah pointed to the last page.

Sadie Shaw peered at the page uncomprehending a moment, then feeling for her spectacles on the table nearby, put them on and readjusting, tried again.

"Yes," she confirmed then. "That's my signature. The way the S is done is mine."

"You're sure? You remember writing it?"

"The S is mine so I must have written it, mustn't I?"

"What about the other signature – Mrs Slade's? Do you remember seeing her sign?"

Sadie Shaw frowned again and Hannah described with some exaggeration Olga Slade's dyed black hair, her overweight and garish clothes, her hard face and beady eyes.

"The housekeeper you mean? Yes, I never liked her much. She gave your father some whisky I remember and dropped some on her dress."

"You saw her sign then?"

"I don't remember that – no."

"Did you see my father sign then?" Hannah persisted, feeling increasingly exasperated. She seemed again to be getting nowhere. "It states that you witnessed the signature."

"If that what it states, then I must have seen him sign."

"Was there anyone there supervising?"

"Supervising?"

"Like a solicitor,"

"I don't remember a solicitor, no."

"So it was just you, my father and Mrs Slade then?"

"I think so – yes."

"What about my brother Hugo? What was he doing?" Noticing Sadie Shaw looking more nervous, Hannah pursued. "I mean someone must have been in charge reading out instructions. That couldn't have been you and Mrs Slade, could it?"

"There's no harm in reading out instructions, is there?" There was a trace of the querulous in Sadie Shaw's voice now.

"No harm in itself – no."

"Maybe it was Hugo then. Now I come to think of it – yes, Hugo was there. I remember him, yes, handing a pen to your father."

"Did he say anything to my father?"

"I don't remember."

"Is there anything special you remember about the evening – anything at all?"

"I'm afraid my memory isn't as good as it was, Miss Delaney. One evening is very like another when you get to my age."

"But you must remember something surely. I mean signing a document is rather special."

"I've signed many documents in my life, Miss Delaney, and when you sign a document you don't expect to be questioned afterwards."

Sadie Shaw turned with relief as Mrs Brown came in with biscuits and tea. She knew more than she was saying, Hannah was sure, – another potential who didn't want to be involved. To her irritation, Mrs Brown hovered, reluctant now she'd emerged from the kitchen to return. But Mrs Brown or no Mrs Brown, Hannah was determined that she wasn't finished yet.

"How did my father seem when the will was signed?"

"Seem?"

"Did he seem cheerful for example or depressed?"

"Could a man, as sick as your father was, be cheerful? I don't think so, Miss Delaney."

"All right then let me put it another way. Do you think he signed the will willingly or so you think he was coerced?"

"Coerced? How do you mean coerced? Who could have coerced him?"

Sadie Shaw continued to display her innocent eyes but there was an unease, an agitation, Hannah sensed, behind them now.

"You've told me that Hugo was present when the will was signed. Please try to remember what happened. Was my father being pressured, do you think, by Hugo? Did Hugo do anything or say anything?"

"He offered me a drink." With a trembling hand, Sadie Shaw started to pour the tea from a silver teapot into fine, china rose patterned cups.

"Did he say anything though in relation to the will that could have influenced my father?" Hannah felt she wanted to scream now with exasperation. She was sure Sadie Shaw could remember now if she wanted to. If she could remember being offered a drink and the whisky on Olga Slade's dress, she could remember other things. Why didn't she?

"Please try to remember." Trying to stay calm, Hannah urged again. "It's important."

But something of her own exasperation she could feel transferring itself. A spurt of tea jetted onto the plush mushroom carpet as Sadie Shaw put down her silver teapot.

"Miss Delaney." Her voice was quivering with both resistance and incipient anger now. "I have to tell you that I'm not supposed to be put under stress. I have a heart condition and I have to avoid pressure. If you ask me any more questions, I shall have to ask you to leave. I don't know where all these questions are leading but I have my suspicions. I did my best as a witness. I signed a document. I don't expect now to be treated as a criminal and asked all these questions."

Despite her exasperation, Hannah felt some sympathy for Sadie Shaw's view. She was after all old and had probably been used. But if she didn't get help from Sadie

Shaw, whom would she get it from? And wasn't the will after all a legal document, which should be questioned? A witness logically should expect to be questioned. But what part did logic play when it came to the point? Could she get Sadie Shaw to see the logic of being a witness who should expect questioning? Sadie Shaw was putting on an act, Hannah was sure, but supposing she did have a heart attack? Could she take the risk by persisting? Was she going to get anywhere anyway?

Finishing her tea, as Mrs Brown retreated to the kitchen for a cloth to wipe up the tea from the carpet, Hannah wrote down her name and Sally's address and telephone number on an envelope.

"If you remember anything," she made a last plea, "please let me know."

Carefully then she folded the paper and put it in a china jar within reach of Sadie Shaw but away from the clearing eyes of Mrs Brown. It was unlikely she knew it would ever be used. Sadie Shaw knew more and could have told her more than she claimed but clearly didn't want to be involved. Or was she part, Hannah wondered, of the web itself in a way not yet clear.

As Mrs Brown slammed the door behind her and she walked back downstairs and out to join Sally at her car, Hannah had the sense of waking too late to a web already spun.

Chapter 11

"How did it go then?" Sally smiled encouragingly as Hannah got back into the car.

"She either doesn't remember or doesn't want to – probably the latter."

"You think Hugo's been getting at her then?"

"I feel someone has. She's old but not as old and forgetful as she makes out."

"Well, there's still the other witness."

"Not much hope there, I'm afraid."

"You may be surprised. She could let something slip unawares. Anyway," Sally beamed as she started up the engine, "I've got some good news for you. A message came through on the cell phone just now from Andy, one of Richard's friends in London. He said Richard's going to phone you later this evening to sort out plans for his leave."

"Phone where?"

"My place. Sorry – but what else could I say? He could hardly get through to you at the cottage, could he, unless you're both telepathic."

Back at Sally's, Hannah hovered, feeling at a loss in the pristine kitchen as Sally cut up onions and peppers for her latest stir–fry. Despite all its facilities and the crisp

whiteness of its walls, she found herself already wishing she was back in the kitchen at the cottage. It was primitive, stained, but it had character, memories and suggestions of a past, which Sally's kitchen completely lacked. I don't belong here, she thought, belong to this age or place and she felt Sally's efficiency draining her, getting on her nerves. Wandering into the garden, she knew she'd made the right decision to leave.

It wasn't until nearly midnight that Richard finally rang from Hong Kong to tell her that he'd be able to get away earlier than planned.

"Things have gone much better than expected and Chan's given the go ahead which means I'll be with you now in 2 weeks – maybe even less. So think, my darling, where you want to go – Paris, Munich, New York – I've decided it's going to be your choice this time."

His voice surged with enthusiasm and she hadn't the heart to tell him that she didn't want to travel anywhere or that she'd planned the course, which would curb any holiday in September. So she told him about the cottage, elaborating on the long grass, the poppies, the thatch and the seclusion and peace.

"Of course," she added then conscious she'd avoided the drawbacks, "it's not exactly well equipped."

"As long as it's got you. We'll be on our travels anyway most of the time." And Richard felt literally he didn't care in that moment as long as he could have her again in his arms, in his bed. He couldn't imagine the cottage at all. Hannah's description seemed more dream than reality but then her descriptions usually did. He would have to wait and see for himself.

"And how's all the investigation going?"

"Not too well." And she admitted her discouragement with Dr Craig and Sadie Shaw.

"You ought to have a good search round Yadrahna," Richard urged. "If your father was coerced, he may well have left a second will later that he'd know you'd find."

"Maybe." But Hugo, Hannah thought pessimistically, knew the potential hiding places as well as she did and his clearance operation so far had not been casual.

"However it turns out anyway, you mustn't worry. It won't be a disaster even if you do lose Yadrahna. We'll be able to afford a property just as good if I stay on here. I'm well in with Chan now and he's expanding into the Philippines and Canada. The world's our oyster if we stay with him. There's no point in looking back."

Richard's voice swept on full of confidence and optimism – a voice that didn't doubt his ability to succeed. And he would succeed, Hannah knew, would control one day a corporation of his own. But in his plans she saw again the concrete teeth of the Hong Kong waterfront buildings biting into the sky and she longed all the more for Yadrahna and to know that it was hers.

As she put down the phone, Hannah felt a fresh urgency to get back into Yadrahna and to search as Richard had suggested, a sense she'd been wasting time when other vital documents and letters could have been destroyed.

Luke had told her he would not destroy any more papers without her seeing them but how many were there that hadn't passed through his hands? And how much, she wondered again, could she trust him. The strange concentrated look he'd given her as she'd left the kitchen

garden – still she found it disconcerting. Interest was it or dislike? Either way she didn't want to depend on him too much; yet it was obvious he could be of use.

It seemed all the more necessary now also to see Olga Slade about the will – not that it was likely to yield much by way of confession but she had at least to try before returning to Ashford.

The next morning on her way to see her mother, Sally dropped Hannah back at Bramble Cottage with instructions that Hannah should ring her every Friday evening from the call box at the end of the lane on the main road. "If I don't hear from you," she expanded, "I'll come at the weekend to check you're all right."

"Thanks, Sally, thanks." And Hannah felt genuinely grateful and reassured by Sally's caring and support; at the same time relieved that she was free at last to do as she wanted.

It was Saturday and she decided to make an unobtrusive visit to Yadrahna straightaway to try and find her bicycle and to check if Luke had saved any papers.

The easiest way was to follow the route of the cars from Wynton up Winter Hill. But she preferred to avoid Winter Hill if she could when walking alone, especially its hairpin bend after what had happened to her mother. She didn't in any case want to be seen, especially by Hugo.

She took instead a badger path she knew to the east of Wynton up through an area of the woods where the beeches were thicker, closer. It brought her eventually to the sheltered rear of Yadrahna. Creeping along the edge of the shrubbery, she listened carefully for signs of life.

It was then she was aware of the sound of sawing coming from the vicinity of the garden sheds by the kitchen garden.

Peering through the shrubbery at the back of the sheds, she could just see Luke in the gap between the sheds bent over a large log of elm, which he was steadily sawing in a rhythmic movement, which seemed to absorb all his attention, all his body. He was stripped again to the waist, the muscles of his back and shoulders rippling again as when he'd forked the fire but there was no sunlight this time – only a sombre dappled light from an overhanging elm and a greying sky. Yet Luke, oblivious it seemed of the grey, was smiling to himself. What was he thinking of, Hannah wondered. She felt she wanted to surprise him, demand an answer to her question. But there was something in his preoccupation that made her hesitate, afraid to interrupt the rhythm and she decided to see first if there was anyone else around.

Skirting round the shrubbery within sight of the drive and garage, she saw that there were no cars parked outside, no sign of either Olga Slade's blue Renault or Hugo's Daimler. It was a chance she hadn't expected to get back inside the house again and taking the familiar cloverleaf designed iron key out of her purse, she ran up to the oak front door and put the key in the brass lock. But as she tried to turn it, she felt resistance. For a moment she thought stupidly she'd brought the wrong key but the cloverleaf design was unmistakable as was the Y scratched on one of the clover leaves. It was the lock that had changed.

She stared at the door a moment in disbelief. The front door of Yadrahna had always been open to her ever since she could remember, open to her childhood, to her teens

and twenties, open to the past and, she'd always hoped, the future. Now it was as if she was a stranger on the doorstep, rootless.

She didn't doubt it was Hugo and Olga Slade trying to prevent any further investigation but her certainty didn't take away the yearning pain she felt in the pit of her stomach and it was some time before she could bring herself to try the back entrance. When she did, it was to find what she now suspected, that the lock here too had been changed and all the windows on the ground floor were likewise secured. Depressed and disconcerted, skirting the shrubbery, she returned to the garden sheds.

The sawing had stopped and she could see Luke some distance away now stacking the logs of elm he'd cut into a pile. Hoping he wouldn't see her, she slipped quietly into the open door of the first shed to see if her bicycle was there. Instead of the untidy muddle of flower pots and tools she'd expected from the past, the shed had been tidied with the terra cotta flowerpots stacked in neat rows and the tools hung on nails. On the bench by the window, pots of compost and cuttings were in the process of preparation. A hanging of sacking shielded the end of the shed and Hannah decided to see if that was where her bicycle had ended.

Hopefully, she flicked back the sacking. She had a glimpse of three tiers of shelves rising up like steps from the floor and on each shelf a row of terra cotta pots with identical plants in them – tall, carefully tended plants with opposite leaf stems and slender, toothed palmate leaves.

There was no sign of her bicycle and suddenly it dawned. The rows of plants were not plants for the garden but marijuana.

As she stepped back in surprise, Hannah was aware of movement past the window, of the doorway of the shed darkening, then Luke's voice tense and hostile.

"What the hell are you doing?"

"Isn't that a question rather I should ask you?" As she turned to face him, accidentally she knocked one of the pots of marijuana from the end of the second row onto the floor.

"Oh, it's you," his voice dropped a notch into sarcasm, "the ex lady of the house."

"Yes, it's me." Ignoring his sarcasm, she added, "Quite a business you've got here, I see."

"Well, what if I have? What's that to you?"

"Nothing except you could get quite a sentence for this lot. It is illegal, you know."

"No really?" With mock surprise, he pushed past her and scooped up the earth and marijuana plant from the pot she'd knocked over and placed them carefully in a new pot back on the shelf again. "So you're planning to shop me, is that it?"

"I didn't say that." She hesitated feeling herself on unfamiliar ground. "But we could do a bargain."

"And what did your ladyship have in mind?"

"I keep quiet and you get me a copy of the new front door key. As you're no doubt aware, the locks have been changed."

"I wasn't, as a matter of fact. As I told you, I don't go into the house, except by invitation."

"You could still get a key though."

"Could is not quite the same as can though, is it? And isn't your bargain a bit one sided? There's no problem in

keeping quiet is there? But to get a key and get into Oxford with it and to get a copy without anyone knowing takes quite a bit of planning and time and money."

"I'll pay for the key. I didn't intend you to end up out of pocket – though I doubt you'll do that with this lot to sell."

"It's not that lucrative – I can tell you."

"Enough – I'm sure. And there's another thing. I need my bicycle. It used to be in the garage nearest the house."

"You mean you think I've got it?"

"I didn't say that. I just thought you might have seen it, that's all."

"There was a bike a few days ago in the coal shed by the cellar."

"A woman's mountain bike was it – blue?"

"I think it was blue – yes. But you wouldn't be able to ride it. Both of the tyres were punctured and one of the wheels bent."

"You think someone's been riding it then?"

"Dumping it more like."

"I see." She paused, looking at him. "Do you think you could do me a favour?"

"I thought I was already doing you that with the letters."

"You've saved some then?"

"A few." From an empty terra cotta pot high up on one of the shelves, he drew down a clutch of letters wrapped in a plastic bag and handed them to her. "That's all there was that wasn't magazines and forms."

"Thanks, thanks a lot."

"Always pleased to be of service." He gave a mock bow.

"Then you'll continue to save them?" Against her will, she could feel herself pleading.

"As long as you keep quiet, I'll save."

"We know where we are then, don't we?"

"Do we? My guess is that we think we know but that's not the same as knowing, is it?"

"You mean you don't trust me?"

"I mean – what happens when you've got the information and things you need?"

"I'll keep quiet I promise if you get the key and my bike and save the letters."

"And that's all?"

Was he being sarcastic or serious? She wasn't sure. She decided to press all the same from his question and make one further demand.

"It would help if you could find me the address of the previous housekeeper – Emma Mason. She was with my father for 5 years before the Slade woman ousted her."

"So she was ousted, was she?"

"That's my belief – yes but I don't know where she's gone and it's difficult for me to find out without letting people know I'm around."

"What do you want her for?"

"I want to know more about the early stages of my father's illness. If you could think of anyone who might know her new address."

"I hardly knew her. She was only here a couple of weeks when I first came."

"But you liked her?" It was suddenly important to Hannah that he'd liked Emma as she had.

"She was better than the present old bag – sure."

"Do you think you could try and find out where she's gone, anyone, any place she had contact with – like the bakery."

"If I go there," more reluctant now he conceded. "I could ask but I can't promise anything. Your family or more particularly your brother is not exactly popular round here."

"Why?"

"There's talk of the land being sold for development."

"For development?"

"You didn't know then?"

"Know what exactly?" It came back to her then what she'd set aside, not wanting to believe – the carefully sketched map she and Sally had found with Hugo's belongings in his room.

"It's to be turned into a block of flats for old people apparently. The developer's had his eyes on it for years but your father wouldn't sell."

"You're joking!"

"No, I'm not. Ask the local branch of Friends of the Earth if you don't believe me. They're concerned because the area round the pond is an SSSI."

"How did you learn this?"

"Because of FOE, because we've gone into SSSI's as part of the course."

"What course?"

"The environment course I've been doing."

"You're a student then?" She felt her hostility lessen, that she should have guessed.

"Why? Shouldn't I be?"

"I didn't say that."

"Well, anyway, I shan't be for much longer once my dissertation is out of the way."

"It's just for the money then you're here?"

"It'd hardly be for love of the inmates, would it?" He turned to the door, then back to her again. "Tell me. Are you always like this?"

"Like what?"

"Asking questions all the time – like some investigator."

"Isn't it better to try to be sure of one's facts?"

"You still don't believe me then?"

"I don't know what to believe. I – " she stopped, feeling tears gathering in her eyes. It seemed incomprehensible that Hugo should want to betray their father in this way, to sell off all her father held dear. What had possessed him and why?

""I'm afraid it's true." She was conscious of him looking at her more intently now with concern, the mockery gone. "Of course he may not get his plan accepted and through the system but Hugh Jamieson has his cronies on the council apparently according to FOE."

"Hugh Jamieson?"

"You know him then?"

"I don't know him personally no, but he's the executor of my father's will."

"It all adds up then, doesn't it? They've got things sewn up between them – your brother and Jamieson or think they have."

"You think that Jamieson has a lot of influence then?"

"I'm not an expert in local politics but bastards like him usually make sure some years ahead they've oiled the wheels."

"I suppose so." Hannah felt a darkness closing in on her, her joy and relief at finding the cottage gone. It was all much worse than she'd imagined. Hugo had struck not only at her but at her father's deepest wishes that Yadrahna should remain in it setting unchanged. But why? Was it purely money that had driven him or more?

She was aware suddenly of the sound of a car in the drive, a trace of metallic blue through the trees. Olga Slade had returned.

"I'll have to go. I want to catch her before she slams the door. You'll get the key and the bike for me, won't you?"

"The bike, yes. The key – I'll try. I can't promise."

"But I've promised you."

"That may be but the terms are hardly equal, are they?"

"Perhaps not." Hannah hesitated at the entrance to the shed, uncertain what to make of him, how much she could trust him, conscious at the same time that she needed his help. "I'd be grateful all the same if you could get the key. It's very important to me and I don't want to lose any more time. I'll come back the same time next week. If meantime you manage to get a copy made, can you let me know? I haven't got a phone but – " Hannah hesitated, realising she would have to let him know where she lived.

"But what?"

"You can put a note through the door of a cottage at the end of Hawthorn Lane – a cottage called Brambles. A friend of mine lives there."

"You mean you don't?"

He regarded her for a moment with amused scepticism but made no further comment and hearing the garage door slam, Hannah took her leave and making sure she wasn't

seen in advance, retraced her steps through the shrubbery to the front of the house again.

Hiding behind a lilac bush, she watched Olga Slade carry a box of groceries from the open boot of the car into the house, removing the key to the front door as she did so and locking the door behind her. When she came back to collect the second box, she repeated the same process, carefully looking over her shoulders to see there was no one around before re–entering the house and locking the door again. She's like a puppet, Hannah thought, a puppet of Hugo, carrying our instructions, not from thought but from fear. Fear of what though exactly? What hold had Hugo over her apart from the doubtful security of her job? What did he fear exactly being found in the house that the locks had to be changed? Was there in fact another will not yet found?

Watching Olga Slade repeat the process a third time, Hannah felt tempted to rush her at the door and push her aside while she was vulnerable with the next box in her ample arms so that she could have the house for a while to re–explore. But there was no doubt a plan, she reflected, for such a contingency and it would only draw attention to her own agenda. No, better to slip in when they were unaware so she had plenty of time alone. For now it was on Olga Slade as the witness she had to concentrate.

As the housekeeper walked from the car to the front door with the fourth and final box in her arms, Hannah emerged from the shrubbery, forcing a smile.

"Good evening , Mrs Slade."

Olga Slade was too intent on the contents of the box to drop it. It was a box full of her favourite wines and liqueurs

together with a bottle of Pimms which she intended to imbibe later that evening at Hugo's expense. Despite all the warnings, however, she couldn't hide her surprise as she struggled with the box to the door. Her eyes bulged and, as if squeezed by their pressure, sweat poured down her cheeks giving their powdered overlay an effect of salmon coloured mould.

"What are you doing here?" Still clutching the box of drink, Olga Slade glanced over her shoulder though whether from fear of further challenge or hope of support Hannah wasn't sure. After hesitating and looking around, eventually she put the box down and stood in front of the door on guard. "Mr Delaney says that everything's to be done through the solicitor."

"I know what Mr Delaney says but it wasn't Mr Delaney I came to see. It was you."

There was a flicker of apprehension for a moment in Olga Slade's black beady eyes and Hannah continued. "You were a witness I gather to my father's will."

"There's no harm in that, is there?"

"No harm at all," Hannah tried to soothe, "but sometimes witnesses need to be questioned when there's a problem or facts to ascertain."

"Well, it's no use questioning me. I can't help you."

"Let me try briefly then to explain." Hannah paused a moment trying to look directly into Olga Slade's eyes. "As you may or may not realise, this has been all my life my home and my father, before I went to Hong Kong, told me that it would come to me in his will. He told me that my brother would have an equal value by inheriting his investments. Naturally it came to me as a great shock

when I saw the will made on the 1st May leaving virtually everything to my brother. I don't think this was my father's intention. In fact, I'm certain it was not his intention from all he told me – which is the reason why I feel the need to investigate the way in which the will was made."

For a moment Hannah thought she detected a flicker of understanding behind the apprehensive black eyes but Olga Slade's voice was soon echoing the plum voice of Hugo.

"I've nothing to say."

"I'm not expecting you to make a judgement. I just want to know what happened on the day you signed as a witness – that's all. Was there a solicitor present for example?"

"I can't remember."

"But you must know if other people were there. Perhaps it would help if I told you that Mrs Shaw, the other witness, says there was no solicitor."

"That must be it then if that what she says."

"Had my father been given a drink prior to the will being signed?"

"I can't remember."

"What kind of state was he in? Was he feeling ill or in good spirits?"

"I couldn't say."

"All right then. Let me put it differently. Did he know what he was doing?"

"Of course he knew what he was doing. He wouldn't have signed the will otherwise, would he?"

Nervously, against the tenor of her words, Olga Slade's eyes shifted as she looked to where the drive joined the

main road. She's expecting them, Hannah thought, Hugo and his mother. She's on edge because they're due any minute to arrive, on edge because she's hiding something but what exactly?

"Was my brother present when the will was signed?"

"I've nothing to say."

"Who gave the instructions on where to sign?"

"I've told you I've nothing to say."

"Did you actually see my father sign?"

Patiently Hannah waited but Olga Slade's full-bloodied lips were sealed this time like a clam.

"On an entirely different note then," Hannah pursued. "Perhaps you could let me know why the letters given to you by my father to post were never in fact posted at all."

"Letters? What letters?"

"I think you know, Mrs Slade. The letters he wrote to me."

"I don't know anything about any letters. Now please go. Mr Delaney will be here shortly and he's told me not to let anyone in the house."

"No one being me. Is that it?"

"He's told me that you've been left certain things in the will and would have your share."

"That's completely untrue."

"Well, there's nothing I can do about it. Now please go."

Suddenly from inside the house the phone started to ring. Nervously again Olga Slade glanced up the drive. It was another chance Hannah thought to push inside but again reminded herself that little could be achieved if she didn't have the house to herself and she watched without

moving as Olga Slade fumbled with the key and squeezed herself inside, locking the door again behind her.

Hannah felt tempted to hide the box of drink Olga Slade had abandoned in her haste to get inside. But the prospect of denying the housekeeper an orgy of alcohol was overcome, as she stared at the closed door, by the bleak sense that she'd achieved nothing of significance from her efforts to elicit facts from Olga Slade only an increased awareness of the housekeeper's obduracy. She still had no proof at all of Hugo's pressure on her father though she was increasingly certain pressure had been applied. How though could one make people talk if they didn't want to? And why didn't they want to? Why couldn't Sadie Shaw and Olga Slade see the injustice and understand? Did they really expect never to be questioned or challenged as witnesses? How could she get anywhere if no one was prepared to co–operate? Neither Dr Craig nor Sadie Shaw nor Olga Slade wanted, it seemed, to help or be involved.

Was Richard not right that one could always buy another house as good as Yadrahna eventually from earnings overseas? Why keep on when there was little hope of getting anywhere, when the plot had been too deeply, carefully laid?

But as she set off back to the cottage in the gathering dusk Hannah knew at heart that she wouldn't be able to give up now, that she'd started on a journey and whether it ended in success or failure she'd have to see it through. How else would she be able to stop the looming threat to Yadrahna against all the wishes of her father? And wasn't it in essence hers? No, she couldn't and wouldn't give up now.

Deep in thought, in the uncertain light, mistakenly Hannah diverted from the main badger path by which she'd ascended and found herself instead on another pathway that passed close to the main road and the hairpin bend she'd sought to avoid.

It was the hairpin bend from which her mother five years before had skidded in her car and plunged through the beech trees to her death. It was a death that had made no sense to Hannah then, with the loss she'd felt and the horror of it all; and it made still no sense to her now as she took in again the steep gradient through the trees. For how could her mother's car have overturned when its path had been blocked by the beech tree it had initially hit close to the road? And why should her mother not have been able then to escape with the sunroof down? And how had three 2 inch nails in the first place become embedded in her tyres on such a remote country road, causing simultaneously three punctures? It was all still a mystery unexplained – a mystery Hannah feared would remain a mystery, for no witnesses had been found to the early stages of the accident and only Hugo for the later stage when the car was already burning and overturned. Why, she wondered again, had it happened. There'd never been a real or adequate explanation.

As she hovered beside a beech tree, thinking back, she was aware of a car revving up the hill with the headlights full on and glaring. Quickly, not wanting to be seen, she slipped behind the tree. As the car rounded the bend, close to where she was hiding, she saw that it was Hugo in the driving seat of his Daimler and next to him the hawk like profile of his mother.

Chapter 12

It was dark by the time Hannah reached the cottage. She had forgotten to take her torch and had to feel her way over the dilapidated porch and door to locate the keyhole. Flakes of paint and cobwebs clung to her fingers and she could smell, more potent than the lavender and thyme nearby, the long drawn out darkness of the cottage like a cry for restoration.

As she put the rusty key in the lock, she was aware of a rustling sound in the yew tree behind her. She turned in alarm, fearing someone had followed her through the woods from Yadrahna but there was no sign she could detect of human form or movement. As she peered into the darkness, suddenly without warning her face was brushed with a rush of feathers as an owl swooped down past her and scooped up a mouse from the long grass on the opposite side of the garden.

What a fool I am, she thought, but still she could feel her heart thumping from her imagined fear and hurriedly she let herself into the cottage and locked the door from inside.

It was even darker inside the cottage and feeling her way to the kitchen she knew at once someone had been. There was smell of food – not the wrapped odourless food she'd bought from the supermarket but of freshly baked

cake and pastry. As she found the switch and turned on the light above the kitchen table, she saw then a cheese and courgette quiche laid out ready for her and a large fruitcake with a note affixed in uneven block letters.

'JACK RYDER WILL COME AND SORT THE SOCKET UPSTAIRS ONE DAY THIS MONTH BETWEEN JOBS. I DON'T KNOW WHEN IT WILL BE. IF YOU ARE OUT HE CAN COME TO ME FOR A SPARE KEY. I HOPE YOU CAN MANAGE TILL THEN. Annie Hobbs

There was no mention of the food. How kind she was, Hannah thought. But why was she taking all this trouble? Natural inbuilt kindness was it that would always welcome strangers? Or was there a reason not yet clear? Whatever it was, Hannah felt touched after the indifference and resistance of the witnesses, felt someone cared. And both the quiche and cake were delicious, far better than she could ever cook herself. Before she'd realised it, she had eaten her way through half the quiche and two large slices of cake.

She remembered then the letters Luke had saved and clearing the table, settled under the kitchen's dim light to sort them through.

There were five letters in all. Three were letters she herself had written to her father between March and May – letters which her father had clearly never received and read for both were still sealed. The other two were in airmail envelopes addressed to herself at her Hong Kong address with Richard in her father's writing. Both had stamps affixed but no postmark. Both had been opened.

Taking the thin airmail paper out of the two envelopes, Hannah saw that both letters were in her father's familiar italic style but less steady than she'd known before with downward sloping lines and strokes which were tremulous and unfinished at times. One letter was dated 10th May, the other the 26th May. Straining her eyes under the dim light, Hannah read the 10th May letter first.

My dear Hannah,

I haven't heard from you for a long time now. I wonder if you have received yet my previous two letters. I do hope all is well and that you are taking care of yourself. Please let me know how you are and set my mind at rest.

I don't know how you are placed with your part time teaching post but I should very much like to see you within the next few weeks at the end of May or early June. I am not in fact feeling too well at the moment. The medicine I have been given makes me feel rather groggy.

Mrs Slade is efficient enough in removing dirt and stain but she lacks Emma's humour and warmth. Strangely Emma has not written since she left, though she promised to and I have mislaid her address. Perhaps you have her address. If so, please let me have it. I want to keep in touch.

Between you and me, I think Mrs Slade is an alcoholic and is trying to get me that way too. It helps reduce the pain but I can't seem to think straight sometimes.

I signed a document the other day, which I am not happy about. I didn't feel well and myself at the time and I want to put it right.

Do you remember the Tennyson poem we used to read together? Read it again in the anthology especially the second line and it will speak to you I think of what I have in mind. Please write and come and see me as soon as you can.

Yours with love Dad.

The letter of 26th May was much shorter.

Dear Hannah,

I wonder if you have received my last letter. I urgently need to see you and speak with you. Things are not right here. I feel entrapped and enclosed. I go into hospital on 6th June. Please come soon.

Dad.

Rereading the letters a second time, Hannah was overcome with grief and pain at what her father had endured, at the cry from the heart, which she'd not responded to. The thought that all along he'd wanted her, needed her and she hadn't gone to him was unendurable and increasingly she blamed herself for not responding to the prompting of her heart, her fears in Hong Kong that something was wrong.

She should have followed her fears and not listened to Richard. Richard had acted, she recognised, for the best, as he saw it, in trying to give reassurance but wasn't it false in a sense to reassure without knowledge of the facts and hadn't her fears been all too justified?

Exhausting her tears at length, she became more conscious of the manipulation that had gone on behind the scenes. Hugo and Olga Slade had clearly vetted all the post, tried to prevent any communication between herself and her father. Regardless of the pain they'd caused, the fact that she'd not been able to say even goodbye to her father, they'd coldly pursued their plans for the will so she'd be kept in ignorance of both the will and his illness. And as the realisation dawned of the extent of the manipulation, an anger grew in her, deeper than she'd felt ever before and with it, as the night wore on, a greater strength of resolution that she wasn't going to let Hugo get away with it.

Trying to analyse what use she could make of the letters, she studied them a third time. The reference to Emma, her mislaid address and the fact her father hadn't heard from her now seemed all part of the plan, suggesting that Emma might have something important to say and it seemed all the more urgent now to Hannah to get Emma's address and to find her.

Her father's reference to a document he hadn't wanted to sign Hannah was sure was the will. Without his specifying the will though could it be used for evidence of his unwillingness to sign? And why hadn't he specified the will? Had he feared someone else reading the letter and left it cryptic for that reason? There was something rather

cryptic too about his reference to Tennyson as if he was afraid too much might be gleaned. What Tennyson poem, Hannah wondered, did he mean. She and her father had read so many Tennyson poems. She knew, of course, the anthology he meant. It was the anthology bound in black leather that she had given him for his 66th birthday, the one he'd sometimes kept in the hidden cupboard by the fireplace in his bedroom. She hadn't looked in the cupboard when she'd checked his room on her visit with Sally to Yadrahna. In her hurry, she realised now she'd forgotten to check it. She wondered if it had come under the scrutiny yet of Olga Slade's prying eyes. Perhaps not. It wasn't all that obvious. In fact, if one hadn't known of the cupboard's existence one would have thought of it simply as part of the oak panelling bordering the fireplace. There was a chance that the anthology was still in the cupboard, that she'd find it if she could but get back into the house. It was what her father she was sure wanted for was he not indicating a link between the document/will and the second line of the Tennyson poem? What the poem was, what the link was, she was yet to find out but it was there, instinctively she knew that now, as something important that she should not ignore.

But supposing, it occurred to her, that Hugo had found the anthology and taken it away, taken other documentation away that could include other wills, taken them away altogether to his house at Windsor. How would she retrieve them then? His Windsor home was virtually a Fort Knox on all sides – impossible to penetrate without a key to the front door and who but Hugo could supply her with a key? He had no close

friends to her knowledge, no other relations apart from herself, his mother and Marcus – no one apart from Olga Slade to whom he'd ever entrusted a key, except his ex wife Laura.

Laura – that was it – she'd visit Laura and see if she had a key.

It was over eight years now since she'd last seen Laura – not since Laura's divorce in fact from Hugo. She'd heard subsequently that Laura had got married again to a Probation officer and had a little girl but had had no detailed news, no contact. She'd liked Laura, would have liked to remain friends with her but sensed that Laura didn't want to be reminded of Hugo in her new life so no contact had been attempted. Hannah felt now justified that she had a reason. Where was Laura though now in her new life? Was she in Banbury still or had she moved?

In a whirl of plans and speculation regarding Yadrahna, Windsor and Laura, Hannah found it difficult that night to sleep. The rather sagging lumpy mattress didn't help nor the scratching noises in the wall of her bedroom and at 3 a.m. when she'd been wondering and tossing for over two hours, she felt something crawl over her face. Shaking her bedclothes and feeling for her torch, she saw by its light a huge black spider scuttling away from the bed across the floor. It was 4.a.m. and nearly light by the time, exhausted, she eventually fell into a deep sleep.

She awoke at 9.a.m. to sun shining through the window of the bedroom and to a banging on the porch door. Hastily she flung on her dressing gown and went downstairs and opened the door to find Annie Hobbs beaming at her with a bowl of pears and apples in her hand.

"I'm sorry if I've woken you up, my dear."

"It's all right. I'm normally up by this time. It's just that I somehow couldn't get to sleep last night."

"You're worrying I shouldn't wonder but whatever it is it's not worth losing your sleep for."

"No, you're probably right."

"But the bed is comfortable I hope." Annie Hobbs' enquiring blue eyes softened a moment in concern.

"It's a bit soft but I'm sure I'll get used to it." The mattress seemed of minor consequence now compared to the other problems confronting her.

"I've brought you some fruit from the garden but the main reason I've called is that your friend Sally rang a few minutes ago to say she wants you to ring her between 1 and 2 in the lunch hour. She says it's urgent and you mustn't forget."

"I won't and thank you, Mrs Hobbs, for all the food you left for me last night. It was delicious and I'm very grateful for all the trouble you took."

"It was no trouble, my dear, no trouble at all." Annie Hobbs regarded Hannah a moment with a questioning look in her eyes as if she couldn't quite make up her mind, then handing Hannah the bowl of fruit, she turned back with reluctance down the overgrown pathway to the lane.

Later that morning, according to instruction, Hannah rang Sally in her lunch hour to learn that the college where she was to do her course wanted to see her urgently about the confirmation of her place and the payment of fees.

""The secretary of the Personnel section rang saying they'd like to see you in person," Sally explained. "So I said

I'd pass on the message and you'd probably be able to go during the week."

"You think they want all the money for the fees up front?" Hannah began to feel alarmed now about the total cost and whether she would in fact be able to afford the fees as well as books and travel. And supposing the cottage was sold and she had to pay the true cost of accommodation? She had the money she'd saved from her teaching and two thousand in her building society account but apart from that only £300 in the bank. It might stretch but only just. Yet increasingly the course seemed the right thing to do, the way to a job she would enjoy more in the future. Richard would no doubt lend her money if she asked him but could she ask him when she hadn't even told him about the course and did she want anyway to go on depending on him? No, she'd try, she decided, to manage from her own resources.

"I don't know," Sally responded, "but I'm sure they'll help you sort something out. There's a very positive attitude now to helping people in higher education. But that's not the only reason I rang. Richard rang too last night saying he'll be here on Saturday, maybe even earlier if the computer's sorted."

"Saturday?"

"Yes, aren't you pleased?"

"Well, yes, but the cottage isn't ready. The lighting doesn't work yet upstairs. The electrician's not been."

"What does the lighting matter compared to Richard? Honestly, Han, sometimes I think you're blind. Richard wants you to stay anyway at the Hampstead flat."

"But I can't leave the cottage."

"Why not?"

"I can't explain in detail now," Hannah said, conscious she was using up her change. "It's to do with a further search at Yadrahna. I've also got to go to Banbury and Windsor."

"Well, if you take my advice, you won't put them before Richard. He's coming, don't forget, specially to see you."

"Yes, I know. I.." Hannah's voice trailed, unsure how to respond. She felt she couldn't cope both with Richard and the problem of Yadrahna and the will. She wanted to concentrate now on stopping Hugo and his plans and not be diverted. Richard she knew instinctively would not see the importance of Yadrahna as she did. Unless she could persuade him. There was always a chance she supposed.

"Would you like me to drive you to the college?" Sally's voice brightly offered down the phone.

"No, no – thanks all the same, Sally."

"Well, ring me then on Friday if you haven't heard anything before. Good luck with everything and take care."

Putting down the phone, Hannah decided to go straight into Oxford to the college without going back to the cottage and caught the next bus. At the college she found forms waiting for her to sign, committing her to the £4,000 fees.

"You can spread it out – £1,500 for the first term, £1,500 the second term and £1,000 for the third," the secretary of the department told her cheerfully, "and quite a number of the books you can get second hand." She handed Hannah a formidable book list of books to be read before the term started. They were books on industrial relations, training and development, employment law and recruitment

– subjects Hannah had no knowledge of at all. She felt suddenly alarmed, wondering what she was letting herself in for and, in fear that her ignorance would be all too easily exposed, in panic she bought five thick volumes from the reading list, reducing considerably what little remained to her in the bank. It can't be helped, she thought, trying to be philosophical. I'll live off the land like Mrs Webb did or get an evening job in a pub. Which pub though where she could be sure not to be recognised by Hugo?

Passing Ashford & Swan's shiny brass sign, she hesitated for a few minutes, wondering whether to make another appointment but thinking again of the fees, she decided – no, she'd wait until she searched Yadrahna again and if the chance came Hugo's house at Windsor.

After waiting an hour at the bus station she took a bus to Banbury to try to see Laura but there was no answer from the freshly painted white door of the terrace house where she'd known Laura to have lived seven years before; only a suspicious face with glasses and tight silvery permed hair glaring at her from a window of the adjoining terrace house, watching her every move.

Eventually after she had rung three times, the face emerged from the adjoining front door as a limping woman in her seventies asking who she wanted to see.

"Laura Davidson and her husband."

"Laura Davidson!" the woman echoed with reproof, as if she'd dragged a second hand skeleton out of the cupboard. "Laura Davidson left four years ago."

"Oh dear, you don't by any chance know where she went do you? I'm trying to trace her for something important I need to know."

The woman pursued her lips. All that she would concede was that the people in the house might know.

"What's their name then?" Hannah persisted. "I can perhaps ring them then when they return to find out."

"We don't give one another's names to strangers. If you want to find out you'll have to call back when they return and ask them direct." And without more ado, the woman turned back into her house, emphatically locking the door behind her.

Hannah arrived back in Wynton feeling hot, tired and irritated that she'd wasted both time and money and with no prospect still of getting into Hugo's house.

But as soon as she reached the cottage, shutting the decaying gate behind her, she felt restored by the long grass and the bright red of the poppies and the smell of lavender and thyme. And suddenly, like a miracle it seemed, in the porch against the peeling door was her bicycle, its chrome shining as new, its wheel realigned and its tyres pumped with air. Never had it looked so restored, so serviced and new.

It could only have been Luke. She knew that. No one else even knew of her desire to have her bike again. Yet why had he taken so much trouble? All she'd asked for was the bike itself. She hadn't expected him to take so much care and do so much work on it. He had even fixed a new wheel. And how had he found the cottage, been so sure it was hers?

She felt both excited and alarmed by the fact that he had come, that he could come again and find her when he wanted. Would he want to though without the excuse of another bike? She smiled to herself thinking of the sun on

the rippling muscles of his back as she wheeled the bike into the kitchen.

Leaning it against the blackberry stained wall by the ancient cooker, she noticed then a folded piece of notepaper projecting from the saddlebag. Extracting it, she unfolded it and read: "The Slade goes to Oxford tomorrow afternoon but there's a dinner in the evening at 7.p.m. Your brother has invited Hugh Jamieson and a surveyor. Entry is now possible but no info on Emma Mason."

There was no signature but like the bike she knew it could only have come from Luke. Only Luke could have given her such information. Yet the handwriting surprised her with its upward sloping lines, its upright slant and tall capitals suggesting he was independent, idealistic and ambitious even. She'd expected writing indicating someone more practical and down to earth. Yet wasn't he after all only playing the part of a gardener for cash – a role only temporary, not his real self.. What was his real self, she wondered. The more she looked at the writing, the more it interested her and the more she felt she wanted to know about him and was sorry she'd missed him.

That night she slept more soundly. No spiders dropped onto her from the ceiling, no scratching disturbed her and she dreamt of her father again, of his voice calling to her, not from the streets this time of a crowded Wanchai but from the quiet of the kitchen garden where Luke was raking the ashes of his bonfire. When morning came, it was clear to her she would do what Luke had suggested in his note and go back that afternoon to Yadrahna.

Chapter 13

Hiding in the shrubbery, Hannah waited till she saw the now familiar blue Renault chuntering down the drive and out onto the road leading down to Wynton and Oxford, a sour face Olga Slade at the wheel. With relief then she edged her way round to the kitchen garden. She heard the clock down in Wynton striking two.

It was a sultry cloudy day and her white T–shirt clung to her like a damp outer skin from the long climb. But it was nothing like the oppressive heat of Hong Kong nor did it take away her anticipation. She could feel her heart beating faster as she located Luke eventually by his pile of sawn up logs, eating his sandwiches and perusing what appeared to be hand written notes. In the process of preparation in front of him was a line of seed trays. What was he planting, she wondered – marigold or marijuana? It didn't seem to matter now. All she wished was that he'd take off his shirt and she could see the muscles on his back again.

"Hello there."

As he looked up, she was aware immediately of a charge between them, of his eyes, deep brown like her own, regarding her with awakening interest and desire. She felt she wanted to respond, reach out to him but before words could come, abruptly then he'd turned away, afraid

of committing himself, of a feeling he couldn't rationalise or absorb into the current rhythm of his life with its pressures of work and financial need. And the moment passed, slipped back into the mode they'd established of caution and doubt.

"So you've come then." He refolded his notes, trying not to look at her.

"I wanted to thank you for doing my bike. You've made it like new. I wasn't expecting all the care, the time you've put in."

Embarrassed, he shrugged. "I don't like seeing clapped out rubbish on the road. It endangers other people."

"I see." She was conscious of a deliberate distance in his words now, that she had implied too much. "Well, I can't be a danger now, can I?" She smiled trying to win him over but, avoiding still her gaze, he packed up his remaining lunch and strode over to the shed.

A few moments later he emerged, holding out to her a shiny new steel key.

"You managed then?"

"Wasn't it part of the bargain?"

"Yes, but it can't have been easy."

"It depends on the old bag's mood. If you chat her up, she'll fall."

"So you chatted her up then?"

"It gave me time when she went to the phone to substitute a similar key. I told her then I had work to do. I was away two hours in Oxford. She didn't even notice."

"You're sure?"

"She was still on the phone when I returned. I simply came through an open door and substituted the key."

"Well, I'm very grateful." Hannah wedged the key into her belt purse, suspecting that it hadn't been quite as easy as he'd described. "What do I owe you?"

"It's all right."

"No, this wasn't a two pound job."

"All right then. It was £9."

Carefully Hannah extracted from her purse a £10 note. "It doesn't matter about the change."

"I don't need to be patronised you know just because I'm working part time." Promptly he handed her back a £1 coin.

"I wasn't patronising."

"Weren't you?"

"No. If I seemed so, I'm sorry. It wasn't intended."

"As far as I'm concerned, this was a business arrangement."

"Agreed."

"You'll keep your word then and not grass on me?"

She wanted to tell him that she'd never had any real intention of grassing on him at all.

"I won't grass on you. I promise."

"Right. That's settled then." He looked at his watch. "I don't want to hurry you but if you want to take advantage of her being out, you'd better make use of the key now. She could be back within two hours and your brother will be arriving any time later this afternoon. As I mentioned in my note, he's arranged a dinner this evening."

"You're right. I'll go now. But could you warn me if you hear them?"

"I'll come to the back and whistle when I hear them in the drive. O.K.?"

"Thanks. And thanks for all you've done."

She felt she wanted to kiss him in gratitude but feared she'd further embarrass him. He didn't want, she guessed, a display of emotion, but as she slipped out of the kitchen garden and looked briefly back to wave, his eyes, she noticed, were gazing at her with intentness again and she felt he was with her as she let herself with his key into Yadrahna again.

Locking the door behind her and slipping the key back in her belt purse, Hannah was conscious at once of an alien atmosphere in the house, of a stale smell of perfume mixed with smoke and sweat and a strange unnatural silence as if the house was waiting in anticipation.

She felt she wanted to open all the windows, let in fresh air again, the sound of the wind and birds singing, to cleanse the air of Olga Slade and all she stood for, to defy Hugo. Then her father's Edwardian mantel clock warned her that it was already half past two and she could be trapped if she didn't hurry.

Briefly she checked her father's study and the sitting room to see if any of his belongings had been returned but both rooms were still sanitised with no sign of him – only the photo of Hugo and Marcus.

She went then directly to his bedroom and over to the oak panel by the fireplace in the centre of the room. The concealed cupboard had never been obvious to her, nor was it obvious now as she felt with her fingers for the exact point where the ridge of panel slid back and opened on the recess beside the fire. But at last, having felt her way over the whole panel, the wood gave way as a door and revealed a deep recessed cupboard extending beyond

even the depth of the fireplace. As her eyes adjusted to the darkness, she could detect in it no sign of the black leather bound poetry book she'd given her father, only a layer of dust and some yellowing sheaves of paper in a recess on the opposite side to the fire.

Disappointed, she was about to shut the panel when it struck her that the sheaves of paper were old letters that could be of interest. Reaching back into the cupboard, she collected them together. It was then under the last sheaf that she felt what she was looking for – the rough leather surface of her father's anthology which had been hidden under the letters. Drawing it out with the letters, tensely she flipped through the well–thumbed pages, trying to detect which poem it was she was meant to decipher but she could find no marks giving significance to any poem.

Then near the end, she came to what had been one of her father's favourite poems: "Break, break, break" and clearly underlined in pencil was the second line: "On thy cold grey stones, O Sea." At the side of the line she read: "cave 2 x 2."

It sounded to Hannah like some kind of metre but it wasn't a metre she'd ever heard of – unless of course, she speculated, it was literally a cave but she didn't know of any cave either, certainly not a square one as suggested by the 2 x 2.

She looked through the remaining pages of the other poems for elucidation. There were no other markings, however, no other suggestions. It was the only line with attention drawn to it.

Puzzled, she looked through the sheaves of paper she'd drawn out with the book. They were pages of three

letters, all written in the spring of 1912, in the same careful, formal, upright script. Each gave as its address Yadrahna with the salutation "Dear John" and each was signed at the end "Your loving father." But there was nothing very loving Hannah could detect in the content of the fading ink on the yellowing pages. Carefully she read the first letter dated 19th February 1912.

Dear John,

I was deeply shocked by your disclosure to me. You have had all the advantages of an excellent public school education and, prior to that, an upbringing at home to be proud of and which, I would have thought, would have enabled you to withstand the temptations and allurements of people of a lower class. We did not bring you up with such care and hope to be entrusted with the running of the firm and the estate for all this to be dissipated by an alliance with someone so obviously unsuited to you.

I must make it clear to you now that there is no possibility at all of your mother or myself agreeing to this very foolish alliance that you have requested. Indeed, I will have to go further and state that, should you persist in such a course, against our will, we shall no longer consider you to be the heir either to the estate or the business which will then pass inevitably to your brother. I hope I make myself clear on this point.

By persisting in your request to marry an unfortunate servant you are placing in jeopardy

your chances of marrying Margaret Hargreaves who would be an ideal match from her social and financial standing as well as character.

I know that it is difficult at your age, not to be carried away by one's feelings but what you seek, I can assure you, is only the infatuation of the moment. It would not, indeed could not, last as a long-term satisfactory union. Please believe the words of someone who has had more experience than you of the world.

Your loving father.

The next letter was dated 2nd April 1912.

Dear John,

I am disappointed that you appear to have taken no heed of warning and that you are persisting in the folly of your request.

I am willing to concede that Hannah has been a good servant but that does not imply that she would be a suitable wife. She has had little formal education. You say that she is very intelligent but without adequate training and experience she is unlikely to be able to take on the quite arduous duties of running the house and estate to a satisfactory standard. My enquiries have also caused to emerge the unsavoury fact that she was born illegitimate.

She is pretty I grant you but prettiness without class background, education and financial means

will not serve well in a long–term marriage for people of our class. When her prettiness fades and she resorts to coarse manners again, you will not find it easy to extract yourself in order to make another alliance.

No, I remain adamant that Hannah is not a suitable match for you. If you persist in your infatuation, I will have no alternative but to dismiss her.

Your loving father

The final letter was dated 15th May.

Dear John,

I have not disregarded, as you suggest, the fact that Hannah is carrying a child – a child she claims is yours.

I have in fact made enquiries and have learnt that Mrs Vince, the blacksmith's wife, who has been unable to have children, would be willing to bring up the child as her own.

Hannah can have the baby, knowing that it will have a good home. She can start then afresh, somewhere new – let us hope with more sense of her position than hitherto.

I feel, however, I have to warn you not to be so naive as to believe that the child is necessarily yours. Such a claim is a favourite ruse of young women in her situation to better themselves and

you could well ruin your prospects only to realise that the child is not yours at all.

I trust that you will think more sensibly about your responsibilities and duties now both to the firm and the estate and that you will convey to Hannah now that the relationship must end.

Provided she delivers the child to Mrs Vince after it is born and makes no further claim upon this family, I will be willing to give her a good reference to work in another family. I think you will see, on reflection, that this is a generous offer and one which will enable you to resume your courtship of Margaret Hargreaves.

Your loving father

Hannah read through the three letters with a growing sense of dismay and apprehension as if she was back herself in 1912 with the outcome still unknown. She had no doubt, absorbing the letters that the Hannah referred to was the Hannah whose name was carved in the attic, who had disappeared in the summer of 1912. Her cry of love and desperation – it made more sense now, had a reason and instinctively Hannah felt her heart go back to her in sympathy against the ultimatum of the father and his rigid adherence to the class system. How absurd he was and yet had he not triumphed, had his way? They'd never married despite the child. She remembered her father looking the name up once in the parish records. Yet neither according to the records had he married the intended Margaret Hargreaves. What had happened to him then? What had

happened above all to Hannah? Why and how had she disappeared? All she knew still was a probably reason. The letter gave no clue as to a response or whether the baby had in fact been adopted by the blacksmith's wife. There was a blacksmith still in Wynton but no one to Hannah's knowledge by the name of Vince.

Absorbed in the letters and the past they conjured, she didn't notice the time passing. Not until the grandfather clock in the hall struck half past three did she realise she might have little time left to explore further.

Putting the letter and anthology in her bag and closing the panel, she tried to resolve again the riddle of cave 2 x 2. But no inspiration, no answer came and she decided to check Hugo's room again to see if he'd concealed a more recent will in his drawers. Passing on the way the guest room where Olga Slade had installed herself, she noticed the door ajar and stepped inside. She was aware again, as in the hall, of a cacophony of sweat and cheap perfume but what struck her most was the number of outfits draped over the bed and chairs and hanging not only in the wardrobe but all around – a gaudy display of emerald greens, golds, deep blues, reds and purples in materials that shimmered or glared demanding attention, nothing subdued. Only the ceiling, evading her touch, asserted still the quiet white elegance that her father had valued. It was like a whore's den, she thought, and without conscience, she inspected the desk and its drawers. In the second drawer she found a scatter of bank statements. There were regular payments she noticed from the end of March of £600 on the 30th of each month, then on the 4th of May a credit payment of £2,000. There was no way of telling if they were all from

Hugo but she made a note of the dates, then went quickly to Hugo's room.

In contrast to the dissonance of Olga Slade's room, Hugo's was ordered and tidy with nothing it appeared out of place. There was no sign of the map which had been on his desk when Sally had been with her, no sign in his drawers of any documents or another will. The only objects, apart from the phone on the desk were some novels of Flaubert and Gide in the teak bookcase. Cursorily looking over the titles, Hannah's attention was drawn to one of Gide's, "Les Caves du Vatican." Les Caves – the cellars she translated and suddenly it dawned. The "cave" her father had referred to was the French for cellar and the "cold grey stones" were the stones in Yadrahna's cellar beneath the trunk where he'd kept for years his cricket gear – stones they'd once lifted together to find the Victorian necklace he'd given to her mother – stones yes, which would measure 2 x 2 from the far corner wall of the cellar.

Excited, with renewed hope, she turned from the bookcase and was about to leave Hugo's room and make her way down to the cellar when she was aware suddenly of a whistling below the window. Peering out, she saw Luke looking up to her with an expression of concern, heard him calling quietly, "They're in the drive – your brother and the Slade. You'll have to hurry."

Signalling her thanks, she ran straight for the stairs, intent still on getting to the cellar. But at the top of the first flight down she heard to her dismay the front door already opening and the dissonant voices of Hugo, Marcus and Olga Slade rising from the hall. There was a tramp of footsteps across the hall to the kitchen, Marcus's she guessed. She was

tempted for a moment just to walk on down the stairs, to defy them and not be cowered, to walk past them and out of the house but an instinct of fear and uncertainty warned her that it would only betray her intent and sharpen their resolve. Quietly instead she slipped back along the landing into Hugo's room and hid herself under the bed.

There was nothing else under the bed apart from a pair of slippers which she pushed out in view to forestall any searching but the bed was low with only a few inches between the mattress and springs and the floor and she found it difficult to maintain a comfortable position without her feet being seen. Eventually, fearful of being detected now, she turned on her side, drawing up her knees and curving her body round them like a foetus in the womb.

There was a long silence after the voices, which seemed to Hannah like hours. Then just as she was wondering whether it would be safe to venture out again, she heard the bedroom door open and footsteps pad over to the bed.

From below the bed, she could see Hugo's black suede shoes shifting, as if uncertain, between the desk and the bed. Why was he hesitating, she wondered. Did he know she was there? Logically, she told herself it was unlikely. The carefully brushed suede shoes so near to her hesitating seemed all the same a threat and for the first time she began to feel afraid of Hugo, afraid of what, unpredictably, he might do.

Almost with relief, she heard Marcus's tramping footsteps, his strident voice as he pushed open the door, demanding attention.

"Luke won't let me use my air rifle in the shrubbery," he complained.

"Well, use it in the field then," Hugo's voice rumbled reluctantly over the bed.

"There's nothing to shoot in the field."

"I'm sure you'll find some rabbits if you look."

"I don't want rabbits. I want birds. They're better practice and there's loads of birds by the pond."

"What kinds of birds?"

"Greenfinches, tits, blackbirds, thrushes – hawks sometimes. There's masses of them. It'll make no difference if I shoot a few."

"Well, he probably thinks it will make a difference."

"What does it matter what he thinks? You're the one in charge."

"I'll have a word with him tomorrow."

"But I want to shoot now," Marcus protested.

"All right then," Hannah heard Hugo sigh as he submitted. "Tell him you've got my permission this weekend. But don't put his back up. I don't want him to go till I've found a replacement."

"Thanks, Dad. I'll try and get you a pheasant for tomorrow's lunch."

As Marcus's voice faded, a flush of cheap perfume wafted to Hannah beneath the bed.

"What time exactly do you want dinner, Hugo?" Olga Slade's mercantile voice breezed through the door, hovering over the word 'exactly' as over a lush private joke between Hugo and herself.

But Hugo was not amused.

"I told you on the phone. Jamieson and Hargreaves are coming at 7 and we'll eat at 8 – just Jamieson, Hargreaves, mother and myself. Marcus can have his with you at 7."

182

"So I'm not included then?" Olga Slade's voice descended into a sulk.

"It'll be purely technical and financial. You wouldn't be interested."

"It's about the estate, you mean?" Olga Slade probed with more interest.

"What does it matter what it's about? Your job is to produce the food."

"And some other services I think." Her voice lilted for a moment with a hint of threat. "Talking of which – the jewellery you gave me in part payment – well, I had it assessed and the pearl necklace is a fake. It's not genuine pearl at all nor the ear rings."

"So what? The rest was I don't doubt. You've had more than a fair whack anyway."

"Not when one considers the gain – for you."

"Gain? What gain?" Hugo's voice grated with impatience. "I haven't got it yet and until I do – you'll have to be content with your lot."

"I see. Well, obviously we shall have to speak further on this. By the way, I meant to tell you. Your sister called this last week."

"Did she now? I hope you told her where to get off."

"I didn't tell her anything or let her in if that's what you mean."

"Just be careful you don't. There's still a way to go before thing's are tied up so just keep your mouth firmly shut."

"I don't talk. You know that." Olga Slade's voice descended again to a whine. "But I don't like being fobbed of with fake jewels."

There was a silence for a moment, then Hannah could hear Hugo straining to control his voice.

"There's been no fobbing. What you lost on the pearls, you'll no doubt gain on the Victorian necklace and ring and more than a tidy sum. What more do you want? I've promised you a cut if things work out."

"As long as you remember. That's all. I haven't got the resources that you have for my old age."

"Yes, yes, I know all that. Hadn't you better get on now with the dinner?"

As Olga Slade receded with her discontent downstairs, Hannah heard from under the bed the sound of gunshot coming from the shrubbery, followed by the clanging of the front doorbell in the hall.

"Christ! Does he always have to be so early?" Hugo muttered amid a volley of expletives as he searched for a clean shirt and tie. Donning his green corduroy jacket then, he paused, as was his custom now, in the doorway, to assess the exact position of the phone on the desk and the desk chair. It occurred to him then what he hadn't noticed on entry that his slippers had been moved from under the bed or had he moved them, he wondered, without realising. I've too much on my mind he thought and a further clanging of the front door bell reminded him that Jamieson was waiting – a man he couldn't afford as yet to annoy or alienate and to Hannah's relief he turned, shutting the door behind him and followed in Olga Slade's wake downstairs.

Hannah remained cramped under the bed for several minutes, fearing Hugo might have forgotten something and unexpectedly return. Whatever happened, she

resolved, she didn't want to be caught and exposed and put him yet further on his guard. She was fairly certain he hadn't been aware of her under the bed but the search of the cellar she decided would have to be left to the next visit when there was nobody around. She certainly didn't want to be discovered with vital evidence in her hand and have it snatched away or destroyed. The problem was how to get out of Yadrahna without being seen.

Amid further rifle shots from the shrubbery, she could hear the voices of Hugo and his mother and a man she presumed was Hugh Jamieson rising from the drawing room below but the drawing room door was close – too close – to her main hope of exit, the front door and there was little hope of slipping out of the back door unseen with Olga Slade in the kitchen close by. She decided to wait till they had all gone through to the dining room then escape while they were eating from her father's bedroom down the drainpipe outside the drawing room.

Stretching out her legs, trying to get comfortable again, Hannah reflected on what she'd overheard.

She wasn't surprised by Hugo's reaction to Marcus. Hugo had always given in, in the end, to Marcus's demands and let him have his way but it sickened her that the way now should be to shoot birds that had always lived without fear at Yadrahna and had as much right to live as he. The thought that Marcus would have free rein if Hugo got the estate appalled her.

For every reason now she had to stop the estate passing into Hugo's hands. But how if she couldn't find another will? She tried to think carefully over the conversation Hugo had had with Olga Slade. There was an obvious strain

there. It wasn't the united opposition she'd visualised. Olga Slade was clearly discontented – a discontent that could be used. There was information she had, moreover, that Hugo didn't want divulged. How though could she be persuaded? How, Hannah wondered, could she herself persuade when the woman was being paid off with her mother's jewellery – jewellery that should have been hers. The thought of the Victorian necklace with its delicate filigree of gold that she'd found with her father, that had been her mother's favourite, now in the scarlet nailed hands of Olga Slade, stabbed her like a knife in the gut, releasing again her pent up anger and pain.

She felt she wanted to cry, to act, to avenge the total injustice of it all but helpless could do neither, could only await the moment to escape.

She had been lying for over three hours under the bed when eventually she heard the voices receding from the drawing room and the scraping of chairs on the polished wood floor of the dining room on the opposite side of the hall.

Emerging from under the bed then, as quietly as she could, she tiptoed out of the room and across to the end of the landing to her father's bedroom. It was a relief to be out of the trapped impersonal conditions of Hugo's room but, to her dismay, trying to open the sash window by the drainpipe, she found it jammed, then noticed that a lock had been affixed but with no sign of a key. There was no hope now by way of the drainpipe. The only alternative seemed to be to make a dash for it out of the front door while they were eating. She had the substitute key still in her pocket but looking over the banisters she observed that

the original steel key was now in the lock so she wouldn't have to waste time with the substitute. But on the other side of the hall the dining room door had been left open as Olga Slade emerged in a sullen mood with a stack of dirty dishes.

The light was fading but it was not yet dark. There was a risk that if she was seen she'd be recognised unless –

For the first time since entering Yadrahna that day she smiled to herself as she returned to Olga Slade's room. Carefully she selected a black shimmering dress hanging from the wardrobe door and slipped it over her clothes. It was far too big; she looked absurd, but it would do.

From the back of the house, checking to see what had happened to her, Luke looked up as she surveyed herself in Olga Slade's mirror by the window and piling up her hair stuffed it into one of Olga Slade's purple hats. Whatever was she playing at, Luke wondered. She was mad or was she? Half guessing her game, he made his way stealthily through the shrubbery to the front of the house to be ready to help if need be.

Unaware, assuming that Luke had gone home, Hannah put the finishing touches to her disguise – a black and purple scarf that secured the hat and half covered her face. More confident, she glided in the shimmering black dress to the top of the stairs. For a moment she could feel what it was like to be Olga Slade wanting to make an impression, wanting to swagger her hips and draw attention. But she was not Olga Slade she reminded herself nor would she ever want to be and she had to move by stealth.

Fortunately the lights in the hall were not yet switched on and though the dining room door was still open she

managed to creep down the stairs in the grey subdued light without any notice being taken.

Then as she moved silently over to the front door and was about to turn the key, suddenly, Olga Slade, her mouth set still in a scowl, stamped back from the kitchen with a tray of fruit and ice cream. She didn't at first notice Hannah. Intent on maintaining the equilibrium of the fruit salad on the tray, it wasn't until she was about to enter the dining room that she was aware of a ghost from the past, an identical dress to her own. So uncanny did it seem, so preposterous to her literal mind that she could only stare for a few moments, disbelieving.. Then as Hannah, seizing her chance, turned the key and ran out into the drive, nearly dropping the tray in her surprise and alarm, Olga Slade rushed into the dining room.

"Someone's been here in my dress – my black dress." Her voice trailed to a wail as Hugo angrily got to his feet.

"What the hell are you talking about, woman? Explain yourself for God's sake."

"Someone's been here," Olga Slade repeated. "Listening," she added, trying to get to grips at last on the reality, "a thief."

"Which way?"

More agile than Hugo, his sharp eyes and lean features alert to expose any law breaking not his own, Hugh Jamieson got to his feet. Trembling, Olga Slade followed, pointing vaguely up the drive.

"All right. Leave it to me. We'll get whoever it is."

Followed by Hugo, Hugh Jamieson spurted off up the drive towards the shimmering figure he could just see now disappearing round the bend in the drive before it straightened again to join the main road.

Behind her Hannah could hear voices, like the yapping of hounds, the scrunch of footsteps on the gravel drawing closer. If she could but reach the main road and cross over, she could lose them in the confusion of trees and tangled undergrowth of Rassler's Wood. But the long clinging fabric of Olga Slade's dress, reaching down to her ankles, slowed her down and as she reached the road four cars in succession prevented her crossing. After the fourth she was about to make a dash for it when she felt a bony hand grip her shoulder. "Got you, you thief."

Jamieson was amazed by how slight the person was but he couldn't see the face which was wreathed in scarves. Always identify and photograph, he reminded himself, and felt for the disposable camera in his pocket. But as he did so he felt both his arms wrenched back and held in a lock that made him cry out in pain. The next moment he was pushed with force from behind down into a laurel bush and the compost freshly spread that morning on the earth below.

"What the hell!" As Hugo stumbled up too late to see his friend's assailant, he too was seized in an arm lock from behind and jerked down on the other side of the drive into a berberis and Luke, smiling to himself at Hugo's loss of face and discomfort, ran on up the drive and across the road to check that Hannah was unharmed.

Safe from the bony grip of Jamieson and limping from a twist in her ankle as she'd tried to hasten up the drive, Hannah knew someone had intervened as she'd been released and heard the shouts of triumph change to indignation. But she hadn't seen who it was or dared to wait. Pressing on, she crossed the road and plunged down

into Rassler's Wood, shedding the purple hat and scarf as she went, finally stopping to disrobe herself of Olga Slade's black dress. She didn't realise it was Luke till she heard footsteps crushing the dried leaves behind her and Luke's voice reaching out to her to reassure. "It's all right. They're not back yet on the trail."

"So I have you to thank."

She paused, not wanting him to see her limping. But he'd seen already and guessed from the strain in her voice and eyes in the growing dark that there was a pain in her heart she had to deal with, more insistent than the strain of muscle.

"It was nothing. They didn't even resist."

"You surprised them."

"And they could still surprise us." Quietly he collected up the trail she'd shed of purple and black and looked back up to the main road. He couldn't see or hear any movement but he felt afraid for Hannah.

"I'll see you back to the cottage."

She didn't feel like talking but she was relieved that he was with her. She felt shaken by Jamieson lunging at her and the whole way she was forced to be the intruder in what she saw still as her home. And still after the effort she had no evidence, no proof of Hugo's pressure on her father or another will. She'd seemed in her father's room to be near for a while to a break through but in reality she was as far away as ever and would have the problem of getting back into the house again. Would it ever end? Would she get anywhere finally if she did keep trying? Or was the plot too well laid and it was all, she thought with despair, a waste of time.

Taking her arm on the side she was limping, Luke helped her down through Rassler's Wood. As they paused to cross the main road to join the lane to Bramble Cottage, a police car raced by. Luke wondered if it was on its way to Yadrahna and was relieved Hannah had shed her glaring disguise. He felt certain that neither Jamieson nor Hugo Delaney had seen his face when he'd assaulted them but suspicion, he was sure, would inevitably fall on him when they tried to deduce who their attacker had been. But what did it matter? He'd only another month to go and he'd be away from Delaney and his dubious practices for good. Or would he? Hadn't he a duty to help Hannah if he could? She was after all, it appeared, the wronged party.

Holding her arm more tightly as they crossed the road, he felt again her vulnerability and attraction, felt he wanted to help her, yet feared at the same time it would complicate his life when he wanted it simple, free and untied to go to India.

Reaching the cottage, Hannah felt in her belt purse and pocket for the key but no trace of the key could she find.

"I'm sure I put it in," she asserted, feeling foolish.

"Perhaps it fell out when you were set upon."

"Oh no. That means they could find it. They'd be able to get in."

"I doubt they'll find anything now in the dark. I tell you what. I'll go and have a quick look. I've got to get my bike anyway and there's a torch in the saddlebag."

"You mean your bike's still in the garden?" She couldn't hide her concern then that the bike would be found and suspicion fall on Luke himself.

"Don't worry. I hid it away down the lane in the undergrowth so they'd think I'd gone but I need to get it back."

"If you're really sure."

"There's not much alternative is there if you're going to get in."

"Be careful, won't you? The police could be there and you could get involved."

"Don't worry. I've had plenty of experience on Road Alert evading the police. They won't search the whole countryside, I can assure you, merely for the theft of a black dress. But in case they do," he handed her the bundle of Olga Slade's clothes he'd collected from the ground, "make sure you hide them or better still burn."

Trying to sound jaunty, carefree, he turned and made his way back up Hanger's Wood again.

It was almost dark and Hannah watched him disappear up the lane with apprehension. He'd been good to her, indeed had saved her from an unpleasant exposure and consequence and she didn't want him to suffer for it, get into trouble on her behalf. He seemed resilient, able to take care of himself but one could never tell how things would work out.

As she sat waiting on the rotting wooden board that served as a seat in the porch, she suddenly remembered that she hadn't taken the key with her at all. Feeling under the stone by the first clump of thyme to the side of the porch, she found it then lying where she'd left it in her haste to get to Yadrahna earlier that afternoon.

What a fool she was. What a fool Luke would think her. How could she let herself in now, be waiting inside

when he returned empty handed? She felt she couldn't and remained waiting for him on the rotting plank, thinking back on the events of the day. If only, she reflected, she hadn't delayed so much, had been more business like and efficient, she could have explored in the cellar and beneath the stones before Hugo and Olga Slade had returned. Somehow she was going to have to get back into Yadrahna when no one was around but how? She would need Luke's help again but would he be willing to give it now, after her stupidity regarding the key?

She was thinking of him as she saw the light of his dynamo fade as he pushed his bike through the wicker gate. Like a trophy, by the light of his torch, he handed her the key he'd found, he explained, in the drive where the scuffle had occurred. But it wasn't, Hannah could see at once anything like the large iron key to Bramble Cottage. The key Luke had given her was a yale key attached to a ring with an orange tab – an orange tab, she recognised now from way back, that was the distinctive feature of Hugo's key ring for the key to his house in Windsor.

"You're brilliant!"

"It was just lying there in the drive."

"There were no police then?"

"I saw a police car leaving but no one searching. They'd all gone back inside. Anyway, I'm glad it's the right key."

"It's not in fact." Hannah smiled and explained apologetically how she'd never lost the key at all.

"Then why – "he stared at her, bewildered.

"Because it's the key to Hugo's house – the key I wanted and never hoped to get."

"You mean you're going to try and get in there as well?"

"If I can – yes."

"Isn't it going to be rather a risk though going to the house, I mean breaking and entering and all that?"

"I won't be breaking in, will I, with the key?"

"Do you think you'll find anything though?" It occurred to him that Hugo Delaney might go hurrying off to Windsor once he realised he'd lost his key. The question was how soon he would realise.

"Maybe not. I feel I've got though at least to try. So far I've got nothing by way of hard evidence to help my case at all." She tried to hold back her tears. "It's all so impossible, so frustrating."

"Can't the solicitor help more? He must have some authority surely to investigate behind the scenes."

"It's a matter of cash. I've got to keep the costs down, which means doing as much as I can myself."

"I see." Luke wasn't sure that he did in fact see. He'd no experience of wills and their anomalies and injustice, no map in his mind of such territory that would enable him to suggest a means of dealing with scheming like that of Delaney, no knowledge of Hannah's personal and financial affairs. But he could feel the distress in her voice, in her pale pinched face in the moonlight – vulnerable, wronged. And he felt again he wanted to help her, that he should help. Wasn't it all part of an outdated system that bastards like Delaney were able to twist the system and get away with it, fending off just efforts?

What use would he be though when in a matter of only weeks now he'd be gone? And before he went there wasn't just his dissertation to complete but his remaining debts

to pay off which would take all his time, juggling extra evening jobs. He hadn't time to be involved.

"Well, I'd better be on my way. I've got to see my tutor first thing in the morning."

"Your dissertation you mean?"

"I've got a few more changes to make. Then he's going over it with me."

"I'm sorry I've held you up."

She felt she wanted to ask him in to make amends for the key. But part of her she could feel wanting to be alone, to be back with her father before the nightmare had begun, to feel his arms, his reassurance again. She missed him so much. The pain stabbing her again never seemed to go away.

"You haven't." Hesitating, Luke smiled. "I only wish I could be of more help."

"You have helped and I'm very grateful." Through her grief, like a receding wave, Hannah could feel his doubt, his hesitation, that he had other problems on his mind and she knew the moment was not right for them, that it might come but not now.

"But you still want to get back into the house or am I wrong?"

"I need another visit – yes."

"So you need to know the Slade's movements again?"

"If you've the time to let me know."

"She'll be more suspicious now but she can't stay in all the time. I suggest though, since you're determined, that you search your brother's house as soon as you can. He may have already discovered he's lost the key."

"I'll go tomorrow." It all seemed obvious now – not something she had to think about.

"Please take care." Luke looked into the darkness deepening in front of her eyes, then, forcing himself, he turned and picking up his bike, wheeled it up the lane to the main road.

Chapter 14

Exhausted from her exertions, Hannah slept soundly again that night, despite the lumpy mattress, the scratching and spiders. She awoke to a fresh breeze coming in through the open window that stirred her with renewed hope that she might that day at last find something significant on which to act.

Carefully checking that she had Hugo's key with the orange tab and enough money for transport, she dressed herself as inconspicuously as she could in blue jeans and a beige T-shirt, swept her hair back in a scrunchy, then piled it into the crown of the one hat she owned of floppy straw with a wide brim, which could be used, she decided, if need be, to obscure her face.

She made herself some sandwiches, checked the timetable she had for a bus and was about to shut the bedroom window, prior to leaving, when she saw, to her surprise, Annie Hobbs standing at the bottom of the garden by the collapsing wicker gate talking to a tall man with lean features and glasses who appeared to have just joined her. She couldn't hear what they were saying but she could hear the tone of their voices coming to her on the breeze, the hard impatience in particular of the voice she'd heard the night before in the drive – the voice she knew at once was that of Jamieson.

How did he know she was here? How could he know unless he'd followed Luke and herself through Rassler's Wood in the dark? More importantly, why had he come? With a cold sinking feeling, she watched him put his arm confidentially round Annie Hobbs' shoulder as if he already knew her, was assured of her compliance and Annie Hobbs was nodding, smiling at him.

They drifted out of sight for a few minutes, then, to Hannah's surprise, Annie Hobbs was tripping back up the overgrown path towards her, as if nothing had happened and was waving up at the window.

"Your friend Sally phoned, my dear. She wants you to ring her by 10. She says it's urgent."

"Just a minute. I'll come down."

Hannah closed the window, fastening it as best she could and went down to the porch.

"Who was that?" she demanded.

"The tall thin gentleman you mean?" Annie Hobbs smiled, undeterred by Hannah's brusqueness. "He's an estate agent – Mr Jamieson."

"What did he want?"

Annie Hobbs frowned now, bewildered. "He didn't want anything. He came to enquire if Mrs Webb's niece is ready yet to sell the house."

"And is she?"

"As I told you, my dear, she 's waiting to get a good price and planning permission if she can."

"Planning permission for what exactly?" Was Annie Hobbs making up the conversation, Hannah wondered, to divert her.

"I couldn't say, my dear. She's never confided in me her plan."

"But this Jamieson is out to buy the property if he can?"

"He's shown a lot of interest."

"Is that all he was interested in just now?"

"What do you mean, my dear?" Annie Hobbs pale blue eyes were just too innocent, Hannah thought.

"I mean did he ask any questions about me?"

"He wanted to know how long the tenancy was."

"And what did you tell him?"

"I told him you had an agreement for a year."

"It's not strictly true though, is it?"

"No, but I knew you wanted it for a year."

"And you don't want him to buy it, is that it?"

Annie Hobbs hesitated. "Some people buy up all the land and they don't heed what folks like us want. It doesn't seem right to me."

"It isn't," Hannah agreed, uncomfortably aware now she'd misinterpreted Annie Hobbs association with Jamieson. "You're quite right and thank you for putting my case."

"You're not cross then I gave your name?"

"My name?"

"He asked if you were called Hannah Delaney – which I thought was strange." Annie Hobbs looked at her with puzzled eyes.

"So what did you say?"

"I told him straight, my dear, that it was not the kind of place he'd find a Delaney."

"Which he accepted I trust?" Hannah felt a bleakness again in the pit of her stomach. Her doubts about Annie James's complicity had gone but she'd been right after all

that Hugh Jamieson was on her trail. Was it wise now to go out for the day? She still had Olga Slade's dress and her hat and scarf under the bed, which would undoubtedly be found if the cottage was broken into and searched during a prolonged absence. More importantly her father's letters and his poetry book with the key to the will in the cellar would also be found.

"I don't know, my dear. He's a strange man but you mustn't worry. He probably just wants to get you as a tenant out of the way. But you must stay firm. Bramble Cottage is right for you. I know."

"Yes." Hannah looked into Annie Hobbs's eyes again, ashamed now she'd doubted, not appreciated the older woman's openness and care and as Annie Hobbs turned to go, she remembered the question she'd wanted to ask about the servant Hannah's child and the Vince family that supposedly had adopted.

"Vince." Annie Hobbs bent her head to one side, like a bird listening, waiting. "Vince," she repeated again. "There were once Vinces here. Blacksmiths they were. I believe they had a daughter later in life but they're all gone now or left the area. What happened to her I can't say. The vicar knows a lot about families in the area. He may be able to help you. Now don't forget about phoning your friend Sally will you."

"I won't."

Back in the bedroom, Hannah decided that it would be caving in to give up her plans to go to Windsor and search Hugo's house. When again would she have the chance with the key in her hand, with Hugo still at Yadrahna, hopefully still unaware? No, she had to go, despite the

vulnerability of the cottage if she was to make any headway and a new determination took hold of her that she would follow now every lead, every clue, whatever the problems and obscurity, that she would give herself to the task with the same determination that Hugo had done to deprive and double cross her.

Her father's poetry book and letters she wrapped in a polythene bag and checking no one was around watching, buried them beneath a clump of nettles in the garden, with care that no sign of digging could be seen. Stung but satisfied then, she stuffed Olga Slade's clothes in a carrier bag. She would sell them she decided at a second hand clothes shop in Windsor to pay for the fare.

Absorbed in her venture, Hannah almost forgot the message she'd received to ring Sally. It wasn't till she was at the bus stop waiting for the bus into Oxford that the telephone kiosk prompted her. Hastily for the bus was due any minute, she rang Sally's number.

"Thank goodness, Han. I thought you were never going to ring," Sally's voice rushed in relief..."Listen. Richard's arriving this evening at 16.00. Can you get to Heathrow to meet him?"

"This evening! But I thought it was next week he was coming."

"It was. But apparently the job unexpectedly finished and he could get away and thought he'd give you a surprise. So what do you think? Can you manage it?"

Out of the corner of her eye Hannah could see the bus approaching slowly but surely down the main road – a bus she couldn't afford to miss if she was to have the time she needed at Hugo's house.

"Look, Sally, I'm sorry I've got something arranged which I can't change. In fact the bus is just arriving."

"But it's Richard, Han, Richard."

"I know but this is urgent. It's probably the only time I'll be able to get into Hugo's house to check for evidence. I've got to take my chance."

"You mean you can't go to Heathrow, even later?"

"I couldn't guarantee it, not without a car, not today."

"We can't leave him waiting, Han."

"He won't wait. He'll go to his flat at Hampstead. He won't mind."

"He's come to see you, Han, not the flat."

There was a pause in which Hannah could feel Sally's silent disapproval pounding at her down the phone. She was aware at the same time of the bus slowing to a stop, that she had little time.

"Why don't you meet him if you're concerned?"

As soon as she'd spoken, Hannah regretted it, felt guilty as inevitably she always did in the end both with Richard and Sally, however slight the confrontation. But to her surprise, Sally was taking up the suggestion, almost humbly without resentment.

"Would you mind if I did?"

"Of course not."

"When will you be back then at the cottage?"

"I'm not sure – say 7."

"Right," and Sally resumed her crisp, clear voice of organisation. "I'll meet Richard and drive him to the cottage for 7."

"Fine" and slamming down the receiver, Hannah ran for the bus, clutching the bag with Olga Slade's clothes,

catching it just in time as it was pulling away.

During the journey to Windsor, Hannah reflected on Richard's impending visit with a growing sense of apprehension. She wanted to see him again yes, but not now, not yet. She didn't feel ready for him, wouldn't be able, she knew, to adapt to his needs, his assumption of what their life together should be. Travelling, seeing people, showing the status of money – it no longer appealed. She felt she wanted to be alone now for the most part, to be close to her father in the peace and quiet of the countryside, to devote herself without diversion to pursuing the truth about the will and putting it right.

Would Richard understand? She doubted it, unless he'd changed, could change and adapt himself to new circumstances. There was always the possibility, she supposed. Hadn't one of the main tenets of her father been that people had an infinite capacity to change and see another's view if the compassion was there? He'd also stressed though the need for rationality, that one should not be fooled by feeling into deceiving oneself about one's importance in the universe. How rare he was, she thought, that he'd been able to combine rationality with feeling, that he'd seen the insignificance of life and not been daunted by it into indifference and scepticism. Some had mocked him for his support of Sartre's concept of individual responsibility but wasn't Sartre right that ultimately one had to accept individual responsibility for the wrongs of society and try to put them right without the comforting prop of belief in an ultimate god?

But where did Hugo fit in the Sartrean scheme of things? Why had he sought to grasp all for himself? Why had he

turned to a path so different from their father? Revenge was it on a society that had not recognised him as an artist to the degree he wanted? Revenge spurred on by his mother for their father's marriage to her own? A feeling of inadequacy, helplessness? But didn't everyone to a degree feel helpless and inadequate – some with cause far greater than Hugo? Or was he pursuing his own ends regardless in a self–interest carried to an extreme? Was this what evil was – self interest to the obliteration of all other concerns? But supposing the self was satisfied, would the evil still be there – an insatiability that motivated itself? Though aware of evil intent, still Hannah felt she couldn't understand Hugo. Even as a child, when first she'd been aware of him as a boy of 13 or 14, he'd seemed unlike other children – cold and remote.

As she drew nearer to Windsor, she feared that Hugo might have returned from Yadrahna, though it was still the weekend, or that he might surprise her while she was searching inside.

It was with a shaking hand, still clutching the carrier bag with Olga Slade's clothes, the brim of her straw hat pulled down to obscure her features, her long hair still bundled in its crown, that in the lunch hour eventually, Hannah inserted the key with the orange tab into Hugo's door. There was no sign of his Daimler outside, no sign of the house being occupied but across the street she could see as she looked around behind her a woman in the front window of the house opposite, carefully noting her movements.

The woman would not, Hannah felt confident, be able to describe her in detail, apart from her clothes. She felt conspicuous all the same and opening the door hurriedly closed it behind her to shut out the prying eyes.

It was over four years now since she'd been inside Hugo's house, when he'd first bought it as a house he'd seen with potential to renovate. She was struck at once by the dramatic changes in the decor, in the atmosphere, in the coolness above all induced by the varying shades and patterns of blue in the hall and the lounge. Midnight blue, royal blue, ice blue, turquoise and every shade between in vases, chair covers, curtains – even pictures and dried flowers – all seemed designed to draw one down into a sub aqua world with its own temperature and rules. Only the rosewood desk her father had given Hugo retained a residual warmth and Hannah shivered slightly, feeling literally cold, feeling that the blue was hostile to her presence and would betray her if it could.

Everything was in place, immaculate, dusted – a blue appointments diary on the desk at an angle precisely in line with the phone; Hugo's passport projecting from a teak letter rack as part of an exactly visualised decor; an encyclopaedia unthumbed, unopened in simulated blue leather on the one casual table. No sign of discarded pieces of paper or materials on the floor. The lounge was like a museum without labels and Hannah knew she'd have to be careful not to leave any sign she'd been.

She started by searching the drawers of the rosewood desk. Hugo had way back, she'd known, in one of his more public gestures, defiantly rejected modern technology and the filing system that went with it but she hadn't expected to find his drawers in a state so at variance with the order he'd imposed above in his decor. Invoices, receipts, bank statements, personal letters, official letters were all jumbled together throughout the drawers regardless of date, size or

objective as if bundled out of sight was to be forgotten. Or was there a purpose in the very disorder – a deterrent to searching?

Determined not to be deterred, she sorted every piece of paper until she found eventually in the third drawer the bank statement she'd wanted confirming that £2,000 had been transferred from Hugo's account on 3rd May, the day Olga Slade had received the same. A bribe to the witness? It was more than relevantly close to the date of the signing of the will and it certainly didn't fit the regular monthly pattern of payments of £600 into Olga Slade's account. But if a bribe what about the other witness, Sadie Shaw? There were no other equivalent amounts withdrawn to suggest two witnesses equally bribed. She needed to consult Mr Ashford she decided. Carefully she folded the statement and put it in her bag.

She concentrated her attention then more on the strange assortment of letters. There were a number of letters from editors of newspapers rejecting a contribution Hugo had made on the grounds that it might offend a racial minority, a number from art dealers and organisers of exhibitions tactfully but firmly rejecting a painting either for sale or display, which surprised her for she'd understood that Hugo had made a living essentially from commissioned work for firms, from portraits, landscapes and interiors of the firm itself. Was it all just a fantasy, a "had been" that had no future and a dubious past? There was little she could see, briefly glancing through the letters that was encouraging, no praise or promise offering substantial sums, no suggestion that he was an established artist at all. What was he living on then? Some other work? Or his mother?

In the fourth drawer down beneath a cover of dated building society statements of his own, she found, more neatly organised and up to date, a clutch of statements pertaining to the building society account of his mother. It was, as she'd suspected, that his mother's inherited wealth was far greater than her father had even guessed, was providing at least £50,000 a year – enough for both of them to live on – enough for him not to have to try and take all her father's wealth as well.

For a moment as she'd read the letters of rejection of his art, she'd felt a stirring in her heart of sympathy for him, a sympathy she always felt for those who'd tried and failed. Now it seemed to her that the art was just a front to give him credibility to the outside world when all the time he was living literally parasitically off his mother for an easier life and, despite her nervousness in the cold blue room, she felt her anger grow.

Resolutely then she persisted with her search through the remaining drawer. To her disappointment, most of it consisted of irrelevant receipts mixed with an involved series of letters regarding his mother's pension payment which Hannah felt impelled to examine but which she couldn't understand. Then just as she was going to give up hope of finding anything revealing, buried beneath some insurance leaflets in the final drawer, she found a letter dated 27th June from Hugh Jamieson, to her surprise in his own handwriting.

Dear Hugo, it read,

Many thanks for your letter of 21st June, giving your blessing to the conversion of Yadrahna,

subject of course to planning permission being obtained.

I don't however visualise any serious difficulty on this score. There's bound to be some protest from FOE regarding the SSSI, possibly also from the CPRE and from Heritage regarding the house itself. But these organisations have only limited appeal regarding manpower and resources in the area – only a few vocal individuals – no more.

The majority on the council I am fairly confident will take a different view and see the beneficial effects of development. There's serious shortage of accommodation for the elderly in the area and I think if we stress the fact of development in fulfilling a sound social need, our plans will be accepted, subject of course to a few minor changes.

It would be worth your while, however, to drum up some support from anyone you know in the area and get them to write to the planning committee members on the enclosed sheet.

I'll be in touch with you shortly when I have finished the plans for you to see which can now be on a larger scale. It would be as well though, till they are approved, to keep discussion within the bounds of only those you can trust. I think I can rely on you to be discreet. Meanwhile good luck with your persuasion.

H.J.

Looking at the date Jamieson had mentioned, that Hugo had written on 21st June, Hannah realised with a shock that it was the same day exactly her father had died. The very same day her father had died, Hugo had offered Yadrahna for development completely against her father's wishes. How could he have done such a thing? How could he have been so calculating and callous? Yet wasn't the letter also evidence of a calculation that she herself could use? Without scruple now she put the letter with the other information she had gained in her bag.

Looking at her watch, she realised then that she had already been at the house nearly now two hours – two hours in which she'd been able to search uninterrupted but for how much longer? She would have to get moving faster if the rest of the house too was to be searched.

The kitchen was unlikely she thought to yield much at all. She couldn't resist though having a look round the door to the rear of the lounge and was amazed at the change Hugo had effected, at the tasteful expensive pine cabinet that had replaced the erstwhile gloom and battered brown. But despite the sun streaming in through a south facing window, there was an imposed order in the decor with everything in its place as if it was meant to be photographed for a magazine rather than lived in and she felt chilled again not wanting to stay or linger.

Upstairs she tiptoed. The blue persisted, seeming to absorb even the sunlight and she felt nervous again and afraid as she opened the door to Hugo's room, that she might find him lying there in the bed, making some sarcastic remark to her as to why she was there. The room to her relief was empty but arranged uncannily like the

bedroom Hugo had taken over at Yadrahna, with the desk by the window and the telephone at the same angle.

Careful not to move any obvious object, she searched the drawers but found nothing, to her disappointment, relating to the will at all, only leaflets and advertising. She looked under the bed and checked the chest of drawers but to no avail. Determined not to give up, she felt then in the pockets of Hugo's trousers and jackets in the wardrobe. Most were empty but in one of his green corduroy jackets, in the inner pocket she found a worn leather alphabetical notebook with a number of addresses inside. Quickly she thumbed through to see if the name Emma Mason was inside. It was but so sloping to the right was Hugo's writing that she found it difficult to read the address beneath. She could just make out "Stone Cottage" but the village or town remained a mystery, starting with a shape that could have been a B or P an R even or an F or E. It was scrawled then with a long thin stroke at the end. The county, however, was Oxon and she had part of the code. It was a beginning she thought with more optimism.

She looked through the notebook then for Laura's name and address and to her surprise found it without problem. 51 Cranmer Road, Banbury. So Laura, though in a different road, was still in Banbury after all and not so far that she couldn't be visited again. And she would, Hannah decided, visit again, for more than anyone, Laura would know what had been in Hugo's mind, what really he was like.

Hannah was tempted for a moment to take the address book with her but decided in the end on caution and wrote the two addresses down.

She felt she should leave then, that it was pushing her luck to stay. She couldn't resist though on the way down stopping to look in Hugo's studio. It was a studio transformed from what she'd remembered. painted and repainted white and blue but there were no paintings on the two easels, that dominated the room and the paints had all been neatly packed away in a corner, the brushes dry.

Bending down, Hannah had a look through a pile of water colours. Most of them were of the Thames near Windsor or of the castle, conventional paintings without particular talent or style, the type turned out for tourists wanting a memento and easily pleased. Had he sold any, Hannah wondered, or was this too a front?

She noticed then a canvas with an oil painting on it turned to the wall. Curious as to its isolation, she bent down and turned it over. She remained crouched a while then frowning, not able quite to take it in for the face staring out at her was alien but with eyes she felt she knew. It was a hard face with contorted features with an exaggerated hooked nose and a witch's projecting chin. But the eyes were not contorted. They were eyes deep brown like her own and she recognised at once the long cloak the supposed witch was wearing, the inimitable grey, white and silver band edging the cloak her mother had worn – the cloak she had rescued just in time from Luke and the fire.

Shaking, she put the canvas back against the wall again, forcing herself to look in Hugo's mother's room and the bathroom. But she couldn't get the face on the oil canvas out of her mind nor the hatred that had impelled it and she found herself drifting now, uncertain where to look further.

She was hesitating on the landing upstairs when she was jolted into a state of alertness by the ringing of the bell at the front door. Standing to the side of the landing window, she looked down through the net curtain to see waiting on the doorstep below the woman who had been peering at her from the house opposite. She was a woman shabbily dressed, with wispy hair and a worried expression – a woman, Hannah thought almost with sympathy, who was probably only doing her duty as a neighbour and she felt tempted for a moment to open the door, to explain her whole situation and why she was there, to try and reassure her and dispel the worry on her face. But instinctively she knew it wouldn't work as she visualised. All too clearly, she'd learnt from her other encounters on the case, that nothing was certain, predictable, following the rational course towards justice that it should, that one should expect, and she couldn't afford to take risks, not now that she'd got some evidence.

Ignoring the bell, she waited until the woman eventually turned away back towards her own house again. It struck her then, putting herself in the woman's place, that she'd soon be on the phone to Hugo or the police. Quickly she gathered up her bag with the documents and seeing no face at the window of the house opposite, she let herself out of the front door, taking the key with her and hurried away down the street towards the main Windsor shopping area.

She'd just turned the corner out of sight of Hugo's house when she remembered she'd left by the desk in Hugo's lounge the carrier bag with Olga Slade's clothes she'd intended to sell to pay for the fare. She was hesitating

wondering whether to go back for it and take the risk again of being seen, when on the opposite side of the road, just turning into the last stretch to Hugo's house she saw the Daimler with Hugo himself at the wheel and beside him his mother looking out of the side window in her direction.

There was no recognition in her uncompromising hard stare, no shift to suggest she'd been taken by surprise but Hannah knew, looking into the penetrating grey eyes that Elvira Delaney had seen her, had guessed where she'd been and would take, if she could, her revenge.

Chapter 15

Hannah felt concerned and on edge as she travelled back to the cottage. The visit to Windsor had not been a failure. She had confirmation of Hugo's payments to Olga Slade, in particular the £2,000; she had a clearer idea of Hugo's and his mother's resources and she had Laura's address and enough of Emma's to locate her if she persisted. There was information beyond vague insinuation to pass on to Ashford. She had not been caught, moreover, in the house red–handed.

But she couldn't get Hugo's painting of her mother out of her mind nor Elvira's Delaney's eyes. Now that they knew she'd been to the house, what action would they take? What action had already been taken at the cottage?

Thinking of the cottage, she remembered then the visit of Richard and Sally, that she'd nothing to eat for them. In her hunger of the night before, she'd consumed all Annie Hobb's quiche and most of the cake.

Stopping off at Oxford to change buses, she bought some yoghurt and another quiche. It didn't look anything like as good as Annie Hobb's quiche but it was better than nothing, she decided, and would have to do. Running back to catch her connection then she slipped and fell, tearing her jeans and dropping the quiche on the pavement,

dislodging the neat slices. The connection then made a detour of all the villages surrounding Wynton. It was 7.30 when eventually, tired and dishevelled, she made her way again up the overgrown path to Bramble Cottage.

The first thing she noticed was a large piece of paper fixed with blue tack to the peeling porch door with a heading '19.10' twice underlined, followed by Sally's large writing:

"We waited till the agreed time. Richard's famished so we're going to The Bull on the main road for a drink and something to eat. We suggest you come and join us in the dining room or bar when/if you get back before we return."

Sally and Richard

Hannah re-read the message more with irritation than disappointment. She was after all only half an hour late and had done her best to be back on time. She hadn't meant the time to be taken so literally. She had expected them to be waiting – yes – and perhaps with some impatience. Both Sally and Richard tended to order their lives by time – she knew that – but not to take themselves off altogether. It wasn't as if it was raining. They could have sat on the grass or in the porch.

The idea of going to find them in The Bull didn't appeal at all. It was the kind of place Jamieson, even Hugo, might well visit and she certainly didn't want to advertise her presence, not with Jamieson already suspicious of her being at the cottage. Had he been while she'd been out?

The front door, to her relief, had not been tampered with and there was no sign in the kitchen that anything had been disturbed, no sign, as she nervously explored upstairs, that anyone had searched her drawers. Everything was as she'd left it, her case under the bed, her books, her make up and underwear in the same position, the window closed. But there was a strange smell she couldn't make out – a smell suggesting burnt wire and a large dark patch of brown around the power socket in the kitchen now as well as the one in the bedroom. Was the electricity fundamentally defective, she wondered, or had it been tampered with?

She felt afraid to put the electricity on now in either room, afraid of what she'd find probing further. It would take little she knew for the timbers of the cottage to go up in flames. She felt she ought to contact Annie Hobbs again and urge her to get the electrician to come the next day But Jack Ryder, whoever he was, appeared strangely elusive and immune to appeal. "He'll come in his own good time," Annie Hobbs had assured her when she'd asked a second time but when that time would be there was no indication nor likely to be it seemed. Resigned, Hannah decided she'd just have to manage till the event with candles and getting out the brass candlesticks and white candles Annie Hobbs had left her, she set them out ready, two in the kitchen and two in the bedroom. She laid out then what remained of the crumbled quiche, hoping the candlelight would subdue to an extent it defects, then went back to the garden.

She heard Richard and Sally approaching down the path well before they came into view, Sally's voice brightly responding to Richard's more assured but subdued tones.

In the shadows of the crab tree, she watched them come through the wicker gate, Richard in his cream coloured travelling suit, carrying a compact streamlined suitcase, Sally in a new strikingly fashionable short skirted suit of duck egg blue. They looked like an established couple, she thought, as Richard held open the wicker gate for her, then took her arm, sheltering her from the trailing entwined brambles. A couple in tune but not with the garden and she wanted to laugh as they looked doubtfully down at the overgrown pathway, fearful of tripping, of the obstructions to their elegance and image en route to the door. And Richard did look elegant in his cream coloured suit, accentuated by and accentuating his newly acquired tan, his carefully cut, casually styled hair. He was striking, handsome but deeply sceptical she could see at once by the way he winced as he looked ahead now at the decaying cottage, unable to hide his doubt as he turned to Sally asking,

"Do you think she's back?"

"Yes, I'm sure." Confidently Sally pointed to the front door. "Look our note's gone." She turned to him then and squeezed his hand. "It'll be all right. You'll see."

"I'm sure you've done everything you can to make it so."

There was a warmth of gratitude in Richard's words that took Hannah by surprise, made her sense a bond between them of concern about herself that excluded her. She was conscious of her torn jeans, of the fact that she hadn't washed or brushed her hair, of dismay close to alarm on Richard's face as she stepped out of the shadows on to the pathway in front of them.

"Welcome to Brambles." She forced a smile. "I'm sorry I wasn't here."

She could feel Richard struggling with his antipathy to the place, the circumstance, the unexpectedness of it all, so at variance with what he'd visualised. She could feel him needing time, could feel herself needing time to explain.

"But you got our note?"

Looking at Richard, Sally felt uncertain now of her intended role to oil the wheels. Could one oil wheels, diverting, it seemed, down different tracks? Afraid of silence, of Richard's disappointment in her, without waiting for an answer, she continued, "You should have joined us at The Bull. They produced a good meal and quite reasonable too."

"I'm sure." Hannah could feel Richard's eyes boring into her. With disapproval was it or scepticism? She wasn't sure. He seemed a stranger now standing beside Sally and the overgrown nettles in the fading light – a stranger remote from the life they'd led together in Hong Kong. "I would have come", she tried to explain then, "only it's not a good idea for me to make myself too well known here in public at present."

"That sounds ominous," Richard commented. She looked like a new age traveller, he thought, like one he'd seen once on television. Beautiful – she'd always been beautiful but there was a wildness now about her, a disregard that worried him. He had to get her out of here, back to normality. Someone, something was turning her head.

"What's the mystery then?" he asked.

"It's probably concerning the will, is it not?" Sally intervened.

"It's related, yes," Hannah agreed.

"In that case I think it's best if I leave now, leave you two to it."

"There's no need for you to go really," Hannah felt obliged then to say. "I've got a quiche if you're still hungry."

"No, thanks all the same. I've got to fit in some work I missed today."

"It's very good of you, Sally, to have given the time." Richard smiled at her with appreciation. "Would you like me to see you to the car?"

"No, really. I'll be fine. You've obviously got a lot to catch up on. Just let me know when you need another lift anytime or if I can help in any way." Sally paused a moment, her eyes resting on Richard, then Hannah, then back again to Richard. Resolutely then she turned back down the overgrown path.

She paused at the wicker gate to wave and Richard waved back, watching till she'd disappeared from sight down the lane.

"She's been so good." He put down the suitcase and turned to Hannah. "I can't get over it, her meeting me like that and giving up all her time. There aren't many who'd do that."

"No," Hannah felt impelled to agree. "She's been a good friend." Yet the way Sally had looked at him, been aware, was it primarily for friendship, she wondered. Were motives ever that simple?

"More than good. I'd say exceptional."

"Why don't you call her back then?"

"Back? What do you mean?"

"Look, I'm sorry, Richard, I didn't meet you. I know it appears I've let you down and Sally's by comparison a paragon. But the fact is I couldn't come at short notice. I had to go to Hugo's house while I had the opportunity, the time."

"Yes, I know that. Sally explained. I didn't expect you to come. I know you've got to sort the will. I wasn't praising Sally to demote you. I was just acknowledging what she's done – for us both. There's nothing to be concerned about."

"That's all right then." Or was it, Hannah wondered.

"I've come to see you, Hannah." Richard stared at her upturned face a moment, trying to probe, to decide whether she still loved him. But the expression of her eyes in the gathering dusk eluded him. He sensed her holding back, unsure, tentative, felt again his own uncertainty. In the cool light of analysis, of practicality, it wasn't perfect, he knew that, but he still loved her, wanted her.

"To see you," he repeated and taking her into his arms, he kissed her, a long drawn out kiss that drew him back again into the uncomplicated warmth for a while of the early months when he'd first known her, had seen her as the answer to his dreams of love, of beauty.

Then an owl hooted, swooped into the long grass beside them, diverting him. Drawing back then, she took his hand and led him into the cottage.

"I'm sorry we can't use the light," she explained as he fumbled with his case in the hallway. "The electrician's coming though any day now," she added brightly, hoping Richard wouldn't see for the moment the defective sockets.

The shadows cast by the candlelight in the kitchen accentuated the shadows under his eyes and he looked strangely lost, incongruous, in his cool, cream coloured suit in the grimy kitchen and she felt she should have been more welcoming.

"Would you like some quiche?"

"No thanks. I'm not hungry."

"Do you mind if I do?" Ravenous now, she stuffed the crumbled quiche into her mouth while he took in the bramble stained walls, the archaic stove, the chipped primitive sink, the pervasive smell of damp and decay. Whatever was she thinking of renting such a place when Sally had so generously offered her a decent room in a location of convenience? He felt he wanted to ring for a taxi, to get out of the place straightaway, only he knew there was no phone and he felt too tired now, hadn't the energy to go and find one. It was over 36 hours now since he'd had a proper sleep. Tomorrow, he thought, tomorrow he'd get her to see sense and get her out of here.

"You don't like it here, do you?"

She poured him a glass of fresh orange, wishing now she'd had the chance to prepare for his coming. She hadn't even a bottle of wine or some Stilton which he liked.

"It's not what I would have chosen. No." He noted an ominous hole in the timber propping up the alcove where the stove was, the darkened paintwork round the socket in the wall. "It doesn't look all that safe to me."

"But it's cheap."

"Not as cheap surely as staying with Sally."

"No, but I feel free here. I can do what I like, be myself."

"Don't you think though that one has an obligation to other people sometimes?"

"What do you mean?"

"Sally's been very good to you, helped you. I don't think you should hurt her feelings."

"How have I hurt her feelings? I've explained everything. I need to be here anyway, near Yadrahna."

"Do you think that's wise?"

"Wise?"

"Being so near – isn't it going to make the whole situation more upsetting for you?"

"I've got to get back inside Yadrahna, Richard , if I'm to make a case." She remembered then the key to Hugo's house she had to give back to Luke so he could 'find' it in the drive and the key she needed from him for the cellar. She had to see him again but how now with Richard here?

"What are you hoping to find?"

She tried to explain then as they went upstairs the hope she held of another will in the cellar, told him briefly about her investigations to date, about her frustrations and at times despair. She didn't mention Luke by name, only that the gardener in antagonism to Olga Slade had 'lent' her a key.

And Richard listened, as much as he could, with attention, trying to puzzle out her frame of mind. But the crumbling nature of the room distracted him and he had to keep bending his head to avoid the low timbers. Carefully folding his trousers and arranging his jacket on the only chair, he lay back at length in exasperation on the creaking bed.

It all seemed to him bizarre what she'd said – a self–created pose, a psychological rather than a legal probe.

Perhaps it had to be from her view. The legal case was not promising, unlikely to succeed, not worth the effort she was expending. Wills were very rarely changed. He knew that from the cynical comments of his uncle who'd been a probate lawyer. Undue pressure was virtually impossible to prove. Yet something positive had to be done to give her hope, clinch the matter, stop her wasting her time, their time now, his hope of establishing their relationship on a firmer base.

"You know what I think," he offered, when she'd finished. "I think you should go and talk to Hugo and ask him direct if he'll agree to a more equitable settlement. He must know it's not fair if he has got, as you say enough resources with his mother. He could well agree to a readjustment. He might even be trying it all on. All this cloak and dagger stuff – is it all worth it – if you're going to end up paying any winnings back in lawyers' fees?"

"I suppose it does sound strange." Hannah took off her torn jeans and lay down beside him. "Of course I don't want to pay unnecessary fees but I can't honestly see Hugo caving into an agreement – not after all he's plotted and planned."

Close to Richard, she felt safer again but he didn't obliterate the hatred she'd seen in Hugo's painting of her mother and his own mother's face in Windsor. It was all far deeper than mere outwitting and games for money – a realm she was sure beyond rational agreement.

"Perhaps not," Richard conceded," but isn't it worth a try – if I come with you?" He turned to her kissing her nose and smiled.

"Maybe." She felt then she had to agree.

"That's settled then," Richard asserted, feeling better. "We'll find out if he's at Yadrahna tomorrow, and strike while the iron's hot, while I'm here. Then we can plan our holiday and your return to Hong Kong."

Drawing her down into his yearning, he made love to her then as when he'd first known her, dispelling fear as she responded, till the candlelight flickered and extinguished itself and, exhausted, he fell into a deep prolonged sleep.

Chapter 16

Hannah woke from a fitful sleep, on the edge of the bed, to sunlight filtering through the rose–patterned curtain of the bedroom window. Flecks of dust stirred in the beams, hovered with hints of decay over Richard's pristine cream suit, his carefully arranged jacket and trousers on the wicker chair. The suit drew at once the focus of eye from Hannah's casually flung clothes, as if to a still life painting on incongruity, on assertion and decline.

What would happen Hannah wondered if it was just left there for months or years like the shawl in Virginia Woolf's deserted house? Would it harmonise eventually with mildew and time or continue to assert itself, as Richard did, rejecting the drag of past image?

What would happen to Richard? To Richard and herself? The past, the present, which mattered more? How could one break away from the past as Richard wanted?

Uneasily as she turned back to Richard in the centre of the bed, there came back to her again the questions that had kept her wakeful: how was she going to tell him about the course, about the fact that she didn't want to return to Hong Kong at all?

She couldn't, not now. He'd slept in her bed, was sleeping still so soundly even as she stroked his cheek, his

arm. She doubted she'd wake him even if she pinched him. Yet his face was not peaceful. There were lines of frowning on his forehead, as if he was striving even in his dreams. Even round his mouth, lines of effort were making their indelible mark.

She felt she wanted to wake him, tell him to relax in his dreams, absorb the drift of the cottage for a while instead of striving. But he needed sleep. Thirty six hours he'd gone without on the journey and he would sleep, she was sure, if left till midday. Time to see Luke and discuss with him what could be done to get back inside to the cellar.

Quietly resolved, Hannah slipped out of bed and dressed, leaving a note for Richard on his suit, and, once more closing the cottage door behind her, made her way back through the woods in the morning sunlight to Yadrahna.

There was no sign of Hugo's Daimler in the drive, only Olga Slade's blue Renault parked close to the back door. Reassured that there appeared to be only Olga Slade in residence, Hannah crept through the shrubbery by her usual route to the kitchen garden. The potting shed door was open and she could hear Luke whistling to himself inside, could see him through the open doorway, with his back turned to her, stacking together seed boxes and piling them on shelves. I'll give him a surprise, she thought.

As she reached the door, she was aware suddenly of a dog barking. Turning she saw then bounding towards her from the cabbages and kale at the far end of the kitchen garden a large, dark Alsatian, its teeth bared.

An Alsatian had once bitten her leg as a child and she sensed this one was not controlled or benign, that it was

there to get her. Barely in time, as it gathered speed, she dashed into the shed and slammed shut the door, breaking as she did so two terra cotta pots in her way.

Luke turned in surprise. He'd expected her but not so soon, not in this sudden, dramatic way and he wanted to laugh, to take her in his arms, to tease her and reassure that no harm would come with the door now closed.

Closer he saw that she was genuinely frightened and more alert than she was, he saw through the low window of the shed, to his irritation and alarm, the unwelcome figure of Marcus with his air gun, following in the Alsatian's wake.

"Quick!" he urged her to the back of the shed behind the sacking, then outside, closing the door carefully behind him, confronted Marcus and tried to pacify the dog.

It was the kind of dog, he recognised at once, as having been trained outwardly for aggression but inwardly wanting affection and attention. He spoke to it quietly, trying to calm it down as it sniffed round the door. It had arrived, at Olga Slade's instigation, only the day before and he didn't know it yet, sensed an unpredictability that could go either way. Had Marcus seen Hannah, he wondered.

The boy's grey eyes were cold, hostile like his father's and already to Luke's disgust, as he spoke, he was assuming his father's arrogant, plummy tones.

"What happened? Why did he bark?" Marcus raised his air gun in a pose of threat.

Luke shrugged, trying to sound casual. "Probably heard a sound he's not used to – a pheasant perhaps."

"I haven't seen any pheasants."

"It's probably just as well with that implement you're carrying around – which reminds me – I should have told you before. It's illegal to shoot song birds. You've killed at least three thrushes and four blackbirds, haven't you?"

"What if I have? It's my land."

"It's your land is it now? Well, let me tell you, your land or not, the ownership of the land is irrelevant. You can't just do what you want."

"Who says?"

"I do. More importantly – the law."

"I don't have to take orders from you. We employ you as a servant."

"What did you say?" Luke felt he wanted to thump the boy, knock him out – arrogant little bastard that he was and cruel.

"I said you're our servant and if you're rude to me you'll lose your job."

Keep cool, Luke told himself, staring back into the boy's hostile grey eyes, in the only safe retaliatory measure he knew. How long he stood there he didn't know. It seemed as though hours had passed when he heard Olga Slade's voice calling from the wrought iron gate at the entrance to the kitchen garden that Marcus was wanted by his father on the phone. His hands still trembling from his imposed restraint, Luke watched the boy go, then turned back into the shed.

"It's O.K. He's gone."

"Does he always talk to you like that?" Hannah asked, emerging from behind the sacking. She had heard Marcus's words quite distinctly with a sense of shame. Marcus was after all her nephew, related, even if he didn't feel like it.

"If he has the chance. He doesn't like anyone interfering with his slaughtering activities."

"It's not right he gets away with it."

"No, but I can't afford the luxury just yet of getting the sack. I still need money to pay off my debts."

"Couldn't your family help?"

"My family? Have you any idea what it's like to live off a state pension? My father can scarcely afford to feed himself let alone take on my debts."

"I see."

"Do you? I doubt it." His voice, to her dismay, had an edge now of bitterness, shutting her out. "You've been used to a life of relative luxury, haven't you, living here? I know you've got problems now with the estate but you've never been really short, have you, wondered if you could afford a loaf, some milk?"

"Not in the past perhaps but I'm not well off now."

"Join the club then," he bantered but he wasn't convinced. She could see it, feel it in the scepticism, the lingering bitterness in his eyes. Marcus's insult had touched a raw nerve, set up a wall between them that would not be removed by pleas in minutes or hours and she decided to change the subject.

"I've brought back the key." She handed him back Hugo's key with the orange tab, trying to sound bright, unaffected.. "It was very useful. Thank you."

"You found what you wanted then?"

"Not exactly but I found some things, yes, and it helped me, let's say, indirectly, helped me to understand my brother's frame of mind."

"Which is?"

"He seems to harbour a deep resentment, almost hatred."

"Even I could have told you that."

"Could you? How?"

"The way he talks. He has a massive chip on his shoulder. The way he looks. He's calculating I'd say and cold."

"He's not susceptible to reason then, you think?"

"Why do you ask?"

"A friend has suggested approaching him direct, asking him to give me my share without using the law at all."

"And does this friend of yours know him?"

"No. Why? You think it wouldn't work?"

"If he's got the prospect of a large sum of money and has obviously planned for it, he's hardly likely to give up now, is he?"

"That's what I think."

"Then why bother?"

"My friend thinks it's worth a try to save lawyer's fees."

"And would this friend of yours come with you?"

"You think I couldn't manage on my own?"

"It's nothing to do with managing or not." Luke turned away in irritation. "It's your brother. He's not the type to take kindly to being cornered or exposed."

"You think he could be dangerous, you mean?"

"I don't know. I don't know him well enough. It's just an instinct that he's irrational, obsessive."

"Obsessive in what way?"

"As I said, I don't really know him. He's the sort of person, I suspect, one doesn't really know. He can't communicate, can he? He's a loner. He doesn't like people."

Luke stopped, aware of her staring at him. Disbelief was it or surprise? Surely she already knew. "I'm sorry if it's not what you wanted to hear but you did ask."

"I'm not criticising. I think you're right. I suppose I just didn't want to admit it, that's all."

"Well, anyway," Luke hesitated, "I think it's best not to see him alone. When are you thinking of seeing anyway?"

"This evening if I can, if he's here."

"He's supposed to be coming back this afternoon."

"Will you be here? This evening I mean?" Had he got a girl friend, she wondered. What did he do when he wasn't at Yadrahna apart from work?

"I don't live here, you know." She thought for a moment he was angry, then he smiled. "Anyway I thought you'd got a friend to come with you."

"I have." She gave a casual gesture of dismissal. "I wasn't expecting you to stay."

"That's all right then. I've got a meeting as it happens at 5 with someone who's going to fill me in on VSO."

"VSO? You mean you've got a job abroad?" She had a sudden dread in the pit of her stomach that she wouldn't see him again, that the next time she came, he'd be gone.

"I thought I told you. I'm due to go to India at the end of the month on a contract for two years."

"Two years but" and she wanted to protest, plead with him to stay and help her, tell him she needed him, needed his support but she couldn't find the words and dare not admit them.

"It's the usual time."

"Is it? I didn't realise."

"Well, anyway, that's the plan."

"I see." She felt numbed, at a loss. "But why India?"

"There's a scheme that interests me there which would encourage hand dug wells which would allow the ground water to replenish itself and I want to help with the reforestation."

"It sounds – "She tried to find the right word.

"Interesting, a challenge, worthwhile?" He gave a mocking smile.

"I wouldn't have thought," she retaliated, "you'd have wanted to call it worthwhile."

"I wouldn't. It's not worthwhile, anyway. It's common sense to preserve resources – a matter of survival."

"It's definite then you're going?"

"If I can pay off my debts and raise the money for the fare – yes."

"So you'll be here a couple more weeks?" She wondered whether she dared ask him again to help her into the house. It didn't seem fair in a way risking his need for money now.

"I can still help you get into the cellar," he offered guessing her doubts. "But they've changed the locks again."

"Again?" She could hardly believe it – the determination to keep her out but didn't it mean all the more that there was a need, a reason for her to get in, that Hugo for some reason was afraid?

"They're more suspicious now as well. When I went in today, the old bag was watching me like a hawk."

"I realise it's difficult. It's just that," she tried to hold back her tears, "I just can't bear the thought of all this being built over and destroyed. My father – he put his life into this

place. It's part of him, his meaning, his meaning at any rate to me." She started to cry, unable to stop herself, her sobs shaking her slim frame as if seeking to break it, break her.

Watching her, Luke was taken aback by the suddenness of her absorption, by the shame and inadequacy he felt in his own reaction. He'd worried about Marcus who was of no real importance when he should have considered her feelings which were just as raw as his own. And he wanted to put his arms round her to comfort her but he felt foolish now, uncertain, afraid she'd misinterpret him. His hands hanging awkwardly, he hovered, trying to find a way through.

"You mustn't give up, you know. Bastards like your brother have to be opposed, however long it takes. Your solicitor must feel that surely and have some more ideas."

"I haven't been back to him. I need to search first in the cellar."

"Do you really think there's anything more to find?"

"I don't know for sure but I won't know till I've tried, will I?"

He looked at her eyes reddened and swollen now with crying. "I'll try and get hold of the cellar key. I can't say when it will be but I'll keep trying."

"Thanks."

"You'll still, I take it, be at the cottage?"

"Yes." She remembered then Richard lying asleep still in the creaking bed and forced herself to the shed door. "Most of the time. If I'm not, you can always leave a message in the porch."

"I'll leave something cryptic then, like I've got the VSO job, then you'll know."

"Fine." She paused looking at him, wanting to stay, yet feeling impelled now to go. "And thanks for rescuing me."

"I didn't," Luke corrected, smiling. "You rescued yourself."

Outside the Alsatian continued to sniff at the door. Grasping its collar, Luke held onto the dog tightly as she slipped away into the shrubbery and back through the woods to the cottage, not letting go till he was sure she was well beyond being pursued. Who was the friend, he wondered, coming with her to see her brother and how important was he to her? He wished he'd persuaded her now to stay on a while, had asked her to come to see him in his room in Oxford.

Chapter 17

Richard was sitting propped up by the two pillows on the narrow iron bedstead, dressed in his underwear, when Hannah returned, a pile of books beside him on the mattress. Bending over then to kiss him, she saw that they were all the course books she'd temporarily concealed under the bed – books on employment law, interviewing, management planning and industrial relations.

"Ah – so the wanderer's returned." There was an aggrieved tone in his voice, wanting attention. "Where've you been?"

"I've been," she hesitated, wondering how to avoid mentioning Luke, "I've been to Yadrahna."

"To Yadrahna? So early?" Despite his irritation, he felt impressed. "Well, you certainly don't believe in wasting time. And is he there, this brother of yours?"

"Not at the moment no but he will be apparently later this afternoon."

"Good. The sooner we see him, the sooner we can get our lives in order." Richard closed the book he was reading on employment law, swung his legs over the creaking bed and proceeded to dress himself again in his cream coloured suit. As he brushed his hair, looking into the stained, cracked mirror on the wall, with studied casualness he

asked, "What made you buy such a collection of books? Employment law in the 90's is hardly your scene surely?"

"Isn't it? I should have thought it was everyone's scene now considering the insecurity."

"But you're not insecure."

"I haven't a job I could be sure of, that I like, not here at any rate." She had to tell him, she knew. Sooner or later it would come out and he'd guess if he hadn't guessed already. Forcing herself, she blurted, "I'm planning in fact to do a course – a course in Personnel work."

"But you're already qualified as a teacher."

"That doesn't mean to say I want to teach forever. I certainly don't want to wear myself out teaching here."

"There won't be any need for you to teach here, Hannah. We won't be here and by the time we come back hopefully we'll have enough money for you not to have to work at all."

"You'd prefer me to be dependent then?"

"I'm not saying that."

"What are you saying then – that I shouldn't expand, try something I'm more suited to?"

"You don't know, though, do you, that you're suited to Personnel Work?"

"I'd like to try it all the same."

"Well, may be in couple of years when we return, if you still feel the same then."

"I'm not thinking of a couple of years, Richard. I want to do the course now. In fact I've already booked to start this autumn."

"This autumn?" Richard turned to her from the mirror in disbelief. "But you've never said anything."

"I wasn't sure enough."

"But you are now, you mean?"

"I've been accepted and I feel I need to do it – yes."

"I see." But Richard didn't feel he did see. He felt a confusion rather of anger and dismay, of being shut out and let down. "And where is it then, this course?"

"In Oxford."

"And that's why you've taken on this wreck, is it?"

"It's not a complete wreck, Richard." She couldn't resist smiling. "And it has the merit of being cheap so I can better afford the fees."

She was aware of him staring at her, uncomprehending and even more he seemed alien in the daylight, in the dust of sunbeams streaming through the window, in his cream coloured suit – alien yet vulnerable as if the ailing walls of the cottage and the dust had perceived him now as a threat and were closing in on him, wanting him out. She felt simultaneously the need to both confront and comfort him – a confusion in herself as to how to deal with him.

"I can't understand what's got into you – the way you're talking, the course, this place. It's as if there's some other influence at work on you. Is that what it is? Is there someone else?"

"If you mean someone I'm going out with, sleeping with – no. The only people I've seen have been connected with investigating the will."

"Maybe that's it then." Richard's blue eyes lightened with relief, the knowledge he was nearer now to understanding and he felt he'd judged too harshly in haste. "Your father's death – I hadn't really taken it into account. I'm sorry."

He went over to where she was standing by the window looking out onto the garden and put his arm round her hunched, thin shoulders. "I should have realised. It's your father, isn't it, that's making you feel like this – insecure?"

"In some ways – may be." She felt she hadn't the heart to argue about it, to disillusion him. And in some ways what he said was true. She'd felt the loss of her father too painful to describe. She wanted the elementary things in life now, not the peripheral as before. Appearance didn't matter – only putting things right, putting right her father's will – the real will that was the sum of what he was, what he wanted, had wanted to achieve and to last into the future.

How though could she explain everything to Richard? It was all too complicated, too rooted in the past, in the minds of herself and her father, so that Richard couldn't really understand even if he wanted. It was no use explaining because she couldn't. One couldn't put everything into words. Words were always inadequate when it came to the point, could always be misinterpreted. One could only feel a situation, live it and Richard and herself, she knew that now, lived in worlds apart.

"You could always do the course in Hong Kong," Richard conceded at length. "There's bound to be a similar one there somewhere. Then we could still be together."

"Is that what you really want, Richard?"

"I want to be with you but not here."

Richard followed her gaze out onto the overgrown garden. The thought of her being here for a year while he was in Hong Kong appalled him and he felt he couldn't talk about it anymore. There was still time, though, he tried to

reassure himself inwardly, time to make her see the sense of returning with him, if he was patient, if he could get her away to his flat in Hampstead, away from this crumbling edifice, its associations and unknown influence.

Trying to be positive, he proposed that they should go out to lunch at The Bull and leave talking about it again till they'd seen Hugo. Readily Hannah agreed. She didn't want a major upset with Richard before seeing Hugo, the prospect of which was alarming her more than she dared to admit. She felt she had to go through with Richard's suggestion to confront Hugo, that she owed it to him to try at least to win Hugo round to a compromise. Intellectually, in theory, it was the right thing to do, to try all avenues to an agreement. One could never be sure it wouldn't work till one had tried. Yet the more she thought of Luke's words about Hugo, the more she thought instinctively he was right, that Hugo was unlikely to listen to reason.

It was with apprehension rather than hope that she walked silently with Richard later that afternoon after lunch back through the beech trees of Rassler's Wood to Yadrahna.

They heard the firing just as they were crossing the main road into the drive – the distinctive, sharp, penetrating, plosive sound of an air rifle. It was coming from the area of the thicket, Hannah estimated, close to the pond. It was Marcus she didn't doubt, knowing Luke was out of the way. And instantly she felt the same anger Luke had felt, that she had to stop Marcus, regardless of Hugo. Taking Richard's hand, she led him through the shrubbery.

"What's up?"

Bewildered, as they reached the pond, Richard stared down at the still green water studded to his surprise with the bodies of dead and dying birds. One he could see jerking its wings in a vain attempt to lift itself into the air again. Eleven Richard counted – blackbirds, thrushes, blue tits, even a robin.

He noticed then on the other side of the pond the figure of a boy with an air gun – a sturdy, pale–faced boy, standing quite still, oblivious of their approach, it seemed, with an intent look of concentration as he aimed his air rifle at the branch of a hawthorn tree above him some eight feet away. To his concern, before he could stop her, Hannah had broken away from him and had stealthily crept up on the boy. Abruptly then, before the boy realised she was there, she had snatched the air gun out of his hands and flung it down into the pond.

"How dare you kill all these birds, you little monster! You know it's not allowed."

For a moment Richard thought the boy was going to go for her throat. His hands were clenched in an upward movement and his eyes blazed at her with hate. Then he saw Richard and that he was outnumbered and jumped into the pond. Waist high in the water, at the edge of the pond, he felt with his feet for the gun, stirring up mud and swirling the bodies of dead birds. Then, triumphantly, he lifted the gun out, spat at Hannah, then ran dripping towards the house.

"Hadn't we better stop him?" Richard suggested, concerned now that his hopes of an agreement would be jeopardised.

"What's the point?" Hannah looked at the bodies of the birds washed now to the edge of the pond. She felt she hated Marcus, like Luke did. "It won't work anyway."

"We're here now. We've got to give it a try." Richard looked with annoyance down at his cream coloured trousers, spattered now with mud.

"All right, if the door's open but I'm not going to act the beggar, asking to be let in."

To Hannah's surprise the front door was wide open and she walked with Richard straight through to the lounge.

Marcus had already, as she'd expected, established himself centre stage with a trail of muddy footprints on the carpet and was protesting at her action at the pond. Following his words with her mouth open and standing opposite the door with a tray in her hand was Olga Slade. At the cabinet beside her, Hugo, dressed in his green corduroy jacket, was pouring himself a gin and tonic. His lips curled as he caught sight of Hannah. As if to nullify her entrance, he went on pouring his drink but he had paled slightly, Hannah noticed, seeing Richard, and his eyes shifted with unease, sideways and then back again towards the west window.

It was then that Hannah noticed his mother ensconced in her father's favourite upright chair by the window. She was leaning forward, her bony hands resting on the knob of a brass studded walking stick, her hawk like profile, her black eyes sharp with an antagonism that seemed to dominate the room and made Hannah feel simultaneously angry and afraid. She decided to speak before they could.

"He's not allowed to shoot birds. It's an offence. He could be prosecuted."

Hugo's eyes slithered back again to his mother. Hannah could feel him weighing the situation, wondering how

to get rid of her. She was glad Richard was with her but wished that Luke was still in the grounds as well, nearer at hand. Richard was already looking perplexed, unsure.

"But that's not the main reason," she continued, "that I came."

"For the first time Hugo spoke, his voice oiled now, prepared. "Why did you come then?"

"I came," she stated bluntly, "to discuss the will."

To her surprise Hugo smiled. "It's no use coming to me about the will. It's a legal document in the hands of the solicitor. It's nothing to do with me." He waved his arms in a gesture of disclaiming. "If you don't like it," he paused with an affable shrug of detachment," you'll have to see a solicitor and take it to court. People can leave their money to whomever they like. Isn't that right, mother?"

"It most certainly is," Elvira Delaney confirmed, her assumed aristocratic voice rising on a crescendo of contempt.

How pretentious she is, Hannah thought, pretentious but no fool. Her eyes like knives. She'd kill me if she could – only I'm not going to let her. She's behind it all but she's not going to win. I'm not going to give in no matter how hard she looks.

"I'm not doubting the validity of free choice," she stated as calmly as she could. "But I don't believe this will, so called, was from free choice. You know as well as I do, Hugo, that our father wanted me to have Yadrahna. In fairness, so that you would have an equal share of the estate, he decided to leave you his investments. That is what he told me and what I understand he told you."

"He told me nothing of the kind. Did he mother?"

"Of course he didn't." Elvira Delaney raised her brass studded walking stick pointing it at Hannah. "It's all lies. Don't listen to her."

"It's not lies. It's the truth," Hannah countered. "It's what he wanted and what he told me before I went to Hong Kong."

"Well, he obviously changed his mind then, didn't he?"

"No, I don't believe he did. And you must know in your heart, anyway, Hugo, that it's hardly fair for one person in a family to take everything. How would you feel, if someone, if I had done that to you?"

"Done what exactly?"

"Manipulated, persuaded an old man when he was ill."

"Manipulate? Persuaded?" Hugo raised his eyebrows. His voice was smooth, still in control, but his neck and face were flushed now with an incipient anger. Or fear was it, Hannah wondered. How little she knew him. She tried to look into his eyes but they shifted restless from his mother to Olga Slade to Marcus then back to his mother again as he continued: "How could I persuade when there were two witnesses? They wouldn't have signed would they if they'd seen me persuading. Ask Mrs Slade here. She was a witness." He turned to Olga Slade. "Did I persuade Mr Delaney before he signed the will on May 1st?"

"No, of course not," Olga Slade quickly replied, looking down at her tray of glasses as Hannah tried to catch her eye.

"There you are." Hugo gave a smile of satisfaction. "and I don't doubt the other witness will say the same. The fact is that father signed of his own free will so it

243

must have been what he wanted. He wasn't mentally ill or incapacitated. He had a sound disposing mind."

He's got the jargon, Hannah thought, has looked it all up beforehand.

"Maybe," she conceded, "He wasn't mentally ill but he was certainly very physically ill and drinking far more than usual by all accounts. Someone must have given him that drink which would certainly have affected his judgement."

"As I said," Hugo shrugged again with detachment, "if you want to take the matter to court, by all means do so."

"I don't think Hannah necessarily wants to go to court, do you, Hannah?" For the first time Richard spoke, his voice conciliatory, calm.

"Oh doesn't she?" Hugo turned sarcastically to Richard. "And what business is it of yours?"

"The business of someone concerned to see fair play." Richard looked at Hugo doubtfully a moment then continued, "It's clearly a very one sided will and should therefore be adjusted. It would be far better if it could be adjusted by mutual agreement rather than by the antagonism produced by a court case."

"So you're suggesting I should hand over what has been freely bequeathed to me. Is that it?"

"I'm suggesting that in the interest of family harmony you should do the right thing and give Hannah her share, which I understand is Yadrahna."

"Oh you are, are you? Well, let me tell you – I've got no intention of giving up anything left to me in the will – nothing at all."

"You really think it's fair to take everything?" Hannah challenged. She was grateful to Richard for speaking up for her but afraid now he'd become the object of abuse and humiliation.

"Of course it's fair," Elvira Delaney's voice rose again from the confines of the upright chair. "Your father ruined our lives by the course he took. We deserve some compensation – more than deserve for his worthless actions."

There was venom, more than venom, in the way she pronounced 'worthless'. Shaken, Hannah turned to Hugo. "Is this what you think – what she's said?" She couldn't bring herself to say mother for Elvira Delaney no longer seemed a mother but some vicious harpy with her claws in the present as well as the past, "that our father was worthless?"

"Well, he didn't do anything for me, did he?" Hugo's smile had changed to a sneer. "The only person he was ever interested in was his precious daughter, wasn't it? Did he ever bother to set me up?"

"He bought you your studio and helped you in other ways."

"How come it then that he wasn't willing to finance me for a degree?"

"Perhaps he thought," Hannah hesitated. She remembered all too clearly her father's words that Hugo had no academic talent, that he would never last the course, that it would only encourage him longer to live off other people. "Perhaps he thought you'd be happier doing something more practical. He always did his best anyway to help you."

As Hugo sneered, she knew there was little or no hope of the agreement Richard had urged. They were set against

her, determined. There was no point in being tactful now or cautious. She would say what she wanted.

"He did his best to help you," she repeated. "And he left you in the will plenty to live on. But not content you wanted not just more but everything. You wanted Yadrahna as well and what for? So that you could sell it for development in a way totally against his wishes. It's true, isn't it? All the planning and plotting, it's been to gain Yadrahna to sell it for development – my inheritance!"

"Your inheritance, is it?" Hugo echoed, stalling. He didn't want to get involved in revelations of his plans with Jamieson. They weren't yet finished, by no means certain. To his irritation, his mother, now stirred, was less inclined to be circumspect.

"And why shouldn't he develop it?" she rasped. "It's his to do as he likes now. If it brings in money, we deserve it – after all we've gone through."

"Gone through! My father looked after you both very well. He was a good caring man."

"Caring?" Elvira Delaney snorted, casting aside her aristocratic tones. "All he cared about was his little bit on the side."

"He was totally faithful to my mother," Hannah retaliated. She felt she wanted to shout out then how much they'd loved each other, her mother and father, how deep their love had been. She wanted to shout it because it was true, to assert it against the intent she felt enclosing her; but the hostility in the room withered the words before they could come and she knew she couldn't have borne the mockery, the failure to understand, the denigration of her father's goodness.

"But he wasn't faithful to me," Elvira Delaney asserted.

"You mean you want Yadrahna as a kind of revenge?" Hannah turned to Hugo.

"If you want to put it that way," Hugo evaded, "please yourself. As I said, if you're not satisfied, take it to court."

One more try, Hannah thought. It was obvious it had all been thought out and planned to cope with any challenge in court. Hugo was clearly confident he could win. She had though to be 100% sure.

"You're not willing then to come to an agreement without going to court?"

"No, I'm not."

"I think we should go." Richard took her hand, trying to draw her to the door. But Hannah felt suddenly overcome by a helpless rage rising within her. The hatred, the resentment, the meanness, the denigration – it all made sense psychologically but rationally no sense at all. And Hugo wanted to take away not just the substance of a building, its stones, its timbers, the grounds in which it lay but the past, her past and the will and spirit of her father and all he'd meant to her. With tears in her eyes, finding it difficult now to control herself, she shouted at Hugo, "You ought to be ashamed of yourself for what you've done. You've manipulated a sick and vulnerable man. You lied grossly about his death just for gain. You withheld letters to him."

"Withheld letters? I don't know what you're talking about."

"Don't you? How is it then that I managed to find them unopened?"

"Oh, so you've been to my house, have you?"

"I told you she had," his mother rasped again from the chair. "I told you I could smell her as soon as we entered the house that day. I told you I'd seen her in the street."

"Let's go." Richard tugged at her arm, fearful of the situation getting out of hand and what else Hannah might reveal to her disadvantage.

"So not content with snooping round here, you actually broke into my house?"

"What if I did?" Hannah pulled away from Richard to face Hugo. "It was all justified. It showed me what you are, the way you feel in the hatred in your painting. You're dissatisfied within yourself Hugo."

Suddenly Hugo's grey eyes were no longer shifting but focused on her with the hate she'd seen in the painting, his face enflamed, his voice, his whole body tense, shaking with anger. "Get out!" he shouted. "Get out!"

Hannah was aware then of Marcus's voice joining in shrilly, trying to emulate his father's, of Olga Slade's, of Elvira Delaney's, triumphant and distorted from her father's blue upright chair. "Get out! Get out!" Like a Greek chorus, gaining strength from one another, they shouted, their voices, their bodies, gradually pressing her to the door.

Desperate, she called back in her heart to her father, to his spirit, willing him to help her but she could no longer feel his presence in the room. Desperate, she wanted to resist, to stand firm, not let them cower her but Richard was taking her arm more firmly now, urging her away.

"There's no point. We won't achieve anything. Let's go."

She felt she wanted Luke then to give her the strength

she needed, saw the muscles on his back rippling in the sun again, as on the day she'd first seen him. Turning back at the door, defiantly she faced them.

"I'm not going to give in to all your plotting and planning, Hugo. You may think you've got away with it, that you've won, but you haven't – not yet and you won't."

She was about to throw a parting shot at Elvira Delaney, when she was aware of Marcus raising his air gun again and pointing it at her feet. There was a sharp plosive sound as the pellet struck the side of her shoe.

Seeing Marcus with a malicious grin on his face take closer aim, Richard pulled her more emphatically this time through the door and shutting it behind him, he forced her through the hall and our of the front door and up the drive.

"Quick into the bushes!" Just in time, behind them they heard Hugo's derisive laughter, then Marcus's pellets striking the gravel where their feet had been.

Back at the cottage, Richard tried to clear the mud from his cream coloured trousers, despondently changed into some jeans.

"I'm sorry. I shouldn't have suggested it. It was a mistake. I see that now."

"You weren't to know, Richard. I was a fool anyway admitting I'd been to his house."

"It would certainly have been better if you hadn't. I should have warned you."

"Warned me?"

"It doesn't do to reveal your hand, Hannah, before a potential court case. Nor your feelings if you want to win someone over to a compromise."

"I was never going to win Hugo over, Richard, whether I revealed my feelings or not."

She sank back on the bed, feeling drained, suddenly exhausted, at the same time deeply uneasy and disturbed by the encounter she'd had with Hugo. His face as he'd focused on her was the same hatred he'd expressed in the picture he'd painted of her mother she'd found at his house, an expression not just of feeling but of intent – an intent that wanted her out of the way, the intent of a force deeper and darker, it had seemed, than mere self preservation and dissatisfaction with a status quo – a force that had driven away even the presence, she'd always felt in the room, of her father.

Why? How? Was Hugo evil or was she imagining it? Could it only be self preservation, self interest? What other fears did he have? What other intentions?

Desperate, through her tiredness, Hannah felt she needed to talk to someone who knew, who knew Hugo, who could tell her what really he was like, what she didn't understand and feared. There was only one person, apart from his mother who knew him – Laura. She had to go and see Laura and speak to her.

"Maybe not," Richard conceded, his words washing over her consciousness, some heard, some not. "It's all the more reason now to leave it all with the solicitor and detach yourself. You've found out what you can. You need to give him now the information. All this breaking into Yadrahna and Hugo's house – it's not going to put you in good light and it's obviously distressing you and taking it out on you. You've lost a lot of weight, did you know that? And it's showing on your face – the

strain. It's a legal matter. You must leave it now to the solicitor."

"Who could well find it more difficult than me to get the evidence. And it will cost, if I leave it all to him, vast sums of money."

"You know I'll help you with the cost. Be sensible, Hannah. Leave it to the people whose job it is to sort these matters and give yourself a break – a break from here. You've done what you can. Now leave it – leave this place. If you stay you'll only be tempted to go back to Yadrahna and you might not escape so lightly next time."

"You think I should let Hugo get away with it, you mean? Which he will do if I don't find the other will."

"I'm not saying that – of course not but even if he does, if the case in the end goes against you, it's not the end of the world. Why do you think I'm staying on in Hong Kong if not to make money – money which will be equal in the end, if not surpass, the value of Yadrahna."

"It wouldn't be Yadrahna, though, would it? It's Yadrahna I want Richard."

"All right then, we'll build another Yadrahna if that'll make you happy."

The daylight was fading now and Richard could feel himself becoming increasingly oppressed in the gathering gloom of the cottage, a sense that his energy was being sapped by the smell of dampness and decay, a sense that Hannah was slipping away from him in the decay. He could understand in part how she felt. It was natural that she should want Yadrahna, having lived in it as a child, natural that she should want to stop her grasping, unpleasant brother developing it but he

couldn't understand her obsession with it. It wasn't as if Yadrahna was a specially beautiful building or a listed one. And it certainly wasn't comfortable and warm to live in with its stone flagged floors and high ceilings. Remote and out of touch, it wasn't the kind of place he wanted to live in at all. He'd feel buried as he did here in the cottage.

"There can't be another Yadrahna, Richard. That's the point."

"Well, anyway." Suddenly Richard felt he had to get away. "I suggest we go to the flat and discuss it all there. You'll see things better in perspective away from here. We can plan our holiday then and go away while the solicitor sorts things out for you."

"You mean now?"

"Why not?"

"There won't be any buses to London now."

"All right then. Tomorrow morning. We'll get up early and go." Seeing her unresponsive, he pressed, "We can go to a show and have a celebration."

"It's a nice idea. It's not that I don't appreciate it, Richard, but I can't. I don't want to leave here now. I've got to go and see Laura."

"Who's Laura for heaven's sake?"

"Hugo's ex wife."

"And how does she come into it all?"

"I feel, I hope she'll be able to tell me about Hugo, what he thinks, what he really feels, what's behind it all."

"And this is important to you?"

"Yes."

"More important than me?"

"I didn't know there was a choice. I'm just trying to investigate that's all while there's still a chance to put things right."

She wished he'd go, leave her alone, leave her to sleep. She didn't want to be questioned, challenged. She'd worked it out already what she'd do. But she'd hurt him. She could see it in his eyes and she felt guilty that he'd come all this way to see her, apparently still wanting her. Yet it wasn't right. She knew that now. They were living on residues of feeling from the past, which had no real relevance now. Yet how could she express it, put it in words aloud to him? She felt she couldn't, not now, not yet.

"All right then." Things weren't going well. Richard could see that from Hannah's words, her expression. She wanted to be alone, without him. But he couldn't just walk out, go back to the flat, not knowing when or even if he'd see her again. He had to give it another chance when she wasn't so absorbed, give her time to think and come to her senses. The whole business with the will was getting out of hand.

Trying to overcome his disappointment with the present, Richard resorted from habit to the future.

"All right then," he repeated. "I suggest I go to the flat for a couple of days and see mother and sort things out there while you go to Laura. Then I'll come back on Tuesday or Wednesday, let's say, and see how things are and how you've got on. How would that be?"

Relieved there'd been no scene, Hannah nodded.

"Promise me though one thing."

"What's that?"

"That you're telling the truth when you say there's no one else."

"I'm telling the truth. There's no one else." Trying to shut Luke from her mind, Hannah turned on her side on the creaking bed and closed her eyes.

Chapter 18

As she rang the bell of 51 Cranmer Road, Hannah felt apprehensive again about her reception. There were no silver haired neighbourhood watch friends this time observing her. But it had occurred to her more than once on the bus to Banbury that Laura might not want to be reminded of Hugo's relations, having severed her relationship with him. There were the years, too, that had passed between them. How could she bridge in an instant the nine years since she had last seen Laura? Would she even recognise Laura?

As the door opened, she felt the surge of the past again, the waves swirling, searching the uncertainty, the hidden crevices of the present. The tall slim woman standing in front of her in the doorway was undoubtedly Laura. She had Laura's flecked hazel eyes, her pale, almost ghostly white skin, Laura's distinctive auburn coloured hair but the chic short style she'd had with Hugo had been replaced by a cascade of loosely curled hair over her shoulders and she was dressed far more casually than Hannah remembered in jeans and a loosely fitting amber coloured shirt that matched her hair. She looked to Hannah younger, more relaxed. Holding her hand beside her was a little girl of five with the same hazel eyes and auburn coloured hair.

She looked at Hannah curiously a moment. "I feel I should know you."

"You do. I'm Hannah." Fearful Laura might suddenly reject the visit, shut the door in her face, she rushed on. "I'm sorry to turn up unexpectedly like this but I wonder if I could have a word with you. I believe you could help me."

Hannah could feel Laura hesitating, her eyes focused momentarily with apprehension. Then to her relief, Laura smiled.

"You'd better come in."

She led Hannah through to a modernised kitchen at the back of the house, where the little girl detached herself and started to play with some beakers by the window.

"Would you like some coffee?"

"I'd love some, thanks."

Hannah felt suddenly weak from lack of food and drink. She'd run out of bread and essentials at the cottage before leaving, which hadn't helped her parting with Richard – a parting that had left her feeling yet more guilty and drained as he'd trudged off in the rain down the muddy lane to a crowded bus. He'd be back, he said, but she had meanwhile to face up to her illusions about the cottage, the course and Yadrahna. What illusions, she wondered, as Laura handed her a welcome cup of fresh strong coffee. Did not Richard have his own illusions – the illusions above all of economic success and expansion as the panacea? What were illusions anyway when there was no final universal arbiter of reality and fact? Did Laura have illusions? Did she have them still about Hugo?

"How's David?" she asked, trying to find a way through.

David, Laura's probation officer husband, Hannah had heard about but never seen.

"He's fine except for being permanently overworked." Laura scooped some biscuits on to a plate and sat down facing Hannah with her coffee at the narrow kitchen table. "He's got an extra case to deal with in fact this morning. But that seems to be the way of it in the probation service nowadays."

"But you're happy with him?"

"Very." Laura was surprised by the directness so soon of so personal a question. But then Hannah had always been direct, she remembered, and in a way she welcomed it, found it refreshing, a change from circling, evasive cliches, felt she wanted to be direct herself. "He's a good man. I've never regretted leaving Hugo if that's what you're wondering. The only problem," she paused a moment regarding Hannah with more caution, "is the influence Hugo still exerts over Marcus."

"Marcus?"

"I gather you've been in Hong Kong. You probably haven't seen him."

"I have in fact. I saw him only yesterday. But I don't think I'm very popular with him." Hannah recounted what had happened with the air gun at the pond.

"You stopped him shooting then?"

"Tried to. I know you probably don't agree with my interfering."

"But I do. I'm glad someone has interfered. I hate the way he goes shooting birds and Hugo encourages him."

"Does Marcus spend a lot of time then with Hugo?"

"Every weekend. Unfortunately I agreed to it in the access arrangements."

"And you don't like the effect?"

"No, no, I don't." Laura's eyes darkened, it seemed to Hannah, with a concern beyond habit or mere resentment. "I know he's your brother and you probably don't want to hear ill of him but I find he has a very aggressive effect. Marcus always comes back very difficult and uncertain of himself, almost unmanageable I'd say. By the middle of the week he tends to have settled down, then we start all over again the next Monday."

"Does Marcus like him, do you think?"

"I'm not sure I'd say like. It's more a hold he has over Marcus. He bribes him with material goods. He always seems to have plenty of money. Perhaps from his mother – I don't know. I gather from Marcus she still lives with him."

"Yes, she does. She was at Yadrahna in fact yesterday when I called."

"At Yadrahna? But surely she's not back with your father?"

"My father's not at Yadrahna, Laura. My father died last month."

"Died? But Marcus never said anything. I mean – I thought it was odd they were spending so much time apparently at Yadrahna but it never occurred to me – your father – I'm sorry – I'd have gone to see him. I wish I'd known. I can't understand it, Marcus not saying anything. I suppose he must have forgotten but how could he? Something so major." Laura's hands were trembling as she poured some more coffee, trying to absorb the implications. "I suppose you'll be living at Yadrahna now then?"

"No, I won't be living at Yadrahna – not unless I'm successful in challenging the will."

"What do you mean?"

"I mean that Hugo managed to manipulate the will to the extent that he's to inherit everything including Yadrahna."

"But I thought the house was due to go to you and that Hugo was to have the investments. It was something understood. Even I knew that."

"It was what my father told us all at some stage and what I'm sure he intended but Hugo had other plans." Trying to keep as calm and brief as she could Hannah outlined to Laura the circumstances of her father's death and what had happened in the final encounter with Hugo until she felt able to put the question that preoccupied her, the question to which only Laura she felt would know the answer.

"Why does he hate me so much, Laura? His face was full of hatred in those final words we had. Why?"

Laura was confused. Hannah could see it in her eyes, a confusion that had its roots way back in fear. She wanted to help, to purge the past of its reminders of Hugo; she also wanted to forget, to press the memories of him down. Yet Hannah had a claim – the claim of another woman she saw wounded, deprived of justice – someone to whom she could also perhaps impart at last her own fears about Hugo and what had long disturbed her.

"It wasn't just you he hated. It was everyone. One of the worst aspects of being married to him was that we had no friends. Everyone was torn to shreds."

"Why particularly though did he hate me?"

"I think it began with your father remarrying, his mother being ousted as it were. She fed then his resentment of your mother and you. You became a kind of rival in his mind, pushing him out. His mother hated, of course, your mother. I've no doubt in my mind that she'd have harmed her if she could. You could have cut it with a knife – the intense feeling she had. I've no proof of it of course but I've often wondered about the accident your mother had."

"Wondered what?"

"Whether it wasn't arranged."

"You mean Hugo and his mother – they planned it?"

"I don't know. I've no proof but it fits their feeling, their hate."

"But she skidded on a bend."

"Yes, but why did she skid?"

"She had three punctures caused by three nails apparently in three of the tyres."

"Precisely. Three whacking great nails which one doesn't usually find just lying on a country road. Which would have had to have been placed at an angle to enter the tyre. And don't you think it a bit odd that Hugo happened to be driving just behind her yet failed to save her from the fire?"

"I thought he had helped according to the inquest and the press."

"According to Hugo who fed the inquest and the press."

"But the inquest surely would have picked up anything suspicious."

"Not necessarily and your father by all accounts was too upset at the time to probe. That doesn't means to say there was nothing to probe."

"But" – Hannah felt overwhelmed by a new dimension that had never occurred to her, reluctant to take it in. She couldn't take it in. All she could think for the moment was how to protect, to justify her father. "Dad was so good to Hugo and his mother. He made such good provision for them."

"I agree but there's no logic in these things, is there? And as far as you were concerned, Hugo was very jealous of you, of the fact that you went to university and he didn't, that you could travel abroad and he couldn't. His whole attitude, Hannah, was full of resentment, putting people down. I felt I was being stifled, crushed. And everything had to be on his terms, as he wanted, the way the rooms were arranged – everything. He was so cold, dominating. I had to go. You understand that, don't you?"

"I think I do now." Hannah remembered the effect of the rooms in Hugo's house. "But I suppose I didn't at the time."

"I know I've probably harmed Marcus in a way leaving him. There's not a day that goes by when I don't feel guilty about the effect but I couldn't have stuck it any longer – the coldness, the domination, the disparagement of everyone, everything. I began to feel he was evil."

"And do you still feel that?"

"I feel he's corrupting Marcus, yes."

"Can you not limit his time with Marcus?"

"Not with access arrangements as they are. He'll always get his way in any case in the end. That's how he is and how he functions. The only interest that matters to him is his own. The law won't help. The only way one will ever get a fair deal with him, the only way you'll ever get a fair deal from him is if he's dead."

The word 'dead' dropped between them like a stone and Hannah could find no words for a moment to respond. The undercurrent in Laura's voice was close to Hugo's own hate and she felt afraid, afraid of them both and their effect.

"It sounds awful, I know, but he's corrupting, Hannah. The only wish I've ever had over the past ten years is that he'd just drop dead."

"He's only 38, Laura."

Hannah felt she wanted to go now, pull back from an abyss that seemed to be wanting to pull her down.

"But alcoholic and overweight and with a dodgy heart. It's quite plausible he could drop dead from shock."

"You're not suggesting..."

"I'm not suggesting anything." Cautiously Laura withdrew into a smile of reassurance. "But it wouldn't take much to tip the scales, would it?"

"Wouldn't it?"

Hannah was aware of Laura looking at her with expectation, almost relief, as if shifting a burden that had long weighed her down, of an insidious pressure in her words, despite the smile, that made her feel it imperative to get away before anything more was said implicating her.

"I think I'd better go." Hannah forced herself to her feet, feigning a hasty glance at the kitchen clock. "I've an appointment, I'm afraid." At the door, she paused. "I'll get in touch if there's anything to report."

"Yes, do." Laura smiled again. "But don't leave it too late."

Chapter 19

Back at the cottage Hannah couldn't get Laura out of her mind. Far from gaining the reassurance and information she'd sought, she now felt more deeply than ever disturbed with more questions than answers.

It was true that Laura had given her reasons for Hugo's behaviour and confirmed her suspicions but, in wanting Hugo's death, she seemed to be making a direct appeal – an appeal Hannah knew she had to dismiss right away but insidiously it kept returning as she reflected, with ever deepening unease, on Laura's suggestion that her mother's death had not been accidental but planned.

Twisted though he was, could Hugo really have gone to such lengths and how to be certain of such an outcome? Nothing had been suggested at the inquest nor had her father shown suspicion. Overwhelmed with grief, he had not wanted, nor indeed had been able, to analyse and delve. Nor had anyone else, including herself, cast doubt. The car had skidded after punctures caused, according to a police report, by three nails embedded in the two front tyres and one back tyre. It had been presumed that her mother had unfortunately got the nails embedded in a builder's yard she had visited the day before.

The more Hannah thought about the three nails now,

the more implausible it seemed to her that they had been embedded simultaneously in the tyres by chance. Yet how could Hugo have been so certain that her mother's car would come off the road at such a point where it was bound to plunge as it had? Moreover, if it was true that he had deliberately planted the nails, how could she ever prove it? Hugo's story had been plausible enough to pass police scrutiny and no witnesses had come forward. Without witnesses and after such a long time, where, how, could she begin to challenge Hugo's version?

The more she thought of the prospect before her and the slim chances of success, the more depressed she felt and the more mentally and physically exhausted. She felt hungry but couldn't bring herself to eat, tired but unable to sleep. All night she tossed in the narrow creaking bed, trying to resolve a meaningful course of action, but nothing seemed clear, resolvable. The only objective she could define with any prospect now of gaining evidence was to get into the cellar at Yadrahna but she still had no means of entry and the chances of Luke getting a copy of the cellar key now seemed increasingly remote. He would try she didn't doubt. He was the kind of person who did what he said he'd do but they would have taken more precautions now, would be on their guard, watching him, closing in on the options and was there not a limit to what she could expect of him?

Exhausted, the next morning, she sat out in her nightdress on the rickety garden seat by the kitchen window, hoping the fresh air would revive her, trying to marshal her thoughts for the day. The two weeks since she had first seen Mr Ashford, the solicitor, were now up

and she was due to see him again that afternoon to report on progress. What was she going to tell him? What could she tell him of real use and significance? She'd found out more about Hugo's character and motivation but despite all her efforts, all the people she'd seen, she still had no hard evidence of pressure or collusion and there was the added complication now of her mother's death. Should she tell Mr Ashford about Laura's suspicions? Was there any point in telling him without witnesses?

Closing her eyes against the sun, she tried to sort out in her mind an order to recount to him of the people she'd seen and what they'd said, of the questions she should ask. But the sun, already high in the sky, she could feel draining rather than reviving, burning into her pale skin almost as strongly as the Hong Kong sun had done. She was about to get up off the seat and go indoors again when she was aware suddenly of a shadow across her face intercepting the warmth and brightness.

Startled, she opened her eyes. For a moment, dazed by tiredness and surprise, she couldn't make out who or what it was standing in front of her and she felt a flash of panic and fear that it might be Jamieson come back again.

Then she heard, like cool water, breaking over her fear the voice of Luke trying to reassure, was aware of his intent brown eyes staring down at her, staring as if they were penetrating right through her nightdress and body on the rickety garden seat.

"I'm sorry. I didn't mean to frighten you." His eyes checked down the garden path to the gate, then back to her still staring. "I wouldn't have come so early but I thought it might be urgent."

"Urgent?"

"I've brought the address." He held out an envelope.

"Address?" She had a strange sensation of floating, of being cast off adrift on a waving sea of green.

"The address you wanted of the housekeeper – Mrs Mason."

"Emma you mean?" With a surge of hope she refocused, taking the envelope from his hand. From inside she took out a square of paper with a carefully written address on it.

"Mrs E. Mason, C/O A.W.Wilson, Plum Cottage, Atherton, Nr. Barton, Oxon." Underneath was a telephone number. "It's amazing. How did you do it?" She smiled up at him.

"I asked in the village every time I had a drink and eventually an old man came up with the name of someone he thought would know. It wasn't a great labour."

"It was good of you all the same. Thanks." She felt she wanted to throw her arms round him in gratitude, but he'd stepped back from her as if wary and she felt uncertain again of how he'd react and interpret her. Something was holding him back that only he could tell her and until he did, if he did, better to play safe she decided. She didn't want to force things, to alienate him. She looked down evasively at the address again.

"I didn't realise you were working at Yadrahna today."

"I'm not."

"You came over specially you mean?"

"It's not far."

"But with all the other jobs you have to do..."

"I enjoy, I need the exercise." He tried to smile, to diffuse the desire he felt rising. He could see the triangle

of brown hair beneath the thin white cotton of her night dress, her breasts pressed against an oval pattern on the material as if it was a skin about to be shed. If only, he yearned, she would shed it so he could be sure.

She looked so cool, so detached, so in control, despite the vulnerability of her slimness, her frame. He wanted her yet felt afraid – afraid it was too soon for her, that she'd reject him and he couldn't bear, he knew, to be rejected by her. The time would come – or would it? Despairing, he thought of his imminent posting to India.

She smiled, puzzled by his expression "Would you like a drink?"

"I wouldn't say no."

He followed her into the kitchen where she poured him a fresh orange, then, excusing herself, went upstairs to change. When she came down again, she was wearing shiny black shorts and a close fitting orange T shirt and she'd brushed back her hair so that it hung sleek and smooth and loose over her shoulders.

He felt he wanted to tell her how beautiful she was. Instead he said: "How's it going then?"

"Going?" She poured some orange for herself, cut a slice of bread and cheese for them both.

"Your investigations. You are still investigating I take it?"

"I'm still investigating – yes."

"With any success?"

"I – " she hesitated a moment, then before she could stop herself, blurted, "I think my mother may have been murdered."

"Murdered!" The word dropped like a stone into the silence of the bramble stained kitchen, astounding Luke,

shaking him. "Your mother? But I thought it was your father you were investigating."

"It is but something's emerged which makes me think – I've no proof but I think it's true."

"Can you get proof, do you think?"

"Not easily no. It's over five years ago now."

"What happened?"

"I'm not sure exactly. That's the problem." Feeling her way, she told him about her visit to Laura and Laura's suspicions.

"And do you think she's right – that your brother's capable of murder?"

"I think he could be – yes." She sat down, trying to focus on the essence of his question. It was a question she knew she needed to answer, not only for Luke but herself. "I have this feeling more and more that there's a kind of evil force inside him."

"How do you mean?"

"It's difficult to explain. It's like a pressure I sense with him, a force that wants to control everyone else's space on his terms and if he can't control will destroy."

"Like something controlling him, you mean?"

"In a way, yes. It's almost as if he was possessed. I know it sounds ridiculous."

"Not ridiculous – no."

"But you don't believe me?"

"I don't believe in absolutes of good and evil – no. But I think people can be motivated by extremes of self interest, self preservation and perhaps fear so as to seem evil."

"You think there's always a rational reason then?"

"I think there's usually a biological or survival mechanism at work, yes. I don't believe in the paranormal or an outside force driving one if that's what you mean."

"You don't believe in a god then?"

"It depends what you mean by god. If you mean a creative dynamic force driving the universe then yes, but a personal god interested in me and my actions and guiding them – no. I think that's just invention, wishful thinking. We've got ultimately to take responsibility for our actions, not shift the burden on some mythical being when we're down."

Luke paused, amazed at the turn the conversation had taken. Evil wasn't a subject he'd ever really talked about in depth yet here he was holding forth, pontificating when all he wanted was her beauty, to take her in his arms.

"Don't you think though that there are some things that humans can't put right?"

"One can't stop a meteor perhaps falling from the sky or an earthquake destroying houses but in the human sphere itself one should be able and should certainly always try to put things right."

"Always?" she challenged. "What about murder – if someone's already slipped through the net?"

Luke felt himself struggling now in deeper water. He knew where he stood on most issues with scientific rationalism as his framework and the green perspective as his moral base. But murder, putting right an injustice, was a subject he felt beyond his grasp. Yet clearly she needed to talk and he wanted to help her if he could. "I don't know but I think it's important to find out the truth if one can and try to put things right."

"But supposing one can't find the truth to prove it legally I mean. Should one take the law into one's own hands?"

"I don't know. I've never thought about it. It depends I suppose on how important it is to you or to someone you care about." Uneasily Luke tried to grasp at some hope and practicality. "You mustn't give up you know. Just because things haven't gone too well for you. It doesn't mean they won't change. I haven't forgotten the key to the cellar. It's just that it's more difficult now to get inside."

"What about the outside door?"

"It's locked from inside. I think there's only one key and the blasted dog keeps yapping around every time I go to investigate. But don't worry. I know it's important to you and sooner or later I'll catch the old bag when she'd been drinking. It'll be easy then."

"It's urgent, Luke. You do realise that, don't you? If you feel you can't do it then I'd better try myself." Hannah shuddered inwardly as she visualised Hugo pawing his way through the contents of the trunk, then moving the trunk and finding the loosened stone, then the will wedged beneath it. She'd no doubt what he'd do with it, could see him, the smile of malice and satisfaction as he watched it slowly burn, watched her hopes of Yadrahna and its past burn away. And inevitably he would find it, given time, as he searched his way slowly, surely, in the cold mechanical way he had through the contents of the house.

"No, don't do that." Luke felt suddenly alarmed. "It's not safe for you. I'll get the key as soon as I can. And when you go to Mrs Mason, I think I should come with you."

"Why? You can't think I'm in danger there too?"

"Not obvious danger perhaps but why don't you ring Mrs Mason now and sort when you're going then I'll know." Luke smiled trying to reassure. "You don't have to worry. I'll keep guard here while you're gone."

"O.K. then." Why not, she thought. Why not show she could trust him? Apart from Ashford and Sally and Richard in their ways, he was probably the only person now she could trust in relation to Yadrahna and the will and waving back to him she made her way up the lane to the now familiar phone box by the bus stop.

There was no answer for a long time from the number Luke had given her then to her relief eventually the voice of Emma's brother, quietly calm as Emma's, telling her that Emma was out at that moment cleaning but she'd be there the next day in the afternoon for tea if Hannah would like to call then around 4.

The thought of seeing Emma again lifted Hannah's spirits. If anyone had understood her father, it was Emma and Emma would know what had happened in the early stages of his illness. She might even be able to help her with significant information as a witness.

In a more optimistic frame of mind, Hannah made her way back down the lane from the phone box to the cottage. It wasn't until she'd almost reached the wicker gate that she was aware of voices, to her surprise, coming from the garden. Who could it be? She hadn't passed anyone in the lane, either coming or going and no one had entered the lane that she'd seen from the phone box. She paused a moment and listened. She could hear Luke's voice slightly on edge, she thought, subdued as if reluctantly answering questions, then a stronger male

voice overriding him, demanding, "Oh come now. You must know her plans. One doesn't hang around as you are without knowing." With dread in her heart then she recognised the hard, impatient voice again of Jamieson. What was he doing back again and how had he got there without her seeing him in the lane? Where had he been hiding and how much had he heard of her conversation with Luke about the cellar? How had he known she'd leave for the phone – unless – No, Luke surely couldn't, wouldn't want to be in league with him. He'd rescued her after all from Jamieson and yet something about the way he'd persuaded her to go to the phone, something about the way he and Jamieson were standing now as if in conspiracy in front of the dilapidated porch threw up in front of her a spectre now of doubt.

Angrily, feeling betrayed, she pushed open the wicker gate, drawing attention to herself and strode up to the two men.

"Is there something you wanted?" She focused her eyes on Jamieson.

He was shorter than she'd imagined from his pursuit of her in the drive, of a leaner build than Hugo but his eyes and features had a sharpness, a determination that would probe, she sensed, till he got his way and she felt at once wary of him.

"Yes, there is as a matter of fact. Jamieson's the name." He extended his hand, changing his stance with all the speed of an accomplished actor to one of affability and charm. "Howard Jamieson. I've come in fact as I was explaining to your friend here to have a look over the property with a view, let's say, possibly to buying."

"I see. Well, I afraid it's not my function to show people round. You'll have to ask Mrs Hobbs the caretaker about that. I'm sure you could make an appointment with her."

"Oh I don't think there will be any need for that." With a smile of assurance, Jamieson drew from the top pocket of his jacket a folded letter which he held out tantalisingly in front of Hannah, adding, "You see I have a letter from the late Mrs Webb's niece saying I can look over the property at my convenience. My calling on you is by way of courtesy you understand."

"Let me see." Hannah grasped the letter from his hand. It was a brief typewritten letter which stated briefly: "Mr Howard Jamieson of Jamieson and Co, auctioneers and Estate Agents, has my permission to look round Bramble Cottage at any time convenient to him between the hours of 9 a.m. and 6 p.m.." There was a carefully laboured signature at the end – too laboured Hannah thought. Almost certainly it was forged. But to reject it, if it wasn't forged, could be to risk annoying Mrs Webb's niece with the possible consequence of having her tenancy terminated and she didn't want to risk that. She decided to cover herself and let him look over the cottage but watch him carefully as he did so. Her father's letters, though hidden, were still vulnerable to theft. She would take them all with her she decided to Ashford that afternoon.

"All right then. I'll show you round but I haven't much time."

"I shan't take longer," Jamieson forced one of his ingratiating smiles," than is necessary, Miss – Miss Delaney, I believe, isn't it?"

They were already in the darkened hall as he spoke her name and for a moment in her tiredness she almost accepted it and gave herself away, forgetting her assumed name. Then the sharp probing in his voice and eyes warned her and with a jolt she realised he was going to trick her if he could, that she had to be more on her guard. Uncertain, she glanced back at Luke still in the garden and corrected, "Robinson's my name, not Delaney."

"Really? You surprise me. You're just like a Miss Delaney who used to live at Yadrahna. You know it – the house above Rassler's Wood on the hill?"

"I'm afraid not, Mr Jamieson."

She could feel his lean face with it sharp features closer to her now, bending over her, peering at her in the subdued light, the smell of garlic and stale onion on his breath, the smell of perspiration mingling. She felt she wanted to vomit, only with effort asserted, "My name's Robinson, Mr Jamieson. Now if you want to see the house..."

Carefully she positioned herself behind him as he paced the bedroom. He wasn't really interested in the building as it stood. She could see that straightaway. His shifting restless eyes were drawn outside to the space and dimensions more of the garden, though he was interested too, she noted, in her possessions, her case under the bed and the window frame. To her dismay, suddenly, he started to probe and prod at the window frame, dislodging as he did so, the latch from its fixture. The main screw then came loose and dropped down into the nettles in the garden below.

"Heh, hold on." It was a deliberate act, she didn't doubt, to make her vulnerable. "You weren't given permission to break the house up."

"The house is already broken, Miss Delaney. It's riddled with wood rot and wood worm in case you hadn't noticed." Unconcerned, he turned to her with a deprecating smile. "Oh dear I should have said Miss Robinson, shouldn't I but...."

"But what?" She had a sense of his playing with her like a cat with a mouse, not from need but from instinct, the sheer pleasure of playing.

"You do look like Miss Delaney, you know. Tell me, if it's not a rude question, have you by any chance been in Hong Kong this last year?"

"Where I've been, Mr Jamieson, is no business of yours."

"Perhaps you could tell me your age then."

"I've no intention , Mr Jamieson, of telling you anything about my private life at all." The nerve of him. She felt she wanted to push him with the screw he'd dislodged out of the window.

"A pity. I'm sure it would be interesting." His eyes lingered with a deliberately brazen gleam over her breasts. "You have a certain attractiveness, you know. Perhaps we could have an evening out or in, if you wish."

How much was he mocking her, Hannah wondered, how much trying to make use of her for his own ends and Hugo's. She felt tempted to play long with him, to see how much she could find out herself but his affectation, the very smell of him, his association above all with Hugo, all repulsed her and she knew she could never convincingly pretend with him.

"I don't wish and I don't have any free time, Mr Jamieson. Now please go."

To her relief, he seemed suddenly anxious himself to get away and a few minutes later took his departure but when he'd gone, she felt concerned again about the window, the vulnerability of the cottage now without the latch.

"Don't worry. I'll bring my tool box tomorrow." Luke tried to reassure her as they searched in vain in the nettles beneath the bedroom window for the missing screw. But he was conscious of doubt in her eyes now, that she didn't fully trust him. Surely, he thought, she couldn't think he had anything to do with Jamieson and his visit. It was absurd, a mere coincidence. Or was it? Something was clearly going on, something probing, planned, beneath the game of buying the cottage but what? Scare tactics or something more sinister? Jamieson had clearly recognised her but what else did he know? What did he have to fear from her? More importantly, what did she have to fear from him? How safe in fact was she at the cottage even if the latch was mended?

Luke looked at his watch at length, conscious of the time passing, of the need to be at the pub for his job – a job he couldn't afford to lose.

"I'm afraid I'll have to go." Luke hesitated, trying to catch her eye as she continued determinedly searching the clump of nettles. "Would you like me to cycle over with you tomorrow to find Mrs Mason?"

She looked up briefly at him, still uncertain. "If you've got the time but there's no need if you're busy."

"I'm not that busy. I'll try and be here by two."

"And if you're not?"

"Then I suggest you follow the main road to Barton and I'll catch up with you." He went over to his bike and

took map out of his saddlebag, pointing out to her a route he thought was safe.

"Take care, won't you?"

"I'm not a child, you know."

"I'm not suggesting you are. It's more what other people will do."

Nothing seemed to have gone as he'd hoped or wanted but at least, he reflected, he was seeing her the next day and could perhaps be of help to her. He folded the map and put it back in his saddlebag, then, wheeling his bike round to face the lane, he said goodbye.

She was still standing amid the nettles, her arms blistered with patches of red from the stinging, her face flushed from searching, her eyes still sceptical of him. Yet even more beautiful she seemed to him and, despite her doubt, his own doubt, he knew he wouldn't be able to resist coming back again and that he loved her.

Chapter 20

As soon as Luke had gone, Hannah felt uneasy about the way she'd treated him since Jamieson's visit. Her first impression of him with Jamieson now seemed increasingly misguided. It was highly unlikely, in fact, the more she thought about it, that Luke would want to associate with someone like Jamieson for money. Why then had she been so ready to misjudge him? Was she getting the whole thing out of proportion as Richard had indicated?

She was about to give up her search for the screw when suddenly she found it in a rusty piece of piping at the back of the clump of nettles below the bedroom window. She wished Luke was still around so she could show him. How patient he'd been helping her with the searching. He deserved more than suspicion. And she was grateful to him for listening to her, that she'd been able to talk to him about her fears of Hugo and evil in a way that had helped, that made her feel she wanted to go on talking to him.

Was it wise though to trust him more than necessary with her plans? Was it wise to trust anyone? Was there anyone she could trust ultimately but herself? So much could go wrong by chance with Luke trying to get the key to the cellar. Though Luke himself might not intentionally reveal her objective to either Hugo or Olga Slade, they

could well deduce it if he was caught trying to get hold of the key.

How else though could she get the key? She'd never get back now into the house, disguised or undisguised, with their present precautions and watchfulness. No, she would have to trust Luke, in this at least, wholly. But the more she trusted, the more the risk seemed to grow – the risk not only of losing Yadrahna as her right and home but the risk that Yadrahna itself could be destroyed with Hugo's plans and everything with it that she loved from the past and its associations with her father.

If only, she yearned, putting the screw on the kitchen table, if only it were all straightforward and simple, the result of effort and persistence, like finding the screw. If only her father were here now to help her. He would know whom to trust and to what level, would know from his experience and knowledge of Hugo how to unravel without blundering the web Hugo had spun. If only she could talk to him, reach through to him, be with him even momentarily, learn from his wisdom what her next move should be.

But he wasn't with her nor would he ever be now.

As she went upstairs to change, the inevitability struck her afresh and everything seemed grey and bleak again, pointless. Even the waving grass in the garden, which had attracted her to the cottage, had a dark blighted look about it now, as if it had been drawn down, like Persephone into an underworld below. What was the point of it all – the point of trying? Hugo would win in the end because he'd set his mind to it, had planned it in advance with care.

She lay back on the bed, instead of changing, feeling drained, exhausted, that she hadn't the energy to make the journey to Oxford. She closed her eyes, slept a while, then awoke, thinking of Luke and Luke's words then came back to her. "You mustn't give up, you know, just because things haven't gone too well. It doesn't mean they won't change." Could they change, she wondered, even now. And even if they didn't, didn't she owe it to her father to press on and at least try?

Tired still, she forced herself off the bed and changed into a subdued beige cotton skirt and blouse and brushed back her hair. She paused a moment by the window and wedged some paper in the hinge to keep it closed, then, digging up her father's letters from their hiding place beneath the nettles in the garden, she left the cottage, locking the door behind her and went up the lane to the bus stop.

As she passed Annie Hobb's cottage, Annie Hobbs came down to greet her at the end of her garden by the lane.

"I was hoping to see you, my dear. Your friend Sally rang a few minutes ago , asking if you'd ring her this morning."

"Did she say what it was about?"

"No, only that it was important that you rang this morning."

What could be the urgency, Hannah wondered. She'd made no arrangement with either Sally or Richard. With a twinge she realised she hadn't even thought of Richard since he'd left the cottage when she'd gone to Laura's. Could it be that Sally was planning to bring him over

again? She hoped not. She didn't want to have to explain any more or justify, be what they wanted, what she didn't want to be.

"I also wanted to tell you, my dear," Annie Hobbs continued, "that I've had a word with the vicar about the Mrs Vince you were interested in. He suggested you called to see him sometime."

"Did he? Oh right. I'll do that then."

"Is something the matter, my dear? You don't look very well, if I may say so."

"I'm just a bit tired, that's all."

"A young person like you shouldn't be tired." Hannah was aware of Annie Hobbs peering at her with concern, her head to one side, as if listening to a heartbeat under the soil. "Has something upset you?"

Hannah wondered for a moment whether to tell Annie Hobbs about Jamieson and the damage to the window but decided against it. What could Annie Hobbs do about Jamieson anyway? Jamieson was the kind of person who would always find a way with his money and power on the council to slip through an old woman's attempts at restriction. No, if Luke could fix the window, she'd find a way of dealing with Jamieson herself.

"No, I'm fine, thanks." She forced a smile and thanking Annie Hobbs for her concern pressed on to the bus stop.

The bus was already approaching and there was no time to ring Sally. On reaching Oxford, the only telephone kiosk she could find before her appointment was occupied.

As she waited in the now familiar high ceilinged waiting room to see Ashford, Hannah's thoughts went back to Jamieson. She'd no doubt that he recognised her

as Hugo's sister, no doubt he'd enter the cottage when she wasn't there to sift through her belongings. What ultimately though had been his intention in trying to intimidate? Was he just warning her away or something more and how was she going to stop him visiting again on the pretext of wanting to buy the cottage? Did he in fact intend to buy Brambles?

The thought horrified her – the thought of Brambles modernised under Jamieson's control into conventional weekend cottage – its spirit gone, without trace or memory of Sarah Webb. But how could she stop it happening short of buying Brambles herself – a prospect virtually out of the question in her present financial predicament?

Or was it? It was possible she could get a loan, even ask Aunt Eileen to help her. The basic price of the cottage as it stood, between £25,000 and £30,000, as Annie Hobbs had told her, was not expensive in modern terms. The real expense lay in its modernising, in the renovation and rebuilding, in" putting it right". Would she have "to put it right" though? Did it matter? It hadn't mattered to Sarah Webb. She'd lived there for years, virtually all of her life without modern heating or lighting, unperturbed that she'd had no means of fast communication. She'd lived moreover a long and healthy life – the life of an individual not a cipher.

One could in fact live at Brambles without changing anything as long as one had water. Other people managed and with far less and survived on it – women and children in remote areas of India and China and throughout the world, down the centuries, surviving on what the earth yielded without pressure and managing. Why should she not manage on what was in essence much more?

The idea excited her, made her feel a tenuous link again with the people who'd lived in the past, closer than she had to the soil. Then her thoughts came back again to the reason why she was waiting and she knew she couldn't afford yet to be diverted, that the first claim on her still was Yadrahna while there was still a chance of succeeding.

"I'm afraid Mr Ashford's been delayed in court." The receptionist came over to her beaming her well–trained smile. "He's just sent a message with his apologies that he'll be another half an hour."

Hannah decided to use the time to phone Sally and found a phone free this time down a quieter side road nearby and phoned Sally's number.

After a long wait, she heard to her surprise not Sally's but Richard's voice, carefully detached, announcing Sally's number. She couldn't think for a moment what to say. Had he moved in? Was he living with Sally or merely visiting? What inference, if any, could she draw? As he repeated the number, afraid that he would put the phone down, she blurted, "Hello, it's Hannah here. Sally left a message for me to ring."

"Oh right. Well, I'm afraid Sally's not here at present. She's gone shopping."

She could hear embarrassment in his voice now and decided to be direct.

"You're not staying at the flat then?"

"Well, no, not at present. There's been a mix up. The tenant's still there till tomorrow evening. I'm going back then."

"And Sally's meanwhile putting you up?"

"That's right yes. She's kindly helped out."

"Good. I'm sure she'll look after you." She hadn't meant to sound catty. She didn't feel jealous or put out. She didn't mind in fact what they did. She didn't feel she had any claim on Richard any more but her voice she could hear coming back to as aggrieved.

"It's not as you think, Hannah. I still want you to come to the flat with me. The plan is that we'll come over tomorrow to collect you."

"I'm seeing Emma tomorrow, Richard."

"Emma?"

"Dad's housekeeper. She's probably got information I need."

"You've decided to persist then?"

"I'm not going to give up now, Richard."

"Perhaps not but there is my view to consider."

"Which is?"

"I'm not prepared to wait around for ever. I think you should leave it all now to the solicitor and come back with me to the flat so that we can sort out our future."

"And leave things at a crucial stage?"

"They'll always be crucial in your mind, Hannah, whatever the stage because you can no longer detach yourself."

"Would you be able to detach yourself if they directly concerned you?"

"I think I would, yes, but, if I couldn't, I hope I'd have the sense to leave it to the professionals who understand the implications."

"Meaning I don't?"

"I don't believe you have the knowledge or experience in these matters, Hannah. It's unlikely, therefore, you'll get anywhere."

"Why do you always talk to me as a child, Richard?"

"I don't think I do. But if I do, it's probably because you act like one at times. Anyway I don't feel this is getting us anywhere. What I propose is that Sally and I come over tomorrow after you've seen Emma with the intention of taking you back to the flat. If you decide not to come, that's up to you. But I hope you'll think about it and the implications. We had something good going for us, Hannah, and it shouldn't be lightly thrown away just to prove something nebulous."

"Nebulous?" It seemed a strange word to Hannah to use, strangely inappropriate. Before she could protest, however, the phone went dead and she realised she'd run out of money for it and time. She looked at her watch and quickly made her way back to her appointment.

Ashford was waiting for her ensconced behind his mahogany desk, wearing the same grey suit and grey tie as before.

"Let's see now." He glanced over the neat, methodical notes he'd taken on her last visit, laid out ready. "You were going to see the doctor, weren't you, Miss Delaney, and the two witnesses?

"That's right, yes."

"Have you managed to do that?"

"I've seen them but they weren't exactly helpful." Hannah explained as briefly as she could how the doctor hadn't seen her father on the day the will was signed and couldn't vouch for testamentary incapacity. "He did, however," she added," say that my father had been drinking a lot which was very unusual for him and it's my belief he was given the drink against his will. The doctor also told

me that he asked my brother to let me know when my father was dying but my brother deliberately didn't tell me. I don't know if this could be used but I feel it was all part of his plan to keep a hold on my father."

"It could help certainly if there was more evidence to back it up," Ashford ventured with caution. "But on its own, I'm afraid, it's not sufficient. What did the witnesses say?"

"Sadie Shaw," Hannah replied, "claimed to have a poor memory and Olga Slade didn't want to remember at all."

"I'm afraid this is often the case with witnesses. They don't want to be involved or let's say are frightened to be involved and avoid the issue by not remembering. It may be worth going back to them. They might for some reason later wish to remember."

"Might they?" Hannah felt sceptical. She couldn't see Olga Slade ever co–operating and Sadie Shaw would probably feign, if not have, an actual heart attack. She showed Ashford her father's letters that Luke had saved from the bonfire.

Ashford read through the first letter of 10th May carefully noting her father's words, "I signed a document the other day which I am not happy about. I didn't feel well and myself at the time and I want to put it right." It indicated, he reflected, certainly the appropriate state of mind of someone unwilling, if it could be proved to be her father's handwriting, but the document referred to didn't specify the will. The defence would never let them get away with that.

He read the letter dated 26th May. "Dear Hannah, I wonder if you have received my last letter. I need urgently

to see you and speak with you. Things are not right here. I feel entrapped and enclosed. I go into hospital on 6th June. Please come soon.". Again, Ashford reflected, it conveyed the sense of pressure but was it specific enough? It was the usual story of indicators but none clinching, of the sense one always had of the unscrupulous, long careful manipulation behind the scenes, covering its tracks, not able to be proved. But he didn't want to discourage her hope and effort. She was genuine, truthful. He knew that, could tell from the concern in her large deep brown eyes, had known from the moment she'd first entered his office, and he wanted to help her if he could.

"What do you think?" She was looking at him anxiously now. "Do you think they're sufficient as evidence of pressure?"

"They're evidence certainly and a help in building up the picture but I don't think," reluctantly he added, "that they're sufficient on their own – not to guarantee success in court. They're not specific enough, Miss Delaney, about the will itself."

"I see." She felt disappointed, cast down again. The letter had expressed so clearly, it seemed to her, her father's doubt. What could she possibly get that was clearer?

"It's difficult for you to accept, I know, but the onus is on us to prove the pressure and malpractice and the proof has to be of sufficient weight that there can be no doubt that it was the will that was referred to and that it was not according to your father's wishes. You see what we are up against."

"There is though the other will hinted at," Hannah asserted, clutching at hope again. She told him then about her exploration of the cupboard in her father's bedroom,

287

about the Tennyson poem, her deciphering and the deduction from her father's message. It all sounded far–fetched, James Bondish and unreal to her in the telling and she wondered whether he believed her. One couldn't tell what he was thinking, believing. He would maintain, she suspected, whatever she told him, the same unruffled calm but there was more empathy she sensed now in the greyness of his eyes.

"I'm pretty sure," she tried to assure him, "I know where it's hidden. It's just a problem of access and the opportunity to get hold of it."

"If such a will exists, Miss Delaney, and I'm not saying it doesn't, then of course it would greatly contribute to the potential success of your case, especially if it post dates the present will and if the signature can be satisfactorily proved to have been your father's."

"I'll try and get hold of it as soon as I can." Luke willing, she thought, and it struck her suddenly how much she needed Luke now, not only to talk to but for the actual success of her case.

"There's another point, Miss Delaney." Ashford consulted his notes again. "The housekeeper you mentioned the last time you were here. Have you managed to see her yet?"

"No, I've only just got her address but I'm going tomorrow."

"And you think Mrs Mason could have relevant useful information?"

"I think she could have, yes."

"In that case, may I suggest you ask her if she would be willing to testify in court. It's no use, I'm sure you

understand, if witnesses back away when it comes to court. One has to be sure that they are there testifying."

"I'll see what I can do, if she's willing, that is." Hannah wondered whether she should mention Laura's suspicions about her mother's death. But what had she to go on? It was all supposition, nothing concrete at all. The proof non–existent, far less even than for the will. No, she would have to dig deeper herself first. Ashford was unlikely to be interested as things stood. Could she afford anyway to seek his services for another case?

"Good." Ashford permitted himself a brief smile. "Well, I think that's all we can do for the moment. You've made a good start, Miss Delaney with your father's letters. They're relevant but from my past experience of the attitudes of the court, they're not sufficient, as I've said, to guarantee success. However, you are entitled as a child to make a claim and could, under the Inheritance Act of 1975, try to negotiate with your brother for a better deal."

"I don't think he would negotiate."

"Think about it. It's an option, a last resort. There's no immediate hurry. One has the option until 6 months after probate is granted. Meanwhile I think you should go ahead on the lines indicated. You are obviously a person who wants to explore all channels."

"You think there's still hope then?"

"There's certainly hope, Miss Delaney, but at the same time we must be realistic about your chances at this stage. You understand that I believe."

"Yes, I can see that." Hannah found it still difficult to accept the limitations of her father's letters as evidence. At the same time she knew that Ashford was being honest

with her and direct, that he wouldn't mislead her for temporary gain and she respected him for it. She knew where she stood with him. How though was she ever going to get back into Yadrahna to the cellar to recover the other will, which seemed the only way forward now?

"Right." Ashford tidied together his notes. "I suggest you come back in two weeks, Miss Delaney. Meanwhile see Mrs Mason and think about seeing the two witnesses again. Regarding the other will referred to, by all means try to obtain it if you can, if it exists, but I must advise you to proceed with caution for your own safety."

Did it exist, Ashford wondered as he shook hands with Hannah and said goodbye, or was it, as so often happened from a sense of desperation, a figment of imagination, wishful thinking? He wasn't sure. He wasn't sure about Hannah Delaney's capacity to imagine nor indeed about Hannah Delaney herself. He sensed a deep attachment in her to her father and to the house Yadrahna, yet no grasping for the wealth that went with it. She didn't seem motivated by money at all which was refreshing, unusual. She was an unusual person, he thought – a person who could follow a number of different paths, as if she was at a crossroads in her life, still undecided. And her large deep brown eyes – she was certainly a beauty – though not in an obvious way.

As Hannah close the door behind her, Ashford sighed, wishing he was young again and free.

Chapter 21

It rained that night in heavy showers that lashed against the decaying framework of the bedroom window of the cottage. Hannah awoke intermittently hearing an ominous dripping inside the bedroom but felt reluctant to get up and shine her torch for fear of what she'd find.

In the morning she discovered two large pools of water on the floor where the roof had leaked by the north window of the bedroom but the rain had now ceased and the window, to her relief, held firm where she'd wedged it with paper. The damp air though had a hint of chill in it now. Rivulets of water were running still down the wall, like ancient waterways, following the course of past stains and neglect and she knew she would have to do something about the leaks if she was to survive reasonably the winter in the cottage.

Forcing herself to get up, she wiped down the damp wall and mopped up the pools of water, putting out a bucket in case of further rain. She tried to think what else she should do. What did one do with a leaking roof? She could call in a builder but would Mrs Webb's niece pay? She suspected not, that it was a matter of "making do" till the house was sold.

Her thoughts came back again to the idea of buying "Brambles". It seemed mad with all the exposure and no

cash to put it right. She decided to write to Aunt Eileen all the same about a loan to test the water.

It was only a short note, concentrating on the space, the potential, the naturalism of Brambles. She didn't mention the leaks and rotting window frame. Aunt Eileen would, after all, she reasoned, see for herself, if or when she came. She hoped it would be when rather than if but there was no telling with Aunt Eileen what her reaction would be. All that seemed certain was that it would be unwise to discourage her by the mention of dull practical things like leaks and wood rot.

The morning seemed to hang suspended after she'd written the letter and she decided on impulse to take some flowers to her father's grave and try and decide on a headstone for him. She picked some achillea and solidago and mixing them with lavender, rosemary and thyme, put them in one of the jars Annie Hobbs had provided and walked up to the churchyard.

The wreaths left over her father's grave had now withered and weeds were already pushing up through the mound of earth below. The whole grave looked neglected, forgotten and she felt a pang of guilt and regret that she'd not been before to look after it. And so much it needed a headstone. As she moved the withered wreaths to the compost heap, she stopped and looked more carefully at the headstones of the graves nearby, wondering about the wording for her father.

She noticed in a line of graves behind her father's, a weathered headstone with ivy growing over it, that she hadn't registered before with the name John Liddell over it. More carefully then she read the inscription:

IN MEMORY OF A BELOVED SON JOHN LIDDELL 26 YEARS OF AGE TRAGICALLY DROWNED 1912 . MAY YOU REST IN PEACE.

It was the same year as the date on the letters she'd found but was it the same John Liddell who'd written the letters expressing his love for her namesake, Hannah?

The only person likely to know, she reflected, was Rev James. She didn't really want Rev James knowing as yet that she was living in Wynton but as she turned back to her father's grave, the compulsion rose in her again. She had to find out. She had to know about John Liddell and, if she could, what had happened to Hannah.

As she stood outside the vicarage door, she had the strange sensation of the other Hannah urging her on, wanting a peace in some way that she hadn't so far gained.

"Miss Delaney. How nice to see you." Rev James extended his hand, his eyes smiling at her with the same empathy she'd sensed at the funeral. He reminded her again of the Indian healer she'd met on the plane. "Is this a brief visit or have you come back to stay in Wynton?"

"It's neither really. I just wanted to ask you something about one of the graves."

"By all means if I can help." How pale she looked, Rev James thought, and tense as if something was troubling her, complicating the pain of grief.

"Are you sure I'm not interrupting anything?" Hannah was conscious now of a mass of paper on his desk, at the same time a pressure in her head, a fear that the information she wanted would elude her and Rev James be called away before she had it. Without waiting for him to reply, she

said," It's the grave of John Liddell, behind my father's – the one with ivy over it. Can you tell me, did this John Liddell ever live at Yadrahna?"

"He did, indeed, Miss Delaney. He was the eldest son of the second owner of the house. Yadrahna, or Stoneleigh as it was called then, was his home certainly until he was sent away."

"Sent away?" Hannah echoed, the words chilling her. "Why was he sent away?"

"It's an involved story, Miss Delaney. Please, won't you sit down?" She looked very stressed, he thought, almost ill. Her father's death was it or something more? She'd been very close to her father. He'd known that since he'd known Thomas Delaney, that theirs had been a special father and daughter bond – a bond which broken she'd find it hard now to accept. It was strange to him that she should be worrying about a death that had nothing to do with her in the past. Or had it? The echoes, the vibrations from the past couldn't always be predicted.

When she was seated, he went on," As I'm sure you know, Miss Delaney, the conventions of the time were that people married into the same class."

"John Liddell's father had someone in mind for him you mean?"

"Exactly so – a certain Margaret Hargreaves from a well known local family. She was an ideal person by all accounts but John Liddell refused to marry her because he had fallen in love with someone else, one of his father's employees, a maid who worked in the kitchen. It might have been a simple liaison to terminate but the maid, to

the concern of the Liddell family, became pregnant it was claimed by John and John insisted on marrying her."

"Is that why he was sent away?"

"Exactly so. The maid was given some help in having the baby – a little girl who was given for adoption to a family in the village. John was sent off to Scotland to some relatives in the hope that working on their estate would cool his ardour."

"And did it?"

"No, he still refused to marry Margaret Hargreaves, still claimed he loved the maid. Tragically then while he was in Scotland, he was drowned, as the headstone tells us, while out boating on one of the lochs there. A freak storm apparently – his boat overturned and he couldn't swim. Terrible it must have been for the family as if they'd sent him to his death."

"And also for the maid, Hannah, was it not?"

"Hannah, that's it – I was trying to think of her name. Hannah Brown it was. You know about her then, Miss Delaney?"

"I know she had a daughter who was adopted by a family called Vince. But I don't know what happened to her after the baby was born."

"I'm afraid I can't help you there, Miss Delaney. According to one of the servants who gave an account to the next owners of the house, Hannah went back to work at Yadrahna for a few days while the family were arranging other employment for her. It was during that time, so I understand, that the news came through, that John Liddell had drowned. Hannah overheard the news, according to the servant, on the evening before she was due to go to her new employer. No one knows exactly

what happened but in the morning when she was due to be collected to go to the station, she'd disappeared."

"Had she taken her things with her – all her belongings?"

"No, that was the strange thing. Her belongings were all packed ready to go in her attic room but she herself wasn't there."

"Surely a search was made?"

"No doubt but the family were all immersed in their grief and I dare say the search wasn't as thorough as it could have been. What happened, I'm afraid, Miss Delaney, remains a mystery and I doubt we'll ever know now."

Rev James sighed for he would have liked to have known. The mysteries of the past fascinated him especially when there were sacrifices made and the boundaries crossed between the classes and had not John Liddell been unusual in putting love before money – a love that within its confines had lasted?

"No, perhaps, not," reluctantly Hannah agreed. "Thank you all the same for telling me and giving up your time."

"A pleasure, Miss Delaney. If there's anything more I can fill in for you please don't hesitate to let me know or if I can help you with the headstone."

"Thank you."

Hannah lingered after she'd left the vicarage a while longer in the graveyard, thinking with a mixture of admiration and sadness of Hannah and John Liddell, then returned to the cottage.

Restless, she felt she ought to do some reading for her impending course. All the books she'd bought on

management and personnel problems were waiting still unread under the bed. But on opening the first page of the main core course book she was to follow she found she couldn't concentrate, that her thoughts kept coming back to Luke and the next main problem confronting her of re–entering Yadrahna and getting hold of the hidden will. Could Luke really help her? Did he want to? Was it wise to use Luke in this way, to depend on him? Could she in fact trust him?

She felt she wanted to now, that he was a person she could trust; at the same time a thread of doubt still lingering that he was not entirely what he seemed, that she must remain on guard.

She wondered whether he would turn up for the ride over to Emma. She hoped he would and for the rest of the morning tried to keep herself physically occupied cleaning the cottage and preparing sandwiches for the ride. Then dressing herself in jeans and a T-shirt, she wheeled her bike out into the garden. It struck her then how much work Luke had put into renovating and cleaning it. The chrome on the wheels and mudguard shone like new with all the rust removed; the handlebars were now straightened and the saddle firm with all the nuts tightened. Both the tyres then she noticed had been replaced – not just one as she'd thought. She felt she wanted to thank him then and there, to tell him she realised all the work involved. To her disappointment at two o'clock there was no sign of him. 2.15, 2.30, still he had not arrived. He was probably only delayed at work, she knew that, knew that if he was late, the arrangement was that she should go ahead. Emma after all would be

expecting her. She didn't want to let Emma down. More than ever now she wanted to see Emma.

She felt uneasy, all the same, setting out alone, as if Luke was meant to be with her.

The road was still damp with muddy puddles to the side which splashed up over her jeans as cars passed by. But the sun had come out now, lightening the green of the hedgerows and there was a freshness in the air that made her feel a new energy and hope. Following Luke's instructions, she took the main road out of Wynton, then a cross–country route of minor roads and lanes.

It was quieter on the minor roads and Hannah found herself enjoying the rhythm of cycling again, the breeze brushing her cheeks and lifting her hair, a closeness again to the country of her childhood. Only a few cars passed her now, cautious cars mainly of people who lived in the area and knew its hidden turnings.

Then gradually she became aware of a grey BMW keeping the same steady distance of 30 feet behind her, not attempting to overtake.

So far the roads had been level but ahead of her was a hill. Half way up the hill, she got off to walk. To her concern, the grey BMW, instead of passing, continued to crawl behind her, keeping the same distance. She paused then and looked back to see if she could discern the driver and number plate. She couldn't make out the number plate at all. All the letters and numbers were blurred by splashes of a brown substance like mud, but would mud, she speculated, stick so convincingly to each letter. The windscreen appeared to be tinted and she couldn't see the driver clearly, only that he was wearing dark glasses and

had thick dark hair and a lean face. She didn't recognise him from anyone she knew or had seen in the area.

Suddenly her enjoyment of the ride ceased and she felt vulnerable again and alone. She wondered whether to turn back down the hill to try to shake him off but all too easily she knew he could do a quick turn even in the lane and follow and she'd be even further then from someone she knew. No, best it seemed to press on to Emma. She was over half way there now and from the map she remembered that there was a long straight stretch after the hill when she could gather speed.

Trying to keep calm, she pressed on walking to the top of the hill. Then praying that he would leave her alone now, sense her intent on the straight stretch of road, she mounted the saddle and pedalled for all she was worth, keeping as close as she could to the hedge.

Half way along, she heard then behind the engine of the BMW revving, drawing closer. She glanced back, hoping it was the sign at last it would overtake. But instead of drawing out into the middle of the road, to her horror, she saw the BMW driving straight at her.

Frantically, in an instinct to save herself, she twisted the handlebar of her bike towards the hedge. For a moment as the bike jolted off the road onto the long grass, she thought she'd made it.

Then the whole bike shuddered as the near side headlight and wheel arch of the BMW caught her back wheel. With a clash of metal and shatter of glass behind her, she fell into the hedge with the bike on top of her.

A spike of hawthorn jabbed into her neck and she could feel her hair tangled in its jagged branches, a pain

in her left foot where the pedal jammed against her. She felt breathless, shocked, unable to think clearly, make a move.

The BMW had stopped a few feet up the road from her. In apprehension, she watched as the man with dark glasses got out and came round to inspect the near side chassis where a dent and scratch mark were evident now on the wheel arch. Despite the warmth, he was dressed in a long black woollen coat and was carefully avoiding, she noticed, his face being seen. There was something sinister about the way he padded silently all in black round the chassis avoiding looking at her, like a panther indirectly stalking its prey, his thick black hair too thick, too black she noticed now in the sunlight. Who was he? What should she do if he came over to her? It hadn't been an accident she was sure but what had he intended exactly? What was he intending now?

She felt a knot of fear again in her stomach, a desperate urge to get away. As she pushed her bicycle up from her, disentangling her hair, quickly then he got back into the car. There was a long tense silence, as she stood up, aware of him from inside, watching assessing her from behind the tinted glass window.

Then as a Volkswagen came in sight in the opposite direction he started up the engine. The elderly man in the Volkswagen was not particularly observing the details around him and failed to stop or note her situation but it was enough that he'd appeared and, as he passed, the BMW sped off down the road and disappeared from view.

Hannah's first reaction was of enormous relief. Apart from scratches on her neck and a graze and bruising on

her foot, she'd had, she realised, a fortunate escape. Even the bicycle was not a total write off. The back wheel was buckled where he BMW had hit it and there was a slash mark in the tyre but the rest of the bicycle was in reasonable shape from the impact, still shining from Luke's efforts. She wouldn't be able to ride it but she could still push it to Emma's by lifting the back and using the front wheel. Perhaps Emma then would be able to help her get to a cycle shop for a new wheel.

As she looked at the map again, her apprehension returned. The BMW could well be waiting further along the road and there were two miles at least before the turning into Atherton, the village where Emma lived now with her brother. There was also the return journey if the bike could not be sorted. On foot it could well be dark by the time she reached the cottage.

Could she really give up now though? Had that been the intention of the man in the BMW, to force her to abandon the whole visit to Emma? Yet who could possibly know she was going to Emma apart from Emma herself and Luke and Luke after all had been the one who'd helped find Emma and where she lived. It didn't make sense that he should want to undermine his own efforts nor did she want to believe he would.

Then the cameo came back of Luke with Jamieson in the garden talking. It struck her then that, without the frame of thick black hair, the lean face behind the tinted glass of the BMW could well have been Jamieson, that in all probability it was Jamieson. She felt angry then more than afraid, suspicious of Luke again and decided, whatever the problem, she was going to see Emma.

The BMW was not waiting as she'd feared but her foot she found increasingly painful and the bike increasingly awkward and heavy to lift at the back as she pushed. As she hobbled eventually down the hill into Atherton, she felt exhausted, close to tears.

She recognised which was Emma's cottage from the six adjoining flint cottages with white doors and brass knockers by the village green. Outside in the patio garden were all the flowers she'd always associated with Emma – hanging baskets of lobelia, tubs of red and white impatiens and borders of multi coloured begonia mixed with alyssum.

She was hesitating outside, conscious of being late, her feeling confused by memories the flowers brought of Yadrahna again, when she was aware of the whirl of cycle wheels behind her, of Luke's voice then beside her, apologising for not making it to the cottage, of his eyes as she turned, taking in with concern the damaged wheel.

"Are you all right? What happened?"

"Don't you know?"

"Know what?"

"You told Jamieson, didn't you, that I was coming here?"

"Jamieson?"

"The man," she responded acidly, "that you were talking to in the garden, the estate agent, my brother's accomplice in trying to get the estate. Wasn't he asking you about my plans?"

"He was asking yes. But you surely don't think I told him anything?"

"Don't I? How did he know then that I was coming? You were the only one who knew."

Luke lowered his eyes in bewilderment and dismay. "You still haven't told me what happened."

"He followed me. That's what happened and he drove into me on the straight run. He tried to run me over."

She saw Luke flinch as if he'd been struck – a frustrated anger in his voice now.

"I can't believe it. I mean I know they're unscrupulous about money but to do that. Are you sure it was him?"

"Not a hundred percent but pretty sure."

"But you can't really believe that I had anything to do with it, that I should want to harm you."

"I don't know what to believe. All I know is what happened and that you," she repeated," are the only one who knew I was coming here and the route."

"It was obviously just coincidence then or he was waiting outside on the off chance."

"Do people running an office waste their time waiting, losing business without some certainty of a tip off? I don't think so."

"If there's an eventual chance of making money from it then yes and he obviously reckons Yadrahna is a good bet. But I can assure you I have never had anything to do with him."

"Well anyway, I'm going in to see Emma now."

"Let me at least see to the bike then."

"Can you magic a new wheel out of the air?"

"No," stubbornly Luke persisted," but I can cycle into Oxford and get one while you're here."

Hannah didn't reply. She didn't feel she wanted to depend on him any more. But he was pleading now, urging her to let him put things right, to prove that he

wasn't the sinister figure she suspected and in the end she relented. She didn't know what to do with the bicycle anyway and watched, undecided about him again, as he removed the chain of her bike, unbolted the buckled wheel from the axle and strapped it on the carrier over his own back wheel.

"I can't be sure I'll be back by the time you've finished talking. But I'll be back I promise as soon as I can. Please don't try walking back alone. Please wait for me."

I can't do any more, Luke thought, mounting his bike again. If she doesn't believe me, she never will. Why, why, he blamed himself, hadn't he insisted to the bar manager that he'd had to leave on time? Why when she needed him, had he let her down? I won't look back, he decided, forcing himself with determination, without relish, onto the road into Oxford.

Hannah watched him go, longer than she'd intended, then leaning the frame of the bike against the bordering privet hedge of Emma's cottage, she stepped carefully through the profusion of flowers into the patio garden and rapped the shiny brass door knocker of its freshly painted white door.

She heard footsteps at once responding, then the door opened and Emma's plump homely figure was spanning the doorway, swathed in a familiar purple patterned floral apron, her rosy face gleaming, her clear blue eyes ready, as Hannah had always remembered, with trust, without judgement.

Tears in her eyes, with relief, immediately she flung her arms round Emma and kissed her. "Dear Emma, I thought I'd lost you."

"Never." Gently Emma shook her head in denial, stroking Hannah's hair. "I always knew you'd come in the end – if I waited."

"Did you really?"

"Of course. And when your friend came..."

"My friend?"

"The part time gardener – Luke I think he said his name was. He came to check to make sure. He said he didn't want you disappointed to find I was someone else." Emma smiled back tentatively at her recollection of the young man's visit.

"I see."

"He didn't tell you then?"

"No, he probably wanted it to be a surprise I expect."

"That's probably it. And it is a surprise, a lovely surprise." Close to tears herself now, Emma took her hand and led her through to the back room of the cottage overlooking a garden of herbs. It was a small low ceilinged room dominated by an oak table in the centre, an oak settle against the wall and a blue oil fired Aga in its alcove from which there emanated the smell of freshly baked bread and chocolate cake, Emma's known speciality, mingling hauntingly for Hannah with the aroma of rosemary, peppermint and thyme wafting in through the open window.

There were herbs too on the table waiting to be hung, a tray of pots of jam waiting to be labelled and everywhere, in the sparkling windows and the scrubbed flagstones and shining brasses hanging in the walls, the marks of Emma's unflagging industry and care. Yet it was a room that seemed to Hannah to follow the seasons and instinct rather than a self imposed order and she felt at once at home in it.

"You're still as busy as ever I see."

Hannah sat down on the settle as Emma cut them each a piece of chocolate cake and made a brew of peppermint tea.

"I like to have plenty to do. No work is work for the devil as they say." Emma paused wiping her hand on her floral purple patterned apron, her eyes drawn to Hannah again with compassion and concern. "I was so sorry to hear about your dear father."

"Thank you."

"I know it's too late, Miss Hannah, but I want you to know that I tried my best to stay with your father. I didn't want to go and leave him. And I wanted to come to the funeral. I would have come if I'd known in time, to pay my respects, you understand."

"I know you would, Emma. I know the situation. No one told you, did they?"

"That's what I can't understand." Emma shook her head in bewilderment. "I left my address with Mr Hugo. He promised to tell me if anything happened and how your father was. Your father I know would have wanted to see me."

"I'm sure he would. I'm so sorry."

"I'm not blaming you, Miss Hannah. I know in part I'm to blame myself. I should have tried more to keep in touch when I was given my notice but it was very difficult with the new housekeeper."

"Why were you given notice, Emma?"

"That I will never understand, Miss Hannah. When your father became ill, he said so many times he wanted me to stay and look after him. He said it to Mr Hugo and the doctor."

"My brother never gave a reason then?"

"He said he wanted a full time nurse who was qualified but that Mrs Slade..." Emma's kindly face puckered for a moment in lines of resentment. "She's no more qualified than I am."

"So my father's wishes were over ruled?"

"As in so many other things, Miss Hannah. And he wasn't happy. I could see that in the last few days I was there."

"Decisions were being taken away from him, you mean?"

"Mr Hugo let everyone know he was in charge."

"And part of being in charge I believe was to tell you not to let me know my father was ill."

"He said he didn't want to worry you, Miss Hannah, that it would upset your career in Hong Kong and that you'd feel you had to give it up. It made it sound as if he was trying to protect you, Miss Hannah."

"So you went along with it?"

"It was difficult at the time. I felt I wanted to tell you, that you had a right to know. But increasingly Mr Hugo was controlling your dear father's affairs and the purse strings which included my job, Miss Hannah, you understand. I felt I had to do as he said in order to be able to stay with your father. He had taken away the address book so I didn't know your address."

"And my letters? What happened to the letters I sent my father?"

"The first ones I gave to the Colonel in January and February I think it was. Then when it was confirmed he had cancer, Mr Hugo told me to give the letters to him so

that he could read them out to the Colonel in case there was anything in them that might upset your father, he said. I began to realise then at the end of February that Mr Hugo was keeping the letters and not letting the Colonel see them at all. So the next letter I gave direct to the Colonel. I know how much he wanted to hear from you. It was one in which you said you hadn't heard from him."

"I know the one you mean."

"I realised then that you weren't getting the letters he'd written which he'd given to Mr Hugo to post. Well, Mr Hugo then found out that I was giving him your letters – two of them there were. After that he told me to leave."

"So you left Yadrahna in March?"

"That's right. At the end of March it was."

"Did you ever go back?"

"I tried to go back in April to see your father to take him some fruit. He used to love grapes, you remember, but that Mrs Slade," Emma grimaced again at the name, "she wouldn't let me in."

"What did she say?"

"She said he was ill and didn't want visitors, that it would upset him to see me. Upset indeed! I heard him when I went to the door asking for me. I tried to push in but she shut the door in my face. I tried then to find out how the Colonel was through the tradesmen and other old friends but no one called they said any more. They told me they couldn't see him. It was a terrible situation, Miss Hannah. It breaks my heart when I think how lonely your father must have been. Why Mr Hugo was acting like this I'll never understand. To deprive a dying man in such a way."

"It's not difficult, Emma, when you know what he was aiming at." Hannah explained then all she'd found out about Hugo's intentions regarding both the will and the estate.

Emma's reaction was one of surprise followed by indignation. "I'm sure that's not what your father intended, Miss Hannah. He was a good man. He wanted fairness and wanted you to have your share. I know he did. He told me many times that he was leaving you Yadrahna."

"Would you be prepared, Emma, to say that in court – to testify that these were his words and intent?"

"Certainly, Miss Hannah, I would. It is what he wished. I know. I'm sure. He didn't want Mr Hugo to have Yadrahna because of the developers."

"Did you ever hear my brother put pressure on him though to get him to change the will in any way?"

"Mr Hugo was always very careful to speak of such matters alone with the colonel. Sometimes when I left the room he would come and check the door. I never heard him say anything to your father while I was there – no. But he did pressure your father into drinking – that I do know.

"What was he drinking mainly?"

"Whisky, gin, vodka, brandy – Mr Hugo sometimes even mixed them together."

"Do you think the drinking affected my father's judgement?"

"I'm certain it did, Miss Hannah. Even before I left when Mr Hugo had been with him for an evening he didn't really know what he was saying. I know it was in part his illness but he was never the same once he'd started drinking."

"But you weren't there on May 1st?"

309

"No, I wasn't there then, Miss Hannah. I didn't see your father again after I left at the end of March." Emma turned away suddenly, her eyes filled with tears. "I wish I could help you more, Miss Hannah. It will always be a great sadness tome that I wasn't with your father when it mattered, when he needed me."

Hannah couldn't bring herself immediately to respond. It was becoming poignantly more clear to her, as their conversation developed, that Emma had loved her father much more than she'd known, that Hugo had probably feared and got rid of her in part for this reason.

"You already have helped me, Emma," she said at length," and you still can." She paused as Emma wiped her eyes, turning back to the table. "I need to know about something else important to me – my mother's death."

"Your mother's death, Miss Hannah?"

"I was away, if you remember, at the time on my year studying abroad. I didn't get back till the funeral. I never really knew the details because my father was too upset at the time and afterwards he never wanted to talk about it. I feel I need to know now."

"Of course if there's anything I can help you with."

"Thank you." Hannah waited as Emma poured some more tea for them both and sat down on the settle beside her. "I know you didn't come to stay till after my mother's death but you used to come to Yadrahna, did you not, to help my mother from time to time?"

"Tuesdays and Thursdays," promptly Emma replied. "The days your mother did her charity work."

"Do you remember anything about the day she died? Were you there that day?"

"I remember her having lunch with Mr Hugo before going out in the car."

"And my brother followed her?"

"I saw him drive off a few minutes after her – yes."

"Did they seem on good terms while they were having lunch?"

"I think Mr Hugo was making an effort to be nice to your mother."

"Why was that, do you think? Can you remember?" Hannah was conscious of a strain now in Emma's eyes as she tried to recapture the minutiae of the past.

"She had a headache, I remember. She said she wasn't feeling very well and wanted to cancel an appointment. Mr Hugo went to the chemist's for her after lunch and got some tablets for her headache and urged her to keep her appointment. He said he'd follow behind and see she was all right."

"Do you know what the tablets were that he gave her?"

"It's a long time ago, Miss Hannah. I can't recall what the tablets were. But I think they must have made her feel better because in the end she agreed to go."

"At my brother's persuasion?"

"He did try to persuade her, yes."

"So they drove off, she in front and he following a few minutes later. And what was the next thing you knew?"

"About two hours later, Mr Hugo came back and rang for an ambulance, saying there'd been an accident, that your mother had gone off the road at Winter Hill."

"Two hours! But Winter Hill's only three minutes away, if that."

"Mr Hugo was trying to save her apparently and applying first aid."

"Do you believe that?"

"It's what the papers said, Miss Hannah. I don't know what to believe. Some said it was strange. She had three nails, all piercing her tyres. Who would drop such nails on Winter Hill?"

"But the inquest didn't find this suspicious, did it?"

"Not that I know, Miss Hannah."

Hannah was conscious of Emma holding back now, of doubt in her voice, matching her own doubt and apprehension.

"Tell me. Do you think anyone else saw the accident and aftermath besides my brother?"

Emma was silent for a while, reluctant to revive the pain but there were things about the death she knew that had never been resolved, that had nagged and were nagging again now – rumours that had more substance than gossip she knew from her brother, only she'd never dared nor wanted to follow them. Was it not her duty though now?

"Some say," she said at length," that there were lovers in the wood at the time. Lovers who didn't want to come forward because they didn't want their affair known."

"Is it true?"

"I believe it to be true, yes."

"Do you know who they are?"

"I know of them, Miss Hannah, but I don't know them personally – no."

"Do you know anyone who does, who could put me in touch with them?"

"I'll have to ask my brother first, Miss Hannah. He knows people who know them but I don't think they would want to talk in court."

"The affair's not over then?"

"I don't think there's any affair any longer, Miss Hannah, but they may be anxious to preserve their name."

"Yes, I can see that. It wouldn't necessarily mean though appearing in court. I just want to find out the truth of what happened. It's something I feel I need to do."

"I know, Miss Hannah. I would feel the same and I'll do all that I can to help you. I'll talk to my brother this evening and see if he'll agree to give the names and put you in touch."

"Will you? You are good Emma." At last, Hannah thought, I'm getting somewhere, if he'll agree, if they'll agree to talk. There were so many ifs, so much unknown, so much dependent on outside forces, on people's vagaries and whims. Yet in a web of intrigue and darkness, hadn't Emma remained steadfastly loyal to her father and someone she could truly trust?

Would her brother co–operate though? That she would have to wait and see. Promising to ring for his decision the next morning, two hours later, when they'd exhausted further news, gratefully she hugged Emma again and took her leave.

Chapter 22

On the green outside, Luke was already back from Oxford and waiting for her, her bicycle propped up against the teak seat beside him, straightened now and with a new wheel affixed as if the accident had never been.

"You must have flown."

"In a good cause," tentatively Luke smiled, "if I'm now believed."

"I want to believe you, Luke."

"Then why don't you? You must know I'd never harm you or plot against you, as you imagined."

"I think I do but–"

"But what?"

"It's not that simple. The whole business of the will and my brother. One can't be sure of people, fully trust them. Just give me time. That's all. But please don't think I'm not grateful. I am. I couldn't have managed today without you. And I want to thank you for coming to see Emma to make sure it was her."

"It was nothing."

"It was your time which matters to you."

"Well, anyway, how did it go?"

"Fine. It was a more confirmation than anything new but I may have more news tomorrow."

"So it wasn't a waste of time?"

"It would never be a waste of time seeing Emma. She really loved my father. I realise that now. It's just that – "

"Just what?"

"I never seem to get anywhere. I mean get concrete hard evidence. I always seem to be going round the edge. I understand more with each visit to people but it never seems to build up into a solid case – as least as far as the law's concerned."

"Is the law all that matters?"

"It's not all – no. But I'm not going to get any justice or redress am I, without it?"

"Perhaps you should try and think of other ways – I mean if you draw a blank."

"What other ways?"

"I don't know. I haven't really thought about it but my father always used to say that one shouldn't get too set on one route to solving a problem."

"Lateral thinking you mean?"

"Perhaps. Anyway I wanted to tell you that there is apparently a key to the outer door of the cellar. It's been found. I heard your brother and the Slade talking about it and I got the impression it's in the kitchen in one of the drawers."

"You think you can get it then?"

"I'm going to have a try tomorrow when the Slade has her hair done. I can't promise anything but let's say I'm on the case. Right then. We'd better make a move if we're going to get that window of yours done." As they mounted their bikes, cycling out from Atherton, Luke added, "I've got to talk at a meeting tonight so I may not be able to stay as long as I hoped."

"What kind of meeting?"

"It's a FOE meeting on SSSI's. I'm giving one of the talks."

"I didn't know you were a public speaker." Hannah edged to the side of the road so that Luke could cycle alongside her. She was relieved to have him with her, even when he dropped back, letting cars pass by. She still felt nervous and apprehensive that the BMW with its dark haired man with dark glasses might be along the route waiting for her.

"I'm not on a large scale but when I'm asked – well, it's a chance to put one's view."

"What view will you put?"

"That more action is needed if we're to save certain species."

"Will people listen, do you think, I mean to the extent of taking action?"

"Not enough perhaps but we usually get a good audience. Why don't you come?"

"Me?"

"Why not?"

"I'm not really a meetings and cause person."

"Isn't environmental impact a cause that affects us all?"

"I suppose so, yes, in a way you're right."

"Well, then?"

"I'll think about it."

"Well, don't think too long," Luke smiled at her self–classification. "It's this evening."

"What time does it finish?"

"About 10 – 10.30."

"I'm not sure about the buses. Getting back could be a problem."

"You could always stay overnight."

"Where?"

"With me." Aware of her hesitation, Luke added," You needn't worry. I wouldn't pressure you into anything. I'm just offering you space. That's all. Anthea might be able to offer you a room of your own if you wanted. There's students coming and going all the time."

"Who's Anthea?"

"She's a kind of landlady I suppose you'd say."

"I see."

Hannah wasn't sure she did see or what she wanted to see and leaving the matter open she made no further comment. A few minutes later they arrived back at "Brambles".

Luke immediately set to work on the window, fixing the screw Jamieson had dislodged, tightening the other screw and applying wood filler where Jamieson had wrenched and dislodged the central upright. It was only at best he knew a temporary measure. The whole frame needed replacing, a job that would take him three or four days, days he didn't have. It was only eight days now before his flight to India for his VSO posting and he still had his dissertation to finalise on the computer and there was still his father to see and settle before he went. Every time he thought of his father, he felt guilt at how little time he'd spent with him. Yet his father had done all he could to help him in his early days at university. Grief over his mother's death then, a growing problem with asthma and an inadequate pension had taken their toll and though his father had good friends in the street where he lived in Leeds, it wasn't the same

317

as having relations close by to care for you. Luke knew that. Yet what could he do? It was virtually impossible to get a job in England – a worthwhile job protecting the environment without experience. The VSO job would give him at least experience – experience that had meaning, though whether it would count when he eventually returned was another matter. What would count, he wondered. Would he ever get a job where he could realise his principles in practice, make some impact in action as well as words?

He felt a creeping doubt now about going to India, about leaving both his father and Hannah. He felt he wanted to take Hannah to see his father, to introduce them, to talk to her about the whole situation, what ultimately he was going to do or try to do to earn a living that was worthwhile.

Looking down on the garden, he noticed that she was throwing crumbs into the long grass, smiling to herself as a robin in response hopped out of the hedge. She'd changed from her jeans into a long flowing skirt and loosened her hair again over her shoulders. I've got to persuade her, he thought, to come to the meeting and stay.

Carefully he finished filling the wood and tightened the remaining screws. He was about to go downstairs to join her, when he was aware of voices approaching in the lane.

"There's someone coming," he called immediately down to her. Fearing it might be Jamieson again, Hannah turned then, to his relief, and hurried back into the house and closed the door.

A few minutes later Luke observed a smartly dressed

man and woman push through the wicker gate into the garden. They were both tall with short fair hair, both in beige suits and with competent, intent expressions. Who were they, Luke wondered. They couldn't be friends. Their smartness and intentness seemed out of tune, out of sympathy with both Hannah and the garden. They were probably estate agents he decided or yuppies on the look out for a bargain weekend retreat in the country. Either way he wasn't going to let them spoil his last few minutes with her before he had to leave.

"There's no one here," he called breezily down from the window. "We've nothing to sell and nothing we want to buy. Goodbye to you, yuppies." Laughing, Luke closed the window as Hannah scrambled upstairs.

"Who is it?"

"No idea. They look pretty harmless though."

Cautiously, Hannah came over to the window and looked down, following his amused gaze, onto the garden.

"Oh, my god. I'd forgotten."

"You know them then?"

"Of course I know them." Hannah drew back from the window, wondering what to do. Richard had seen her, she was sure. She would have to confront him now. It would all have been straightforward if Luke hadn't proclaimed himself. "Why," she turned on him," did you have to shout like that?"

"I didn't know, did I? It was only a joke." The release he'd felt drained away in irritation. "I didn't know you had friends in the city."

"They're not in the city. They're just ordinary people in marketing and I.T."

"Well, they've obviously come for a purpose."

"They've come to persuade me to go to Hampstead to his flat – at least that's what I think they've come for."

"So you know him well then?"

"As well as it's possible to know someone, I suppose."

"You mean you've lived with him?"

"I lived with him for a while in Hong Kong, yes."

"Why didn't you tell me?"

"Why should I tell you? What relevance is it? I don't intend to go."

"But you're still seeing him?"

"So you want everything cut and dried, do you? Relationships severed neat and tidy when they're not quite perfect or ever likely to be."

"I didn't say that."

"No, but you implied it." Below she could hear now Richard banging on the door, calling her name, saying he knew she was there and wanted to speak with her. "I didn't come here," she vented her irritation on Luke, "to be told who I should or shouldn't see."

"I know you didn't and I didn't mean that or," Luke added dispiritedly," to imply it."

"Well, anyway, I think it's best if you go now. I shan't be able to talk to them if you're here. They'll misinterpret."

"Does it matter?"

"Yes, because it's not true is it? You're not here living with me."

"Very well." Luke gathered together his tools. "If that's what you want. And the meeting? Are you coming?"

"I'll see when they've gone. I don't know."

"Well, I'll be off then."

He paused a moment staring at her. He felt he wanted to rip off her clothes, force her onto the bed, take out on her all his pent up frustration, disappointment and anger. I'm a fool, he thought, getting involved. Yet as he strode without speaking past Richard and Sally still waiting in the porch, he knew more than anything he wanted her to come to him that evening and stay.

"Who's that joker then?" Irritated that he'd been kept waiting, Richard watched as Luke wheeled his bicycle away down the lane.

"He's the gardener at Yadrahna. He came to do some work on the window." Hannah opened the door, leading them into the kitchen.

"Is that all he came for?"

"It's not your concern, Richard, even if it wasn't." Trying to keep calm, she offered glasses of grape juice or orange, but they both, with a wince at the glasses, declined.

"Meaning you're having an affair with him, I suppose?" Richard challenged.

"I don't mean that at all – no." Hungry, as they hovered, she cut herself a chunk of cheese. "He's just a friend, as a matter of fact, helping me out."

"Well, I must say you choose some strange friends left to your own devices. Calling out of the window like that. Yuppies indeed!"

"It was only a joke, Richard."

"It was ignorant all the same. You're letting yourself slip, Hannah, moving with people like that. And this place – it's falling down around you. It's not right for you. Surely you must see that." Richard turned to Sally for confirmation.

Sally responded, Hannah noticed with a smile but it was a smile more of unease than reassurance as if she doubted her own position with him. She's in love with him, Hannah thought. It was obvious in the way she couldn't take her eyes off him. She's always been in love with him.

"I can see it's dilapidated, yes."

"So you're seeing sense at last then?"

"Sense?"

"Sense enough to come to the flat at Hampstead."

"I've already told you, Richard.."

"Look," Sally interrupted suddenly, moving to the door. "I think it's best if I go back to the car. I'd rather you two sort this out alone."

"That's very thoughtful of you, Sally." Richard turned to her with a grateful smile. "Thank you."

"She's been a tower of strength," he commented when Sally had left. "I don't know what I would have done without her."

"May be you should marry her then."

"How can you talk like that so glibly, Hannah, as if one can just change one's affection. I love you. Don't you realise that?"

"May be it's more an idea of me you love, Richard."

"What do you mean? Do you think I've invented some phantom out of the air? Does it mean nothing that we've been together?"

"It's not that it means nothing, Richard." Despairing, she tried to think of a way to avoid hurting him. "It's, it's that I feel different now. I feel I've moved on."

"To this joker, I suppose."

"I don't mean specially to anyone else."

"Why was he here then?"

"You're not listening, Richard. You've got fixed ideas of what should be, what I should be. Can't you see that I want, that I need some space to find myself as well as to sort the will and Yadrahna? I can't commit myself to anything else now. I don't want to."

"So you don't want to come to Hampstead then?"

"No."

"You do realise, don't you, that if you don't, we're finished? I'm not going to humiliate myself by coming again."

"I wouldn't want you to humiliate yourself, Richard. All I want is for you to understand."

"Well, I think I know what's behind it all, despite what you say." Abruptly Richard moved to the door and out into the porch, brushing his suit with his hand as it touched the decaying wood. "I hope things work out for you." He hardened his voice in dismissal. "It won't be any use running back to me if they don't."

"I've no intention of running back."

Quietly Hannah watched him go, then went upstairs to the bedroom. She tried to think what to do, whether to go or not to the meeting but nothing seemed clear any more. Then the pain returned, the longing for her father. On the bed, she sobbed herself into a state of exhaustion.

When she awoke, it was getting dark but she knew now she wanted to go to the meeting, that she didn't want to be alone in the cottage, that she wanted company, the company of Luke.

She would be late, she knew. She decided all the same to go and catching the next bus to Oxford, she made

her way to Edmunds Hall where Luke had told her the meeting would be held.

The hall, to her surprise, was almost full, not only with students but with people middle-aged and elderly as well.

Her eyes were immediately drawn to the front of the hall where Luke was already on his feet talking, his voice reaching back with a concern, strangely assured to her after the hesitation of their parting.

"It's incredible that half of our ancient woodlands have been destroyed since 1945. And yet even now this destruction continues. Official statements indicate that one in five of our most important wildlife areas are being damaged each year. The laws that should protect them simply aren't working."

There was a murmur of assent from the audience and the chairman beside Luke, an elderly man with receding wiry grey hair and a beard, nodded his assent. Trying to remain unobtrusive, Hannah skimmed her eyes over the seats near the back of the hall to see if she could locate an easily accessible chair.

"At stake," Luke continued," is the future of nearly 6500 sites of SSSI. They are just 9% of our total land area but they are hugely important because they are the last refuge of our ancient wildlife habitats and they are home to many of our rarest species of animal and plant life. The European Otter, the Manx Shearwater, the Red Kite, the wild cat, the early Gentian, the white clawed crayfish among others are all under threat now literally of extinction."

Noticing an empty seat three from the end of the second to back row, as quietly as she could, Hannah crept forward to sit down. To her consternation then as she was

about to squeeze into the row, the man at the end stretched out his legs and she tripped knocking into a woman in the seat in front of her. There was a gasp of annoyance. Several heads turned in irritation and to her dismay Luke stopped talking.

"Is there a problem?" the elderly chairman called out concerned. I can't answer, Hannah thought. Blushing, she kept her head down, wishing she hadn't come. Luke must have seen her or had he? Keeping her head bent low and away from him, she edged her way into the empty seat. To her relief, as she sat down, he started talking again but his voice had a nervousness now, a tension, and she knew from the way he kept glancing in her direction that he had seen her. She tried to focus on what he was saying rather than the way and gradually it seemed to her his voice gathered strength again.

"The problem is that the SSSI status does not ensure that an area is protected. It simply provides a means of informing owner and occupier that there is important wildlife on their land. Landowners and developers and the government itself can still get away with damaging and destroying SSSI's."

Suddenly it occurred to Hannah through Luke's words, that Yadrahna's own SSSI, the area round the pond, was now under threat from Hugo's plans. Were not Hugo and Jamieson the very developers intending to get away with it if they could? Was it not an additional reason now to persist, perhaps even an argument against the present will itself?

She found herself listening now to Luke more intently and for the first time raised her head looking directly at him.

"Pressure," he continued, "is still growing. That is why we need a Wildlife Act. To get wildlife protection, we need government legislation. We want the government to introduce a Wildlife Bill. This needs full protection of SSSI's, including management orders to protect important habitats when voluntary agreements break down. It needs the introduction of protected areas for important marine wildlife, improved protection for important species and support for those managing important wildlife areas, including better incentives for owners and managers of land to protect the environment for the public good."

"It won't be easy," Luke continued, his voice much stronger now and more convincing. "There are powerful interests which will resist the enactment of a Wildlife Act and they will use every opportunity to stop it being applied. To win against such odds, we need all the funds we can raise, help on the ground, lobbying of M.P.'s and letters to the press. I ask you all to give and do all you can to help. We can't afford to lose our wild places. Thank you."

There was prolonged clapping as Luke sat down, followed by interested questions on the various campaigns which Luke dealt with very ably, Hannah thought. She felt impressed by his dedication and persuasiveness, by his grasp of the facts and implications in response to questions, by his concern above all about the threat to more fragile species, to the rest of life and its survival. What more important cause was there when extinction rang its knell, when we were all as species linked and implicated?

She felt she wanted to tell him that she agreed, that she wanted to try to help if she could the local Friends of the Earth, that she was sorry she'd been rude to him.

As he went to sit down then in the front row, she noticed a woman stand up and take his hand and kiss him – a striking woman with wavy auburn shoulder length hair and wearing a flowing lime green dress. Together they sat down in the front row, talking, clearly involved and animated. Who was she, Hannah wondered. Luke was bound, she knew, to attract other women. He was an attractive man. It would be strange indeed if no one else was interested in him. She felt a stab of jealousy all the same at the recognition, a sudden pain in knowing she wanted him, that he might not want her, that this woman might have a greater claim and power.

The elderly man was speaking now on the rain forests, on the need to preserve the biodiversity, on the devastating effects of the beef industry in the clearing of forests, on the need for more stringent laws to reduce the clearance of land. Much more could be done, he asserted, to recycle paper, to reduce the consumption of developed countries, to involve the people of the rain forests in sustainable use of their products. He urged the need to elect politicians generally committed to green politics, long terms measures instead of endless economic growth as a concept.

His voice had a quiet authority, a sincere belief as Luke had in what he was saying. He wasn't a man, she knew instinctively, who would be deflected from his principles by money. He knew what he believed and would hold to it, yet recognised the problem, the potent claim of vested interest.

She admired him. He was an old campaigner, dedicated, yet she found it difficult now to concentrate. She got the gist of what he was saying but missed the detail. She couldn't take her eyes off the auburn hair which kept tilting towards Luke.

She wondered whether she should go. The last bus back to Wynton would leave in half an hour. She could make it quite comfortably if she left within the next few minutes. Yet she couldn't bring herself to stand up and attract attention again.

To her surprise suddenly the meeting ended. She noticed a group mainly of young people gathering around Luke and the woman with auburn hair. I'm not going to make a fool of myself, she thought, and turned with the drift of the audience to the exit door.

She was about to step out into the darkness beyond when she felt a hand on her shoulder. Turning, she saw Luke, alone, smiling down at her in the shadowed light of the entrance.

"You got away then?"

"Yes." She hesitated. "I'm sorry about the commotion and being late."

"It doesn't matter. You came. That's the important thing."

"Is it?" She felt she wanted to tell him how effective his speech had been but wasn't sure how he'd take it. Praise, she suspected, wouldn't convince or interest him.

"Of course. I want you to meet the others."

"It's a good cause obviously but – "

"But what? You are going to stay on, aren't you? I thought – "

He stopped as a group of young people coming from the hall surrounded him. Then the woman with auburn hair was taking his arm. "There's someone from Perspectives wants a word with you, Luke," she said. "We thought we'd go on then to Jason's. Would you like to come?" Hannah was aware suddenly of the woman regarding her with interest, extending her hand. "I'm Anthea by the way."

"Yes, do come," two other voices from the group then urged.

She felt she wanted to join them. They seemed friendly, warm–hearted. But what would happen later? What was Luke's relationship with Anthea who appeared to have some kind of claim on him? It could be simply friendship, association for a cause but it could equally be more and how was she to know? She certainly didn't want to share Luke nor did she want to be dependent on him for the night, not knowing. I'm not going to make a fool of myself, she resolved.

"Thanks but my last bus leaves in a few minutes. Perhaps another time." She was aware of Luke staring at her in bewilderment; then a reporter claimed him for comment and seizing her chance, she slipped out into the darkness.

It was a dull journey home and as she got off the bus and walked down the lane to the cottage, she began to wish she'd stayed on in Oxford after all. As a group they'd welcomed her, the first to have done so since she'd returned to England and they were obviously concerned and interested in what mattered, in the future well being of the planet and she felt she could identify with them. There was no real evidence that Anthea was Luke's girl

329

friend just because she'd kissed him. Would Luke ask her anyway if they'd been lovers? I'm a fool, she thought, as she pushed open the wicker gate.

To her surprise, shining her torch towards the door of the cottage, she saw that it was already open. She tried to think if she'd forgotten to lock it but couldn't remember.

As she focused her torch on the lock and door frame, she saw then that the keep of the lock had been wrenched off the frame and was dangling now on the mortise on the door, leaving a hole where it had been of splintered wood.

Whoever had entered with such force, it occurred to her then could still be there. Nervously she hesitated in the doorway listening. All she could hear was a tap in the kitchen dripping and the creaking of the shifting board on which she stood.

"Is anyone there?" she called at length.

It seemed to her as she waited then, without response, that the house itself was waiting, breathing, but without alien breath and she plucked up courage finally to venture inside.

Bending down by the table in the narrow hallway, she felt for the candle in the brass candlestick and the box of matches she'd put ready for her return. Lighting the candle then, she made her way upstairs.

She'd partially prepared in her mind for an intrusion since Jamieson's visit. But her mental preparation failed to take away the physical shock she felt as she saw in the candlelight her clothes scattered in disarray over the floor, her case pulled out and upended, her letters and documents ripped from their envelopes and torn, the scroll of the horse she'd bought for her father in Wanchai trampled

on, slashed. Even the new course books, which she hadn't even used, had been deliberately, it seemed, damaged in anger as they'd been wrested from under the bed. The bed itself had been stripped with the sheets piled on the floor, the mattress slit open as if it had held some secret store of stolen money. Thank God, she thought, she'd taken her father's letters already to Ashford but as she gathered up the wreckage, she realised with dismay that her passport had gone together with her address book, that some of her clothes were unfit now to wear.

Shaking, in tears, she went down to the kitchen. She was aware at once in the doorway of the smell of tomato, of a dampness on the flagstones underfoot. Bending down then in the flickering light of the candle, she saw splashes of tomato ketchup all over the kitchen flagstones, interspersed with mounds of coffee and tea emptied from her jars. On the floor by the pantry was a pile of broken crockery – all the mugs and plates that Annie Hobbs had provided. In the pantry itself the cheeses she'd bought for the coming week were crumbled on the floor and mixed with broken biscuits. A bottle of milk tipped over was till dripping its contents onto the floor and over the cheese.

Trying to avoid the mess and broken pieces, Hannah manoeuvred herself back to the table and put down the candle. It was then she saw the notice – a large sheet of white paper on the table with the words inserted in capital letters "GO BACK TO HONG KONG AND DON'T MEDDLE IN AFFAIRS THAT NO LONGER CONCERN YOU."

She felt numb for a moment, too distressed to cry, then a slow growing anger as she absorbed the violation to

both herself and the cottage and its weakness – a violation that would now cost her in replacing both the lock and crockery for Annie Hobbs – a cost she could ill now afford.

She had no doubt it was Jamieson allied with Hugo or someone employed by them and that they were intent now on frightening her away.

Well, she resolved, ripping up the notice, she wasn't going to be frightened away. She was going to stay and see it through. Lighting another candle, she started to clear up the floor of the kitchen.

Chapter 23

Despite her resolution not to be intimidated, Hannah slept that night only fitfully and in the light of morning her apprehension returned. How, she wondered, was she going to be able to secure the damaged door against enforced entry? The chair she'd pushed against it might warn her of an intruder but could not deter. There was the problem too of all the broken crockery, which necessitated letting Annie Hobbs know what had occurred.

On the way to the phone to ring Emma regarding the witness, she stopped at Annie Hobbs' cottage and told her briefly there'd been a break in but without indicating she suspected who it had been. To her surprise, Annie Hobbs' reaction lacked its usual bright sympathy. It was as if a pact between them had been violated as she warned shaking her head.

"If Mrs Webb's niece hears about this, she won't be pleased. She won't be pleased at all. If there's any trouble she said to me, then whoever's there must go."

"But surely," Hannah protested, "a break in's hardly the fault of the tenant."

"Maybe, maybe not." For the first time, to Hannah's dismay, there was a gleam of suspicion in the older woman's eyes. "If you take my advice, you'd best say nothing about

what happened, nothing at all. If it gets back to Mrs Webb's niece, I don't doubt she'll ask you to go."

"You mean I've got to pay for the door?"

"If you want the door mended, my dear, I'm afraid there's no other way. Mrs Webb's niece told me she wants no expense, no expense at all till the house is sold."

"So you think now," Hannah ventured, "that she might want to sell it as soon as she can?"

Annie Hobbs peered at her more sharply. "Do you know someone who wants to buy?"

"Possibly," Hannah hesitated, "if the price is right." Uncertainly she wondered what her aunt's reaction had been to her letter. She didn't hold out much hope but you could never tell with Aunt Eileen. Hard headed though she was, she had the odd instinct that didn't quite coincide with material objectives. There was still some hope – hope she'd need if her case against Hugo eventually failed. And Annie Hobbs knew, she could tell by the sharpness of her eyes, that it was herself she was thinking of as the prospective buyer.

"I tell you what, my dear," Annie Hobbs gave the impression of relenting now. "I'll replace the crockery if you'll find someone to repair the door." With a smile of complicity, she promised to deliver some plates and cups later in the day.

There seemed no alternative but to agree and trying not to think of the cost, Hannah proceeded on up to the phone. Annie Hobbs was probably right, she told herself. It was unwise at this stage to risk being ousted by the elusive Mrs Webb's niece but her doubts surfaced again about Annie Hobbs herself as she recalled again the conversation

she'd witnessed between the old woman and Jamieson at the end of the garden at Brambles. How well in fact did she know Jamieson's intentions? And how serious were her intentions of getting the elusive Jack Ryder to save the cottage from the dangers of fire? Briefly Hannah wondered whether to go back and urge on Annie Hobbs the danger of the browned socket but it seemed now pointless. If Jack Ryder hadn't turned up, she decided, by the end of the month, she would get an estimate herself and act on her own.

To her relief, phoning through to Emma, she found Emma not only in but able to give her the name of the witness to her mother's accident and her phone number.

"My brother says, though," Emma warned," that she'll talk to you privately but she doesn't want to give evidence, he means in court. Please don't persuade her, he says."

"I won't." Hannah tried to sound reassuring though it was more to herself, she realised, than to Emma. Was this going to be yet another encounter that led nowhere, that she couldn't use?

Apprehensively, she rang the number Emma had given. The phone went on ringing for a long five minutes before a quiet tense voice answered.

"Helen Wilkes speaking."

"I'm sorry to bother you, Mrs Wilkes, but my friend's brother, Alfred Mason, said you would be willing to speak to me. Hannah Delaney's the name."

"I told Mr Mason I might yes, on certain conditions."

"Could I ask what those conditions are?"

"That we meet alone, that there's no tape recording or photography and no follow up."

"You wouldn't be prepared to keep the situation open then?"

"If you mean by open – witnessing in a court case – no."

"I see." Was it worth it, Hannah wondered, to find the truth, even a truth and not to be able to use it? Probably not, not in the legal sense, and yet wasn't it still important to know for its own sake, however frustrating the outcome?

"It's not that I want to be awkward or obstructive." Hannah could feel the woman reacting to her disappointment with more sympathy now. "There are reasons," she continued," why it would be damaging to let the story out in court. One has to protect the living, in the media jungle, as well as the dead."

"Yes, I suppose so." Struggling to understand, Hannah added, "I'd still like to see you."

"Very well then but we're going away on holiday tomorrow. It'll have to be when we return."

"When will that be?"

"In three or four weeks, say four."

Four weeks – it seemed to Hannah a lifetime and she knew she couldn't wait that long. Risking Helen Wilkes's good will, she ventured, "I know it's a nerve asking you when you're busy but could you possibly see me this afternoon?"

"This afternoon?"

"It wouldn't take long." Close to tears, Hannah pleaded. "Half an hour perhaps – no more."

There was a long silence, then more kindly, Helen Wilkes' voice came back to her responding.

"Very well then, I'll meet you at the lay by on Winter Hill where it happened at 3.30. It's the only time I have. I'll be in a beige Polo. Please don't keep me waiting."

"I won't."

Afraid of being late, Hannah arrived at the lay by at 3.00, promptly wishing she hadn't. There were not many cars passing but the drivers of those that did peered at her curiously, wondering, she suspected, what she was doing here and she felt nervous lest Hugo himself should pass in his Daimler and seeing her, guess at her intent. She thought at one stage she saw the car that had driven into her bicycle passing on the other side of the road and was relieved when Helen Wilkes's beige Polo at length drew up beside her.

Helen Wilkes had greying, short, wavy hair and lines of strain etched at the corners of her eyes and down her cheeks. She was about forty five Hannah guessed, but still a beauty with classic high cheek bones, a broad forehead and straight nose and large grey eyes – eyes that were regarding Hannah with caution now. Her voice was tense as it had been on the phone.

"I hope you've done what I asked, Miss Delaney."

"I haven't brought a tape recorder if that's what you mean."

"And no one's with you hovering around?"

"There's no one – only me."

"Good, well as I told you, I haven't much time. You'd better tell me exactly what it is you want to know."

Cautiously Hannah sat down in the passenger seat beside her. "I want to know what happened on the evening of 6th November five years ago when my mother's car went

337

off the road. I want to know if it really was an accident. If you could tell me what you saw."

"And if I tell you will you be prepared to let it rest?"

"It depends, doesn't it, what you tell me. But as far as you are concerned, yes. You made your terms clear."

"It won't be pleasant. You may wish you hadn't heard."

"I still need to know, to understand."

"About your brother you mean?"

"My brother and the whole situation."

Helen Wilkes regarded her in silence a moment, her large grey eyes cautious still but with more empathy now.

"I can only tell you what I saw from the place I saw it but it will be enough I think."

Leaving the Volkswagen in the layby, Helen Wilkes led Hannah up to a large beech tree overlooking the bend, some thirty feet away, where Hannah knew her mother had come off the road. They sat down on some moss beneath the beech tree and looking intently down at the bend, Helen Wilkes continued.

"I was here with Frank. I hadn't seen him for some weeks and I wasn't noticing much else. The light was beginning to fade. It was about half past four. One could still see but some of the cars passing had their lights on. There was a long period of quiet I remember with no cars at all. Then a white Golf came down the hill. We didn't take much notice. It wasn't going fast but suddenly as it manoeuvred the bend there was a squeal of brakes, then a juddering sound as it lost control and tipped off the road. There was a sound of breaking glass then as the nearside wheel and headlight crashed into the beech tree there. I remember thinking how lucky it was the beech tree had

broken a much more dangerous fall. And we could hear a woman's voice calling out as if she was trapped but not badly injured.. Frank said then we'd better go over and help her.

He was just getting up to go when we saw another car that had been following pull up at the bend as if intending to help the trapped driver. Frank waited then thinking the other driver would do what he'd intended and pull the woman out.

"And didn't he?"

"No. He just stood there on the edge of the road, not going to her assistance at all. A full five minutes it must have been and he just stood there watching her while she called out to him to get her free. Frank thought at first he must be trying to make a plan of rescue and assess the situation but as the minutes ticked by it became obvious that he wasn't intending to do anything at all but just leave her."

"Then why didn't you and Frank.."

"Frank was on the point of going when suddenly a sheet of flame ripped through the car. There was a terrible scream and all at once the whole car was ablaze. We could feel the heat even from here. There was an explosion then as it caught the engine and the whole wreck buckled away from the support of the tree and went plunging down to where it was found at that beech tree down there. It was all too late then. There was nothing we could do."

"And the man who let her die? What happened then? What did he do?" All the pain her mother must have suffered – she tried not to think about it, to put it to the back of her mind, as determined she tried to focus on Helen Wilkes' story.

"He stood watching still for a while by the side of the road, watching while the car burned. Then another car came down the road and stopped. He put on an act then of running down through the trees to see what he could do."

"My brother you mean?"

"It was all in the papers the next week. Hugo Delaney, the hero, who tried to save his stepmother."

"So he managed to convince the other driver?"

"And the editors, it seems."

"How did you feel then?"

"I felt bad, of course, but what could we have done? Exposing your brother would have meant exposing Frank and our affair. It didn't seem – it wasn't worth it. Your brother after all hadn't committed an actual crime. He was guilty of moral cowardice yes, but not a crime that could be proved."

"Wasn't he? Surely letting someone die when you could save her is a crime."

How could Hugo have done it, Hannah wondered, to someone so close. What could have been in his mind? Had he really planned it all as an accident as Laura suspected? The three punctures – had they not been rather too well timed?

"Perhaps I was wrong I agree that he got away with a false reputation but Frank mattered to me more. I knew I couldn't live with Frank being harmed. I still couldn't. I thought it would all come to light anyway, that you, his family, would realise."

She's shifting it all, Hannah thought, back to me. Yet how could she have kept silent so long? What sort of love was it that let someone get away literally with deliberate

callousness and disregard? And yet Helen Wilkes was looking at her with sympathy, with regret for a past that could not be altered.

"I was naïve, I suppose," Hannah confessed then. "I'd been called back from abroad. The police report gave no hint of anything suspicious and it was so awful for my father. I couldn't think beyond our grief. I never dreamt," Hannah faltered as the past pressed in on her now with images she 'd sought to stifle, "I never dreamt that my mother had been abandoned in such a terrible manner." And suddenly she was with her mother in the car, could feel the clamp of metal on her foot trapping her, the fear of plunging, then the terrible pain of the flames searing her eyeballs, her breasts, her hair – pain beyond enduring. "I can't bear it what she suffered."

She didn't know how she got back to the cottage. Vaguely she was aware of Helen Wilkes taking her arm and leading her back to the car and driving her down to the end of the lane, uncomfortably trying to comfort and reassure.

Then she was stumbling alone, shaking, feeling she could hardly breathe, down the dried rutted mud of the lane and in through the wicker gate, through the wild grasses of Brambles.

Not until she reached the porch did she see him – Luke standing like a guardian in front of the broken doorway, holding out a large bronze key. "They're going to be out tomorrow afternoon." Boyishly he smiled at her.

She knew immediately it was the key she'd sought, the key she needed to fulfil her objective, the key to the cellar at Yadrahna. She knew she had much to thank him for but she could only stare at him in pain, unable to respond.

It came to him then how ill she looked and shattered, that she needed looking after. She looked any moment she might faint. Concerned he took her into the cool of the kitchen to sit down. Going back to his bicycle then, propped up by the kitchen window, he poured her an infusion he had in his flask of peppermint tea.

"Here drink this. Something's happened, hasn't it?"

Patiently he waited as slowly in a daze she drank the tea. It had something to do with the broken door, he decided. Someone had broken in and frightened her, which meant it had to be repaired and soon for her peace of mind. But how? He had no suitable tools in his saddlebag for such a job and it was obvious it was going to need a new lock. He remembered then that there was an old lock similar in the box of oddments in the shed at Yadrahna. There were also some pieces of wood he could select from and use. If he walked up through the woods so he wasn't noticed, he could collect the lock and some tools at the same time for the job.

"I think I could sort the lock for you."

"Could you?" She felt a desperate need to sleep now, to let him take charge.

"It means going up to the shed to get some tools. I shan't be long though and while I'm gone I think you should lie down. I'll fix the door temporarily with some plastic cord."

"Thanks."

She could hear him below humming to himself as she lay on the narrow bed, then the shock of what she'd overheard overcame her and she slipped into an uneasy sleep.

Chapter 24

To his irritation, on emerging from Rassler's Wood behind the shed, Luke could hear voices coming from close to the shed in the kitchen garden – voices he recognised at once as those of Jamieson and Hugo Delaney. Apprehensively, he wondered whether Jasper, the guard dog, was on the loose with them and roaming around. He hoped not. Unresponsive though the dog was to commands, it wasn't to smells and would soon, he knew, if around, flush him out with its barking.

Peering through the laurel to the side of the shed, he saw, to his relief, no sign of Jasper around them, no sign of its ominous panting. But Hugo Delaney and Jamieson were standing directly in front of the shed door, their heads close together as if engaged in a long conversation. There was no hope of getting into the shed while they were there, no hope of getting the lock or the necessary tools for the cottage door. But why were they there?

Creeping as close to the shed as he could, listening, he realised they were talking about him.

"You're still doubtful about him then?" he heard Jamieson say.

"I'm still certain he was the one helping her the night she got away. You said yourself you saw him with her at the cottage."

"Yes, but it didn't strike me he knew much about her. He's just got the hots for her I'd say."

"The more fool him." Hugo Delaney gave a cynical laugh. "You'll never guess. I saw the silly bitch this afternoon wandering with some other woman in a daze like a mad woman on Winter Hill."

"Why do you suppose that was?" Jamieson asked.

"I don't know but I don't trust her even if she does appear to have lost her marbles." Luke was aware of a hint of menace now creeping into Delaney's voice. "You still haven't got her out of the cottage, have you?"

"It's not that easy, Hugo. She's a determined person and she has the right to be there. It's not as if there's a legal screw I can use. And Steadman did after all force the front door and get the passport for you."

"But no evidence or letters about what she's up to. And she's still there."

"I could get Steadman to have another go, I suppose."

"Yes, but it needs to be something more effective this time."

"Like what exactly? Don't you think you might be in danger of forcing him to reveal our part in it – if you go too far?"

"He won't talk if we pay him. But he's got to do what he's paid for and frighten her off once and for all." There was an ominous pause, then Delaney added, "Or I'll have to do something about it myself."

Luke could hear no more as they walked back to the house but it was enough and he felt shaken with fear for Hannah. Who was this man Steadman and what was he likely to do to frighten her away? The thought of Hannah

vulnerable in the cottage and alone at the mercy of her sinister brother appalled him. He had to get the door fixed and fixed effectively without delay. Impatiently he watched, waiting till the two men were out of sight. Making a dash then into the shed, he closed the door behind him, in case they unexpectedly returned, and searched out a piece of wood and appropriate tools.

To his dismay, as he was about to leave, looking out of the shed window, he saw Jasper, the guard dog, prowling now round the vegetable garden and periodically sniffing at the shed door. He had to wait another half hour before eventually it gave up and trailed off, following the two men into the house. He'd been away, he realised, two whole hours, instead of the half hour he'd intended – two hours in which someone could have broken in again to Brambles.

He ran all the way back then through the woods. At the cottage, he found a tray of crockery in the porch with a note from Annie Hobbs, saying she hoped the door would soon be mended. To his relief, the plastic cord barrier he'd devised was still intact and upstairs Hannah sleeping still, unharmed. Looking down on her, he saw though that she was frowning as if in pain, that she wasn't sleeping peacefully at all.

He remembered then what he'd overheard Hugo Delaney saying, that she'd been wandering in the woods as if demented with another woman. Why? What had happened? Still she hadn't told him.

He felt he wanted to wake her then, to tell her how much he loved her, that he'd help her if he could to get through it all, that she could come to his lodging in Oxford, away from the danger.

Then he remembered he was supposed to be going to see his father in Leeds in the morning as a final visit before India, to help him settle in his new accommodation. Quickly he tried to calculate. He could still go in the late afternoon he reckoned after he'd settled Hannah and still be there for the following day for the move so he didn't let his father down. He'd go and ring when he'd finished the door. Forcing himself back downstairs, he started to repair the damaged frame.

Conscious of working against time, Luke chiselled out the splintered wood of the frame where the keep had been. More carefully then, he shaped the block of wood he'd brought from the shed to fit the hole. He'd just given it a final sanding and nailed it in place ready for the dislodged keep, quite pleased with his efforts when he heard suddenly a cry from the room above where Hannah was lying and Hannah's voice calling in fear: "No. Stop him. Stop him."

Immediately dropping his screwdriver, Luke bounded up the stairs to find Hannah sitting upright in the bed, her face strained with bewilderment and fear. She stared at him a moment, then started to cry.

Gently Luke put his arm round her, sitting down beside her. "It's all right. There's no one here. You're safe. Don't worry."

Gradually her crying ceased but it brought no reassurance and he was startled when next she spoke.

"He left her to die, Luke."

"Left who? What do you mean? Who?"

"My mother. Hugo – he left her trapped in her car." She tried to tell him then what Helen Wilkes had told

her. It came brokenly in jagged sentences. She had to keep stopping to recover but all the more true and devastating it seemed to him in its brokenness. And he could feel, as she spoke, as she did – the trauma, the pain, the flames. But how, he wondered, was he going to be able to help her. He felt as if he was looking into a pit –a pit with Delaney in its darkness and he felt he wanted to search Delaney out and kill him before he had the chance to harm any more or kill Hannah herself. But how? He'd never even thought of killing anyone before. To his horror then he heard Hannah echoing his own thoughts.

"I feel I want to kill him, Luke."

"No." Instinctively he drew back, jolted. Wasn't it exactly what her brother wanted – to ensnare her, to ensnare anyone concerned in the web he'd spun, to determine their actions, drag them all down? No, there had to be a better way. Desperately he tried to think clearly, constructively of a way to give her hope.

"No, you mustn't think like that. It won't help. You can't kill him. You're not the sort of person who could live with it if you did."

"He's lived with it and quite happily it seems."

"Perhaps because he has no conscience but you have. You need to focus on outwitting him."

"He's planned it all too carefully, Luke."

"But we have the key now. And if you can get in tomorrow afternoon while they're out, get the will from where it's hidden and get it to the solicitor, you can leave it then to the law."

"Supposing though the will isn't there after all – that he's found it?"

"There are still things you could do – like going back to the witnesses. You mustn't give up hope. You owe it to your mother and father. But there's something even more important."

"What do you mean?"

Luke hesitated a moment then said, "I don't think you're safe here. The door will hold hopefully for a casual intruder when I've finished but not for someone again determined."

"Yes, but they won't come while I'm here, will they?"

"One can't be sure." She looked so strained still, so exhausted, he didn't want to tell her what he'd overheard for fear of stressing her yet further. "I mean I know you like the wildness and the peace and it's cheap and all that but it's not worth the risk."

"Risk?"

"Look you could have my room in Oxford while I'm in India. It's not expensive and it'd be more convenient for you for the course. And I'm sure Anthea could find you another room till then. Why don't you give it a try while I'm away in Leeds?"

"In Leeds?"

"I've got to be away for a couple of days helping my father move. We can get into the cellar when I return."

"It may be too late then, Luke."

"There's a risk I suppose. I don't think it would be wise all the same searching Yadrahna especially the cellar on your own. I could keep watch if there's the two of us. It'll be safer, more predictable."

"Maybe." Was anything going to be predictable when it concerned Hugo, Hannah wondered. She sank back in the bed, feeling she hadn't the strength to argue.

"When did you last eat?" She looked thinner, he thought, as well as drawn and pale.

"I can't remember."

"You don't look after yourself properly, you know." I sound like an old woman, Luke thought. He smiled but felt increasingly anxious about her. How was she ever going to get over it? The shock alone was enough but her brother uncontrolled still, unpredictable, intent on harming and denying her, how was she going to deal with him, let alone come to terms?

Concerned, Luke went downstairs to see if there was something for her to eat in the kitchen but all he could find was some mouldy cheese and some stale bread. No wonder she was thin, he thought.

Determinedly, he set about finishing repairing the doorframe, nailed in the wood he'd reshaped for the hole, then re-fixed the keep. To his satisfaction, the door locked without problem and he set off up the lane to the village store where he bought as much fresh bread, cheese, apples and orange juice as he could with the £4 he had left in his wallet. Stopping at the telephone kiosk then he rang through to his father. His father, as always, was selflessly uncomplaining and without recrimination adapted to the changes in his plan. If only Luke wished, he had more time for them both, for Hannah and his father and could bring them together. They would like each other, he was sure.

Back at the cottage, he found that Hannah had fallen asleep again. In the fading light, she seemed to be sleeping more peacefully now. He ought to get back to finish his dissertation. He'd only have four days once he got back

349

from helping his father move to get it finally checked and corrected on the computer ready for printing. It was going to be tight, more than tight, but he knew he couldn't leave her now after what he'd overheard.

He made some sandwiches for her from the bread and cheese he'd bought ready for when she awoke and poured some orange. Upstairs then he sat in the creaking wicker chair Hannah had by the window, watching, waiting.

It was about midnight and he was just dozing off in the darkness, when he heard the swing of the wicker gate on its broken hinge. Startled, he refocused on the garden. He couldn't make out anything for a moment. Everything was still in the garden, the moon covered with shifting clouds throwing shadows that deceived. Then he was aware of a more substantial shadow making its way up the overgrown pathway to the porch, a shadow that gave the impression at once of sinister intent rather than opportunism, of strength, of muscular fitness and build.

From beneath, in the porch came the sound of the man turning the knob of the door, a curse and a kick when he realised it was locked. Then he was directly below Luke at the kitchen window. There was a brief silence as he hovered a moment undecided, trying to peer inside. As the moon came clear then of the clouds, Luke glimpsed a glint of steel in the man's hand, the thick blade of a knife which he was edging into the window now, trying to get inside.

Luke couldn't make out the features but there was something familiar he thought about the shape of the head and the receding hairline. It wasn't Jamieson he was sure but, whoever it was, it came to him urgently he had to stop him getting in with the knife.

As silently as he could, he crept down the stairs to the kitchen. To his horror, the man already had the window open and was about to climb in. Picking up the first thing he could feel, Luke hurled the bucket of drinking water waiting in the sink straight into the face outlined in the window. There was a cry of anger as the man dropped back in surprise. Quickly Luke reached out with his left hand for the latch of the window. He felt a piercing pain as the man's knife caught the top of his index finger but managed to draw it back and slam shut the window again. In a loud voice then pretending he had a cell phone, he called out, "Hello Police. There's been a break in at Bramble Cottage, down Lavender Lane, Wynton. A man with a knife. He's still here yes. The lane's opposite the telephone kiosk and bus stop, The last house. Come quickly."

Looking back out of the window, as he finished his supposed call, he saw the man stumbling away down the path, heard to his relief the clang of the wicker gate again on its broken hinge. If only, he regretted, he'd seen the man more clearly, had brought his torch. For the moment at any rate the man had gone but Luke had no doubt from the alertness of his approach that he'd be back, that even more now Hannah needed protection.

Returning to the bedroom, he sat down again at the wicker chair by the window. To his amazement, Hannah hadn't even stirred but he was relieved for her sake. He needn't even tell her, he reflected, as long as he could persuade her to go to his room in Oxford. He was conscious of a throbbing pain in his finger but felt too tired to get up again. As dawn was breaking and the shadows lifted from the garden, he fell into an uneasy guarded sleep.

★

Hannah woke to the sun streaming in through the bedroom window and Luke standing over her gently stroking her hair.

"Sorry", he smiled tiredly at her, his eyes focused as from the depths of a deep cave. "I'll have to leave soon."

"Leave?" The intense pain she felt the night before from Helen Wilkes's disclosure had subsided but she still felt a dull aching and apprehension. She didn't want to be alone. She wanted Luke with her.

"I've got to catch the 10 o'clock train from Oxford. " He handed her a glass of orange juice he'd poured ready the night before. "Here drink this. You need some liquid in you and food."

She noticed the gash across his finger, freshly again bleeding.

"What happened? What did you do?"

"I jammed it in the window."

It wasn't true, she knew. One didn't get a gash like that from a window especially a window at the cottage. More like a gash it was from a knife. But why was he lying to her? Taking in the wicker chair by the window she realised with a jolt that he must have been keeping watch all night. Keeping watch for whom and who had come?

"It's you who needs the drink, Luke." Climbing out of the bed, she searched out the first aid kit she kept in her suitcase, carefully applied antiseptic and bandaged his finger. "And you need to see a nurse or doctor. It may need stitches. It looks nasty."

"I'll go in Leeds this afternoon."

"Leeds?"

"I'm going to help my father move. Remember?"

"I think you should see someone before that. Maybe we should go to the surgery now."

"No," Luke decided, despite the pain, he had to be firm. "There's not time. I'll be all right. Don't worry. The main thing is that you install yourself in my room while I'm away. How about coming with me now?"

"I'm not ready, Luke. I'd hold you up. I need some time." Time for what exactly Hannah wasn't sure – only that deep down she didn't want to leave the cottage, that somehow it seemed wrong to go just now, that she needed to think things through.

"Promise me though you will go – I mean to sleep tonight?"

"I promise."

"Good." Reassured Luke handed her his two spare keys and his address in Lockwood Road. "I'll try ringing tomorrow evening."

"How long will you be away?" She felt again she didn't want him to go, apprehensive of being without him.

"Two or three days – no more. As long as it takes to settle my father. I need to be back anyway by the 24th."

"For your dissertation?"

"For my dissertation – and you." He watched her drink the orange juice, then gently put his arm round her and kissed her cheek. "I shall miss you."

"And I you." She tried not to think of his going to India. The three days in Leeds were already too long and as she watched him push his bike up the lane to the main

road, she felt a pang of longing for him to be back closer to her again, an incipient fear that he might not return.

"Take care," she called. But already he had gone, caught up in the ever speeding flow of traffic into Oxford.

Restless, Hannah hovered in the garden then, wondering whether to stay at the cottage or go, as Luke had wanted, to his room in Oxford. She had nothing urgent to do at the cottage, apart from washing and sorting her clothes and some food. She could go straight to his room on the next bus from Wynton. She had his key, his reassurance but she also had the key now to the cellar at Yadrahna and the more she thought of the large bronze key Luke had extracted for her, waiting on the table upstairs by the creaking bed, the more she felt reluctant to leave and go to Oxford.

Luke was right, of course, she reflected, that it would be safer and more sensible to wait till he returned so he could keep watch for her while she explored the cellar. But it would mean three more days of waiting, of inaction – days in which Hugo would have time to find the will for himself – days that mattered, that could count.

Was it fair, anyway, to expect Luke to give up yet more of his limited time to help her? Was she not relying on him too much? Why should she not manage now on her own?

And was it not a fact, as Luke had told her, that the Slade and Hugo would be out that very afternoon, the Slade to shop and Hugo to collect his mother? The days immediately following Luke's return might not be so certain. Why not take the chance now while their absence was certain? If she was careful, nothing need go wrong.

The cellar could easily be searched in the two or three hours that Hugo was away collecting his mother.

The thought of lifting the appropriate stones in the cellar, now her mind was focused, excited her. She was in reach now of achieving a break through. If she kept her cool, she could manage on her own, would manage and surprise Luke when he returned, surprise maybe even Ashford.

Yes, she decided, she would go to Yadrahna that afternoon but she would keep her promise to Luke to go to his room in Oxford that evening.

Trying to calm her apprehension, at midday she changed into the practical attire she had – a dark green track suit, which would keep her, she hoped, inconspicuous. Then she brushed her hair and tied it back in a scrunchie. She would take only the minimum with her, she decided, – her travelling torch, her penknife, a plastic envelope to protect the will and a tape measure for the exact distance of the stones from the cellar walls.

Downstairs, she ate two of the sandwiches Luke had prepared, leaving the rest for her return. She hesitated in the doorway, wishing Luke was with her. Then the flames of her mother's car came back to her and, locking the door behind her, she knew she had to go, that for both her parents' sake, as well as her own, she had to try and outwit Hugo and now, as soon as she could, before he achieved his objective.

Chapter 25

Concealed by the laurel bushes in the shrubbery, Hannah watched with relief as Hugo Delaney's Daimler purred out of Yadrahna's driveway and out onto the main road, precisely at 2pm, the Slade scowling on the front passenger seat. But there was no sign that she could see of Marcus or was he having, Hannah wondered, one of his many demanding tantrums lying down on the back seat. The answer soon came in the familiar plosive sound of Marcus's air rifle coming from the direction of the pond. Blasted child, Hannah thought, but at least he was preoccupied for the moment not prowling about looking for something to do. Then she heard the dog yapping in the persistent irritating way it had when Marcus was egging it on or provoking. Would it stay with Marcus though if it heard the unlocking of the cellar door?

Hannah felt again in her track suit pocket the large bronze key that Luke had given her, then looked back again at the house. There were three ravens on the roof, she noticed, looking down against a darkening sky and below all the downstairs windows had their curtains drawn as if deliberately to shut out the light. Why, she wondered. Her father had never drawn the curtains against the sun and it made the house with its high windows look forbidding

now, unfriendly, holding secrets that could not be known. It made her think of the other Hannah again. Though she'd learned a lot more about John Liddell, Hannah's lover, from Rev James, she still didn't know what had happened to Hannah herself. Would she ever know now? She doubted it but still she felt she wanted to know, a nagging desire still to find out what had happened on the night Hannah had heard of John Liddell's drowning. The problem was how after all this time. If Rev James who'd given the time and resources to it hadn't been successful, would she ever be?

Suddenly, Hannah was aware of a rabbit darting across the lawn in front of the house, closely pursued by Hugo's yapping new dog and a few minutes later, Marcus himself with his air gun, trying to keep up with them as they ran towards the field on the other side of the house. It was her chance, she reckoned, perhaps her only chance while they were out of earshot. Clutching the cellar key, cautiously she looked back down the drive again, then crept out of the laurel and skirting the wall of the kitchen garden, made a dash for it across the exposed grass and ground to the back of the house to the cellar door.

Her hand was shaking as she pushed the key into the lock of the sturdy oak door. For a moment in her fumbling, she thought it wasn't going to fit, then she turned it slightly to right, then left, as Luke had suggested, and the door creaked open.

She was aware at once of a chill in the air, of the old familiar smell of mustiness and damp, of materials long forgotten and in decay. Through the light of the open door, she could see then the worn stone steps leading

down and beyond the last step in the corner, boxes of old equipment, of discarded curtains and old clothes, a pile of broken deck chairs and two worn armchairs. Behind them in the corner – the trunk she needed to move. It looked so far, to her relief, as if nothing in the area of the trunk had been tampered with or removed.

But as she pressed the light switch at the top of the steps, removing the cellar key to inside as planned and locking the door behind her, she saw, to her surprise, by the neon lighting illuminating the rest of the cellar, a huge metal wine rack dominating the space to the left of the steps and extending up to the steps leading to the hall – a rack rising to within an inch of the cellar ceiling and containing she saw, on closer inspection, from their labels, bottles of high class, high quality wines.

It came to her then that Hugo must have had the rack specially constructed for Yadrahna, that it would never have fitted into his own house in Windsor – which meant he must have been installing himself for months, not weeks, and installing himself in style. Angry, she felt she wanted to take the bottles of expensive wines and smash them on the stone cellar floor, to pull down the whole edifice, all the planning that had gone into undermining both herself and the house she loved.

Then she heard the yapping of the dog again close to the cellar door and the urgency of her task reasserted itself.

As quickly and quietly as she could, Hannah lifted the discarded deck chairs from off the trunk and pulled away the boxes and the two armchairs around it. Gripping the handle of the trunk then she tugged at it, trying to pull it away from the corner. There was a clinking sound inside

as she tugged but no responding movement and though she tugged again and again, the trunk, as if glued to the floor, refused to budge, even an inch, let alone the 2 x 2 feet her father had specified. She paused from her efforts in dismay. To empty it was going to take valuable time and make a noise but there seemed no alternative.

Opening the lid, she saw the reason for the problem, that the trunk wasn't filled with cricket bats and sports gear as she'd remembered but with carefully crated bottles of vintage whisky, brandy and port. She couldn't believe it. The whole trunk was filled with them – specially designed crates, each containing four vintage bottles. But why hidden in the trunk? From the Slade? From Marcus? And if Hugo had penetrated the trunk after all, might he not also have explored beneath it?

Desperate now, conscious of the time passing, Hannah set about lifting all the crates out of the trunk onto the stone floor. Trying to keep her movements quiet and to find space for the crates nearby, it took far longer than she had anticipated and by the time she'd finished she felt again like smashing them all for the delay. But at last the trunk was empty and she was able to shift it with ease. Taking out her tape measure, carefully she measured the 2 x 2 feet distance from the corner her father had specified in the anthology she'd found in the hidden cupboard of his bedroom.

Then, with the aid of her penknife, she lifted what she thought was the correct grey stone. To her disappointment, there was nothing she could see beneath the stone at all – no documents, no paper – only the earth bearing the imprint of the underside of the stone. Had she imagined it all? Had

her father misled her? Or had Hugo got there first and destroyed the one document that could help her? It wasn't beyond him. Nothing was beyond him. She knew that now but there was no obvious sign he'd lifted the stone, no disturbance she could see of the soil – unless. It struck her then that her father might have intended it to disappoint if Hugo got there first. Her heart thumping, she started to dig with the blade of her penknife into the soil. One inch down – still nothing. She noticed then, half an inch deeper, a transparent piece of plastic. Gripping it with her thumb and finger, she pulled it out from the soil – a carefully folded A4 plastic envelope with a folded document inside.

Her hands trembling, she removed the document from the plastic cover. It had only one page, written entirely in her father's italic hand, a hand she could see at once had been written with effort and had been shaking at times but which she knew unmistakably was his from the embellishments and curves of his capital letters.

Her eyes skimming down the page she read:

This if the last Will and Testament of me, Thomas John Charles Delaney:

1. I revoke all wills I have previously made.
2. I appoint as my executor my solicitor, Nicholas James.
3. I give the following legacies:
    a) To Marcus, my grandson £10,000
    b) To Emma, my housekeeper £10,000
    c) To my sister Eileen Brownridge our father's chest and mementos

4.   I leave Hugo, my son, all my insurance and guaranteed bonds.

5.   I give to my daughter, Hannah, unconditionally the property of Yadrahna and all the contents and furniture therein. If my daughter, Hannah, does not survive me, I give my property, Yadrahna, to The National Trust.

Signed: Thomas J. C. Delaney

Dated 17ᵗʰ May 1996

Witnessed : B.J. Williams
                         M. Mills

Hannah looked at the date again. The 17ᵗʰ May was over two weeks beyond the 1ˢᵗ May. There could be no dispute now of her father's intentions with the more recent date. And the will moreover was witnessed. She recognised the signature of Williams, the gardener, who'd worked for her father for many years. Mills, though, – was it the postman? She wasn't sure. She didn't recognise the name as that of a friend. Whoever it was, it was remarkable achievement. So much planning it must have taken, with Olga Slade and Hugo constantly on the watch, and how had her father managed to get down the steps, to move the trunk when he was so ill? Had he done it at night? In the day? How had he eluded them, managed the almost insuperable obstacle of getting Williams, himself and Mills secretly together? Tears came to her eyes as she thought of his struggling, his efforts, virtually alone, to defeat Hugo's scheming.

Then like a wave her heart lifted with the realisation that his efforts could carry her now forward, that she had

the evidence, the hope at last herself now of defeating Hugo's scheming.

Carefully, she folded the will back in its plastic cover, then slipped it down inside her track suit trousers so that it couldn't slip out.

She had just stamped the stone back in place over the disturbed soil and was pushing the trunk back into the corner again, when she was aware of the sound of a car engine in the drive above to the right of the cellar. Surely, she tried to dismiss the thought, it couldn't be Hugo back already. Looking at her watch then she saw with concern that it was in fact the time Luke had warned her that Hugo might return.

She hesitated, uncertain whether to make a dash for it, with the risk of being caught, leaving the excavation exposed, or whether to wait and put everything back again in the hope that Hugo wouldn't even realise she'd been.

The thought of being caught now appalled her. They were bound to realise she'd come for something and try and search her. No, it wasn't worth the risk. She'd wait until they were all settled inside then creep out, with Hugo none the wiser, lulled.

As quickly as she could, she started to put the crates back in the trunk again. She had just put the last crate in and had covered the trunk again with the discarded deck chairs and pushed back the boxes of curtains when she heard Hugo's voice quite distinct now coming from the hall above the stone steps on the other side of the cellar.

"Why's the light on in the cellar?"

"Light?" she heard Olga Slade echo in the disgruntled way she had when challenged.

She heard the door from the hall then open. There was still time to make a dash for it up the steps to the outside door but she felt rooted to the spot with fear and indecision at the sound of Hugo's voice and a doubt that she'd make it.

"Look. I told you – full on. Have you been down here again?"

"Of course I haven't." Olga Slade's thick voice came adamantly in denial. "You can count them if you want."

"Maybe I will."

Hannah could just see now Hugo's black suede shoes on the third step down from the hall. It was too late now to conceal herself convincingly behind the trunks and boxes, too late to escape without being heard. As Hugo's black suede shoes felt for the next step down, she slipped into the shadows on the wall side of the wine rack.

Half way down the steps, Hugo looked across at the trunk where he kept his vintage bottles. He noted that one of the deck chairs was not in the exact position where he'd left it. He was about to call up to Olga Slade to challenge her again when, pausing to assess other possible changes, he was aware of a movement behind the wine rack, of a figure then pressed against the wine rack trying to hide – a woman's figure judging by its height and slightness. He could see then from the angle where he was standing through the open patterning of the metal – the long brown hair.

His pulse speeded a moment in fear that others were waiting with her, waiting to get him but as his sharp eyes penetrated the familiar shadows, searching each gap between the boxes of curtains, soon he realised that there was no other real hiding place, that she was alone.

Why had she come? What was she after that he didn't know? And how had she got in? Who had helped her? As he paused on the step, his hatred grew and with it a deeper fear that she might yet find the means to thwart him.

Then he smiled to himself as a plan formed in his mind. If she'd come uninvited, unknown to him, uninvited, unknown she could stay.

Giving no hint of suspicion, Hugo padded with an air of nonchalance down the rest of the steps, across the cellar floor and up the steps the other side. He could hardly believe her oversight, that the key was still in the door and she hadn't taken it.

Making sure the door was locked and secure, whistling to himself, he withdrew the key then and put it in his inner jacket pocket. Wary that she'd noticed, he kept the shadow within the corner of his eye as he padded back again across the cellar floor.

As he mounted the steps again to the hall, it suddenly struck Hannah what he'd done and what he intended. He must have seen her, she realised then. Why else had he taken the key? She'd be trapped at their mercy. Creeping out from behind the wine rack, as Hugo neared the top of the steps, she scrambled up the steps behind him. Hearing her, Hugo turned, blocking the door, and, as she tried to squeeze past him, using all the force he could muster, he kicked at her with his black suede shoes. As she went sprawling back down the stone steps, he turned off the cellar light and bolted the door behind him.

Shocked, at the bottom of the steps, Hannah leaned against the rough limestone wall in the darkness, trying not to cry. Her forehead throbbed where she'd hit it against

the wall in falling and she could feel blood trickling down her cheek from the wound, a pain in her ankle where she'd twisted it, a pain in her wrist where she'd tried to break the fall. Her torch, to her dismay, was no longer in her pocket.

She felt faint and vaguely nauseous. The bleeding from her forehead frightened her. In an effort to stop it, she pressed the palm of her hand over the wound as she remembered once being instructed in the guides but it had little effect. The blood kept trickling down her cheek, dripping through her fingers. What would happen, with increasing alarm, she speculated, if she couldn't stop it.

Even more frightening now, impenetrable, was the darkness between herself and the outside cellar door – the door to which only Hugo now had the key. There was no trace of light, not even from beneath the door at the top of the steps to the hall. Hugo had put something there, she was sure, to ensure she wouldn't see. What else had he done, she wondered then in fear, what else intend. He was bound to suspect something from her visit and she still had the will in her possession but for how much longer if she didn't get away?

In panic, at a fresh spurt of bleeding, Hannah unzipped her track suit top and pulled off her white T–shirt. Folding it as best she could like bandage, she tied it round her forehead, pulling it tight. As she felt for her track suit top to put it back on again, her fingers closed to her relief over the torch that had fallen from her pocket.

The plastic over the bulb was broken and as she pressed the switch the bulb emitted only a faint light – a light that would soon extinguish itself but for the moment it was enough.

Forcing herself to her feet, one hand still pressed over the T shirt binding her wound, Hannah stumbled by the light of the torch across the cellar floor past the wine rack and up the steps to the outside door.

Leaning against the wall, she paused, trying to draw in deep breaths against the faintness creeping up on her again and reached for the light switch. But as she pressed it down, nothing happened. Puzzled she tried again. Still no light.

It came to her then what inwardly she feared, that Hugo had been to the fuse box, that there would be no light in the cellar now – only the uncertain light of her torch.

Crying, she switched the torch off to save it, in desperation knelt by the old oak door and as loudly as she could through the keyhole called for help in the hope that someone, anyone would hear.

Close to the pond, Marcus could hear her as he paused throwing stones. He felt no compulsion or interest in going to her aid. Her father had anyway instructed him to ignore any women's voices he heard.

Exhausted by her calling at length, Hannah slumped back against the wall again. Through her deepening apprehension, she was aware suddenly of a movement outside the door. Leaning forward she could see still the minute patch of sky through the keyhole, then something dark covering it and the sound of heavy breathing. She pulled at the bolt at the lower end of the door in the hope that the door might have been opened without her realising but though she tugged as hard as she could, the door remained securely shut as before. Looking back

through the keyhole she could see the minute patch of sky again – no sound now of breathing. Whoever had been there had apparently gone. Gone where?

It occurred to her then, trying to revive her hope that perhaps the hall door was now open, that Hugo having frightened her, might be willing now to relent a bit and let her go. He couldn't keep her here indefinitely. Someone sooner or later was bound to find out. Would they though? No one in fact knew she was here – not Luke, not even Sally.

Trying not to think about the consequences, switching on the dim light of the torch again, Hannah forced herself back down across the cellar again. Her T–shirt to her relief had stopped the bleeding but her forehead still throbbed and she felt a recurring faintness and dizziness as she slowly climbed up the steps again to the door leading to the hall.

She paused on the top step, leaning against the wall to recover her strength and turned off the torch. She could hear voices coming from the kitchen – the voices of Olga Slade and Hugo keyed up in some kind of altercation but the noise of the radio blurred to her ears the exact nature of what they were saying

Carefully, quietly, she turned the knob of the hall door and pushed. For a moment her hopes rose as it yielded an inch within the frame. Then she was pushing against the resistance of a lock that was unyielding.

Angry, in her disappointment, she started to shout and bang on the door. "Let me out! Let me out!" Stopping to listen, she was aware that the voices too had stopped. There was a brief silence as she waited, then abruptly loud

music coming from the radio, trying to drown her voice as she started shouting again.

How long she went on shouting she wasn't sure. In a helpless rage, she heard herself threatening to break all the bottles of vintage wine but there was no response.

Leaning back, exhausted and nauseous again, against the wall, she tried to think afresh what to do. Her whole situation seemed vastly more ominous now. Hugo had no intention, it was obvious, of letting her go and as the flames of her mother's car swept back with Helen Wilkes's story through her throbbing head again, it came to her then with growing fear that Hugo was going to use the darkness and cold of the cellar as he'd used the flames, leaving her if he could to die, pretending he didn't know she was there.

It was no use calling to the Slade or Marcus. They would do, she was sure, all Hugo demanded and take no notice. Her only hope was to dig and break her way out or to wait for Luke till he returned and try till then to survive.

She hadn't any hope of digging or breaking her way out. She knew that right away. There were no tools in the cellar – nothing to dig with, no axe to break down the door and she felt she hadn't anyway the strength now. No, she could feel all her instincts now telling her to conserve her strength, to try to survive for when Luke came. She didn't doubt Luke would come, when he realised, when he knew. She knew she could trust him now, that he had nothing to do with Hugo. Would he come though in time?

She was conscious of feeling increasingly thirsty and cold, of wanting to lie down somewhere safe and warm. Like an animal she felt wanting to seek out its burrow.

But there was no burrow in the cold stones of the cellar, nothing to drink except Hugo's vintage wines.

Assess your resources, her father had always said, make a plan. His words came back to her now and she remembered the bottle of mineral water she'd seen on the lower level of the wine rack before the lights had gone out, remembered the curtains she'd shifted in the boxes by the trunk.

Switching on the torch again, she struggled back down the steps again. Locating the mineral water, she extracted the bottle and pulled some curtaining from one of the boxes. With a final effort, she heaved the curtaining up to the top of the steps leading to the outside door. There wasn't room to stretch out but she knew she'd feel safer here – farther from Hugo, closer to Luke. By lying with her legs curled up like a foetus, she'd manage, she decided.

She took a drink of the mineral water then placed the bottle carefully upright in a recess in the wall to the right of the door. Bundling up the curtaining, she made a makeshift mattress and pillow, using the heaviest curtaining to cover her. The curtaining smelt of dampness, decay and mould but she didn't care. Exhausted, she closed her eyes, not noticing she'd left on the torch and within minutes had drifted asleep.

She dreamt of Hugo. She was lying stretched out on an operating table and he was bent over her with a skullcap on his head and a mask over his mouth. All she could see of him were his eyes – his cold grey eyes piercing her with hate. And he was holding in his right hand a sharp red knife, a surgeon's knife poised over her breasts. He was going to sever her breasts suddenly she realised. He was

going to maim her, kill her and no one was stopping him, no one holding him. She tried to bend her knees, to kick out at his groin but her legs she felt clamped by steel bands nor could she move her arms, her hands. Any moment the knife was going to cut into her –

Hannah awoke to her own cries echoing back to her in the darkness. For a moment, shivering in fear, she had the impression of Hugo's knife in her dreams having blinded her – so cold it was and dark – dark beyond her imagining. Feeling round her in panic, her fingers touched then the brocade of the curtaining and it all came back to her with the musty smell – her struggle up the steps and her sleeping.

How long had she slept, she wondered. What time was it? She felt over the stone close to the door where she'd left the torch. The torch was still there but as she pressed the switch she realised with dismay that she'd forgotten to switch it off, that prematurely through her own neglect it had finally extinguished itself.

Trying to feel her way carefully, for fear of falling down the steps, she knelt by the door and pressed her face against the keyhole. She could detect no light outside though whether it was night or something had been put there she couldn't tell. She listened against the door, trying to distinguish any sound that would indicate the time but all was quiet – no bird song, no traffic.

Despondent, she leaned against the wall, pulling the curtaining back over her again. She felt cold. Her head still throbbed from the wound and though she felt nauseous, increasingly she was conscious of pangs of hunger now. How stupid she was, she reflected, not having taken Luke's

advice and brought some rolls. But at least, she tried to comfort herself, she could drink. She felt for the bottle of mineral water she'd put in the recess of the wall, took a few sips, then cautiously put the bottle back again.

In an effort to divert herself from thinking about her hunger, she tried playing a mental scrabble, visualising the letters laid out on the cellar floor but within a few minutes she found she couldn't concentrate, that her head ached too much and her mind kept going back to Hugo.

How was she going to get away and outwit him? Would she be able to get away? And if Luke didn't come, who would?

As the night wore on, the realisation came to her that she could die in the cellar – die without anyone knowing or coming in time. Die without having begun really to live, to achieve anything of meaning.

What had she achieved in fact with her life? Nothing, she thought, that amounted to much. Some moments of teaching here and there – a few odd students who'd responded but she'd never really got anywhere with anything, never really given herself to anything – a cause, a group, even a single person, to help, to make a difference.

Her relationship with Richard had never been true because she'd never shared his assumptions. The only relationship where she'd really communicated had been with her father. With Richard she could see more clearly now she'd just drifted in and out of his life without meaning.

Now Luke –

Luke who was as unlike Richard as anyone could be, who would never seek to conquer in a material

conventional sense but who knew deep down, she sensed, what he stood for. As she thought of him now again, looking down at her in the cottage when she'd woken, his eyes filled with kindness and concern, she knew that she loved him, that she wanted above all else to keep herself alive for him.

Increasingly cold, she wrapped herself more closely in the brocade curtaining again, took another sip of the mineral water and tried not to think about her hunger.

As the night wore on, sleepless, it came to her that she couldn't go on simply waiting for three days for Luke to return. He might not return. He might have to stay on with his father. His father could be ill. Despite Luke's reliability, nothing was certain, predictable. Luke like everyone else was subject to events beyond his control, his own wishes. Should she put herself in a position anyway of relying on Luke? Hadn't that been her weakness all along with Richard – relying on him too much? What sort of state anyway would she be in in three days? Could she last that long in a state of alertness? As long as she was captive, she was vulnerable and the will, despite her concealment, could be taken away by Hugo.

No, she had to make an effort while she still had some strength. How though? She had no light, no tools, nothing that could be used as a ram to break open the door. Part of the cellar, though, she reflected, was above ground level. Its outside wall, moreover, following damage in a storm, had been reconstructed, like the scullery, with bricks and mortar, not stone. If she could dislodge some bricks and mortar by the top steps where she was lying, she could perhaps make a hole eventually large enough to climb

through. Dislodge with what though? Her penknife, her only tool, was scarcely up to the job. Something larger, more pointed was needed to dig with any effect the lime mortar out from between the bricks.

She remembered then the old poker in the fireside set she'd moved to get at the trunk. Cautiously edging her way down the stone steps, she felt round the trunk again over the discarded deck chairs till she located at length the poker's brass handle. The handle felt dented but the steel shaft strong and firm and pointed still at the end. If she could but find something hard to bang it into the wall. There's been no sign in her search of a hammer but one of the broken stone paving slabs, she reflected, might do. Carefully, she felt around the trunk in the darkness till she located a piece of jagged stone, that seemed large enough, that she could use.

Feeling her way again up the stone steps, tentatively at the top she started to probe with the poker and stone the wall to the right of the locked oak door.

Chapter 26

It was the darkness that got to Hannah most, the sense of helplessness she had at being excluded from the rhythms of light and shading she'd always till now taken for granted. She literally couldn't see anything. Every movement, every probe with the poker had to be felt first and checked with her fingers. And her fingers were sore now with feeling the grainy lime mortar. The mortar came away more easily than cement mortar would have done but it was a painstakingly slow tedious process. After two hours of hammering at the poker, with the broken slab, she'd dislodged only two bricks from the first inner wall and there were two more thicknesses of brick beyond it.

The problem was the header bricks spaced after every two stringer bricks, which meant she couldn't clear the first thickness sufficiently to get at the second. There was always going to be, she could feel, a header brick spanning the first and second thicknesses. The only solution she could think of was to attack each header brick sideways as she removed the two stringers and break the whole header up at the point it entered the second thickness. This she proceeded to do with a growing sense of frustration at the slowness of it all. At the end of another hour she had broken up only one header. Her arms ached from holding

up the poker and banging it and she felt weak, a tautness in her stomach from hunger. Desperately she wished again she'd brought the sandwiches Luke had made, instead of leaving them behind. How stupid she was, she blamed herself, for not coming more prepared.

As she stopped to sip some of the mineral water in the alcove, she could hear outside the cawing of ravens on the roof and intermittently the sound of a car driving past on the road down to Wynton. It was obviously light outside now, she concluded, which meant the Slade and Hugo would soon be up and about and she would have to be more careful about making a noise. She pressed on more skilfully, faster, this time dislodging two more stringers and a header, then hearing voices, coming from near the door leading to the kitchen, decided to stop for a while to try and hear what they were saying.

Carefully, feeling her way down the steps and across the floor of the cellar, she crept up the stone steps, down which Hugo had knocked her, then bent down with her ear close to the keyhole of the door. Tentatively, for a moment she turned the door knob in the hope that perhaps unknown to her the Slade had unbolted the door but it was as firmly secure as before.

She could hear then, to her surprise, the voices of the Slade and Hugo, coming quite clearly from the kitchen – the Slade's petulant and whining, Hugo's on edge, on the defensive.

"You promised," she heard the Slade say. "You know I won't have a proper pension. You know how hard it is for me. It's why I agreed in the first place. I wouldn't have agreed otherwise."

"Promised!" Hugo's voice had assumed its usual contempt and indignation when faced with challenge but there was a strange uncertainty about it, Hannah detected, out of keeping with his plans. "I promised nothing except you could have a roof over your head which you were only too pleased to accept, as I remember."

"Of course, I was glad to have some accommodation that went with the job. It's not easy at my age being left with no home and no pension. But it's not right if you don't keep your word."

"What word? I said I'd reward you if I could, if things went my way and I still might but circumstances have changed."

"Changed? What do you mean?"

"Things are not so certain now."

"You mean all this façade we've been through – there's been no point?"

"I wouldn't say that."

"Then why can't you pay me the second instalment?"

"I haven't the funds to pay you."

"You must have to run this place."

"I tell you, woman, I don't have the funds to hand."

"In that case," Olga Slade's voice started to probe with more threat. "I shall have no alternative but to make things known."

There was a prolonged silence then Hannah heard Hugo's move with more menace on the offensive.

"Make known what exactly?"

"The will, the way you forced your father to drink, the fact you're now trying to starve out your sister…"

"I wouldn't if I were you."

"But you're not me are you? And I want my money."

"You'll have your money in due course when the situation is resolved. But it won't be resolved if you go blabbering to all and sundry."

"You can't let her stay there much longer."

"I don't intend to but it's got to be long enough for her to realise.."

"Realise what?"

"That she's got to accept the situation."

"She's unlikely to do that and supposing she finds something down there. Another will? You said yourself there could be another will."

"And so there may be but she won't get very far with it if there is. I intend to search her before I let her out. Just give it another day and we'll know what she's been up to."

"As long as we do." Olga Slade's words trailed on a note of scepticism and Hannah heard no more as their voices receded away from the kitchen.

Had Hugo intended her to hear about the search, she wondered. It was no idle threat, she was sure of that, which made it all the more important that she got out as soon as she could. Dare she continue though with the hammering now they were awake?

Tense with tiredness and a growing sense of weakness now and isolation at the thought of the task ahead, she waited, on edge, till she heard the sound of the Daimler's engine in the drive. Hugo was away at least for a while but was the Slade with him?

Hannah decided to risk it and becoming faster now, to her satisfaction, she managed to chisel away six more bricks of the inner wall before the Daimler returned. She

heard Marcus then most of the afternoon taking pot shots with his air rifle close to the outside cellar wall and felt impelled again to pause till she heard the Slade calling him for his evening meal. When she could hear no more obvious human sounds outside, no more birds singing, she began in earnest to attack the second thickness of wall.

All night she worked in the dark with a growing sense of urgency and desperation. In her fear of Hugo waylaying her and taking the will, she could ignore for a time her bleeding sore fingers, her aching back and hunger. Then her hunger would reassert itself in waves of weakness, making the muscles of her arms and legs feel like paper. Her head would spin then, aching from the wound inflicted on the cellar steps by Hugo but she didn't dare lie down or rest to recover. Pausing only to take a few sips from her diminishing supply of mineral water in the alcove, she forced herself back again to the resistant bricks and mortar till her hunger became a part again of the rhythm of hammering.

It was past 6 when eventually she broke through the third layer of bricks and made a hole sufficient to crawl out onto the Yorkshire stone bordering the cellar wall. Already the sun was bright in a blue sky and for a moment she stood mesmerised, dazzled by the brightness after so long in darkness, dizzy again from hunger, her throat dry. Then a movement in the shrubbery alerted her. A fox, a badger – she couldn't see but it seemed a warning. She paused to feel the will secure inside her trouser leg, then pulling her socks up more firmly, limped away from the broken wall and down the drive to the road.

She decided to follow the path down through Rassler's wood, go first to the cottage to get something to eat, then catch a bus into Oxford and go straight to Ashford with the will. But as she followed the usual badger path down, she was aware, as she struggled to keep her bearings, of the crackling of twigs periodically behind her, of the shadowed outline of a man's figure between the beech trees as she glanced behind her – a figure that seemed to be gaining on her. With all the effort she could muster, jaggedly she ran, gasping down through the trees till she reached the main road.

A bus with early morning commuters was just drawing up at the bus stop. She hesitated a moment, then abandoning her earlier plan clambered on board. Unnoticed by her as she fumbled in her jean's pocket for some change, a man with dark hair climbed in after her and went down to the back of the bus. To her dismay, all she could find in her pocket were two 50p pieces, which was not enough for the fare right into Oxford. She would have to get off on the outskirts, the conductor said. She noticed then other people on the bus looking at her strangely as if there was something the matter with her. But she felt too tired and weak now to analyse the reason or to care.

Getting off at the allotted stop in north Oxford, she felt she hadn't the strength to walk to the city centre. She had to get something to eat – a sandwich – anything. Passing two schoolboys consuming iced buns, she felt she wanted to snatch the buns from them, in panic asked one of the boys for a bite but he merely stared at her, then giggled and went on eating.

At the corner of the road she thrust her hand into a rubbish bin but there were only greasy pieces of paper and

plastic wrappings – nothing edible. It came to her then from the road names that she wasn't far from Luke's room at Anthea's, that Anthea might be able to help her if Luke wasn't there. Was Luke back from Leeds, she wondered. She tried to remember what day it was but felt confused. As she strained to remember, clutching at the dustbin, the throbbing in her head returned.

She asked an elderly woman the way to Lockwood Road. The woman pursed her lips and motioned to a road nearby, her eyes uncertain whether to empathise or disapprove. Do I look that bad, Hannah wondered. She could feel dried blood in her hair still, a sharpening pain in her temples as she staggered along the last stretch of the road the woman had indicated. At last she could see it then, the brass number 46 shimmering over a light green door.

Forcing her self up the steps, Hanna felt a wave of nausea, the pain in her head intensifying, Shaking, she pressed the white bell, then collapsed fainting against the light green door.

Solicitously, a man with lean face and dark hair bent over her, feeling in the pocket of her jeans. Then the door opened and she fell back on the doormat at Anthea's feet.

Chapter 27

Luke thought constantly of Hannah while helping his father move, talking about her to him and promising to bring her to see him when he returned from India.

"If I'm still here, lad," his father had wryly smiled.

"Of course, you will be." Would Hannah, though, Luke wondered. What did she feel about him? He still didn't really know – only that he didn't want to be separated from her now, hundreds of miles away.

He kept wondering if she was settled in his room now at Anthea's. He felt he should ring to check but there were so many practicalities to sort out for his father and when he did eventually ring the phone was engaged.

It was late in the evening at the end of his second day, when his father was eventually settled in his flat and his objects of furniture and furnishing installed, that he had a phone call from Anthea telling him that Hannah had not stayed in his room nor made any contact.

Alarmed, trying to calm his father as much as himself, Luke decided to catch the first train the next morning. All the way back, he tried to tell himself that Hannah had probably decided after all, in the independent way she had, to stay in the cottage. But he found it difficult to convince himself. Hannah had after all promised him, despite her

independence, that she would go to his room for the night and stay. What had happened then?

On arriving back in Oxford, Luke went straight to his bicycle padlocked at the station and cycled out to Wynton. The cottage, to his concern, was locked and the windows closed without sign of Hannah and as he looked into the kitchen window he noticed that the kitchen table was exactly as he'd left it on the morning he'd gone to Leeds with the same loaf of bread in the same position, the pile of sandwiches he'd cut ready for her – most of them uneaten.

What had happened? What should he do? Call the police? Call the police though for what? He'd no evidence anything as yet was wrong – except that he knew deep down something was wrong and he had to find out.

Leaving his bicycle, Luke ran stumbling up the path through the woods to Yadrahna – the path Hannah would have taken coming home. There was no sign he could see she'd come that way – no objects she'd left en route behind. Cautiously for a moment he paused in the shrubbery, noting that the Daimler and Olga Slade's blue Renault were both in the drive, then made his way round to the cellar.

The hole he noticed in the upper cellar wall struck him at once as strange. What could be the point, he wondered. It hadn't been in need of repair. As he looked inside then through the three layers of brick, he saw lying on the curtaining at the top of the steps the torch Hannah had had at the cottage and what seemed on the curtaining to be stains of blood.

Alarmed, he climbed in through the hole and inspected the curtaining more carefully. It was blood, he was sure,

and through the light filtering through the hole he could see more blood spattered on the steps leading down but no sign of Hannah herself in the recesses of the cellar. Fearful, he tried to imagine what had happened, how badly she was injured – above all where she could be.

Picking up the torch and a piece of the curtaining for evidence, Luke clambered back through the hole. He could hear Olga Slade now outside the back door of the kitchen, clattering rubbish into the bin outside. His brain instantly signalled a way in and running past the back of the house he pushed his way through the back door as Olga Slade was returning inside.

"What do you think you're playing at?"

Never had Olga Slade looked so ugly, Luke thought, as she pouted now in indignation, her small black eyes like currants in a lardy cake.

"Where is she?" he demanded, ignoring the hands on hips as she tried to bar his way.

"Where's who? I don't know what you're talking about." Olga Slade's face puckered up again but her currant eyes were shifting now, her voice on the defensive.

"You know bloody well who I mean." He felt suddenly he wanted to throttle her. Gripping her shoulder, he twisted her, pressing her back inside the kitchen against the stove. "Tell me where she is or I'll make you pay for it. You locked her in there, didn't you – you and that bastard!"

Luke stopped, shocked at himself but it had worked. Olga Slade was crumbling as he held her, tears of fear and remorse streaking the layers of powder on her cheeks.

"She's gone."

"Gone where?"

Before Olga Slade could answer, Luke was conscious of a padding sound behind him. He spun round to see Hugo Delaney standing in the doorway of the kitchen with a glass of wine in his hand. For a moment he thought Hugo was going to throw the glass at him, so intense was the grey hostility in his eyes. Then he smoothed the rim of his glass with his fingers, seeming to recover himself.

"So it's you back again." Hugo looked with contempt over his glass at Luke. "In answer to your question, my sister went to Oxford this morning."

"Oh did she? How do you know? Did you take her?"

"She took herself, as a matter of fact."

"But you locked her up first, didn't you?"

"I did no such thing. I locked the cellar door, yes, but I had no idea she was there."

"How do you account then for the blood on the steps and the way she obviously had to dig her way out?"

"She should have let us know then she was there, shouldn't she? Isn't that right, mother? We didn't hear her calling, did we?" Hugo turned as Elvira Delaney came up behind him in her wheel chair.

"Even if we had," Elvira Delaney's voice was hard and hawk like as her eyes, "she deserved to stay after all she's done."

"So you were prepared," Luke turned on them both in anger, "to leave her to starve to death – like no doubt you left her mother to burn in her car."

The muscles of Hugo's face went taut for a moment and his eyes darkened in fear. Then to Luke's surprise his cheeks went pale and his hands, his whole body were shaking as he tried to control the glass in his hand.

"You can't deny it, can you?" Luke persisted. "You left her to starve and she would have done if you'd had your way."

Luke noticed patches of perspiration seeping through Hugo's shirt on his chest and under his arm, glistening drops of sweat on his forehead, then he was lurching over to the nearest oak chair at the kitchen table. He slumped down then, dropping the glass of wine as he did so on the stone flagged floor. Pieces of glass scattered to the wheels of Elvira Delaney's chair and the wine trickled like watery blood round Hugo's black suede shoes.

Hugo opened his mouth to speak in denial but the words wouldn't come and he grimaced as if in pain.

From the doorway, Elvira's voice, uncertain now, pleaded with Luke. "Leave him alone. Can't you see he's not well?"

For the first time since he'd known Hugo, Luke sensed a glimmer of conscience, a nerve linking flesh to brain and motivation. But his concern for Hannah was greater than any sympathy he could have felt for Hugo's symptoms.

"You're a bastard, Delaney – an evil bastard!"

Luke kicked aside the broken glass and strode out of the kitchen and back door onto the drive. His words would cost him dear he knew. He'd never get the back pay owed to him now for his gardening. But he didn't care. Clutching Hannah's torch still and the blood stained piece of curtaining, he made his way back down through Rassler's Wood again to the cottage. Hugo Delaney was a bastard but what, he kept searching himself, was he going to do about it? Bastards always got away with it unless one took the wind out of their sails and acted. Act how though? That was the question.

As he came to the bend in the road where Hannah's mother's car had come off the road, he remembered Hannah's strong suspicion that her brother had planted the nails that had caused the skid. If Hugo Delaney could act in such a way, he mused, why should he not be acted upon in a way similar?

Preoccupied, Luke began to work out a plan. By the time he reached the cottage, he began to feel calmer, more resolute. His bicycle, to his relief, was still leaning against the porch where he's left it, untouched, but the sight of the cottage, so quiet and closed in on itself in the bright morning light, made him feel despondent and concerned again about Hannah herself. Even the garden with its abundance of herbs and long grasses seemed strangely lifeless now without Hannah bending over them.

Standing by the porch, Luke was overwhelmed with longing for her again. He had a strange sense she was calling to him though from where he couldn't tell. Desultorily, he wiped away some bird droppings from the old garden seat, then turned back to his bicycle. He was about to wheel it round towards the lane when a peremptory voice suddenly startled him.

"Is this Brambles, young man?"

Luke turned to see an elderly woman advancing up the over grown path towards him with a walking stick aimed like a gun at the cottage. She was smartly dressed in a grey linen suit and silvery grey hair swept back in a knot but what struck Luke most was that she had the same finely shaped features as Hannah, the same high cheek bones and large dark brown eyes. For a moment he thought it must be Hannah's mother but he knew it couldn't be, that her

mother, like his own, was dead. Then who, he wondered, as he answered.

"It's called Brambles, yes."

"Good." The woman lowered her stick. "At least I've found the right place. Now where's my niece?"

"Your niece? You mean you're Hannah's aunt, Aunt Eileen?"

"I most certainly am. And who, may I ask, are you, young man?"

Luke hesitated. It was a simple yet profound question which carried implications he didn't feel capable of dealing with right now and he replied simply:

"I'm Luke, Luke West." He leaned his bicycle against the porch and went up to her and shook her hand. Her hand felt bony, vulnerable but the mind that directed it would not be, he sensed, so easily crushed.

"I don't think you've answered my question, young man. It wasn't your name I wanted to know but your reason for being here, your relationship with my niece. She wrote to me only a few days ago saying she had found an idyllic place. It doesn't look too idyllic to me." Aunt Eileen waved her stick accusingly towards the crumbling porch. "But never mind. Where is she?"

"I only wish I knew. She's disappeared," Luke said. "I think she may be injured."

"Injured? Disappeared? Whatever's going on?"

Luke hesitated. He wanted to cycle into Oxford as fast as he could to find out now and waste no more time. He wasn't sure anyway how much to confide in Aunt Eileen and worry her, how much he ought to confide, how much Aunt Eileen knew already about the whole situation. But

Aunt Eileen was clearly not going to let him go without answer.

"I've plenty of time, young man. No short cuts. I want the whole story." Aunt Eileen gave a dubious glance at the rickety garden seat, then flicking away some dead flowers with her walking stick, sat down.

Luke told her then as succinctly as he could what he's seen at Yadrahna, about his encounter with Hugo and what he'd deduced from his visit.

"I always knew that nephew of mine was up to no good, "emphatically Aunt Eileen endorsed Luke's view, prodding some oregano with her stick in the crack of the stone path. "The question is though – where is my niece?" Aunt Eileen gave a last prod, then stood up, pointing the stick at Luke. "You go into Oxford, young man, and find her. Meanwhile, I'll have a word with my nephew. It's time I gave him a piece of my mind."

Intrepid, with her stick, Aunt Eileen strode back down the overgrown pathway then through the collapsing wicker gate and up the lane to her car.

She's like an early Victorian traveller, Luke thought, determined, never phased. Following with his bicycle, he wondered what kind of reception she'd get from Hugo. He felt he ought to accompany her, but more than ever he wanted to find Hannah. Aunt Eileen seemed more than capable anyway, he mused, in looking after herself. He watched her zoom off in a grey BMW out onto the main road, narrowly missing a motor cycle as she did so. With a final wave, he cycled on alone into Oxford.

He went straight to Lockwood Road to his lodgings where Anthea, to his relief, answered the door.

"She's here," Anthea immediately informed him. "She came earlier. I tried ringing you in Leeds."

"How is she?" he looked into Antheas's tired, concerned eyes.

"You'd better come up. I've put her in the spare room next to yours."

It was a room identical to his own with the same sash windows and the same alcoves and Edwardian lead fireplace and white walls and green carpet but there were none of the random objects and splashes of colour that marked his own. There were no personal possessions, only the white sheets of a single pine bed close to the window where Hannah lay stretched out asleep in the clothes she's arrive in that morning.

Luke was immediately aware of the gash on her forehead, of dried blood clotting her hair and staining her shirt and jeans. Drawing near, he saw how pale she was, that her hair was tangled and filthy, with brick dust and mortar, that her nails were black and her hands cut and raw.

"She fainted on the doorstep," Andrea whispered. "The odd thing was that someone was with her, bending over her as if he was helping her but he ran off as soon as I opened the door."

"What did he look like?"

"Thin faced, thick black hair. No one I'd ever seen before."

Jamieson in disguise, Luke wondered, or was it the other man, as yet unknown, whom Delaney employed to do his dirty work? Whoever it was, he must have thought he was on to something or he wouldn't have followed her.

The second will was it? Luke felt increasingly concerned as Anthea continued,

"I got a doctor to come and check her. He said he thought she was probably a bit concussed and we needed to watch and give her plenty of rest. Mainly he thought she was exhausted from not eating. I gave her some soup and bread and cheese. Little and often he said and not to overdo it."

"How long has she been asleep?" Luke felt he couldn't bear to think what she'd been through alone.

"She's been here five or six hours – most of the time I'd say."

"She's not spoken to you then?"

"Only to ask for you. I think she wants you to do something for her." Anthea smiled and put her arms round Luke's shoulder. "I'll leave her with you. If she wants anything, let me know."

"Thanks, Anthea and for all you've done."

Luke drew up a chair and sat by the bed when Anthea had gone. For over an hour he sat, waiting, watching, wondering what had happened in the hours he's been away. Had her brother deliberately inflicted the wound or had it been an accident? How deep was it and with what effect? Had she found in the end the will she'd wanted and managed to get it out? The more he thought about it, the more remarkable it seemed that Hannah had managed to dig her way out of the cellar in the way she had but it had been at a cost. If only, he wished, she'd waited and he'd been with her, able to share the risks, the effort, the loneliness and pain. He felt he wanted to stroke, caress her wounded head, her breasts, her raw scratched hands and

breathe new life into her, share what she'd gone through. But he didn't dare, following Anthea's instructions disturb her.

He was wondering what he should do about the cottage and where best she should be looked after when he was aware that her dark brown eyes were open and looking at him.

Gently he took her hand and pressed his lips against her palm. "How do you feel?"

"I'm not sure." Tentatively she smiled. "A bit tired."

"I'm not surprised after all you've been through. I can't tell you how relieved I am you're here."

"You've been to Yadrahna then?"

"Yes," Luke hesitated, not wanting to remind himself of Hugo.

"I want you to do something for me Luke."

"You've only to say the word." She seemed to his relief, normal, alert.

"I want you to take the will I found to Ashford."

"You mean you've got it with you?"

"It's here in my trouser leg." Putting her hand down inside the left leg of her jeans, Hannah began to feel down for the plastic envelope with the will inside she 'd found in the cellar. To her dismay she could no longer feel it where she'd placed it just below the knee. "It doesn't seem to be here," she frowned.

"Perhaps it's slipped." Taking off her socks which had been pulled up over her jeans Luke felt up from her ankle but there was no sign of any paper that could be a will. He looked down than at the carpet and noticed a crumpled piece of plastic inside one of the socks he'd discarded.

"Is this it?" He straightened out the plastic and handed it to her.

Nervously she drew out then the single sheet of paper from inside. It was crumpled, a mess, like the plastic sheet covering but to her relief her father's will still legible with his signature intact.

"Could you take it for me now?"

"Of course." At last, she trusts me, Luke thought. He felt moved, humbled, determined not to let her down. "I'll get an extra copy first on Anthea's machine. Is there anything else you want me to do?"

"No, but there's something else I want to do."

"What's that?"

"I want to get up into the attic."

"At Yadrahna you mean?"

"Yes."

"But surely now you've got the will?" The thought of her trying to get back after all she'd gone through appalled Luke.

"There's still some documents and diaries of my father and I want to see if there's anything relating to the other Hannah."

"The other Hannah?"

She told Luke then what she'd learnt from Rev James and the letter she'd found about the tragic love affair between the other Hannah and John Liddell, about the message written on the beam in the attic.

"J in the waters of death – presumably refers to John's drowning then," Luke commented.

"It seems to fit but I feel there's more than that." Hannah frowned, trying to grasp what always seemed

to elude her, that there was another meaning. She felt exhausted but a desire still to go back to Yadrahna to investigate, back again to the cottage, to be near. "`I'd like to go back to the cottage, Luke."

Luke frowned, alarmed again. He didn't want to feel any doubt about her safety now that he was about to deliver the will to Ashford. Surely she could see the danger of being close to her brother.

"I don't think you'd be safe at the cottage," he said. "I don't want to frighten you but your brother may get desperate once he realises there's a second will."

"But if you were there.."

"You mean you want me to stay at the cottage?"

"Yes, yes, I do."

"You realise I'm going to India in three days?"

"I know and you've got your dissertation to hand in. I want you to come all the same if it's only for a night."

"As long as you agree to come back here when I'm in India then, yes. I'll come for my last night. Meanwhile you've got to rest and get stronger first."

Carefully Luke smoothed out the crumpled will and put it back in the plastic sheeting. "I'd better go now to Ashford or he'll be packing up for the day."

Looking into Hannah's eyes as he said goodbye, he could feel already the pain of separation that would inevitably come in three days.

What am I doing, he thought, as he slammed Anthea's door behind him and mounted his bike again. Committing myself, when I can't be committed. India, the time, the place – everything was against it, except the one thing that mattered to him – Hannah herself.

Chapter 28

"I'm sorry to hear you've not been well, Miss Delaney,"
James Ashford motioned Hannah to sit down on the other
side of his mahogany desk. "I trust you're feeling better
now."

"Yes, thank you."

Hannah wondered whether she should discuss with
Ashford the possibility of suing Hugo for wrongful
imprisonment and assault. Would it be worth it though?
Would it succeed? Nobody had seen him push her down
the steps and inflict thereby the wound to her head and
Hugo would be bound to say she'd trespassed and hidden
herself without his knowledge, that he'd locked the cellar
without knowing she was there. No, she decided, she
couldn't afford any wasted efforts with the law. Better to
concentrate her efforts on the will. Wasn't the will anyway
more important?

Nothing had altered in Ashford's room since her
last visit. His desk had the same well–polished orderly
neatness without clutter and Ashford himself the same
pervading grey. He was even wearing she noted the same
grey tie.

It was as if time had stood still and yet so much had
happened. It was eerie, unnerving, yet perhaps that was

what the law was – something to come back to, detached, unchanging, there when you needed it, when the action was over. But there was a difference she thought. Ashford was more optimistic now.

"You're certainly in a stronger position now, Miss Delaney." Straightening his file, Ashford permitted himself a smile. "Mrs Slade, the first witness, has made a statement which suggests that both she and your father were under pressure and that your father was being plied with alcohol which could certainly have disturbed his judgement. There is also, of course, your discovery of the second will which has been dated, duly signed and witnessed and which leaves you, as you'd hoped, the house Yadrahna and its contents. The second will though, unfortunately, does not mention who is to have the residue of the estate. This together with the possibility that Mrs Slade might not be a reliable witness in court suggests that it might be better to try and reach an agreement with your brother about the residue without going to court."

"An agreement?"

"Yes, we could deal with it through a Deed of Variation which is sometimes called a deed of Family Arrangement usually for tax efficiency purposes. You and your brother would sign to the effect that you would have the property and contents, that he would have your father's bonds as stated and that you'd share between you the residue. If your brother can be persuaded to give in, in the face of the later will and Mrs Slade's statement, on what was promised to you, without losing face, he is likely to be perhaps less obdurate than if we go to court, which could of course take a long time and be very costly. It is always better I find

to settle if possible and find a compromise approach rather than going to court."

Hannah wondered if it was possible to compromise with Hugo. Hugo and compromise were two words that didn't mix. But if a settlement could be achieved in this way sooner, why not? If Hugo could be persuaded, if –

"If you think it will work."

"I think we should try," Ashford asserted quietly. Learning that Hannah was not on the phone at the cottage, he suggested that she waited downstairs while he and his secretary tried to sort out a meeting there and then with Hugo's solicitor.

Down in the reception area, she told Luke about Ashford's proposal.

"It's a bit of a risk, isn't it? He's not to be trusted – your brother."

"In a way though he's cornered now," Hannah responded. "He may realise he's got to give way."

But with what effect, Luke wondered. Delaney, he was sure, wouldn't take it lying down. More than ever he felt the need to protect Hannah, a growing reluctance to go now to India and leave her.

He was not reassured by the arrangement confirmed a few minutes later that the meeting would take place the next morning at 11 and at, Hugo's suggestion, at Yadrahna itself.

"Just be on your guard, that's all," he warned her as they stepped out into the sunlight of the street.

"It's in the hands of the solicitors now surely, isn't it?"

"I suppose so." Her optimism disconcerted him. He didn't want to worry her but neither did he want her led on by a false hope.

Their arrangement was that she would take the bus out to Wynton while he cycled so that he could return more flexibly the next day to pack for his flight to Delhi in the evening. It was an arrangement he now regretted. He wanted to be with her as much as he could, to look after to her and see she wasn't hurt.

Momentarily as he cycled out of Oxford, the wind lifting his hair, he felt a sense of freedom. His dissertation was now over, handed in, complete. He had no employment to confine him. For the next twenty four hours, he was free at last – free for Hannah. But as he approached Wynton he had a sense more of threat than freedom, of Delaney casting his shadow across the road ahead of him.

Two miles before Wynton he noticed a green furniture van ahead of him with large letters in gold written over it – Hawk Brothers Quality Removal Specialists Windsor. There followed a telephone number and an address in Windsor.

The word Windsor immediately sparked in Luke an association with Hugo Delaney as he remembered Hannah telling him about her investigation into his home there and as the van went through Wynton then turned up the hill towards Yadrahna, his suspicions mounted that it had come at Delaney's request. Feeling he had no alternative now but to check for himself and find out, keeping a discreet distance, he followed the van on up Winter Hill, saw eventually, as he'd guessed, that it turned into Yadrahna's driveway.

Hiding his bike at the back of the shed by the kitchen garden, Luke crept then through the shrubbery to observe

the front of the house where the van was parked now close to Yadrahna's front door.

For several minutes nothing happened, then Luke saw Delaney emerge from the front door with some paper work in his hand, followed by two muscular, well built men in blue overalls, carrying Thomas Delaney's walnut desk which they loaded into the van.

There followed then, to Luke's concern, a succession of Thomas Delaney's furniture – his chaise longue, his eighteenth century grandfather clock, his walnut bookcase, then the antique furniture from the lounge, one by one each piece carefully loaded till it appeared the van could take no more.

It was calculated theft and retaliation, Luke knew, on Delaney's part but there was little he knew also he could do alone now to stop it. Carefully he noted the telephone number and address of the removal firm and there was something else strange he could see looking across to the side of the house at the open garage door – rows of petrol cans which had never been there before. Why? What use had Delaney for so many cans?

As the men in overalls closed the van door and went back into the house with Delaney for payment and tea, quietly Luke skirted round the back of the garage, then inside and checked the cans. They were, as he thought, full of petrol. As he smelt each one checking, he noticed then a transparent plastic box of 2 inch nails – the size of the nails he remembered that had punctured the tyres of Hannah's mother's car. Why had Delaney got them out again now? Luke hesitated, looking around, then stuffed the box into the pocket of his jeans.

Hearing voices then, he slipped back into the shrubbery. A few moments later the van was driven away and Delaney turned back into the house and locked the door. There was no sign Luke could see of the Slade.

Heavy-hearted, for he knew the news would be upsetting to Hannah, Luke retrieved his bike and made his way down to the cottage. He wondered en route whether to phone Ashford and let him know but what could Ashford practically do about it now? No, it was up to Hannah to decide but he could try at least and lessen the blow and stopping at the village shop he bought some bread and cheese and a bottle of red wine.

Hannah meanwhile pushing open the wicker gate was amazed by how much the garden had grown in her absence. Only five days and the crevices of the path were covered now with mint and oregano, the kitchen window obscured by even taller, thicker nettles. In the herb garden, tarragon floundered now, too tall, and flowering feverfew had taken over and everywhere – over the wicker gate, the overgrown hedge and against the cottage wall the brambles had extended themselves, the berries beginning to darken. I'll make some wine, when they're ripe, Hannah resolved, and some blackberry jam like Mrs Webb.

She felt glad to be back. She didn't want to live in Oxford as Luke had suggested but she wished Luke was here, waiting now. There was so much to tell him, so little time. Where was he, she wondered.

Looking in her bag for the key, she remembered then that Luke still had it. Tired and feeling dizzy from the heat, she sat down on the rickety seat by the overgrown herb garden. She was conscious of the smell of peppermint and rosemary,

of lavender wafting from further down the garden, of the mixture of smells having a strangely calming effect. Unable to resist, she closed her eyes and drifted into sleep.

She dreamt, as she slept, of old Mrs Webb standing over her steaming saucepan of blackberry jam, stirring. Then she saw a young woman coming up the pathway between neat rows of marigold and thyme with a bunch of forget–me–nots in her hand. It seemed in the dream at first to be Mrs Webb projecting back to a younger age but as the face was uplifted towards the kitchen and she saw the sadness in the deep blue eyes she knew with a certainty, as if she'd been there, that it wasn't Mrs Webb but the other Hannah, that the flowers she carried were for her lost adopted child.

And a surge of sympathy went out to her, a longing to alleviate her sorrow for her hair was streaming out behind her against the blue of the sky as if she was swimming now in deep water, struggling to find air. Yet how could that be? Hannah could feel in her dream herself puzzling, trying to grasp an elusive meaning, another dream.

Then suddenly she was awake, jolted, and looking into brown eyes, not blue, the brown eyes of Aunt Eileen with a white parasol in her hand.

"I was wondering when you were going to wake." With an abrupt swish, Aunt Eileen put up the parasol shading out the blue but the intense blue of the water in her dream remained in Hannah's mind.

"Sorry. Have you been here long?"

"Long enough to see that you're looking rather peaky still, young lady. It's no wonder you've been asleep." Aunt Eileen frowned with indignant concern. "Where's the young man?"

"Young man?"

"The young man who was here when I called before. Luke I think he said his name was. He seemed very attached to you. How old is he by the way?"

"I've no idea. We've never discussed our ages." Luke's age in fact seemed strangely irrelevant now Hannah thought about it. She guessed though he must be younger than she was, twenty three or four perhaps.

"You're not thinking of marrying him then?"

"Marrying? Honestly, Aunt Eileen, I've only known him a few weeks and he's about to go to India. I'm not sure anyway he's the marrying kind."

"Whatever do you mean by that? "

"I doubt he'd want to be confined as yet. He's –" Hannah grasped at the nearest phrase she could think of. "He's a free spirit." Immediately she regretted it. It wasn't a phrase that did justice to Luke and the way she felt about him and Aunt Eileen was now predictably admonishing her.

"Free spirit," her indignation rebounded, "suggests going from one woman to another, which is not what you want to encourage at all."

"I'm not encouraging anything, Aunt Eileen. All I'm saying is that marriage is not the be all and end all of a relationship."

"Maybe not for your generation. But you'll wake up one day, you mark my words, regretting you haven't had children."

Still the sad blue eyes of the other Hannah in her dream lingered. "Maybe I'd regret it if I had," she responded.

"What a strange girl you are!" Aunt Eileen laughed, not taking her seriously. "But you always did have views

different from everyone else – right since I can remember. It's the reason I suppose you didn't see eye to eye with Richard."

"We took different things for granted, Aunt Eileen. It wouldn't have worked. Richard's the corporate man wanting to conquer and control everything. I don't think it works anymore."

"Well, let's hope his new partner feels the same as he does."

"New partner?"

"I met him with her in Hampstead. I was going to tell you. He still has his flat there I understand. Sally she said her name was – an old friend of yours I believe."

"They're definitely going to marry then?"

"So they said. They'd just got engaged they told me that morning." Aunt Eileen peered at Hannah more closely. "You don't seem concerned."

"I'm not. I never really loved Richard. I realise that now. I never really communicated or shared things with him." It disconcerted her all the same that Richard had switched his allegiance with such speed after his declaration of wanting her. What did it say for Sally? Would it work, she wondered. Probably yes, she decided on reflection. Hadn't she often in her mind seen them together, sharing their same sense of time and the importance of time, the same assumptions? Hadn't Sally all along wanted Richard? She hoped deep down for Sally's sake it would work.

"I see." Aunt Eileen tried to recover her assurance. "Well, you obviously, as I said, know your own mind. But that's not what I came for. I came to say – yes, I'll consider helping you to buy this place. That doesn't mean

to say I think it's an ideal investment." Aunt Eileen's eyes slanted pointedly back at the decaying porch. "But you're obviously going to need a base whether or not in the end you get Yadrahna – which could well take weeks, months, even years to confirm. And since you seem to like it here I may as well give you now the money I'd have left you in my will."

"That's very good of you, Aunt Eileen."

"It wouldn't be without strings though. Don't get the wrong idea, Hannah. I haven't money to throw away."

"Of course not. I wasn't expecting.."

"I can't go above £40,000. All the restoration work would have to be yours. Basically I would be buying the site and shell of the house. The rest of would be up to you as and when you can afford it. That's all I'm afraid I can do."

"All? But that's fantastic, Aunt Eileen." And standing up Hannah flung her arms round her aunt and kissed her. "I can't thank you enough – really."

"Don't thank me. Thank your father. He helped me when I was in need many years ago. The least I can do is to help his daughter – my own niece." Hannah saw her aunt's eyes suddenly fill with tears. Then embarrassed, she marshalled her parasol into position again. "Well, I must be on my way. Let me know what happens about Yadrahna."

"I certainly will and thank you, Aunt Eileen. Thank you so much."

As she watched her aunt's neat well–dressed figure beneath the white parasol receding down the lane, Hannah had the same sense as Luke had done, that the tide was at last turning. Yadrahna was in theory now hers.

In all probability she would be able to live at Yadrahna but it wasn't yet a reality. There was no knowing what Hugo would do. There could be months of legal wrangling ahead. But in the cottage now she could feel financially more secure. And there, to her relief, stopping to talk to her aunt at the end of the lane was Luke himself.

Immediately she wanted to tell him about her aunt's offer. But as she took his hand, drawing him with her through the wicker gate, looking into his eyes she saw at once that something was wrong.

"What's the matter?"

"It's your brother. He's had the furniture van up at the house, loading all the antique furniture."

"You mean to take away?"

"To Windsor, it seems. At least that's where the van came from."

"But he's no right. The will's not resolved." Hannah stared at Luke in dismay. She should have anticipated, she thought, but how? How could one ever know what was going on in Hugo's mind?

"Right or not. That's what he's done." Luke described what he'd seen, then handed to Hannah the name and number of the firm he'd written down. "I think you should phone Ashford straight away. It's too late to stop the van but at least he'll have the information and know what to do."

"Yes, you're right. I'll do that. I'll go and phone straight away."

At the telephone box by the bus stop, Hannah had difficulty getting through to Ashford and when she did eventually it was to find, to her disappointment, that

Ashford himself was in court and unavailable. So she left a message with his secretary giving the name and number of the van and feeling there was nothing else effective she could do she returned to Brambles to find that Luke had laid out the kitchen table with a tempting array of breads and cheeses.

"Heh stop! You'll make me fat!"

"That's the object." Luke laughed pouring them both some wine.

The nettles covering the window gave the kitchen a strangely subdued light. Coming into the cottage was like shedding a skin, Luke thought. The outside world was no longer relevant. They talked at they ate of her aunt's offer, of her dream of the other Hannah, of the past and what it meant, of the future and how uncertain it seemed. Yet all the past and the future seemed to him focused on the present, on Hannah herself. All he wanted now were her lips, her body, to be part of her, to give himself up to her, to the flame she was igniting in him.

As they finished eating, he stroked back her hair. "Let's go upstairs."

They undressed together and she lay on the bed. Even more a miracle then she seemed to him stretched out naked on the ancient iron bedstead – her breasts, her small flat belly, her thighs white in the shadowed light, like a marbled carving of beauty beyond time.

But time, the present, was more urgent with him now. He wanted her and as he touched her, cautiously at first, then more assured, he felt the coolness of her skin, not of carving but of flame. And the flame rose up in him unquenchable now.

"I love you," he whispered as she opened her thighs to him.

And she wanted him then, as he entered her, more than she'd ever wanted anyone. And suddenly her body was alive, anticipating in a way she'd never experienced before, as she felt him inside her, his penis close fitting, rubbing her vaginal wall. All her longing then she felt released as she strained down, responding to his rhythm, like water racing across the sands to quench his flame. Two elemental forces they met in their climax, each quenched, seared by a new loving, untamed. And Hannah knew she would never want anyone else inside her again but Luke.

As they lay back at peace, the early evening sun slanting in the window, together in words they traced the way their love had started.

"I think it was when I first saw you." Gently Luke stroked back her hair again. "You were really angry and you made me feel angry. I resented being accused. At the same time I knew it was justified and that it was real, had a real cause. You were like an ancient goddess standing there with right on your side. It was strange. Though I resented you, I felt a kind of sympathy."

"But you couldn't resist mocking me," she teased.

"No, it was my defence, I suppose. You did take me by surprise. And you – what did you feel?"

"I hated you for what you were doing. I hated your mockery. But I kept thinking of you later, of your muscles in the sunlight. So something must have happened then but I took a long time to see, to trust you."

"It doesn't matter, as long as you trust me now."

"I trust you more than anyone, Luke." Drawing him close, she stroked his back, thinking of the effect of the sunlight on his muscles again. "You know that, don't you? And I love you." How absurd it was, she reflected, that she'd been frightened to tell him before. Now all she wanted was to tell him over and over again. "I love you. I can't bear the thought of not being with you."

Luke was silent a while, then said, "Perhaps I shouldn't go."

"Go?"

"To India."

"I thought it was all arranged."

"It is but things are different now, aren't they? I don't want to leave you."

"What would you do instead? For work I mean,"

"I don't know. I haven't thought about it. I was going so that I could get experience for a development job when I return."

"That's the way to get in, you mean?"

"It's difficult without experience – that's for sure."

Hannah hesitated, then forcing herself said, "Then I think you should go. You might regret it if you don't – later I mean."

"What about us though?"

"We can still see each other. I could come out in the holiday. I've always wanted to go to India." She told him about the leprosy healer she'd met on the plane.

"It's not cheap, you know."

"I'll find a way."

She turned away, conscious of sadness in his eyes now, afraid she herself was going to cry. The thought of his going

to India was increasingly unbearable yet so in its way was the thought that she could undermine a potential career which was not going to be easy either to enter or sustain.

"Let's get something to eat," she said.

He stroked her thighs, kissing her, then held out his hand, helping her off the bed.

"You're beautiful," he said, as she stood by the window, reflecting. "I want you. I'll always want you. You know that, don't you?"

"Yes," and she drew him back with her down onto the creaking iron bedstead again.

Forgetting food then and India, Hugo and all their problems, they made love the whole evening, each awakening merging into the next, feeling they could never have enough of each other.

It wasn't until it was dark and they felt the pangs literally of hunger that Luke went downstairs eventually and wheeled inside his bicycle and locked the door. In the saddle bag of his bicycle were the nails he'd taken from the garage of Yadrahna. He still felt uncertain what to do about them and after fingering them a moment put them back in the saddlebag. Gathering together the bread and cheese he'd brought for lunch, he made some cheese sandwiches and took them up to Hannah with candles and the remains of the wine.

She looked more tired now, he noticed, and after they'd eaten and made love once more, he suggested she should sleep so she could manage the next morning for the meeting at Yadrahna.

"What about you?" she asked, her eyes already closing.

"I'll keep watch for a while," and drawing up the chair, Luke sat by the window as she slept as he'd done before.

It was two in the morning as he was about to fall asleep himself in the chair from exhaustion, when he heard the familiar creak of the wicker gate again. He looked down on the darkened garden but he couldn't detect any figure as he'd done before moving across the overgrown pathway. Nor could he see any movement amidst the plants and shrubs of the garden. After carefully watching for a few minutes longer, he decided he'd imagined the noise and unable to resist, as he sat back again, he let his eyes close.

It was an hour later when, feeling a twist in his neck from the discomfort of the chair, he sat up abruptly again, aware of the smell of smoke and burning coming from below in the kitchen. Switching on the torch, he grabbed the bucket Hannah used as a waste bin, the only useful utensil he could see and cautiously crept downstairs.

He didn't need the torch he soon realised. Through the half open door of the kitchen, he saw, to his alarm, that the whole of the oak table, in the centre of the kitchen, was on fire, the flames leaping up and already scorching the timbers and plaster of the low ceiling and the nearest wall.

So far the timbers themselves were not in flames but already they were smoking. Skirting round the table with the bucket, Luke made a dash for the sink and turned the tap full on. As the water filled the bucket, he flung it over the burning table. Bucket after bucket he kept filling, flinging till the flames subsided and the table crumbled as a sodden blackened wreck. By the light of the torch, Luke flung then water over the smoking timbers, fearful that the whole cottage could suddenly catch fire. Not till he was satisfied there was no more danger, did he lean

back against the sink, wondering how the fire could have started.

Had a candle been left burning? There was a brass candlestick on the floor by the charred table with a burnt down candle in it but could it really have been the cause? They had used a candle certainly earlier in the evening but not in the past few hours.

Luke shone his torch round the kitchen and by the window to see if anyone had broken in. He noticed then that the window was not on its latch, that it seemed shut but was not secure. It was possible Hannah had forgotten to secure it but he didn't think so because she hadn't, to his remembrance, opened it at all. Uneasily he made sure it was now secure and made his way past the wrecked table upstairs.

To his relief, Hannah had not woken but more than ever he felt her in danger now. Someone had been, increasingly he felt sure, and that someone was either her brother himself or the elusive other person paid to do his work. Either way her brother was not going to rest till he'd got what he wanted. The more his hopes were thwarted, the more he'd try to get at Hannah. And sooner or later, in his obsessive state of mind, he would get her, Luke in fear decided – unless something was done to stop him.

Even if he stayed to protect her, Hugo would still find a way. Without his staying, with no one else aware of him, watching over her, what chance did she have?

No, more coolly Luke began to analyse, it was Hannah's life or Hugo's. If Hannah was ever to feel safe, Hugo had to go. It was no use hoping he would reform or die by his own hand or corruption. People like Hugo rarely ever

did. Self – preserving, unscrupulous, they usually got their way in the end – if you let them, if they trampled long enough. Well, it wasn't going to work that way this time, Luke determined. He'd get Hugo first – even if he paid for it.

Quietly, he got up from the chair and went downstairs and put the box of long two inch nails he'd taken from Yadrahna, ready by his bicycle for the morning.

Chapter 29

Luke looked so peaceful, Hannah thought, so deeply asleep, with his arm flung back in an arc above his head and his dark brown hair all tousled over his forehead. Though she longed to see his eyes open again, looking at her, it seemed an assault to wake him. She would leave him, she decided, a little longer and went downstairs to find some food for breakfast.

She couldn't believe it as she opened the kitchen door and took in the charred sodden collapse of wood that had been the kitchen table. If there was one solid object in the cottage, it was the table where old Mrs Webb had prepared her blackberry jams and jellies and she felt, as she stared, that she was looking at the scene through old Mrs Webb's eyes, a sense of loss tugging at her heart and eyes, which made her realise, despite all its disadvantages, how much she valued the cottage and its past.

It was obvious from the damp walls and water still in puddles on the stone flagged floor that Luke must have been active in controlling the fire. But how had it started? Looking round she could see no obvious clue, except the old candlesticks on the floor. Had they really left a candle burning downstairs? She felt she wanted to let in light and

air to dispel the tired, decaying smell of dampness that pervaded the room.

As she opened the door to the porch, she felt something shift under her feet. Bending down she saw with surprise that it was a box of nails. Plasterboard clout it said on the label. Plasterboard Clout, she thought. That was surely for fixing roofs. Why should Luke want nails for fixing roofs? Looking more closely then she saw the size – a size forever now imprinted in her mind – two inches – the exact size of nails found in the tyres of her mother's car. Could Luke really be planning the same as Hugo, an exact retaliation? Why else, if he wasn't, had he got the nails?

In the doorway of the porch, she felt a chill run through her and, forgetting breakfast, hurried back upstairs and dressed herself for the meeting at Yadrahna.

. She put on a light blue cotton dress. It had a close fitting waist, a collar and a full skirt – a suitable compromise, she thought, of formality and casualness. Yet still she felt cold from her apprehension. Searching for something to go with it, all she could find was her mother's grey cloak that she'd rescued from Luke's fire.

Slipping it with the hood over her head, she looked at herself in the cracked stained mirror. She was about to take it off again, thinking she looked rather too much like Jane Eyre about to set off on her fateful moorland walk away from Rochester, when she was aware of Luke's voice, of his eyes behind her in the mirror, awake and watching from the bed.

"Don't take it off. It suits you."

"Does it?" She looked back at him through the mirror.

"You look like your mother. The photo that used to be in your father's study. She was wearing that cloak."

How amazing, she thought, that he'd remembered such detail. Perhaps she would after all wear it to go through the wood. Still she felt cold.

She went over to the bed and kissed him.

"I see you had quite a night downstairs. What was the cause?"

"I don't know."

"You didn't see anyone then?"

"No."

"But you think it could have been Hugo?"

"Possibly."

"Is that why you've got the nails?"

"Nails?"

"The two inch nails by your bike."

"Oh those." Luke shrugged trying to sound nonchalant, as he swung his legs off the bed.

"Why did you buy them Luke?"

"Oh for this and that – different uses."

"Was one of those uses to go under Hugo's car?"

"Why ever should you think that?" He looked away from her towards the garden.

"Because you know about my mother and the two inch nails and it's a bit too much of a coincidence, isn't it?" Suddenly he seemed to her vulnerable, uncertain, standing there, looking into the garden and she felt afraid for what could happen to him. Going up to him, she put her arms around him. "Please I want to know."

"Why?"

"You could be in trouble."

"All the more reason you don't know, then, isn't it?"

"But I want to share things with you, Luke."

"It's not as simple as that though, is it, when it comes to the law? Ignorance is safer."

"Not for me. I feel part of you now. I want to know."

"All right then. I didn't buy the nails. I found them in fact in the garage where your brother keeps his car and I brought them here and I'll tell you why. Because he's obsessed with getting rid of you, that's why. Do you think I can just sit back and do nothing?"

"You mean you're planning to do what he did to my mother?" She felt a terrible dread in the pit of her stomach. She wanted to be free of Hugo's threats and his power but not by this means, not by Luke.

"If that's what it takes, yes. What's the alternative anyway for dealing with him? You can't appeal to his better nature. He hasn't got one. If we don't get rid of him, he'll get rid of you. It's obvious. That's the way all his actions are tending. You're in danger, Hannah, as long as he's alive and active and hasn't finally got his hands on Yadrahna and the money."

"No."

"What do you mean, – no? It's true what I say."

"I mean no. You can't do it. He may have done all these things but he's still my brother. And you – I couldn't bear you to take the risk."

"There's no point in life if you never take risks. It just means people like your brother get away with everything as he already has with your mother."

"But you may not, Luke. Besides you're different. You've got a conscience. You told me, didn't you, that I couldn't live with harming him? Neither could you. And I don't want you to take risks for me that you don't have

to. I don't want anything to happen to you, Luke – from him or the law. Promise me, promise me that you won't do anything with those nails."

Luke hesitated, then forcing himself said, "Only if you promise not to stay here when I've gone and go to Anthea's. Will you promise that?"

"It looks as if I'll have to, doesn't it?" It wasn't what she wanted but she wanted Luke more and to remain for her free.

"It's a bargain then." Gently Luke stroked back her hair over the grey cloak and kissed her, trying to comfort, to reassure and divert her. "Jane Eyre. Hannah Eyre, Hannah Delaney. The other Hannah – wherever you are if you're still alive."

"You think seriously she could be alive? At 104?"

"Some are. Why not her?"

Why not, thought Hannah. It was possible even now some old people's home still sheltered the memory of that fateful year, so long ago, of an angry father, a baby's loss, a lover's drowning. Yet Hannah felt in her heart it was not really so, that the restlessness she sensed between the other Hannah and herself was not that of life but of a death unresolved.

"Maybe."

She clung to Luke then, not wanting him to go, wanting the life he could give her, that the memory of Hannah could not. But time was pressing and soon she would have to confront Hugo, be at the meeting arranged at Yadrahna. And Luke, though she said she could manage, was insisting on coming up to Yadrahna with her.

They took the well–worn path they'd taken before up through Rassler's Wood.

Several times, hearing scurrying sounds, a snapping of dried twigs, they looked round but each time it was either a grey squirrel or muntjac deer taken by surprise and they continued walking till they reached the road passing by Yadrahna's drive.

There was no sign as yet of Ashford who had arranged to meet her at the entrance to the drive, so they could discuss some points together first in the car before driving up to the front door.

"I'll go and see if he's already arrived at the house," Luke said. "Be on your guard if your brother appears. He's not to be trusted. Remember that."

"You, too, take care." Silently drawing her mother's cloak more closely around her, Hannah watched as Luke slipped unseen into the shrubbery to survey the scene.

She had been standing for a full five minutes on the opposite side of the road to the drive, so she could be seen by Ashford, when from the grounds of Yadrahna she heard the sound of a car revving.

A few moments later, she saw to her surprise the familiar fluted radiator set against the distinctive black bonnet of the Daimler coming towards her down the drive but not at its usual leisurely pace. Gravel was spurting and spraying from beneath its wheels as it wove between the curves of the laurel.

Reaching the road, it shot out then without stopping. For a moment it seemed to Hannah it was heading straight at her as she stood in her mother's cloak on the edge of the road opposite the entrance to the drive. Then abruptly it swerved but not before she saw that it was Hugo at the wheel, his mouth open, his eyes wide staring at her

– with anger was it, surprise or fear? Shocked, she heard then a squeal of brakes as a blue BMW about to turn into Yadrahna's drive jolted suddenly to a halt, just missing the Daimler's bonnet and mudguard. She had a glimpse of Hugo juggling with the Daimler's wheel as if trying to curb a stallion out of control, then the Daimler surged forward on down the hill into Wynton. Questions flashed through her mind at random about the speed he was going and why he was going and where. Why above all the intensity of his staring?

Hannah noticed then with relief Ashford getting out of the blue BMW and coming over to her.

"Are you all right, Miss Delaney?" Ashford asked, slightly unnerved by Hannah's appearance. She looked almost ethereal, he thought, of a different age in the long grey cloak she was wearing – like a nineteenth century governess or the solitary remnant of a warning chorus. But there was no mistaking the reality of the long brown hair, the large brown eyes, dazed with shock was it or fear?

"I thought for a moment he was going to drive straight at you. Who was it, do you know?"

"It was – it was my brother."

"Mr Delaney? But he was meant to be meeting us here."

"Exactly."

"You think then he has no intention?"

"He may have just gone to the post but I doubt it." Hannah felt still shaken, a deep unease she couldn't pinpoint.

She was about to get into the car with Ashford when suddenly coming from the road through the woods below,

they heard a prolonged screech of brakes, a moment's silence, then the harsh impact of metal against wood reverberating through the trees to where they were standing.

"We'd better go and check," Ashford said.

"Yes," though Hannah felt she knew already what had happened. As they parked at the layby close to the bend where her mother had gone off the road, she saw it then at once in confirmation – Hugo's Daimler, bizarrely it seemed to her, wrapped round the self same beech that had impacted on her mother. It was as if the Daimler had tried to scale the tall scarred trunk and the tree in revenge was now growing out of its bodywork, so embedded was the metal of the near side door and the wheel arch.

Hannah stared as she got out of Ashford's car, a moment mesmerised. It was as if time had kaleidoscoped in on itself, backwards five years, then forwards again, that it was her mother crying out through Hugo. And his voice was pitiful like a child's, vulnerable, a voice she couldn't ignore. "Get me out of here. Get me out."

Still wrapped in her mother's cloak, Hannah scrambled down from the road. Pulling open the door, where Hugo was still seated in the driver's seat, she saw then that the impact had buckled the floor of the Daimler right across to his side and that one of his feet was jammed now under the clutch and that his seat belt was also jammed.

An ominous small flame and a trail of smoke were also rising beneath the bodywork where the petrol pipe had fractured and Hugo realised. She could see it in his eyes – the fear intensified by the fact he was no longer in control.

"My foot's jammed," he cried.

"Here let me." As she tried to loosen the seat belt, Ashford bent down and unable to move the dented clutch, forced Hugo's foot out of his shoe.

"Is anything else hurting?" Ashford looked concerned into Hugo's eyes.

"I've a pain here." Hugo put his hand over his breastbone.

"We'll try and take care but we'll have to get you out of here."

Hugo nodded and let himself be heaved free from the car then pulled by both Ashford and Hannah across some leaves and earth to another beech where together they propped him up against the trunk.

Barely it seemed in time. Looking back at the Daimler, Hannah saw that the incipient flames from the fractured petrol pipe had now taken a firmer hold and had penetrated inside to the driver's seat. And suddenly the whole car was ablaze, the warmth reaching to where they were sitting, the flames throwing strange patterns of light and shadow over Hugo's face. Despite the heat, he had turned pale, Hannah noticed, and closed his eyes.

"I'll go back to the house and ring for an ambulance," Ashford said. "Meanwhile I suggest you stay here with him until they come."

What a decent man Ashford was, she thought, watching him go. Kind and practically helpful but unobtrusively so. She couldn't have managed, she knew, without him.

She looked down at Hugo's face. His eyes were still closed. Despite lines of ageing on his forehead and down his cheeks, he looked strangely childlike, innocent, difficult to associate with all the plotting that had gone

on, the angry hatred in his eyes, the way he'd pushed her down the cellar steps. Was there another side to him after all – a goodwill he'd never allowed himself to exploit or reveal?

The shape of his face, the straightness of his nose reminded her suddenly of her father. It had always seemed to her before that he was quite unlike her father – perhaps, she reflected, because she had wanted it to be that way. But now it struck her that there was a definite likeness which made her feel strangely closer to him, less afraid. If only, she wished, she'd been able to speak with him, explain how she really felt, perhaps he would have understood, not plotted as he had. Perhaps she could even have trusted him.

She tried to think how to talk to him and what to say. Say what you really feel her father had once said. What did she feel now – that he was a bastard, a schemer? She felt he was those, yes, but something more in the strange mixture we all have of self–interest and abnegation, something of her father perhaps that might still lift him.

"I want to talk to you, Hugo."

She pressed his hand. For a moment it seemed that he was sleeping still, then he opened his eyes.

"It's too late," he said. His eyes were focussed on a patch of sky between the beech, evading her, looking down at the Daimler smouldering, now a wreck.

"What do you mean – too late?" He looked paler than ever, she thought, and his hand felt clammy and cold despite the heat from the car. She took off her mother's cloak and laid it over him, bunching some fold behind his back.

"Yadrahna – you need to go."

"I'll go in good time. I'm staying here till the ambulance arrives," she asserted. "Yadrahna can wait."

"No." For a brief moment his grey eyes looked at her direct. Appeal was it or aversion in their cool depths? She couldn't tell. Then they closed again and she heard the siren of an ambulance approaching up the hill.

All was movement then. Skilfully, carefully, Hugo was helped onto a stretcher and carried to the ambulance and given first aid. A suspected heart attack, one of the ambulance crew told her, which was probably the cause of swerving and the crash. She was handed back her mother's cloak and told to ring the Waketon Hospital later in the afternoon for a report on his condition.

The police arrived then to investigate the accident and deal with the wreckage. Hannah answered their questions as best she could. It wasn't till they had gone that she paused to wonder what had happened to Ashford and Luke. Both had gone to Yadrahna but neither had come back to her. Why?

Uneasily it came back to her then, Hugo's strange insistence on her going to Yadrahna. What had happened? What had he done? With dread in her heart, clutching her mother's cloak, she started to walk back up Winter Hill.

Chapter 30

Momentarily, through the trees, as she ran, she had a glimpse of Yadrahna's subdued ochre coloured stone, warm and welcoming in the morning sunlight. Then she saw it – the smoke, as she'd seen it in her dream in Hong Kong, billowing from the two chimneys and from the windows of the lounge and, as she emerged from the drive, in full view, the curtains of her father's front bedroom window now aflame. She could hear a crackling sound, a splintering of glass, then Luke's voice calling down to her, his face blackened, from a side window.

"We've called a fire brigade. They're on their way. We're trying to stop the fire getting to the back stairs."

"Take care," she called but already he had disappeared from view. Apprehensively, seeing the front door ajar, she stepped inside and opened the lounge door.

Fanned by the movement of air, a flame immediately leapt up the brocade curtain of the window overlooking the drive, searing it to shreds as she watched in horror. The rest of the room she couldn't see for smoke but she could feel it – an intensifying heat from the carpet and her father's piano now ablaze – a heat which could soon threaten the very foundation of the house and which alone, she knew, she and Luke were powerless to subdue.

But there was no smoke, she noticed, emerging from under her father's study door. She could try at least, she resolved in desperation, to save his study, his antique books. Closing the lounge door, she ran across the hall and more cautiously this time opened the study door.

The room was empty of her father's furniture, as Luke had warned, but all his books were still in place in their carefully crafted glass–fronted walnut cases and shelves and his old rust coloured favourite Afghan carpet still on the floor. But at the far end of the room an insidious flame like a snake was already creeping along the carpet's edge. There was no time, she knew, to lose. Quickly she rushed to the kitchen, filled a bucket of water and returning doused the flame till it was out.

She opened the window then onto the drive and selecting first the most valuable books carried them in her arms, pile by pile, from their cases via the window onto the gravel of the drive. Back and forth she ran, each time with a heavier load, each time more concerned as she heard in her father's bedroom above an increasing roaring of flame. Desperately she hoped Luke had come back now downstairs.

She was conscious of Ashford from time to time in his grey suit, alongside her helping, of his rescuing the Chinese scrolls and Bokhara carpets, which her father had so admired, from the walls of the hall. Then he had to go, he said, to move his car from where it was partially blocking the entrance to the drive.

She had removed two thirds of the antique books and was on her way out of the window with the volumes her father had particularly valued of Bunyan's "Pilgrim's

Progress" when the plaster of the ceiling in the centre of the study gave way and a burning piece of timber crashed down onto the Afghan carpet setting it light again. Flames then leapt down from her father's room above causing to crash more plaster, more timber in their wake. There was no hope now she knew of saving the remaining books.

She limped out onto the lawn outside, despairing watching the smoke billowing out from the study window. Why, she wanted to scream. Where was the fire engine? Why hadn't it come? She was aware then of Luke's blackened face beside her, of his arm round her shoulders.

"I'm sorry. We tried," he said, "but it had taken hold before we came."

"What happened? How did it start?"

"Your brother – he chose certain rooms, then threw in the petrol. Everywhere it was – on the carpets, the walls, the beds – anything he'd left behind."

"You saw him then?"

"I saw him throw the last can before he drove off. He's mad. He doesn't know what he's doing."

"Enough though to tell me."

"Tell you?"

"To come back here."

"What do you mean?"

"Mr Ashford didn't tell you then?"

"Tell me what?"

"Hugo – he came off the road on Winter Hill, at the bend – the exact spot…"

"The same as your mother you mean? But he can't have. We decided not to plant the nails."

"He came off all the same. A suspected heart attack the ambulance man said. I've got to ring to confirm this afternoon."

"So he's in hospital then?"

"For the time being, yes." But how would he be, Hannah wondered, when he emerged.

Through her fear, momentarily with relief, she heard the siren of the fire engine at last signalling its approach. She looked up again at the roofline. Flames were now leaping up from the two chimneys and garishly illuminating the upstairs windows and splintering the glass. The attic windows had so far escaped but for how long? Would the firemen be in time?

Focusing on the attic window from which she'd first seen Luke, she thought of the other Hannah then and her message in the timber, all the objects her father had saved from their childhood in the trunks there, his own collection of insects and stamps, his diaries, his memories of the past.

"For God's sake – no!" the words came out of her in a cry of desperation.

Trying to understand, Luke followed her gaze. "It's your father, isn't it – his things?"

"I can't bear to lose them – the diaries, all he wrote and collected. He put so much of himself…"

"We can still get them."

"No, it's too late now – too dangerous."

"It may not be." Luke tried to sound optimistic. "The back stairs were still clear a short while ago. I could try."

"It's not worth it, Luke." She could feel herself pleading now, felt she couldn't bear anything to happen to him.

"Isn't it?" Looking into her eyes, he felt he'd do anything for her, whether of risk or not. The pain he could see there from the love of her father was like a pain of his own. He felt he had to do something. "I'll have a look anyway and assess the situation."

The fire engine had sirened its way up to the front of the house. Six firemen in yellow helmets descended, detaching ladders and hoses. As one of them came over to speak to Hannah, quickly Luke took the chance and slipped away past the smoke and flames up past the side of the house to the back door.

"Is there anyone in the house, do you know?" The fireman had clear blue eyes, weathered cheeks and a kindly smile.

"No, I don't think so but the attic," Hannah pleaded, "please try and save it first."

"We'll do what we can." He turned to give instructions. The other firemen positioned themselves strategically round the house, hosing water at once onto the flames in the lounge, her father's study and the his bedroom upstairs.

"Have you got a hydrant here?"

"A hydrant ? No, I don't think there is."

"A swimming pool then or a pond? We're going to need a lot more water than we could bring."

"There's a pond."

Reluctantly, Hannah led him through the shrubbery to the pond, hoping he wouldn't have to use all the water. It looked so still, so established, so rich in life and beautiful with the morning sun filtering through the trees. It was the pond where frogs came to mate and she could see four of them close by, hunched up like attentive guardians on

the leaves of the white water lilies. Apprehensively, she watched as he ran a suction hose from the pump of the engine and dropped the end in the pond. The pond was deep, very deep, enough to drown in her father had once warned. It had endured all the extremes nature had been able to throw at it for the past 100 years. Could it endure now being emptied and the complex web of life within?

But there was nothing for it but to go along with the firemen's wishes she knew. He had a job to do and perhaps some of the house as a result could be saved.

It was clearer now, as she stood back, looking at the pond, knowing that something was being done, that Hugo had never intended to come to the meeting, that he'd fled after setting fire to Yadrahna. Why though had he set fire to Yadrahna? A gesture of despair was it or malice, knowing he could never have it now for himself?

With dread in her heart, Hannah walked back to the drive.

Ashford, having re-parked his car where Hugo's Daimler had been, at once came over to her.

"Now that the Fire Brigade has come, Miss Delaney, there's no immediate point, I think, in my remaining. I'll come back to see how things are progressing this afternoon. Meanwhile, I think it's more productive if I go back to the office and contact your brother's solicitor to see if I can find out what has happened and what his intentions are. Do you think he will be long in hospital?"

"I don't know. I'm supposed to ring this afternoon but the phone's out of order now."

"Would you like me to try for you? I could convey any message when I return this afternoon."

"Could you? That would be a great help. Thank you."
I could go to the phone in the village, Hannah thought –
it's not a problem. But she knew in her heart she didn't
really want to, that she was afraid of what she'd hear. Why?
She wasn't responsible for the accident, neither was Luke.
Why then should she be concerned? What was it about
Hugo that made her want reconciliation now after all
he'd done? They were years apart. Not only in age but in
thinking. Yet wasn't he still her brother and for all he'd
done, still vulnerable?

"Right. I'll give the hospital a ring before coming back."
Ashford paused, regarding her with genuine sadness in
his eyes. "I'm very sorry about what has happened to the
house. I know how much it means to you. But at least the
back will have escaped relatively unscathed and nowadays,
much more can be done, can it not, to put things right?
Was the house insured, by the way?"

"I don't know." The insurance had been due every year
in July, Hannah remembered. Would Hugo though have
remembered, absorbed in his other plans?

"Well let's hope for the best. I'll be back, Miss Delaney,
shortly." He shook her hand. "Try to think, if you can, of
what can be done, rather than negative aspects."

"I'll try," Hannah responded but she felt herself
dragged more and more into a hopeless sense of loss as
she watched disconsolately the continued fire fighting at
the front of the house. It seemed the firemen were getting
the better of the flames, reducing their potency and roar.
But the lounge and study and the two bedrooms above
were virtually now gutted and there would only be in the
end, she knew, the stone walls. Walls that had held the

inhabitants of Yadrahna with all their joys and sorrows for over six generations in a past she still hadn't fathomed or explored. Walls that had held above all her father. It was as if the very spirit of the house, expressed through her father, was being destroyed and as her grief for her father surged again, she felt she couldn't bear to watch any longer the smouldering, destructive flames.

She felt overwhelmingly the need to talk to Luke again. But she could find him nowhere now in the grounds. He must have gone down to the village for something, she decided. Heavy hearted, she returned back to the pond.

Chapter 31

To Hannah's dismay, what she'd feared had happened. Apart from a small pool of muddy water in the centre, the water had virtually all been drained from the pond, leaving water lilies, water violets, typha, eichhornia and juncus effusus, all stranded like pieces of wreckage on a primeval mud. Her eyes skimmed the remaining water for other creatures and plants that could inadvertently be sucked into the hose.

It was then that she noticed near the edge of the pond on the other side the curve of something white projecting from the mud. Going closer and bending down from a different perspective she saw that it was a skull with its eye sockets upturned towards her.

Her first reaction was one of shock that there could be a skull in the pond. What was it doing there? Where had it come from? It seemed to her that the upturned sockets, though embedded with mud, were pleading with her to be released.

Looking more closely she saw that it was in fact a remarkably well–preserved skull with all its teeth and its jaw bone intact – the skull she guessed of someone young. Who though and how long had it been there and why?

Uneasily, she stared at the skull, then started to scoop away the mud around it with her hands. It was soft, oozing

mud seeping back again almost as fast as she moved it but she felt eventually a backbone still attached it appeared to the skull and further down the bones of a rib cage and arm.

Uncovering at length the rib cage, she found juncus clinging in a tangled mass round the sternum and one of the ribs. Trying to pull it away she felt then, to her surprise, enmeshed in the dark green corkscrew leaves of the juncus, a thin band of metal with a box like piece of metal attached. It struck her at once that it must be some kind of jewellery that had been worn round the neck. More carefully then she unwound the spiralling leaves from the sternum and manipulated the band of metal slowly up from under the skull.

She had stepped back and was standing with the tangled juncus and metal in her hand on the pathway by the pond when she saw the fireman she'd first met return to adjust the hose. Trained, his eyes immediately saw the skeleton in the mud, more exposed now by Hannah's efforts and he strode at once over to her.

"Don't move anything, Miss," he ordered, concerned. "It's a police job. I'll get onto them on the cell phone." Hastily, the fireman returned to the fire engine to make his call.

When he'd gone, Hannah lay out the juncus and unwound again its spiralling dark leaves. On the pathway before her uncovered now was a small heart shaped gold locket attached to a finely crafted thin gold chain. Taking out a handkerchief, Hannah wiped the locket dry, then cautiously prised it open with her fingers. Inside was a damp piece of brown stained card which had once been she guessed a photo. Looking at it closely she thought she

could detect the two eyes but the features were blurred by stains and there was nothing else inside the locket – no message, only the sodden brown card.

Disappointed, she closed the locket and was about to slip it back onto the rib cage, when turning it over she noticed some lettering on the back. The letters were small, scarcely decipherable. As she strained her eyes, a shaft of sunlight pierced the overhanging willows and elder, illuminating more clearly the minute words. "Hannah" she read then, "with enduring love John."

As the words engraved in gold gleamed back at her, Hannah knew in that shaft of sunlight what she'd sensed in the shadows, that the locket and the bones and skull lying in the mud below were those of the Hannah she'd so long sought. Hannah who'd carved her message of love in the attic, who'd lost her baby to another's care and her lover by drowning, who'd come here that fateful night on hearing of his death to drown herself in sorrow.

How she'd done it, Hannah didn't know – only that she had. And wasn't it the reason why she'd always sensed the other Hannah's presence around as if waiting to be released? Over eighty years she'd waited to be buried with her lover, John.

Enduring love. Enduring – yes, it was the right word in every sense that John had used. Their love had lasted. John had never succumbed to the pressure to marry another for convenience. But it had also been a love that had suffered from the class system of the age.

One could never change the past. Hannah knew that all too well but as she looked at the skull and the eye sockets, still, it seemed to her, pleading, she determined

that she herself would plead with Rev James that Hannah could be buried now where she rightfully belonged with John.

Absorbed in the locket and her thoughts of the other Hannah, she didn't notice Luke's approach till he was beside her. She was shocked then to see a raw, red wheel mark across his forehead and that his left hand and arm up to his elbow were swathed now in bandage.

"You haven't been.." she wanted to protest but found she couldn't. As he laid the canvas bag he'd brought down on the pathway, still holding the locket, she put her arms round him and kissed him, gently stroked his bandaged arm. "You shouldn't have, Luke."

"It's superficial – just for protection, that's all, to please the firemen." Luke smiled. "I think I've got most of the diaries and documents but you'd better check. There's also a box of your father's prints in the drive. They.."

Luke stopped suddenly, noticing the skull and partially covered bones. From Hannah's expression he knew at once that they were not ordinary bones but special to her with meaning. "It's the other Hannah, isn't it?"

"Yes." She held out the locket to him and in the beam of sunlight he read the inscription.

"You think she drowned herself then?"

"Yes. It all makes sense now. The words she carved in the attic –she's been here all this time, Luke, and we didn't know – nearly ninety years."

"You always felt she was close, didn't you?" Luke handed back the locket and kissed her.

"Yes, I did. I wish it hadn't ended though the way it did."

"But they kept faith, you could say. They didn't give in to convention, to what others wanted."

"I suppose there's that, yes."

"That's the reason we remember them. All the others who conformed and lived to a ripe old age, they're forgotten."

"Yes, you're right." Her gaze rested on Hannah, then she turned back to Luke, burying her face against his chest. "I'm so glad you're here. I couldn't bear it – the fire – to watch any longer."

"I know." Luke tried to think of something comforting to say but what could he say, he wondered, when so much she loved with all its associations, especially with her father, had gone. "It's possible to rebuild though, given time."

"I'm not sure. I don't think one can rebuild the past – really rebuild I mean. The past has so much about it that was never designed – crevices and corners, scratch marks like Hannah's. You can't recapture those."

"One can rebuild for the future though." Luke wasn't sure if he was making a statement or asking a question. He sensed a change in Hannah that he couldn't quite penetrate or analyse – a mental shift that had come, he guessed, from her discovery of the other Hannah, as if the past was no longer so important to her. "This setting," he ventured," it would be ideal for an environment centre – a place where people could come and take courses – practical courses, courses for children. You've even got an SSSI."

"If the rain comes." Sceptically, Hannah looked over the dried up pond with water lilies and juncus and typha stranded round it edge.

435

"It will." Despite her sadness, his own unease, Luke felt a growing optimism for her. "And Yadrahna's yours now surely to do as you want with now the will's been found."

"Is it? I'm not sure." She couldn't get Hugo's face out of her mind as he'd been by the beech tree – the fact that she couldn't be sure, still didn't know what his real reaction had been. "I don't think Hugo will give in that easily," she said.

"He may have to now that he's had a heart attack." Luke thought back again to the shaky state Delaney had been in in the kitchen with Olga Slade and his mother. What had finally pushed him over, Luke wondered. His conscience at last or something more?

He felt he wanted to reassure Hannah, give her more hope about Yadrahna itself but one of the firemen was signalling to her from the other side of the pond through the trees. "There's a gentleman in grey looking for you, Miss."

"Right. I'll come." She turned back to Luke. "It's probably Ashford. I'll see what he wants. I won't be long."

She met Ashford as she emerged from the trees coming towards her, frowning with a strained expression in his eyes.

"Ah, Miss Delaney. I went back to the office and phoned the hospital as we agreed." Ashford paused a moment, wiping the sweat from his forehead. "I'm afraid I have what may be unexpected news. Your brother has not recovered from his heart attack. He died, in fact, an hour after going into hospital."

"Died?" Hannah stared at the burning house, unable to relate it now to Hugo, unable to absorb the implications of what Ashford was saying.

"I'm sorry to have to tell you so abruptly." Her downcast expression moved him. Her brother was a blackguard without conscience but here she was clearly shocked and upset. You could never tell, Ashford thought, the latent feeling there in the genes, despite everything, unpredictable like people themselves.

"The police, I should mention, "Ashford continued in control, "want a relative to identify the body. If you'll agree, they'll be grateful."

"You mean now?" Hannah's voice sharpened in dread that she'd lose the little time she had left with Luke.

"No, he's been moved to a hospital mortuary. But if I can let them know you'll agree, they'll let me know later which one."

"If it's later then, yes."

"Right I'll let them know. I'll be back shortly."

Ashford paused a moment looking into her deep brown eyes. He thought of her again, like a ghost from the past, as she stood in her long grey cloak by the side of the road. Had Delaney had the same impression, Ashford wondered, as he'd driven out of the drive.

Back with Luke beside the dried up pond, quietly Hannah told Luke what she'd heard.

"I don't understand," puzzled, Luke responded. "Your brother was shaking – yes – when I last saw him. Why though should he have had a heart attack just before going down the hill? He wasn't old."

Luke tried to visualise Delaney coming out of the drive in his Daimler. Then he saw it all clearly – Hannah standing in her mother's cloak, looking exactly like her mother, before her last fatal drive, when Delaney himself had planted the

nails with the intent of bringing about her end. Hannah herself just standing here, waiting like her mother, had given him the association, the emotional shock and charge, had finally stirred his conscience. Hannah herself unwittingly had caused his end. How could he say it though if she herself did not see? He couldn't. It was like condemning her to blame for something for which she bore no blame and for which she should never have to suffer again. No, some thoughts were better hidden and to remain so.

"At any rate now," he tried to shift the angle, "what remains of Yadrahna will definitely be yours."

"Yes, I suppose so." Only then did it strike her that Hugo was in fact dead, that the plotting was over, the threats to her safety and life. She should have felt, she knew, relief and jubilation, that his sinister influence had gone. But she felt in her heart only an inexplicable sadness at the waste of it all – the waste of his scheming on himself and his life. So much he could have done, she thought. So much he failed to do because of his obsession and destructiveness.

So much he had destroyed of relationships and trust. Why? Why had he done it, acted the way he had? Was it his genes which put his survival first above all other considerations? Or was it other people, other influences and factors: his mother, his lack of real success, even their father through remarrying? Or was there in fact evil in some people, in Hugo himself which couldn't be accounted for, couldn't be changed? Would she ever know now? Would Hugo himself have known? By death he had freed her of fear but not the questions and she felt again the sense of waste and sadness at what might have been with him.

"It's difficult to absorb, I know." Luke lifted her face to the sunlight, kissing away the tears now falling. "In a year you'll feel different."

"But you won't be here, will you?"

"Yes, I will. I wanted to tell you. I've told the VSO I can only stay now a year."

"You mean for us?"

"I had to. It was too long. A year maybe but not two – not without you." With dread in his heart, Luke looked at his watch. It was already nearly four. His coach left at seven and he still had to cycle back to Oxford, pack and get to the coach. "I'll have to go soon."

"I'll come with you."

"No, you're needed here now – the police, Ashford, the house – you're in charge now. I'd rather say goodbye to you here, anyway. It's you, where you belong and I can think of you here."

Taking her in his arms, he felt he wanted her again, that it would never end the wanting.

"You'll wait for me, won't you?"

"How could I not? Dear Luke." She buried her head against him, trying not to cry. "I love you. I'll always love you."

There was no more to be said. No more he needed to know. Implicitly he believed her, knew her words would not be broken.

"I'll see you at Christmas then."

"I'll come to the road."

"No." Gently he kissed her and detached his arm. "I'd rather think of you here with trees. Not cars." He looked into her eyes, then forcing himself, he turned and

walked away. At the oak trees where he'd left his bicycle, he paused a moment and waved back at her. Then he was gone, wheeling his bicycle to the drive and out onto the road.

Hannah waited till he was out of sight. No longer restraining her tears then, she lay the locket back over the other Hannah's bones, ready to be identified. Slowly then, she made her way back to the burning house to find Ashford.

No flames leapt up now from Yadrahna's windows and chimneys. The building smouldered, subdued by the firemen's efforts and skill, hissing now rather than roaring as the water of the hoses sprayed incipient flames. But the damage was obvious for all to see with the lounge, her father's study and the two bedrooms above gutted – the furnishings and the floors between them gone. Only their charred stone walls were left standing. But the stone roof miraculously it seemed to Hannah was still intact together with the two attic rooms below. For how much longer though? The great oak joists spanning and supporting the attic floors, which had so far resisted, were exposed now, smouldering. The back of the house appeared to have escaped unscathed – the kitchen, the dining room and the bedrooms above. Had Hugo reckoned they weren't worth burning or was it merely the spectacle he'd wanted? How could he have done it – to try to destroy the place where he himself had grown up with his own past, his own memories as well as hers? Had he hated her so much or was it finally himself he'd hated?

Trying to comfort herself, Hannah looked inside the canvas bag Luke had rescued. There were all her father's diaries she remembered and other documents as well.

Curiously she drew out two birth certificates bound together by some faded pink tape. The first was that of her father which she'd seen already. The second was that of her mother which was new to her.

Slowly with interest she read the names and dates on the certificate. She noticed then what she hadn't known before that her mother named here Clare as well as Stella had been born on the 19th April 1938 in Suffolk and that her father had been a boat builder.

A boat builder in Suffolk. Her eyes moved more alert then over the names of her mother's father and mother. George Sidney Rope she read and Sarah Vera Rope, formerly the certificate stated – Vince.

In a flash then it came to her – if her mother was the daughter of Sarah Vince, then she was the grand daughter of the other Hannah – the Hannah she herself had so long sought and now found and who was now it appeared related – her own great grandmother. Could her mother have known, she wondered. She didn't think so for her mother had never investigated to her knowledge the Vince family. Wasn't it all too bizarre anyway to be believed, too much of a coincidence?

Yet wasn't it in front of her in red and white – facts that in essence couldn't be denied? And hadn't she all along known it in her heart – a closeness to the other Hannah that she hadn't till now been able to explain? Now she could explain, knew in part the reason for her quest.

"Ah, Miss Delaney."

Hannah turned to see Ashford looking strangely incongruous now in his formal attire amidst the firemen and casually dressed onlookers.

"I'm afraid I'm going to have to go now. I suggest you come and see me at my office next week. Everything's obviously going to have to be reassessed in view of the accident and fire."

Ashford paused, trying to assess Hannah's reaction. He still couldn't remove from his mind the powerful image of her in the long grey cloak by the side of the road.

"Do you intend to stay on in Wynton for the next few days, Miss Delaney?"

"I haven't really thought," Hannah replied. "I'll probably stay on at the cottage I'm renting." Yes, she'd need Brambles even more now as a base. And it was safe now – no danger from Hugo, no need to go and live in Oxford. But something would have to be done about Yadrahna. Perhaps Luke was right, she thought. What remained could be developed into a centre as Luke had visualised, a centre where both adults and children could come to gain a practical understanding of the natural world. It was an idea her father would have approved – building on the past for the future as the Victorians had done in planting Yadrahna's trees. Perhaps she and Luke could run it together, combining their experience and skills. She could even set it up before Luke returned.

"The police will be coming up shortly," Ashford continued," about the identification. No doubt they'll be able to give you some advice about protecting the rooms at the back of the house. I gather they're also coming to see you about a skeleton that's been found. Have you any idea who the person was?"

"Yes, it was a maid who once lived at the house, called Hannah."

"So you've been doing some investigation into Yadrahna's history?"

"She always interested me – yes."

"Why, Miss Delaney, do you think she ended her life in the pond?"

"I don't think it was foul play." Hannah hesitated, trying to feel her way into how the other Hannah must have felt when she was forced to give up her child and on the evening she'd heard that John had been drowned. "I think she died of love and the loss of her child to another's care."

"Of love?" Ashford looked startled a moment, then sceptical. She was letting her imagination run away with her, of course. Romantic retrospection and projection into what was probably an accident if it wasn't manslaughter or murder. He had a curious sensation all the same of the light in her large brown eyes penetrating long forgotten corridors in his mind, unsettling certainties and closed doors and against his established habit of reserve and detachment in such matters, he ventured.

"Loss I can understand, Miss Delaney, but love? Can one really die of love?"

"Love can have a power to surprise, do you not think, Mr Ashford?"

"Perhaps," Ashford conceded. "But the question is," he challenged, smiling, "is it greater in its power than hate?"

"Yes," Hannah affirmed. "I think it is."

She looked at the charred stone walls of her father's study where his antique books had been and her thoughts went out to Luke as he'd turned to wave to her at the pond. Soon he'd be in the coach to Heathrow, then on the plane

to India, half a world away. It would be four months before she'd see him again. But she would see him. She was certain of that now, that they would eventually be together. And together, in memory of her father and Hannah, from the roots of the past, they would rebuild Yadrahna for the future.